Castellan

Peter Darman

Formatted by Jo Harrison

I would like to thank the following people whose assistance has been integral to the creation of this work:
Julia, for her invaluable help and guidance with the text.
'Big John', for designing the cover.
Shutterstock for the cover image.

Contents

List of principal characters

Those marked with an asterisk * are known to history.

<u>Commanders in the Army of the Wolf</u>

Andres: Jerwen

Hillar: Rotalian

Kaja: Saccalian

Riki: Harrien

Tonis: Saccalian

<u>Danes</u>

Albert: Count of Orlamunde and Holstein, nephew of King Valdemar

Rolf: Count of Roskilde and Governor of Reval

*Valdemar: King of Denmark

<u>Englishman</u>

Sir Richard Bruffingham: Count of Saccalia

<u>Estonians</u>

Indrek: Ungannian, deputy to Kristjan

Kristjan: son of Kalju, Chief of the Ungannians

Peeter: Duke of Fellin

Rustic: mystic and follower of the old religion

<u>Germans</u>

*Albert: Bishop of Riga

*Bernhard: Bishop of Semgallia

*Gunzelin: brother of the Count of Schwerin, ally of the King of Denmark

*Henry: Count of Schwerin, ally of the King of Denmark

Manfred Nordheim: commander of the garrison of Riga

Stefan: Archdeacon, Governor of Riga and nephew of the Bishop of Riga

<u>Lithuanians</u>

Aras: Selonian warlord

Arturus: Duke of the Kurs

Butantas: Duke of the Samogitians

Kitenis: Duke of the Aukstaitijans

*Lamekins: Kur prince, deputy to Duke Arturus

*Mindaugas: son-in-law of Prince Vsevolod

Rasa: wife of Prince Vsevolod

Torolf: ambassador of Duke Arturus
*Viesthard: Duke of Semgallia
*Ykintas: prince, son of Duke Butantas
Livs
Fricis: leader of all the Livs
*Rameke: warlord and brother-in-law of Conrad Wolff
*Vetseke: prince, former ruler of Kokenhusen
Oeselians
Bothvar: earl
Kalf: son of Olaf
Olaf: King of Oesel
Sigurd: son of Olaf
Stark: son of Olaf
Swein: earl
Order of Sword Brothers
Anton: brother knight at Wenden Castle
Arnold: Master of Lennewarden Castle
Bertram: Master of Segewold Castle
Conrad Wolff: brother knight at Wenden Castle,
commander of the Army of the Wolf and Marshal of
Estonia
Friedhelm: Master of Uexkull Castle
Godfrey: Master of Holm Castle
Griswold: Master of Kokenhusen Castle
Hans: brother knight at Wenden Castle
Henke: brother knight at Wenden Castle
Jacob: Master of Gerzika Castle
Lukas: brother knight at Wenden Castle
Mathias: Master of Kremon Castle
*Rudolf: Master of Wenden Castle and deputy commander
of the Order of Sword Brothers
Thaddeus: chief engineer at Wenden Castle and
Quartermaster General of Livonia
*Volquin: Grand Master of the Order of Sword Brothers
Walter: brother knight at Wenden Castle
Russians
*Domash Tverdislavich: Mayor of Pskov
Gleb: Skomorokh, follower of the old religion
*Mitrofan: Archbishop of Novgorod

*Mstislav: Prince of Novgorod
*Vsevolod: former ruler of Gerzika
*Yaroslav Nevsky: boyar of Novgorod, son of Yuri Nevsky
Yuri Nevsky: boyar of Novgorod

MAPS

Maps relating to the lands and peoples described in 'Castellan' can be found on the maps page on my website: www.peterdarman.com

Livonia 1222

Chapter 1

The winter ice had disappeared from the Dvina at last; the mighty river now at its peak as melt water surged towards the sea. The formerly barren pastures and meadows sprang back to life to be carpeted with pale flowers. In the forests reindeer moss filled pine groves, lichens and mosses flourished and fungi wreathed tree trunks. Through the woods ran effervescent rivers and streams where otters hunted along their banks. Away from the water wild boar, roe deer and elk roamed among the trees. And in the sky above them black storks, lesser spotted eagles, grouse, white-backed woodpeckers and pygmy owls replaced the wintry silence with their calls. Visually life was returning to Livonia but away from nature the province was dying.

The large, deep harbour at Riga should have been filling with boats carrying furs, flax, timber, tar and hides to be sold in the city markets or purchased by merchants for onward shipment to the towns and cities of Germany and Denmark. Exotically dressed traders from the Russian kingdoms of Polotsk and Novgorod should have been bartering with city officials over prices for the grey squirrel pelts that were so desired by the nobility of Europe. But instead the harbour was empty and no boats came from the Russian principalities to the east. No ships came from the west either for Valdemar, King of the Danes and Master of the Baltic, had placed a blockade upon

Livonia. On his orders no ships left Lübeck carrying crusaders to fight on behalf of the Bishop of Riga against the pagans and ships were prevented from leaving Riga itself carrying goods for sale in German and Danish cities. Valdemar was strangling Livonia and God seemed intent on adding to the kingdom's woes, for the pox had broken out in Riga.

The first signs of the dreadful pestilence had showed themselves at the end of winter in the cramped, foetid backstreets of Riga. At first only one street near the harbour had been affected but then it had spread at an alarming rate, whole families struck down by high fevers, chills, severe headaches, backaches and a general malaise. Soon the men of the city militia, those who had not themselves been struck down, were hacking at the hard earth beyond the city walls to create common graves where the dead were to be interred. Work ceased on the Bishop of Riga's cathedral as he went among his flock, holding open-air masses to implore God to spare His city on the Dvina. But Albert's prayers went unanswered as the graves began to fill and the pox spread to outlying villages. Soon a quarantine had been established around Riga in an effort to stop the dreadful disease spreading east and north. Everyone prayed but God was not listening.

'My uncle's prayers are wasted. Until the source of God's displeasure is dealt with Livonia will continue to suffer. At this rate we will all end up as destitute beggars among the heathens.'

Archdeacon Stefan took another sip of wine from the silver chalice and dabbed his lips with a cloth. He shook his

9

head, causing his double chin to wobble. Manfred Nordheim raised an eyebrow. His master was still putting on weight, notwithstanding the plight of the kingdom. The archdeacon waved over the young novice who had been ordered by the Dean of Dünamünde to attend him during his stay. Manfred walked over to the window to look at the well-tended fields surrounding the monastery.

'What source would that be, archdeacon?'

The novice refilled Stefan's chalice and withdrew to his position beside the door.

'Conrad Wolff, of course. I would have thought that was obvious.'

Manfred stroked his neatly cropped beard and turned back to the archdeacon, who was now shaking his head.

'The Sword Brothers have become a monster that now bites the hand that feeds them. They were created to serve my uncle and now their insolence and arrogance has led to Livonia being blockaded by the Danes.'

Manfred noticed beads of sweat on the archdeacon's lily-white forehead as the latter continued complaining.

'I cannot believe that this Conrad Wolff, this baker's son, has been allowed to bring the whole kingdom to its present dire predicament. I have a mind to send you to Wenden to arrest him so he can either be sent to Reval or be burned in the central marketplace in Riga.'

There was a sharp intake of breath from the commander of Riga's garrison. Stefan's sweating forehead creased into a frown.

'You disagree, Manfred?'

'The Marshal of Estonia has many warriors, archdeacon, not to mention the support of the Sword Brothers. The garrison of Riga is not large enough, I fear, to seize the Marshal of Estonia at Wenden.'

Stefan wagged a finger at his subordinate. 'The Sword Brothers would not raise a hand against the commander of the garrison of Riga.'

Manfred walked over to the table and tore off a chunk of bread that had been made that morning. It was delicious. The monks of Dünamünde lived a good life.

'Last year, at Reval, when the pagans and Sword Brothers decided to fight the Danes instead of handing over the Marshal of Estonia,' he said, 'the grand master himself threatened me when I tried to point out the error of his order's ways.'

Stefan cast his head down. 'Such is the corruption of the Sword Brothers that they think nothing of issuing threats against the servants of the bishop, my uncle. Their greed for power has poisoned their minds against Bishop Albert.'

'Perhaps the pox will wipe them out and the bishop can raise a new, more obedient order,' offered Nordheim.

'I pray that it might happen so, Manfred. But for the moment we need Volquin and his army of miscreants. With no crusaders arriving this year Livonia will be at the mercy of the

Lithuanians, Russians, Danes, Oeselians and the thousands of pagans who inhabit Livonia.'

Manfred stopped himself from laughing. He liked the archdeacon, not least because he had a high opinion of his own importance, which meant that when danger, real or imagined, presented itself Stefan could be relied upon to seek out the safest place. Thus when the pox broke out in Riga he had taken himself to Dünamünde, thirty miles southwest of the city, along with the commander of the garrison and fifty of his men.

'No army will attack Livonia, archdeacon, not while it is being ravaged by the pox. But some might flee it and seek sanctuary beyond its borders.'

'Who?' asked Stefan.

Manfred finished eating his bread and picked up an empty silver chalice.

'The Livs, possibly.'

'No great loss,' sniffed Stefan.

Manfred pointed at the novice and then at the empty chalice. The young boy walked over and filled it. Stefan ordered him to leave the room and close the door behind him.

'Please sit down, Manfred,' he said, 'your continual pacing is tiresome.'

The commander did as he was ordered. Stefan leaned forward.

'I have a small task for you.'

Manfred took a sip of the wine. Like the bread it was most appetising.

'I remember reading of the pox ravaging some north German province, the name of which escapes me. Apparently a whole village was wiped out when a chest containing a consignment of clothes from a neighbouring village was unwittingly sent there.'

Manfred nodded. 'It is common practice to burn all the clothes and linens of those who contract the pox, as a precaution against it spreading.'

Stefan's eyes glinted with malice. 'I want you to arrange a consignment of infected clothing to be sent to Kalju, the leader of the Ungannians.'

Manfred was confused. 'Why?'

Now it was Stefan's turn to rise from his well-upholstered chair and begin pacing.

'Do you know what the role of an archdeacon is, Manfred?'

'To govern Riga?' suggested Nordheim.

'That is one of my duties, yes. But my main purpose is to be the Bishop of Riga's assistant, specifically to take care of business that my uncle does not have time for.'

Manfred sipped again at his wine. 'The bishop wishes to kill Kalju?'

'My uncle,' replied Stefan, still pacing, 'is currently praying for the welfare of Livonia and does not have time to consider pagans. But this Kalju is clearly an agent of Satan and needs to be dealt with. You said yourself that his appearance at

Reval led to the outbreak of violence between the Sword Brothers and the Danes.'

Manfred nodded.

'Then by his actions did this pagan leader declare himself an enemy of both God and my uncle.'

Stefan suddenly stopped and looked earnestly at his subordinate. 'And you and I both know what the penalty for heresy is.'

'I do not wish to pour cold water on your plan, archdeacon,' said Manfred, 'but even if the consignment of clothes reaches Kalju, and even if it infects and kills him, how does his death help Livonia?'

Stefan walked back to his chair and retook it.

'First of all it will be a clear sign that God has struck down this pagan leader. Secondly, it will deprive the baker's son of an ally. He and this Kalju are close, I believe.'

Nordheim nodded.

'Good, it is fitting that the former Marshal of Estonia should know loss, for his very existence results in mounting losses for Livonia. Ensure that whoever delivers the consignment impresses upon this Kalju that it is a gift from the Sword Brothers. Time to drive a wedge between Volquin's order and his pagan allies, I think.'

Manfred finished his wine and ran a finger around the top of the chalice.

'Speaking of which, whoever delivers this package is risking his life. It will be a suicide mission, most likely.'

Stefan waved a hand dismissively at him. 'I'm sure you will be able to find someone for the right price, though only pay half the amount up front. The rest can be collected after the completion of the delivery.'

'The courier will likely de dead by then, archdeacon.'

Stefan laughed. 'Thus benefiting the city treasury.'

Nordheim looked up. 'Livonia would be better served if Conrad Wolff was dead, archdeacon.'

'I am apt to agree with you. But the bishop, virtuous man that he is, seems to be fond of him, no doubt because the baker's son saved his life outside Riga during Vetseke's rebellion some years ago. It took all my time and effort to persuade him to revoke his post of Marshal of Estonia. Loyalty can be a double-edged sword, Manfred.'

But not for the archdeacon mused Nordheim. He was a good paymaster and gave his commander much latitude but he knew that when he was no longer useful the governor would quickly dispense of his services. His task was to ensure that those services were always required.

'If the worst comes to the worst, archdeacon, I can always get you and the bishop out of Livonia.'

'Oh? It may have escaped your attention, Manfred, but Danish ships currently patrol the Gulf of Riga. Nothing escapes them.'

Nordheim smiled. 'I am used to slipping past ships unseen, archdeacon. You have no need to worry on that account.'

'Ah, yes, I forgot you were once a pirate. Well, I'm sure it won't come to that, not if we appease the Danes, at least. Which is why I am determined to rid the world of this Kalju, after which I will send word to King Valdemar that his mortal enemy has been dealt with. I will also invite him to seize Ungannia, which may lessen his animosity towards Livonia.'

Nordheim was unconvinced that Valdemar would even read a letter sent to him by a relation of the Bishop of Riga, but the archdeacon appeared content with his plan so he said no more. Stefan looked around the well-appointed room.

'I like Dünamünde.'

Nordheim had to agree that the monastery was a most auspicious place. It had been built seventeen years earlier and from the beginning had been designed as a citadel as well as a place of orderliness and solitude. Like all Cistercian monasteries it had a cruciform-shaped church, adjacent to which was a cloister: a rectangular covered walkway built around a central garden. The east range was a two-storey building, opposite of which was the range where visitors would be greeted and where guests were lodged. But the archdeacon had his own rooms in the strong tower next to the church. Three such towers had been built at Dünamünde, along with a perimeter wall and wide moat to strengthen the whole monastery's defences.

When it had first been built the monastery had been subjected to numerous Kur raids that had resulted in loss of life and livestock. Now the perimeter wall, moat and towers ensured that the monks who lived at Dünamünde could hold out long enough in the event of a siege until relief arrived from Riga, though the Kurs usually restricted themselves to raids only. The man responsible for improving the monastery's defences had been Abbot Bernhard, formerly the soldier and noble Bernhard von Lippe, who had been abbot for seven years before being created Bishop of Semgallia. The effort to install him in his bishopric had ended in disaster south of the Dvina and now he resided in Riga with Bishop Albert. Just one more reason for Stefan to seek sanctuary at Dünamünde.

'It is a pleasant place,' agreed Manfred.

'And profitable,' added Stefan. 'The flocks of sheep, fields and orchards are very productive. Do you know why, Manfred?'

Nordheim was not really bothered and felt another of the archdeacon's interminable lectures was at hand, but he smiled politely.

'No, archdeacon.'

'Because matters at Dünamünde are ordered according to God's law, that is why. The monks who live and pray here are of noble birth whereas the lay brothers, the secular members of the monastery who carry out the day-to-day tasks such as working in the fields and the outlying farmsteads, are drawn from the lower classes and, worse, local Livs.'

He reached forward to lift his chalice to his lips.

'As it should be, lay members can never don the white cowl or tonsure and they are required to remain illiterate. The natural order of things, you see. That is why Dünamünde prospers, Manfred, because the strict order of things is maintained. You will not find a low-born baker's son raised high here.'

*****

Valdemar held his head in his hands as the messenger relayed the dismal news. His nobles and prelates looked at each other furtively and fidgeted with their hands. The messenger himself had been sent by one of the captains of the two surviving cogs that had docked in Reval's harbour. The ships had been carrying food and supplies for the Danish garrison. Three vessels had originally set out from the port of Lübeck but they had been attacked by Oeselian longships north of Hiiumaa, the island immediately north of Oesel. Normally armed cogs, especially as part of a flotilla, could fend off longships but the captain of the third Danish vessel had panicked and steered his ship on to rocks, causing it to break up. All those on board were lost. The deaths of lowly sailors and soldiers were insignificant of course but the ship had been carrying a choir made up of young boys who sang in Lübeck's cathedral. They were being sent to Reval in an attempt to improve the humour of the Danish king, which of late had deteriorated. But now they were dead and he would never hear their angelic voices.

Valdemar raised his head and waved away the messenger, who bowed and scuttled from the throne room. An awkward silence then filled the chamber as Valdemar reclined in his high-backed chair and sighed.

'God has abandoned me.'

The king's narrow face had a gaunt look and his shoulder-length hair was showing streaks of grey. The death of his young wife Berengaria the previous year had hit him hard. She had borne him four children and he missed her company greatly. His blockade of Livonia had caused great hardship among his Danish and German merchants, which they never tired of informing him. As a result he had left Denmark to seek refuge at Reval, his fledgling city on the northern coast of Estonia. Many of his German nobles, including his most able commander, Count Henry of Schwerin, had absented themselves to go on crusade in the Holy Land, leaving his army short of soldiers and experienced leaders. And now the young choirboys of Lübeck were dead.

'You are a valued servant of God, my liege,' said the Bishop of Roskilde to break the oppressive quiet. 'How else can your great victory at this place be explained?'

The king looked at him with gratitude in his eyes. 'Thank you, lord bishop, for reminding me of happier times.'

Valdemar had arrived at Reval at the head of a great crusading army three years before, and had defeated a pagan army a few days after landing. God himself had sent him a banner to show His pleasure that the heathens had been vanquished. That banner, a white cross against a red background, now hung on the wall behind Valdemar's throne, along with his own standard of three blue lions surrounded by small red hearts on a yellow background. The Bishop of Riga had begged for his help to subdue the Estonians and the Pope himself had granted him the Estonian kingdoms. But Bishop Albert had basely reneged on his promises and the Sword Brothers, the private army of the bishop, had marched against his lieutenants. Worse, the Bishop of Riga had made one of the Sword Brothers the Marshal of Estonia, thus directly insulting him. Valdemar had demanded that this marshal surrender himself so he could face summary justice for his crimes, only to witness the Sword Brothers attacking his own soldiers outside the walls of Reval. So Valdemar had imposed a blockade on Livonia and waited for the Bishop of Riga to crawl on his hands and knees before him to atone for his sins.

'Livonia is being throttled, uncle. The Bishop of Riga will see the error of his ways soon enough.'

Valdemar gave his nephew a half-smile. Only twenty-two years of age, Albert, Count of Orlamunde and Holstein, possessed the certainty and arrogance of youth. Ever since he had accompanied the king to Reval thoughts of fighting the Sword Brothers and pagans had filled his mind. He had amused himself with raids against local villages but had been ordered to desist by the Governor of Reval: Rolf, Count of Roskilde. Butchering defenceless civilians was a pleasant enough pastime for the king's nephew but the ill will that it caused produced a surly, rebellious population. As well as a stream of recruits for the Marshal of Estonia.

'Thus far Bishop Albert has proved himself remarkably resilient,' said the king, 'notwithstanding the cessation of trade and crusaders I have imposed upon his crusader kingdom.'

'Let me march south with an army to impose your will on the bishop, uncle.'

Valdemar looked at his swarthy nephew and laughed, the first time he had done so in a while.

'Count Henry tried that and found the Sword Brothers tenacious opponents. Besides, I will not raise my sword against the Bishop of Riga, who after all is a prince of the Holy Church.'

'Most wise, majesty,' agreed Bishop Peder.

The king cast the bishop a conniving glance. 'Besides, two hundred Danish ships are more than enough to strangle Livonia and bring Bishop Albert to me.'

'Let me at least march south against Wenden, my liege,' pleaded Albert. 'That is where the damnable Conrad Wolff is stationed.'

'Wenden is a fortress, Count Albert.'

It was the first time that the governor of Reval had spoken. Ten years older than the king's nephew, Rolf, Count of Roskilde, was an intelligent, serious individual who had set about learning as much as possible about the Estonians, their language, culture and military capabilities. He had also made it his business to find out as much as possible about the Sword Brothers, especially the garrison at Wenden.

21

'A strong outer perimeter wall and a stone castle on a hill,' continued Rolf, 'with a sizeable, experienced garrison that possesses mangonels and trebuchets. To take such a stronghold would require a large army and a prolonged siege.'

'This Conrad Wolff cannot be allowed to escape my uncle's justice,' Albert shot back.

Rolf stroked his strong jaw. 'This errant Sword Brother must be brought to justice as you say, count, but at this present juncture he should not be the main topic of our discussion.'

Valdemar was confused. 'Oh? Then who should be, Rolf?'

'Those who have recently murdered your subjects, my liege,' replied Rolf. 'The Oeselians.'

Valdemar's ears pricked up at this. He had no appetite for fighting a lengthy war against the Sword Brothers but a sortie against the nearby island of Oesel was a much more attractive proposition.

'You are thinking of a reprisal raid, Rolf?'

The governor nodded. 'Yes, my liege. Burn a few settlements and bring back slaves to Reval to be sold to the Russians.'

Rolf looked at the bishop.

'If the church has no objection.'

Bishop Peder brought his hands together. 'The lives and souls of unbaptised pagans are of no concern to the Holy Church, my lord, as they face certain defeat in this world and damnation in the hereafter. You have my blessing to punish these pirates.'

'Were it not for these pirates, these Oeselians,' said Albert, 'the Baltic would be a Danish lake.'

He walked to stand before Valdemar.

'It is but a short step, uncle, for a raid to turn into a more long-term endeavour.'

Valdemar used both his hands to wave his nephew back, but he was interested in what he had to say.

'What endeavour?'

Albert stood to attention. Rolf thought he looked quite ridiculous but was alarmed by the words that came out of the young man's mouth.

'I propose a campaign of conquest against these Oeselians, uncle. The soldiers of Orlamunde and Holstein are eager to prove their loyalty, my liege. What better way than to finally eradicate the threat of these pagan pirates?'

Rolf was not impressed. 'I would advise caution, majesty.'

But Valdemar was warming to his nephew's proposal.

'Caution, Count Rolf? Does Denmark fear the Oeselians?'

Count Albert's narrow face wore a smirk as the governor chose his words carefully.

'Oesel is a large island, majesty, containing as it does many settlements. To subjugate such an area would require a sizeable army, and at present I would suggest that Reval does not have the number of soldiers required for such an ambitious project.'

There was a sharp intake of breath from the bishop as Count Albert's eyes widened in surprise. Rolf had been chosen by Valdemar to be Reval's governor because of his bravery, intelligence and calm nature. But those qualities now worked against him as he stated what he believed to be the blindingly obvious, which was interpreted by Valdemar as a slight on his military prowess.

The king sprang from his throne to stand before the governor.

'In a war against heathens, Count Rolf, it is not numbers but Christian conviction that decides battles. Was not my own victory at Reval three years ago proof of this?'

Rolf was now seriously worried. 'Indeed, majesty, but then the army was all in one place whereas now it is required not only to hold Reval and the former pagan stronghold of Varbola, but also numerous outlying forts in Harrien and Wierland. I fear that the size of the army that will march to Oesel may be deficient in numbers.'

'Give me command of the army,' said Count Albert, 'my men alone can conquer the island.'

Now it was Rolf's turn to smirk. The king's nephew had brought less than three hundred men with him; barely enough to mount a raid let alone a full-scale invasion. But Valdemar was not thinking of numbers, only revenge and glory.

'How many soldiers can be mustered to invade Oesel, Rolf?' queried the king.

Rolf scratched his head. 'A rough estimation would be around two thousand, majesty.'

Count Albert spread his arms. 'Surely more than enough to crush a few miserable pagans?'

'I am apt to agree with my nephew,' said the king.

'And you would have your holy banner, majesty,' added Bishop Peder, 'the sacred standard that is the bringer of victory.'

Valdemar looked up at the banner hanging beside his own, a simple white cross on a red background. But for Valdemar it had holy powers. He was taken back to three years before when he had been locked in deadly combat with a pagan brute as the sky was filled with thunder and lightning and rain lashed the land. He had thought himself a dead man but, out of nowhere, a banner had flown into the face of his assailant and he had killed his foe. As the pagan lay dead in the mud Valdemar saw his body covered with the cloth bearing a white cross against a red background. And from that day he had taken that device to be not only his personnel standard but also the flag of all Denmark. God had given him this standard. How could an army that carried it be defeated in battle, much less by pagans?

'I will march to Oesel,' he stated, looking at his nephew, 'and you will be coming with me.'

Count Albert could barely contain his delight. 'Yes, uncle.'

Valdemar pointed at the governor. 'You will stay here at Reval, Rolf, to ensure that the Russians do not take advantage of our absence. With Riga closed to their merchants as a result of my blockade I have no doubt that the Prince of Novgorod covets this place.'

'Reval's defences are strong, majesty,' Rolf assured him.

That was certainly true. The governor had spent many months constructing towers along the perimeter wall that surrounded the town, as well as strengthening the fort that stood atop Toompea Hill just outside the settlement. It was true that the walls, towers and fort were all of wooden construction, but it would take an army of many thousands to besiege Reval, let alone storm it.

'What of Wenden and the Sword Brothers, uncle?' asked Albert.

Valdemar shrugged. 'What of them?'

'After we have conquered Oesel will we be marching against Wenden to arrest this Conrad Wolff?'

Rolf shook his head. The arrogant certainty of the king's nephew was breath-taking. How little he knew of the Sword Brothers.

Valdemar rose and walked towards the doors of the chamber, the counts and bishop bowing their heads as he passed.

'Do not concern yourself with the Sword Brothers, nephew. I have heard that the pox ravages Livonia. In a few more weeks the Bishop of Riga will have surrendered Conrad Wolff to me in person when the citizens of Riga, those that have survived the pestilence, are starving and the Lithuanians and Russians are banging at their gates.'

*****

'My lads haven't been paid in six months, master, and to say they are far from amused is putting it mildly.'

Leatherface stood beside the oak desk where Wenden's brother knights were seated and stared at Master Rudolf with unblinking eyes. The aged mercenary had always been free with his tongue, erring towards sedition, but his promotion to command all of Wenden's mercenaries had increased his rebellious nature.

Leatherface looked down at his battered, dirty gambeson. 'I mean look at me. Someone might mistake me for a beggar such is the state of my apparel.'

Rudolf Kassel, Master of Wenden Castle and deputy commander of the Order of Sword Brothers, sighed and raised his brown eyes to the ceiling. The weekly meeting of the brother knights in the master's hall at Wenden was usually a straightforward affair, with brother knights airing grievances, offering recommendations and giving an account of their responsibilities. But of late they had become fractious affairs, largely due to the Danish blockade on Livonia that had resulted

27

in a cessation of the transportation of goods, mostly food, timber and hides, to Riga down the Gauja. This in turn had led to the castle's income drying up, which meant no money to pay for the one hundred and twenty mercenaries that the master employed as part of the garrison.

Rudolf spread his hands. 'What do you want me to do, magic money out of nothing? Until the Danish blockade ends the order has no money to pay its mercenaries. It is the same for all the order's garrisons.'

Leatherface shook his head. 'I'm not an unreasonable man, Master Rudolf.'

'That's debateable,' muttered Henke.

Leatherface shot the powerful brother knight a disparaging glance.

'But,' the mercenary continued, 'if I and my boys aren't paid then we will have to consider our options.'

'What options?' queried Henke derisively. 'You can't go to Riga because the city is under quarantine due to the pox. And even if you could there are no ships to take you to Germany on account of the Danish blockade.'

Leatherface smiled. 'Who said anything about Germany, Brother Henke? There are others who would pay handsomely for our services, such as the Russians. And there's always the Lithuanians south of the Dvina.'

Brother Walter, Rudolf's deputy, was appalled. 'You would offer your services to apostates and heathens?'

'That's the point of being a mercenary, Brother Walter,' replied Leatherface, 'we work for whoever is willing to pay us.'

Rudolf pointed at the mercenary. 'I think you and your men should think carefully on your future actions. At Wenden you are fed, housed and issued with clothing and weapons, notwithstanding that some of you choose to dress like ruffians. The blockade will not last forever, but if you feel that you can no longer work for the Sword Brothers then I must ask you and your men to be gone by the end of the week.'

Leatherface's eyes opened wide in alarm. 'Well, there's no need to be hasty, Master Rudolf. I'm not an unreasonable man. I'll have a word with the lads. I'm sure I can calm their anxieties.'

'Of that I have no doubt,' replied Rudolf.

Leatherface nodded his head at the master, winked at Conrad and departed, shutting the door behind him.

'Arrogant bastard,' hissed Henke. 'He should be flogged in front of his men as a warning of what happens when someone crosses the Sword Brothers.'

'He and his men are good soldiers,' said Conrad. 'Good soldiers deserve fair treatment, not brutality.'

Henke laughed. 'You've been spending too much time among your heathen friends, *brother*. The Sword Brothers cannot be held to ransom. It sets a bad precedent.'

Rudolf held up a hand. 'No one is going to be flogged, Henke. Wenden's mercenaries have been with us for years and have fought by our side on many occasions. If the price of retaining them is a verbal battering from their commander once a week then so be it. Let us hope that the Danish blockade ends speedily so we can all get back to normal.'

'To which end, master,' said Conrad, 'there is someone waiting outside who brings welcome news.'

The brother knights looked at Conrad with eager faces. Any good news was welcome amidst the gloom that hung over Livonia.

'Then being him in,' ordered Rudolf.

Conrad went to the door, opened it and seconds later the huge frame of Hillar entered the hall. He was one of the commanders in Conrad's Army of the Wolf that was made up of different contingents of Estonian tribal members. Hillar led the Rotalians. There were around three hundred of them deployed in the borderlands between Saccalia and Rotalia. Henke rolled his eyes but Rudolf rose and extended his arm to Hillar.

'Welcome Hillar,' he said in Estonian. 'What brings you to Wenden?'

The Estonian gripped Rudolf's forearm with a hand that was as wide as a bear's paw. In contrast to the neatly cropped hair and beards of the brother knights, Hillar's fair hair was long and unkempt.

'I bring news of a Danish invasion of Oesel.'

Rudolf gestured for him to sit at the table, the Rotalian first unbuckling his sword belt as a sign of friendliness. He placed his sword on the floor beside him. Walter poured him a cup of wine and passed the vessel to him as everyone looked on with eager anticipation.

Hillar drained the cup in one gulp. 'I have many scouts in Rotalia and they brought me news that the Danes marched from Reval and crossed the water to invade Oesel. Many ships sailed from Reval to transport the Danish king to the island.'

Henke was unimpressed. 'It was only a matter of time before Valdemar decided to conquer Oesel. It does not help us.'

Conrad nodded at Hillar. 'Tell them how the great King Valdemar fared on the island.'

Hillar reached over to grasp the wine jug and poured himself another drink.

'When the Danes arrived on the island the first thing they did was to start building a fort.'

'Sensible,' said Lukas. 'Oesel is a big island and any conqueror would need a base for operations.'

Hillar took a mouthful of wine. 'Bad mistake. Olaf has the fort surrounded so the Danes cannot escape the island.'

'The garrison of Reval will send ships to aid Valdemar,' said Walter.

Hillar finished his wine. 'The Oeselian fleet has Danish ships trapped in Reval's harbour like sheep in a pen.'

Henke clapped his hands together. 'Excellent. Valdemar will die and the blockade of Livonia will end.'

'No, Henke,' said Rudolf, 'if Valdemar is killed then his son will become Danish king and the blockade will continue.'

Walter was most upset. 'As Christian knights we should help Valdemar in his hour of trial.'

Henke was unimpressed. 'Why should the Sword Brothers help the man who tried to have one of our own executed like a common criminal?'

Conrad smiled. 'Brother Henke, I had not realised until this moment that you cared so much for me.'

Henke looked daggers at Conrad. 'I don't, I was just making a point.'

'That's enough,' ordered Rudolf. 'Hillar, what do your scouts tell you about the Danish fort on Oesel?'

'The Danes spent a week landing supplies and building a stone fort just inland from the beach they landed on. A fort surrounded by a ditch and earth rampart.'

'How many Danish soldiers landed on the island?' asked Walter.

Hillar scratched his beard. 'Two, three thousand, perhaps.'

'I say let the bastard get killed or captured by the Oeselians,' insisted Henke. 'He's no friend of the Sword Brothers.'

Walter's face wore a deep frown but most of the brother knights were unconcerned. It was well known that Valdemar had denounced the order after the savaging it had given his army at Reval. If he died it was one less enemy for the Sword Brothers to worry about. But Rudolf was thinking ahead and

32

sniffed an opportunity. He stood and began walking around the table, speaking to himself rather than anyone in particular.

'Valdemar is besieged on Oesel, the Oeselians lie outside the harbour of Reval, thus making it impossible for the garrison to send ships and reinforcements to relieve their king.'

'The Danes could march overland towards Oesel, Master Rudolf,' offered Conrad, 'though they would have to find boats to transport them to the island.'

Rudolf stopped and shook his head. 'Just as Hillar has scouts in Rotalia I am sure the Oeselians have eyes watching Reval. If the garrison sent a relief party overland I am sure Olaf's ships outside the harbour would assault Reval.'

'Alas for Valdemar,' said Henke, smirking.

'The Oeselians will kill all the Danes eventually,' stated Hillar without emotion.

'Notwithstanding that he has declared himself an enemy of our order,' remarked Walter, 'the death of a king appointed by God is no cause for celebration.'

Conrad begged to differ but held his counsel. Perhaps God was punishing Valdemar for the injustices he had inflicted on Estonia and the blockade he had imposed on Livonia.

Rudolf returned to his chair and smashed his fist on the table, startling everyone.

'Valdemar will not die on Oesel because the Sword Brothers are going to rescue him.'

Those around the table looked at each other in confusion, aside from Walter who was nodding piously.

'It takes a noble nature to ignore the slights our order has endured at the hands of King Valdemar, master, and you have proved yourself a worthy knight of Christ.'

Lukas, who had known Rudolf for many years, since they had been part of the same mercenary band that had terrorised Germany, was more reflective.

'Very noble, Rudolf. Too noble, in fact.'

'Are you insane?' was Henke's only comment.

Rudolf ignored them and pointed at Conrad.

'Muster your army at the Saccalian border, Conrad. We will meet you there once I have summoned the garrisons of Kremon and Segewold.'

'Surely only the grand master can issue orders to summon a muster, master?' said Walter, ever a stickler for protocol.

'In normal circumstances you would be right, Walter,' agreed Rudolf, 'but these are not normal circumstances. Riga is cut off from the outside world until the pox is gone, and therefore no communication is possible with Grand Master Volquin. As deputy commander of the order I am using my authority to assist both the order and Bishop Albert.'

Normally courier pigeons flew between Riga and the order's castles along the Dvina and Gauja. However, fear of infection had resulted in any form of communication between Riga and the outside world being prohibited.

'Send riders to Kremon and Segewold,' Rudolf told Lukas, 'I will draw up orders for Master Bertram and Master Mathias. The meeting is over.'

The brother knights stood and bowed their heads as Rudolf walked from the hall to his private office at the rear of the main chamber.

Conrad walked with Hans, Anton and Hillar into Wenden's great courtyard. It was the first time the Rotalian had seen the three brother knights in their non-martial apparel. The pagan was wearing leather boots, a thick leather cuirass and leather wristbands, with a sword and dagger strapped to his waist.

'Are you and your knights being punished, *Susi?*' he asked Conrad.

The name had been bestowed on Conrad because the Estonians who fought for him believed him to be the reincarnation of the ancient wolf spirit of the forest in human form.

'No, why?'

'Then why are you dressed like women?'

For the meeting all the brother knights wore long dark tunics reaching to the ankles, belted at the waist with tight-fitting sleeves. On their feet they wore plain shoes instead of boots and under their tunics woollen shirts and woollen breeches, as there was still a nip in the air. The only indications that they were members of the Sword Brothers were their mantles, lightweight white cloaks to signify purity, each bearing the symbol of the order on the left shoulder.

'This is our attire when we are not wearing our armour,' Hans told him.

'Sitting in mail, gambesons and aketons for long periods indoors can be most uncomfortable,' added Anton.

'I must ask you to ride north immediately,' Conrad said to Hillar. 'Wait for me at the Pala. Inform Sir Richard, I am sure he will want to join us on our campaign.'

Anton screwed up his face. 'It will take at least two weeks to reach Oesel. Valdemar might be dead by then.'

'If he is, he is,' replied Conrad. 'But Master Rudolf is determined to attempt to save his hide.'

'To what end?' asked Hillar.

'I have no idea,' said Conrad.

They walked from the master's hall across the cobbled courtyard towards the stables on the western side on the castle. Wenden had once been a pagan hill fort but had been captured from the Livs fourteen years before. Since that time a great building programme had been undertaken to turn the stronghold that sat atop an escarpment with sheer northern and western sides into a stone citadel. And now that work was all but complete. A host of workers had been brought from Germany during those years to build the stone castle, now the strongest in all Livonia. Along the eastern wall were sited the chapel, master's hall, dining hall, armoury and smithy. Opposite was the longer western wall; for Wenden was an irregular-shaped castle to fit the escarpment. There were but two buildings along this wall: the two-storey dormitory where the brother knights and sergeants were accommodated and the expansive stables block. The destriers, palfreys, packhorses and mules all had to be sheltered from the elements, especially the prized, pampered destriers that were treated better than the brother knights.

A small army of servants, stable hands and blacksmiths worked in the castle, many of them either living within the castle's outer perimeter defences immediately south of the massive gatehouse, or in the steadily growing village below the castle's northern ramparts. When Conrad had first come to Wenden ten years before there had been no village and the land around the castle was largely dense forest. But now many of the trees near the castle had been felled to provide material for the outer perimeter wall. Huts and buildings filled the area inside it and the village that had sprung up on the opposite side of the escarpment. It too had a wooden wall for it was not so long ago that it had been burnt to the ground during a Cuman attack.

Hillar's horse was tethered to one of the rails outside the stable block but Conrad, Hans and Anton went inside the wooden office sited outside the block. There an officious individual with a pointed nose sat at a sloping desk equipped with inkhorns examining a parchment made from goatskin. It was unfortunate that as Wenden grew in size and importance so the number of officials employed there increased. They were all under the control of Master Thaddeus, the white-haired quartermaster general of Livonia who was now in his early seventies.

The official looked up.

'Ah, brothers Conrad, Hans and Anton. How can I be of assistance?'

'We need three palfreys saddled immediately,' replied Conrad.

'And fodder for at least two weeks,' added Hans.

'Which we will collect later, after we have returned from a more immediate errand,' said Conrad.

The official raised an eyebrow. 'You are going on campaign, brothers?'

'We are,' said Conrad, 'though first we are riding south to the Estonians' village.'

The official turned the quill he was holding through his fingers.

'If you are absent for longer than two days I will need authorisation from Master Rudolf. Standard procedure, you understand.'

'We've just come from the master's hall,' stated Conrad, 'and are here on the orders of Master Rudolf.'

The official looked at the three fearsome brother knights, all with well-earned reputations for being skilled killers, especially Conrad, the man who had slain Lembit and tried to kill the Danish king at Reval, or so he had been told. He drummed his fingers on the desk as the brother knights became visibly annoyed with this nondescript scribe.

'Well,' the official said, 'if it is on the master's business then I suppose I can authorise the issue.'

'You are too kind,' said Anton.

'Of course you will all have to sign for the horses and supplies,' insisted the official.

They nodded curtly whereupon the official barked an order to one of the stable hands, who went to collect the horses. As the three brother knights made their signatures on a separate parchment, Hans making an 'x' as he could not write, three young stable hands led three saddled palfreys into the courtyard.

'You should learn to read, Hans,' said Conrad, shaking his head at the official who had returned to his records. 'The world is changing and you need to change with it.'

His friend was not convinced. 'I am a soldier not a scribe. I have no need of it.'

Conrad asked Hillar to accompany them on the ride south to the village that had sprung up on the site of Thalibald's settlement, some five miles south of Wenden. When the Army of the Wolf had arrived at Wenden following the battle against the Danes it had originally made camp on the large meadow south of the outer perimeter gates. But Master Thaddeus had suggested that rather than enduring months or longer in tents, the Estonians should construct their own village. Rudolf agreed but was desirous that they should build it away from Wenden, which had suddenly become home to an additional six hundred souls. Hillar's Rotalians had stayed near the border of their homeland and seventy Saccalians had been sent to Lehola to reinforce Sir Richard's garrison in case the Danes decided to march south in pursuit of Conrad. But the rest had followed the Marshal of Estonia back to Wenden.

Thaddeus had suggested that the village be built on the site of Thalibald's settlement, Conrad's former father-in-law who had been killed during a raid conducted by Lembit's wolf shields. Overgrown and desolate, there were hardly any traces of what had been the village of Caupo's chief warlord. Thaddeus had asked Conrad if he had any objection to the site being re-occupied but the brother knight had none. His wife and child were buried in the cemetery at Wenden. The site was close to fresh water and surrounded by land that had been cleared for fields, though now overgrown. So the Army of the Wolf had set about building its new home.

The largest contingent was Andres' four hundred Jerwen warriors, with Riki mustering only fifty Harrien men capable of bearing arms and Tonis, the former Wolf Shield, retaining the same number of Saccalian fighters. There were in addition a hundred women and children who had attached themselves to the crusader army during its retreat south from Reval.

The four riders trotted from the courtyard, through the gatehouse and across the drawbridge that spanned the deep, dry moat. They rode down the track bisecting the area within the outer perimeter defences; to the left the well-tended, walled cemetery and beyond it the huts that housed the civilian workers who worked in the castle. On the right stood the huts where Wenden's mercenaries slept and the training fields where the dogs of war perfected their skills along with the brother knights and sergeants. The grounds were a hive of activity, children playing among the huts, crossbowmen testing their weapons against straw targets and spearmen drilling under the watchful eye of sergeants. Conrad doubted whether any spearmen would travel north: Rudolf would want to cover as much ground as possible each day and that meant every soldier would have to be mounted.

They cantered along the dirt track leading south to the village, the other track from the castle diverting west to reach the jetties that projected into the waters of the Gauja two miles away. During the previous spring and summer months, before the pox had blighted Riga, there had been much traffic to and from the city. But now that had dried up completely. Fortunately the Gauja was still full of perch, bream, roach, dace and chub that were caught to feed Wenden's expanding population.

Soon ploughs pulled by oxen would be going into the fields to prepare the ground for sowing the spring crops: barley, oats, peas, beans and vetches. It was fortunate for the villagers that Master Rudolf allocated them a portion of the boar, deer, duck and goose that were hunted in autumn by the garrison's crossbowmen, the meat being salted in preparation for the winter months. When the snow lay thick on the ground the master sent his hunters into the forests to kill wolves, both for their meat and fur.

But now the land was bursting with life as the spring sun warmed the land, bushes and flowers blossoming along with bird cherry, lilac and apple trees. The rivers and streams were filled with ice-cool water and the air was filled with the twittering of birds. It was still fresh in the mornings and evenings, and frosts could last until June. But the iron grip of winter had been broken and villagers looked forward to bountiful harvests, new additions to their families and peace throughout Livonia.

Like countless villages throughout Estonia the settlement Conrad and his comrades rode to had a meeting hall, huts, barns, smithies and animal pens holding pigs, goats and chickens. Pig farming was a very popular Estonian practice so the village contained many grunting and squealing animals occupying fenced-off areas on its outskirts. Though in the winter the livestock was brought into the buildings to save them being taken by wolves and the cold.

Thalibald's village had been strongly defended by a ditch and wooden wall. The Estonians had cleared the ditch of weeds and deepened it, constructing a fresh wooden palisade behind it. There were also crude watchtowers at the gates that gave those on guard views of the surrounding terrain. Sentries in the towers spotted their approach, and so when they trotted over the stout bridge across the ditch a reception party was waiting for them. The six Jerwen warriors were armed with spears and carried round shields that sported the bear symbol of Jaak, once leader of their people but now dead. They raised their weapons in salute as Conrad and the others dismounted.

'Greetings, *Susi*,' said their commander.

Conrad acknowledged him. 'I am here to see the tribal leaders.'

'They are expecting you,' the warrior replied.

Conrad was surprised. 'They are?'

He pointed up at the guards on the top platforms of the watchtowers.

'As soon as you were identified a message was sent alerting them to your impending arrival.'

He clasped his fist to his chest. 'They will be pleased to see you. Lord Hillar.'

'Well, then,' said Conrad, 'let's be on our way.'

When they arrived at the meeting hall in the centre of the settlement a large crowd of mostly warriors had gathered, word having quickly spread that *Susi* was among them. When Conrad caught men's eyes they nodded purposely and the air tingled with excitement. The fact that he was with his comrades Hans and Anton, plus Hillar, who had remained in Estonia, could mean only one thing. They were going to war.

Only the three commanders and their senior chiefs were allowed in the hall. Girls served those present with large wooden cups filled with beer as a trestle table was hastily set up in the middle of the chamber. Riki, Andres and Tonis greeted the brother knights and Hillar then looked at Conrad. He took a large gulp of the cool beer as they sat around the table, the chiefs standing behind their leaders.

'Muster your men. We are marching north immediately.'

The chiefs grinned broadly and slapped each other on the back as those Estonians at the table nodded thoughtfully. Marching north meant only one thing: the liberation of their homeland.

'You should tell them why we are marching north,' said Hans.

All eyes focused on Conrad.

'We are going to Oesel,' he announced.

There was a stunned silence. Hillar, who already knew this, cast his eyes down to avoid the others' gazes.

Tonis, the Saccalian leader, laughed. 'What is there on Oesel for us?'

'We go to rescue the Danish king who has allowed himself to be surrounded by the Oeselians on the island.'

They all burst out laughing.

Riki pointed at the cup Conrad was holding. 'You have been drinking too much beer, *Susi*, it has deadened your mind.'

'Muster your warriors and lead them to Wenden tomorrow. Then we will ride north. No carts; we travel light and fast.'

Andres, the stout commander of the Jerwen, was now totally confused.

'The Danish king wanted you dead, *Susi*. Why would you raise a hand to help him?'

Conrad drained his cup. 'My friends, I understand why you think this order is strange. But I too obey orders and it is the desire of Master Rudolf that we should ride to save the Danish king.'

'Many of my men will not be happy, *Susi*,' said Riki. 'My people have suffered greatly at the hands of the Danes.'

Hillar looked up. 'As have my people. But I took an oath to serve *Susi* and will not break it.'

Riki looked at Tonis and then at Andres. The Rotalian leader was not only physically large; his voice held great sway in the Army of the Wolf.

'The Jerwen are with you, *Susi*,' said Andres, nodding at Hillar.

Riki and Tonis also voiced their support, which silenced the mumblings of the chiefs behind them.

'I know that what we are about to do makes little sense,' said Conrad. 'In truth it makes little sense to me. But I tell you that we will not be spilling blood in vain. The Danes will be held to account for what they have done in Estonia, that I promise.'

The Estonian leaders and their chiefs filed out of the hall, their muted spirits in contrast to the faces full of expectation that awaited them outside. They announced that the Army of the Wolf would be marching north the next day, which was greeted with rapturous cheering. The men were told to gather round their chiefs who would appoint quartermasters for the allocation of supplies for the ride north.

'They will be less happy later when they discover they ride north to save Valdemar's hide,' said Anton glumly.

'What did you mean when you said that the Danes will be held to account?' Hans asked Conrad.

'I have yet to work that out,' his friend answered.

'Perhaps Count Henry is with Valdemar,' said Anton.

Conrad's eyes lit up. 'I do hope so, as I trust that the Oeselians have not killed him.'

'So you can kill him instead?' said Hans.

Conrad grinned. 'Precisely.'

The brother knights arrived back at Wenden in time for Sext Mass at midday, one of seven services that delineated a brother knight's day. Immediately afterwards the knights and sergeants were expected to repair their armour and equipment and do other necessary tasks. However, as the castle was fully staffed with armourers and blacksmiths, who took a dim view of brother knights infringing on their responsibilities, there was little to do before lunch in the dining hall, save for guard duty that every bother knight and sergeant had to perform. Master Rudolf was insistent only members of the order should stand guard over the castle, arguing that mercenaries were more likely to fall asleep at their posts. Leatherface took great exception to this, telling the master that if they did they would be hanged as punishment. Rudolf retorted that it was of no benefit hanging a man if his negligence had allowed an enemy to infiltrate the castle.

Lunch was eaten in the dining hall, with the brother knights fed at the first sitting, the sergeants afterwards. Lukas' young novices served the brother knights at table. Meals were always eaten in silence; the food first being blessed by Father Otto and then a clerk would read from a Bible during the meal. According to the rules of the Sword Brothers meat – mutton, goat, beef, veal – was eaten three days a week and fish was consumed on Fridays. All other meals contained only vegetables, usually in the form of broths, though there were always ample portions of bread, fruit when available, and cheese to accompany the main dishes, washed down with water.

The Cistercian order of monks that had given birth to the Sword Brothers through Bishop Albert ate no meat and partook of sparse meals. But Grand Master Volquin and his castellans quickly discovered that the knights and sergeants of their order needed to be fed like fighting cocks if they were to defeat their enemies in battle. As usual before going on campaign, Hans, the former starving beggar from Lübeck, attempted to empty the castle storerooms of food before he departed Wenden.

The new day dawned bright and cool, the fields around the castle white with frost and the air crisp. After Prime Mass and breakfast the three friends donned their armour in preparation for their departure. Soon the Army of the Wolf would be arriving at the castle, hundreds of men on hardy ponies that had greater stamina than the horses the order imported from Germany.

Rudolf came to see them as they were changing into their martial attire on the first floor of the great dormitory where the brother knights slept. They all stood when he appeared among them.

'Please continue with your preparations,' he commanded.

Just as the order believed that its soldiers should have good food so it spared no cost when it came to their weapons and armour. They may have been poor, pious knights but their equipment was among the best in all Christendom. Next to the skin were worn cotton breeches and a vest, over which was worn a quilted cotton-covered aketon that protected the vest and skin beneath from the long-sleeved mail hauberk that covered the arms, hands, torso and thighs. The mittens had soft leather palms so the wearer could grip his weapons with ease.

'So,' Rudolf said to Conrad, 'you ride north today. How many men does the Army of the Wolf number?'

Conrad put on the linen-covered, quilted sleeveless gambeson over his mail armour. The garment could defeat a glancing sword or axe blow and lessen the penetrating power of an arrow, though not a crossbow bolt.

'Just under nine hundred men, master, including the Wolf Shields I will collect at Lehola.'

Rudolf nodded in admiration. 'The largest force that Livonia can currently muster. You are to be congratulated, Conrad.'

Conrad adjusted the mail chausses that protected his legs, beneath which was linen hose to prevent chafing.

'The Estonians do not understand why they march to assist King Valdemar, master,' said Conrad.

Rudolf picked up Conrad's sword belt and drew the weapon.

'Estonia will benefit from our expedition,' remarked Rudolf, 'in the long term. But at present I must ask you, all of all, to refrain from unleashing your base instincts.'

'Base instincts, master?' said Anton innocently.

'I am well aware that Valdemar was responsible for the death of Brother Johann,' replied Rudolf, 'and indeed would probably have burned Conrad at the stake had it not have been for the timely arrival of Kalju at Reval.'

He handed the sword to Conrad. 'Remember the great knight who gave you this sword and the principles it and he represent. I would not blame you for wanting revenge upon Valdemar. I too have entertained such thoughts. But I would remind you that the very future of Livonia may be at stake in the next few weeks and our actions will determine what that future will be.'

'Perhaps King Valdemar is already dead, master,' offered Hans.

Conrad laid the sword on his bed and pulled on his boots. 'Pray God.'

Rudolf shook his head. 'You would like that, wouldn't you? But if he is dead then his son will become king and Livonia will still be under blockade.'

'And if we rescue him, master,' asked Conrad, 'what then? He despises the Sword Brothers and most likely will use the opportunity to attack us.'

'We should let the Oeselians kill him before we assault Oesel,' said Anton.

'Kill two birds with one stone,' smiled Hans.

Rudolf sighed. 'Like I said, you all must resist your base instincts. Keep your men and your emotions under control. God will not forgive you if you wreck my plans.'

He began to walk towards the door to the dormitory.

'What plans, master?' Conrad called after him.

'You will soon see,' answered Rudolf as he disappeared from the chamber.

'The master is worried that you will try to kill Valdemar, Conrad,' said Anton.

'If a Sword Brother killed a king appointed by God then that would surely be the end not only of Livonia but also our order,' replied Conrad. 'And that I do not desire.'

'The master said nothing about his father, Count Henry,' mused Hans.

'He probably wants to forget him,' said Conrad. 'With a father like that so would I.'

A sergeant appeared at the door.

'Brother Conrad, the Estonians are gathering beyond the outer perimeter.'

Conrad raised his hand in acknowledgment and put on his white surcoat emblazoned with the emblem of the Sword Brothers. He tied the straps of his linen coif under his chin, pulled the mail coif over it and then placed the padded leather headband on his head. The headband made the wearing of a helm more bearable. He then buckled his sword belt around his waist, the others doing the same.

'Time to visit the armourers,' said Conrad.

At the armoury they were issued with their helms and shields, plus Conrad's axe and Hans' and Anton's maces.

'We will need crossbows as well,' Conrad told the armourer, who like most of his comrades was a squat, ugly fellow with huge forearms and a condescending manner.

'Brother knights aren't issued with crossbows,' he answered curtly.

'Three full quivers each as well,' said Conrad, ignoring him.

The armourer grunted and disappeared into the dim interior of the squat stone building housing a multitude of weapons, armour and crossbows. When he returned, with another man who was uglier than he, they slammed the crossbows on the wooden counter, the full quivers alongside them.

'Spare bowstrings,' added Conrad.

The armourer grinned and pulled the rolled-up strings from the pocket of the leather apron covering his thick chest and huge gut. He threw them on the counter.

'Make sure you don't let your heathen bastards anywhere near these crossbows. They're only for God-fearing soldiers.'

The brother knights tucked the axe and maces into their belts and picked up the crossbows and quivers.

'That heathen bitch was in here earlier,' the armourer called after them as they walked from the counter. 'She's getting too high and mighty for my liking. If Ilona wasn't with her I would have given her a slap.'

'I often think that the armoury provides a vision of what hell must look like,' remarked Hans as the three walked back into the courtyard.

The 'heathen bitch' was Kaja, a Saccalian orphan whom Conrad had taken under his wing when he had led the relief of Lehola four years before. The bedraggled girl had been only sixteen then but now she was an attractive, determined woman of twenty who knew her own mind. She was not actually a heathen, having been baptised into the Christian faith. But she had retained her fierce Saccalian nature and backed it up with an intricate knowledge of swordplay, for Conrad and Brother Lukas had taught her to use a blade, which she had strapped to her waist as she sauntered over to the three brother knights. Her blonde hair had been tied into a ponytail and her leggings hugged her shapely legs. She carried an iron helmet with a nasal guard in the crook of her arm. Beside her walked Ilona, the raven-haired beauty, a Liv healer revered for her skill with herbs and potions who had saved Master Rudolf from the flames of Holm many years before.

'This looks ominous,' remarked Anton as the two beauties approached.

'You ride to Oesel, Brother Conrad,' said Kaja.

Hans and Anton laughed.

'You are remarkably well informed,' replied Conrad.

'I'm coming with you,' she declared.

'It would be better if you stayed here,' Conrad told her.

'The Army of the Wolf has never been defeated when Kaja has ridden with it,' said Ilona.

'That's true,' agreed Hans.

Conrad glared at his friend. 'We are going to war, Kaja. I cannot guarantee your safety if you come with us.'

She grasped the hilt of her sword. 'I can do that.'

'The Estonians believe Kaja to be a lucky mascot, Conrad,' Ilona told him. 'Men fight better if they believe luck is on their side.'

'That's true,' said Hans.

'You are not helping,' Conrad told him. 'I'm sorry, Kaja, but you cannot come with us.'

Her blue eyes hardened. 'Am I not free?'

'Of course.'

'Then I choose to accompany you north.'

Stables hands were leading out their palfreys with sacks of fodder fastened to their saddles. Conrad noticed that there were four.

'Besides,' said Ilona casually, 'who will carry your banner if Kaja does not accompany you?'

'That's true,' said Hans.

'Shut up,' Conrad told him.

He was about to reply to Ilona when he saw Rudolf, Walter and Otto approaching, the latter carrying a standard.

Ilona smiled kindly at Conrad. 'Rudolf thought the same.'

Conrad realised he had been out-manoeuvred as the group halted and the severe Otto handed Kaja the standard that Conrad had carried into Estonia four years before. Like the standard carried by the garrison when it went to war, it was stored near the altar in the chapel, for it was a sacred banner.

'Kaja is reckoned a lucky mascot by your men, I believe,' Rudolf said to Conrad. Conrad nodded.

'Well, then,' continued the master, 'I have been persuaded that her presence will aid your cause, which in turn will aid the order's cause.'

'Kneel!' Otto commanded.

Conrad smiled wryly as he knelt on the cobblestones, a beaming Kaja already on her knees with her head down as she clutched the haft of the standard wrapped around the wood and tied in place with ribbons. He had forgotten how manipulative women could be.

Otto asked God to protect them and give them victory, his deep voice filling the courtyard. After he had finished Rudolf and Ilona wished the three brother knights and Kaja luck as they walked to their horses and rode from the castle to lead the Army of the Wolf north.

And far to the south a chest of clothes was spirited out of Riga under cover of darkness and loaded on a cart for transportation to Odenpah.

Chapter 2

King Valdemar's march to Varbola and then to the coast of Rotalia was not so much a military campaign more a procession. The column extended over many miles as it made its way slowly to the coast where it would rendezvous with the boats that would transport it to the northern coast of Oesel. Among the greenery of the countryside it presented a dazzling spectacle, a garish display of red, blue, yellow and orange. Leading the army had been the knights and squires of Count Albert of Orlamunde and Holstein, the caparisons of his knights' destriers bearing his coat of arms: a white nettle leaf on a red background. Their shields, pennants and surcoats carried the same device, and the count had also insisted that the shields of his lesser knights, those men who had the money to purchase their own horses and weapons, should also display his emblem. The count had brought fifty knights, fifty squires and fifty lesser knights to Estonia to subjugate the enemies of the Danes.

Valdemar's bodyguard numbered a hundred mounted knights, men attired in the finest armour and riding the best destriers that money could buy. Added to Count Albert's horsemen it gave the king two hundred and fifty horsemen, more than enough to charge straight through a pagan shield wall.

The king's foot soldiers were all drawn from his Danish and Swedish lands. The largest contingent was the axe men, rough-hewn men wearing conical helmets with nasal guards, mail hauberks and gaiters around their lower leggings. Like the Oeselians they carried a round wooden shield for protection and a large-bladed war axe as their primary weapon. The hundred Danish sergeants were likewise armed with axes and equipped with hauberks, though they also carried swords, wore kettle helmets and carried almond-shaped shields. The spearmen's shields were the same shape as those carried by the sergeants, though larger, and in addition to their spears they were armed with broad slashing swords with a tapering blade. They numbered three hundred and fifty.

Valdemar's best non-mounted troops were his Danish foot knights. These men wore segmented iron helmets with fixed face guards, beneath which was worn a mail coif. Their mail hauberks had integral mail mittens and their yellow surcoats were very broad and had long sleeves. On their legs they wore mail chausses and a thickly padded gambeson beneath their hauberks. Their principal weapon was a sword. The almond-shaped shields they carried were reinforced with slender iron crosspieces held in place by a small iron boss. There were two hundred of these élite foot soldiers.

Valdemar's only missile troops were two hundred Swedish archers, the crossbowmen having been left behind at Reval for the defence of the town. The king gave orders that the archers were to be sent out every day to kill game to be served each evening in the royal pavilion. Thus did the royal army number two thousand, one hundred fighting men, plus a substantial entourage that accompanied Valdemar to ensure that his spiritual and physical needs were attended to at all times.

As befitting his status as one of Europe's most powerful monarchs the king was accompanied by the portly Bishop of Roskilde, a brace of abbots and deans and half a dozen scribes tasked with recording every detail of what would be Valdemar's conquest of Oesel. In attendance were also the court chamberlain, treasurer, justiciar – head of the royal judicial system and the king's viceroy, keeper of the royal seal and master of the horse. To serve him at table were cupbearers and dapifers – servants that brought meat to those seated. To entertain the royal party were jesters, minstrels and bards. Then there were falconers, stewards and heralds. They all amounted to a grand total of three hundred men and boys responsible for making the king's journey and accommodation in the field as comfortable as possible. There were also two hundred Estonians that had been impressed to perform manual duties for the royal procession, such as digging latrines, preparing fires and collecting firewood, though not chopping it as they were not trusted with weapons.

The army with its dozens of carts and wagons managed to skirt the many bog ponds, freshwater springs and lakes on its journey, a vehicle occasionally sinking in the mud and either being hauled out or abandoned, its cargo distributed among the Estonians. From Varbola the army struck west to Matsalu Bay where the ships and boats despatched by Count Rolf from

Reval were waiting. It had been suggested to Valdemar that it would be more convenient to take ship from Reval directly to Oesel but the king was insistent that his Estonian subjects should see him in all his pomp and glory as he travelled among them. No one riding with the king said anything as the army passed through a succession of deserted villages.

It took two days to load the dozens of boats in the bay and two more days to ferry the army and its attendants to the northern coast of Oesel. The relief of the island is mostly flat though the coastline is strongly fragmented and so it took longer than anticipated to find a landing site. However, eventually the ships docked in a bay between two grass-covered peninsulas, where the water was deep enough to accommodate the cogs carrying the king, his chief advisers and commanders. The majority of the foot soldiers were shipped in shallow-draft oared vessels with a single sail that resembled Oeselian longships, but the latter were nowhere to be seen. Upon landing the Bishop of Roskilde held a service of thanksgiving on the beach and then the Danes set off inland.

They did not go far, perhaps two miles before the quartermasters found a moraine plain of rocks and sediment on the edge of a great expanse of forest and near a large freshwater lake. They informed the king that the space between the plain and the trees – a meadow of tall grass – was an ideal site to construct a stone stronghold to provide a base for the subjugation of the Oeselians. The Estonians were immediately put to work collecting rocks for the construction of the fort as the engineers marked out the rectangular site of what would be the stronghold while the king's servants erected the royal pavilion, around which a host of other pavilions and tents were pitched. Soon the space was filled with hundreds of smaller tents, horses, wagons, carts and cooking fires, with a steady stream of soldiers going to the forest and returning with firewood. Sentries were posted as the light began to fade but everyone forgot about the Oeselians who were obviously cowering in their hovels, a people waiting to be conquered.

That night at the royal banquet Count Albert expressed his disappointment at not having to fight the pagans on the beach where the army had landed earlier. Valdemar reminded him that since God had sent him the holy standard his army had never been defeated. This being the case, the news that it accompanied his army had probably cast the Oeselians into the depth of despair.

*****

The king's hall in Kuressaare was filled with Olaf's earls: tall, powerful men with long hair and thick beards who wore mail armour and carried swords at their hips. The hall was a huge wooden building in the centre of Oesel's largest settlement, its steeply pitched roof supported by two interior rows of massive oak posts. The doors were closed but the temperature inside the hall was pleasant enough, the spring mornings still cool though there was no need to light fires in the stone hearth in the centre of the floor. The earls lounged on the tiered benches positioned against the walls, listening intently to their king. Slaves went among them with trays holding tankards of honey mead.

In the centre of the hall stood the squat, broad-shouldered king, his hair and beard now totally white, his skin leathery. Now in his early sixties, his eyes were still alert and his mind sharp. On the nearest bench sat his three sons: Sigurd, Stark and Kalf. The king threw his empty tankard for a slave to catch and wiped his mouth on the sleeve of his tunic.

'The day we prayed that would never come is upon us. The Christians have landed on Oesel and are now in the north of our blessed island building a fort.'

There was a stony silence among the earls. Olaf knew that many were desperate to be heard but they kept quiet out of respect for the king.

'After conquering the Estonian tribes the Danish king has decided that we are next on his list of targets, to be reduced to slavery just as the Estonians have been. Some of you may be wondering why I have not raised an army and attacked the invaders.'

The silence remained but many of the earls were having difficulty holding their tongues. The amount of treasure and quantity of estates they held and the number of warriors they could raise measured Oeselian earls. They captained the king's longships and fought beside him in battle. They were fierce, proud and brave but now they were confused. Eventually one rose from his bench, a bear of a man who was older than Olaf but as hard as the iron helmet sitting on the bench beside him. The king nodded at his friend Swein.

'Forgive me, great king,' he began. 'But many wonder, myself among them, why we have not thrown these Danish barbarians back into the sea.'

There were mooted mutterings from both sides of the hall.

'A fair question, Swein,' answered the king. 'One that my son will answer.'

Olaf nodded to Sigurd and sat down. His eldest son and heir, his long hair pure blonde and his face clean shaven, rose and took his position in the centre of the hall. Now in his mid-thirties, he had none of the arrogance and fire of his dead brother Eric. He had been the embodiment of what an Oeselian warrior should be: reckless, contemptuous of death and impossibly brave. But for all Eric's fame and lust for glory he had achieved nothing except to lead an army to defeat at the hands of the Sword Brothers. It was a mistake that his brother was determined not to repeat.

'My lords,' Sigurd began, 'for over twenty years we have fought the Christian crusaders. Both on the seas and on land. First in Livonia and then in Estonia. Many Oeselian warriors have given their lives in this fight, among them my own brother Eric. Now the Danes have landed on Oesel itself.'

He began walking up and down the centre of the hall, nodding to those earls he knew.

'I have seen the crusaders break shield walls on the battlefield, have seen the deadly power of their crossbows first hand, and felt the earth shake when their mailed horsemen charge. The Danish king comes to Oesel to fight us in battle.'

'And we will give him a battle,' came a voice from the assembled earls. The others cheered and stamped their feet in support.

Sigurd let the hubbub die down.

'We will not offer the enemy battle,' he said slowly and firmly.

Stark and Kalf looked at each other in confusion and then at their father. But Olaf stared ahead, a knowing look on his face. There were murmurs of dissent from the earls.

'We will not offer battle because we will besiege the Danes,' said Sigurd. 'We will grind them down and starve them into submission. How will the Danes be able to march out against us when their warhorses are so weak and emaciated that they cannot carry a man? How will their foot soldiers fare against our warriors when they have not eaten anything in days?'

A brawny man with a thick blond beard and long moustache rose from his bench. He bowed his head at his king and close friend.

'Prince Sigurd,' said Bothvar, 'we have no machines with which to besiege the Danes.'

Sigurd smiled. 'Do we not, Earl Bothvar? In the next few days you will see that we too can build machines just as the crusaders do.'

*****

The scribes that Valdemar had brought with him from Reval called them *paterells*, which was a derivative of *patera*, meaning 'dish' or 'cup', but they were in fact a form of mangonel. Crude and smaller than the machines that the Sword Brothers and Danes used, Sigurd's *paterells* were nonetheless effective. They could throw a stone weighing around ten pounds up to a range of three hundred yards, but before they were employed Sigurd unleashed a fleet of longships to blockade Reval. This ensured that the garrison would not be able to re-supply Valdemar or evacuate his army from Oesel. Sigurd then sent a flotilla of *karvs* – small, highly manoeuvrable longships with thirteen pairs of oars – to burn the ships at anchor that had brought the Danish army to Oesel.

Sigurd's plan had worked perfectly.

Valdemar was now isolated. Soon he would be under siege.

*****

The Army of the Wolf did not ride to Lehola but instead headed northwest towards Rotalia and the coastline of the Gulf of Riga. Hillar and his few men journeyed ahead to rally his army at the rendezvous point where the River Parnu flowed into the Gulf of Riga. The guides led the mounted force

63

through a land of bogs, marshes and thick pine forests, eventually joining the coastline a day's ride from the rendezvous point. The column trotted by the side of long sandy beaches and fishing villages dotted along the coast, some deserted and burnt. Every settlement had a crude hill fort, sometimes nothing more than four wooden walls with a single entrance to provide sanctuary from Oeselian raiders. But of late it had been Danish horsemen that had spread death and destruction.

On the Saccalian border Conrad had collected Hillar's three hundred Rotalian warriors, all of them mounted on hardy ponies allowing the army to cover at least twenty miles a day. The land was predominantly flat and very fertile, rye growing in the fields around inland villages and herds of cattle grazing in lush meadows flanking rivers. They also provided good pasture for the ponies that had transported the Army of the Wolf to Rotalia and which now made camp two miles south of the Parnu River.

The three Sword Brothers slept in a simple pagan tent comprising a rectangle of felt draped over a ridgepole with two vertical poles at each end, the fabric staked to the ground by means of wooden pegs. There were hundreds of such tents, all arranged in circles around tribal chiefs. The shields and banners of the Estonians bore ancient pagan symbols, such as the sun cross, pentagram, plaited lattice designs, elk antlers, eight-pointed star and cornflower. There were also the symbols of the chiefs, now dead, who had once fought the Sword Brothers, the leering red wolf, the bear and stag. As Kaja threw more wood on the fire to heat the stew in the cooking pot, Hans looked around at the dozens of other fires that were helping to mist the dusk.

'Not much of a Christian army, is it?'

'It fights for God,' said Conrad, 'it does not matter what symbols men carry on their shields.'

'They fight for *you*, Conrad,' said Anton, sniffing the air as the pleasing aroma of the stew entered his nostrils.

'What do you say, Kaja?' asked Hans. 'Does this army fight for the Christian God or for Brother Conrad?'

'For *Susi*, of course,' she replied.

'Just think,' continued Hans, 'the Bishop of Riga has a pagan army under his command. I wonder what the Pope would say?'

'And now a pagan army goes to rescue a Christian king who has got himself trapped on Oesel by pagans,' complained Conrad. 'It makes no sense.'

Kaja stirred the stew. 'You would prefer that the king was killed by the Oeselians, *Susi*?'

'I would,' stated Conrad. 'After all, Valdemar desired my death. It is only common courtesy that I should reciprocate the sentiment.'

He looked at the groups of warriors gathered round fires, eating and chatting, stacks of spears and shields nearby.

'It grieves me that many of these men will die saving the neck of that wretched king.'

Hans laughed. 'Who would have thought it, a beggar and a baker's son from Lübeck having a say in the fate of a king?'

'What about me?' said Anton.

'You don't count,' his friend told him, 'on account of you being from a rich family.'

'Hillar told me that the Danes have been hard on his people,' remarked Anton. 'There are many destroyed villages north of the Parnu River.'

Conrad nodded. 'All the more reason to leave Valdemar to his fate.'

'That is not very charitable, *Susi*,' said Kaja, stirring the stew. 'Father Otto says that we are all obligated to perform acts of charity if we want to enter heaven.'

Conrad looked at her and smiled. When he had first met her she had been a half-starved wretch who had lost all her family. But now she was known and respected throughout the Army of the Wolf as a good fighter and a lucky mascot. He glanced at the fine Danish sword in its scabbard strapped to her waist.

'What else does he say?' enquired Conrad.

She stopped stirring and looked at him with her piercing blue eyes.

'That men are brothers and members of the same family.'

'A splendid theory, I have to agree,' said Anton.

'The thing is, Kaja,' said Hans, 'you will find that there is a great difference between what men say and what they do.'

'Even if they are priests, Brother Hans?'

Hans gave her an ironic smile. 'Especially if they are priests.'

She looked at Conrad. 'So you do not love the Danish king like a brother, *Susi?*'

'No, Kaja.'

She started to ladle stew into wooden bowls as the brother knights sat on the ground near the fire. As usual Hans insisted on being served first on account that he was deprived of food as a child and had a lot of catching up to do. She too sat on the ground with a bowl after she had served them.

'Clever how you employed Ilona to persuade Master Rudolf to let you come with us, Kaja,' said Anton casually.

'In truth it was easy,' she said. 'He did not need much persuading. I was delighted.'

'I can imagine,' muttered Conrad.

'The master said that I was a lucky talisman,' she continued, 'and should carry the army's banner. Master Rudolf is a kind-hearted man.'

They burst out laughing. Rudolf was many things: callous, brave, loyal and steadfast. But what he was not was kind hearted. Which made his not only agreeing to but encouraging Kaja to accompany the army north all the more baffling. It was most strange and made Conrad more anxious concerning the mission to Oesel. He was also burdened with the knowledge that Kaja and his brother Rameke were very fond of each other and had exchanged messages during the past eighteen months. Indeed he expected Rameke to make her his wife. If anything happened to her he would never forgive himself. Worse, Rameke would never forgive him.

Sir Richard arrived two days later at the head of over three hundred men, all mounted on either horses or ponies. As ever he was accompanied by the dour Squire Paul, whom Conrad reckoned the eldest squire in Christendom. The Duke of Saccalia rode at the head of forty heavily armed and armoured knights. Each man wore a full-face helm, mail armour and surcoat emblazoned with the coat of arms of their family. Some of the heavy horsemen had journeyed to Livonia with Sir Richard as squires but had been elevated by him to knightly status in a ceremony that was the same the length and breadth of Europe. After a mass the other knights fixed gilded spurs to the aspirant, who was given the belt that was an important emblem of knighthood. Then Sir Richard handed him a sword, kissed him and tapped him on the shoulder. It was a curious thing that despite the religious nature of knighthood, the rank was bestowed not by churchmen but by men who were knights and who had proved themselves in battle.

Sir Richard had made his home in Saccalia, as had those men who had elected to stay with him in the land of forests and lakes. But many among the forty squires who rode with him into camp were native Saccalians who had been baptized and were learning how to fight as 'men of iron', as the locals called the mounted Christian knights. Thus, slowly, did the notion of knighthood and the Christian faith spread throughout Saccalia.

Sir Richard also brought fifty lesser knights, men who had enough money to buy a horse and armour but not enough to purchase an expensive destrier. And certainly not enough to maintain a squire and servants. But like those original knights and squires that had accompanied Sir Richard they had elected to stay in Saccalia to make a new life for themselves.

Lastly the Duke of Saccalia brought two hundred Saccalian levies, young men drawn from the villages around Lehola who could ride and fight in a shield wall. Conrad was amazed to see that not only were they all riding hardy ponies but also that each man was equipped with a helmet, mail or lamellar armour – either leather or iron – and shield. Every man was also well equipped when it came to weapons, carrying one or two spears, a light hand axe, dagger and sword. Conrad had never seen native soldiers, either Livs or Estonians, so well-armed and armoured.

'Lehola's armoury is filled with the weapons and armour we took off the Cumans and Russians when you relieved the fortress,' Sir Richard told Conrad as he chewed on a piece of over-cooked boar. 'Not to mention the weapons the Danes left on the field when they fled back to Reval after hostilities broke out.'

The three Sword Brothers and the other leaders in the Army of the Wolf had been invited to dine with him and his commanders the first night they had arrived in camp. Sir Richard had been asked to travel light so as to reach Oesel quickly, but he and his knights had still loaded their pavilions

69

on the backs of ponies. Indeed, there must have been at least a hundred of the beasts weighed down with food, tents, clothes, weapons and armour.

Squire Paul, his face a mask of indifference as usual, stood behind his lord and served him beer and food. Sir Richard spat out a mouthful of meat.

'It's like eating charcoal, Paul. Too long over a fire.'

'Better than not cooked enough,' sighed Paul. 'At least you won't be writhing around with gut rot tomorrow.'

Sir Richard rolled his eyes. 'No, I will just be faint from starvation. Get me something I can eat, damn you.'

Paul exhaled loudly and sauntered from the tent.

'Paul is still truculent, your grace?' smiled Conrad.

'Truculent? He gets worse by the year,' complained Sir Richard. 'I don't know why I tolerate him.'

But Conrad knew that Paul was unfalteringly loyal to his lord, notwithstanding his sarcastic manner, and Sir Richard returned the sentiment. They were like an old married couple, thought Conrad.

'So, we go to rescue King Valdemar from the pagans,' said Sir Richard.

Conrad picked at the meat on the wooden plate in front of him.

'So it would seem.'

'You do not hold with Master Rudolf's plan?' the Duke of Saccalia probed.

Hans, who had finished his own plate of food, took a handful of Conrad's.

'Conrad believes that King Valdemar should be left to his fate on Oesel.'

Anton took a swig of beer. 'As do I. Why should the Sword Brothers help one who despises them?'

Hillar, Andres, Tonis and Riki sitting alongside the three brother knights banged their fists on the planks that had been laid on trestles to indicate their support.

Sir Richard laughed as his commanders opposite did the same, raising their cups to the bearded warriors. They too had little inclination to save the Danish king. Paul returned with a fresh plate of food and placed it before his lord.

'Perhaps,' suggested Sir Richard, 'Master Rudolf believes that if he saves Valdemar then the Danish king, out of gratitude, will stop throttling Livonia and will lift the blockade.'

Conrad batted Hans' hand away when his friend tried to take more food from his plate.

'Even if that is so, your grace, Valdemar will not relinquish Estonia and Estonia belongs to the Sword Brothers. It would be better if an Oeselian warrior throttles the Danish king and saves us a perilous journey.'

Hans and Anton beside their friend slapped him on the back and smiled. Squire Paul regarded Conrad for a few seconds. He leaned forward to whisper to his master.

'The boy becomes the man. Valdemar may regret letting that one live.'

Sir Richard smiled as a squire placed more meat on the plates of the three Sword Brothers, who proceeded to devour the food like ravenous wolves, especially the lean Hans. The blue-grey eyes of *Susi* glinted with anticipation and menace.

'He is like an angry wolf,' Sir Richard replied.

'Not sure I would like to be rescued by an army of angry wolves,' said Paul.

'Where is Peeter?' asked Conrad, 'I was sorry he did not accompany you.'

'He is well,' answered Sir Richard, 'but I thought it advisable that he remain at Fellin to keep an eye on our eastern border.'

Pope Honorius himself had created Peeter, a Saccalian, Count of Fellin, upon condition that he accepted baptism. Thus it was that a former pagan warlord was now a Christian noble guarding the border with Ungannia.

'What do you hear of Ungannia, your grace?' enquired Conrad.

'Kalju and Eha are well,' Sir Richard replied, 'and Ungannia is at peace and prospers. But I doubt that Kalju has forgiven Henke for the loss of his son.'

'He is a wise leader,' agreed Hans.

The next day Master Rudolf rode into camp accompanied by the masters of Segewold and Kremon. Behind them a long column of horses carried the brother knights of those two castles and Wenden, together with over a hundred sergeants, one hundred and thirty crossbowmen and packhorses carrying supplies, weapons and ammunition. All the sergeants carried crossbows in addition to their personal weapons, which meant that the newly assembled army could muster nearly two hundred and fifty missile troops in total. Conrad, having received a summons from Rudolf, walked over to the Sword Brother camp with Hillar as the garrisons pitched the chapel tent, those of the masters and then the rest in ever-expanding circles around them. Horses were tethered to fences fashioned from branches from felled trees and sheltered from the elements by canvas sheets spread over wooden frames. Very soon the daily rains turned the camp into a sea of mud.

'You'll dirty your nice white surcoat, Brother Conrad.'

The brother knight turned to see a grinning Leatherface in his customary ragged trousers and aged gambeson.

'No such worry for you, my friend.'

Leatherface picked his way around pools of mud to get nearer.

'You decided not to hire yourselves out to the Russians, then?'

Leatherface rubbed his grubby hands together. 'Not with a new campaign rearing its head. I've heard that Oesel is full of wealth.'

Conrad continued to walk towards the tents of the masters.

'Really?' It was not what he had heard.

But Leatherface was most insistent. 'Stands to reason, if you think about it. These Oeselians are descended from the Vikings. Am I right?'

'I have no idea.'

'The point is,' Leatherface continued, 'it's well known that the Vikings plundered every land their longships landed on. And where did they take all that loot?'

Conrad stepped in a large puddle. 'I have no idea.'

'Oesel, of course. It must be dripping with gold. The lads are itching to get there.'

'The Oeselians might object to you plundering their island.'

Leatherface cackled. 'Master Rudolf is clever. He has left all the spearmen behind and armed his sergeants with crossbows to supplement my lads. Using your heathens for cover we will shoot the enemy to pieces. How's my girl?'

'I assume you are speaking of Kaja? She's not your girl and you should not provoke her.'

Leatherface wore a look of innocence. 'Provoke her? Me? When I retire and get my alehouse I'll be looking for a woman with a pair of child-bearing hips to help me out. Women like a mature man with property.'

Conrad shook his head. 'The saints preserve us. Just keep your plans to yourself, don't tell her. Her sword is as sharp as her tongue.'

Leatherface suddenly became serious. 'You made a mistake teaching her how to use a sword, Brother Conrad. She will get ideas above her station.'

Conrad laughed. 'You mean she can defend herself from lecherous old goats like you.'

'And she can shoot a crossbow,' complained Leatherface. 'Just think of a world full of women who can fight like men. Don't bear thinking about.'

'I would have thought an old mercenary such as you would like a woman who has a bit of fight in her,' jested Conrad.

The dog of war slapped him on the back.

'Must be away. The lads are cooking a deer they caught earlier. You take care Brother Conrad, and give my girl a big fat kiss. And before you teach any more girls to fight remember that women and weapons don't mix.'

Hillar, who had little knowledge of German, had remained silent throughout the conversation. He looked at Leatherface as the mercenary walked off whistling, seemingly without a care in the world. The Rotalian had seen the old dog of war before of course, but was still amazed that this man who had coarse manners, scruffy clothes and a haggard appearance held a high position among the Sword Brothers.

'He is very good at what he does,' said Conrad, 'and he holds the respect of the other mercenary crossbowmen that the order employs.'

'Why does he dress like a beggar, *Susi?*'

75

'Always has done. I think he regards his dishevelled appearance as something that marks him out from the rest. Besides, in battle he is someone you would want by your side. He remains calm when others are losing their wits.'

'He should buy himself some new clothes,' said Hillar.

When they arrived at Rudolf's tent they found masters Bertram and Mathias in attendance, both tall like Rudolf though more thickset. The master of Wenden was now forty years old but the castellans of Kremon and Segewold were older by perhaps five or six years. Conrad introduced Hillar to them as Rudolf indicated they both should take a seat around the table arranged in the centre of his tent. Out of courtesy to Hillar the conversation was in Estonian. Rudolf poured them both a drink of beer as they waited for Sir Richard to arrive. The patter on the tent's roof indicated the arrival of more rain before the English lord, who was wrapped in a brown cape when he appeared.

Rudolf closed the tent flaps and tied them together as the raindrops turned into a short downpour, battering the sides and roof of the tent. Then suddenly it was over.

'I thought England was bad when it came to weather,' remarked Sir Richard as he removed his cape and draped it over the remaining chair, 'but Estonia and Livonia make it appear positively arid.'

Rudolf poured beer into his cup.

'I apologise for luring you from Lehola, your grace.'

Sir Richard took a swig. 'Can we please dispense with this "your grace" nonsense? We are all friends here and have shed blood together, so let us not stand on ceremony. So, when do we set out for Oesel?'

Rudolf looked at Conrad. 'We are in your hands, lord marshal.'

'I am no longer Marshal of Estonia, master,' said Conrad.

'In my eyes you are,' replied Rudolf, 'and I think I can speak for my fellow masters.'

Bertram and Mathias nodded grimly.

'So please continue.' Rudolf said.

Conrad looked at Hillar. 'Tell them what your scouts have discovered.'

Hillar made to stand but Rudolf told him to remain seated.

'As Sir Richard says, we are all friends here.'

Hillar gestured with his huge hands as he spoke, using them to cut the air as he told of how the Danes had landed on the northeast coast of Oesel where they were currently besieged by the Oeselians. They had advanced only a small distance inland, establishing a camp and staying close to the ships that had dropped anchor in the nearby cove. But the Oeselians had fired the ships and blockaded the other Danish boats that had sailed back to the mainland, taking shelter in Matsalu Bay.

'My people have also heard that the Oeselians also maintain their blockade of Reval.'

Rudolf laughed. 'Valdemar is well and truly bereft of hope.'

He tapped a finger on the rim of his cup and pondered for a moment.

'Hillar, what would be the best way to transport this army to Oesel so it may come to the aid of King Valdemar?'

Hillar puffed out his cheeks. 'It would take many boats to transport hundreds of men and animals.'

'What if we left the horses and ponies on the mainland?' Rudolf pressed him. 'Can the Rotalians provide me with enough vessels to transport a thousand men to Oesel?'

Bertram raised an eyebrow. 'I thought there are nearly fifteen hundred men in this camp, Rudolf.'

'There are,' Wenden's master agreed, 'but I will leave a few hundred on the mainland to guard the animals and supplies. Besides, we need room in the boats to accommodate our esteemed Danish allies.'

'What is left of them,' said Mathias grimly.

'I know the elders of Lääne County, the region on the western coast of Rotalia,' said Hillar. 'I can ask them to assemble as many boats as their people can gather. From there the army can sail to the island of Muhu, which is but a short distance from the mainland. Muhu lies between the mainland and Oesel. My advice would be to spend one night on Muhu and then sail through the strait between the islands to land near where the Danes are besieged.'

'You know these waters and islands you speak of?' Mathias asked Hillar.

The Estonian nodded. 'Before I joined *Susi* Lääne was my home.'

Conrad suddenly remembered the time, many years before, when he was on a cog travelling to Livonia.

'If we are attacked by Oeselian longships we will be slaughtered, master.'

'He's right, Rudolf,' said Bertram.

But Rudolf had already thought of that.

'Hillar has told us that Oeselian ships are blockading the Danes in Matsalu Bay and in the harbour at Reval, and we know that an Oeselian army is besieging King Valdemar. Unless the Oeselians are devils from hell in human form then I would hazard that they are stretched thin. That being the case I believe we can get to Oesel unnoticed and snatch Valdemar from the jaws of defeat.'

'We risk much for someone who shouts loudly that he is an enemy of the Sword Brothers,' said Bertram.

'Why can't we let the bastard die?' asked Mathias.

'Because he is more use to us alive,' said Rudolf, though when questioned further on the matter he would say no more.

'We go to steal a king,' Rudolf announced. 'Hillar, I must ask you to ride to your people to assemble the boats so we may accomplish our mission.'

As the camp was subjected to another heavy shower and the others filed out of the tent, Rudolf asked Conrad to stay.

'When we get to Oesel try to resist the temptation to kill King Valdemar, Conrad, and order your warriors to likewise refrain from harming his regal body. I know that they are loyal to you.'

'They obey orders, master, have no fear.'

Rudolf smiled. 'Good. And bring that girl that you and Lukas have turned into a fighter with you.'

'Kaja, master? Why?'

Rudolf smiled again. 'You will see.'

*****

The Danish engineers had laid out the ground for what would become the castle of Berengarian, named in honour of the king's late wife, the Estonian slaves being whipped to encourage them to dig the giant rectangular ditch and earth rampart behind it. Inside the fledgling stronghold the king's pavilion was erected in the centre, the Bishop of Roskilde's immediately behind it and around them both the tents of Count Albert, his knights and the men of the king's bodyguard. As the slaves hauled stones from the nearby moraine plain, parties were sent into the forest to hunt elk and boar for the king's table. Patrols of axe men and foot knights were despatched in every direction to hunt for the enemy but they returned with news that villages had been abandoned and the Oeselians were nowhere to be seen. It was as if the island was deserted of human life. The king spent most days consulting with his chief of engineers over how many towers Berengarian would have and how tall they should be, while Count Albert amused himself with hunting wild boar. It therefore came as a rude shock when the Oeselians burnt the Danes' ships, and even greater distress was inflicted on Valdemar when his camp was attacked on the very same evening. Hundreds of screaming Oeselians flooded from the forest and surrounded the camp. The king's men stood to arms. Count Albert was in his element as he stood on top of the rampart fighting off the enemy, who seemed to show a marked reluctance to cross the ditch and get to grips with him and his men. Indeed, the Oeselians made a lot of noise and shot a few arrows but remained behind their shields as they taunted the Danes. And then, as quickly as they had appeared, they melted back into the trees.

The next morning the king, egged on by Count Albert, led his mounted knights out of camp escorted by nearly a thousand foot soldiers. Valdemar had revenge on his mind but the Oeselians were waiting and sprung an ambush that killed a hundred Danes in the first five minutes. Thereafter there was a grim mêlée in which the Oeselians tried to kill the Danish king but were thwarted by the bravery of Count Albert and the king's bodyguard. But in the subsequent retreat to camp the Danes lost a further three hundred men. Thereafter there was relentless pressure as the Oeselians attacked day and night to further whittle down the Danes. On the second day Valdemar lost an additional fifty horsemen and four hundred foot soldiers when he led an attack against the enemy, the latter having dug a trench during the night, into which his horsemen and spearmen fell.

The Oeselians then brought up the *paterells* and positioned them on all four sides of the camp and began pelting the Danes with stones. The machines were small, crude affairs, no taller than a man, but they could hurl stones into the Danish camp well enough. Using the same moraine plain for ammunition that the Danes had pillaged for building material, the Oeselians maintained steady withering volleys of missiles that drove Valdemar's men to distraction. Count Albert led a foolhardy mounted charge in an effort to destroy those *paterells* that had been deployed against the camp's entrance. But the Oeselians had dug three rows of holes immediately in front of the machines and a score of Danish horses broke their legs when they reached them. Albert lost fifty men killed and nearly the same number of horses as the *paterells* lobbed stones at his riders.

On the fourth night the Oeselians launched a general assault against the camp, which was repulsed with heavy losses. But in the fighting the Danes lost a further two hundred men and many horses were killed when an Oeselian party infiltrated the stabling area and inflicted terrible wounds on the animals with their axes. The dawn broke to the pitiful sounds of dying horses crying and whimpering, further shaking the Danes' morale.

'They are finished father.'

Sigurd, his face smeared with blood, though not his own, his eyes red-rimmed due to lack of sleep and a night of hard fighting, was nonetheless in an ebullient mood.

'Keep on shooting!' he bellowed at the nearest *paterell* crew as they rested their hands on their knees. Each machine had a crew of three: two to lower and secure the throwing arm; one to load the basket and release the throwing arm. Sigurd was immensely proud of his fifty machines, which now ringed the Danish camp like a coiled snake.

'If we lose any more men *we* are finished,' muttered Olaf, his right arm bandaged. 'We lost many men last night.'

'But the enemy lost more, father,' insisted Sigurd, 'including all their horses. All that remains is to batter them into submission. Keep shooting.'

Tired warriors, their leather and mail armour ripped and torn, sat on the damp ground and watched with listless eyes as the *paterell* crews continued to lob stones into the Danish camp. The morning air was filled with dull thuds as throwing arms slammed into crossbeams. Occasionally a Danish archer would appear next to parts of a wall that had been started by Valdemar's engineers and built by the Estonians, loosing an arrow at the besieging army that sometimes found its target. Sigurd had given strict orders that no arrows were to be shot into the Danish camp, which would only be shot back. Early on it had become apparent that the Danes had no crossbowmen.

He rubbed the stubble on his chin. 'There will be no more attacks, father. There is no need. We will let hunger and low morale defeat the Danes.'

Olaf grunted. He was tired, hungry and his arm hurt, a gift from an enemy spearman. But beneath his gruff countenance he was happy enough.

He would be the first to admit that he had poured scorn on his son's strategy, especially when Kalf and Stark had berated him that to allow an enemy to set foot on Oesel's sacred soil would offend the gods. But they had been sent away with Bothvar and Swein, who commanded the longships that were blockading Matsalu Bay and Reval respectively. Sigurd had kept his nerve and now had his reward: the Danes were penned in and being ground down and soon the head of their king would be decorating the roof of Olaf's hall in Kuressaare.

On the fifth day the Danes attempted another sortie, flooding over their pitiful western wall to try to reach the *paterells* that were sited beyond that side of the camp. But it had rained steadily during the night and the ground around the camp had turned to mud. The Oeselians, tired, wet and cold, formed up in a shield wall four ranks deep and trudged through the mud to meet the Danish spearmen and axe men. The rainfall steadily increased until it became a downpour as the two sides closed and began hacking, thrusting and slashing with their weapons. The rain muffled the screams, shrieks and cries of men having their bellies ripped open, their jaws cleaved in two and their faces reduced to bloody pulps. More died when they lost their footing in the mud and fell face-first into the dirt, to be trampled underfoot and die horribly as water and mud were forced into their mouths and noses.

After no more than ten minutes of a frantic close-quarter mêlée in which upwards of five hundred men hacked at each other in a downpour, both sides, mutually exhausted, withdraw a few paces, stared in silence with vacant, listless expressions, and then trudged back to their respective camps. The Danes left a hundred and twenty dead in the mud and helped a further sixty wounded back to their sodden, demoralised camp. The Oeselians lost fewer than fifty men and the same amount wounded. Sigurd was delighted.

'With every venture they make the Danes weaken themselves further, father,' he said to a soaked Olaf who had waited with a reserve, axe in hand, in case the Danes broke the shield wall.

Olaf looked at the wounded warriors being helped on to two-wheeled carts for the journey back to Kuressaare where they would at least have their wounds attended to in a dry longhouse. Other carts were loaded with dead for cremation outside the town.

'We are also weakened,' said Olaf. 'We do not have an inexhaustible supply of warriors, Sigurd.'

'Neither do the Danes, father. Neither do the Danes.'

The rain stopped, the sun came out to dry the earth and the *paterells* continued their desultory shooting. More than half were now out of action, either because their skeins were frayed and had lost their tension or their throwing arms had splintered. But twenty-five were still operable and every stone they shot frayed the nerves of the Danes still further. Inside the camp the Bishop of Roskilde and his priests prayed for a miracle, for unless relief came they were surely doomed.

*****

It took nearly a day for Master Rudolf's army to cross the swift-flowing Parnu, now in spate and around five hundred paces wide. A local guide led it five miles upstream to where there was an island in midstream that narrowed the channels on either side of it to less than fifty yards. It took all morning to cut down trees to make rafts to span these channels. One raft was secured to the southern riverbank with posts and ropes and then a second raft was launched into the water and floated to the end of the first raft. This process was repeated until there was a line of rafts from the riverbank to the island.

Rudolf was the first to step on to the island, and promptly sank up his ankles in mud. Remembering the time when the garrison of Wenden had had to make a spring march to the Dvina when the land was soaked, he ordered a corduroy road of logs to be laid across the breadth of the island. It took all afternoon to assemble and position the rafts that bridged the span from the island to the northern riverbank, the army moving across the river as the sun began to dip on the western horizon.

The next day the army struck northwest towards Lääne County and the coast, a two-day journey through forests of pine, birch and fir skirting large peat bogs and bog fields. After the dawn broke, mist formed giving the land an eerie, ghost-like appearance. But as they neared the coast the wind picked up to make the banners of the Sword Brothers and Sir Richard's knights flap. Sir Richard himself wore no coat of arms on his shield or surcoat. His were plain white, as was the facing on his shield.

'I have seen the curious beasts and strange markings on the shields of his knights,' said Kaja as she proudly held the Sword Brother banner that Master Rudolf had instructed her to carry, 'but he does not paint his shield. Why?'

She rode with the three Sword Brothers, Riki, Tonis and Andres in the vanguard of the Army of the Wolf strung out in a long column behind them. Ahead of them was Hillar and a party of Rotalian scouts. Behind Conrad's army came Rudolf with the Sword Brothers with Sir Richard providing the rearguard.

'He believes that his actions before he came to Livonia shamed his family's coat of arms,' Conrad told her. 'So as a form of penance he does not wear them.'

'What were those actions?' queried Kaja.

'It is not for us to gossip about Sir Richard,' Conrad rebuked her. 'You must ask him yourself, Kaja, and if he has a mind to he will tell you.'

Conrad and the others knew, of course. Sir Richard had fallen in love with his friend's wife to be, who had taken her own life rather than be torn between two men. In grief his friend had also taken his own life and Sir Richard had been tortured with remorse. He had taken the cross in Livonia and had proved himself a brave and loyal friend of the Sword Brothers. Conrad often wondered if, like himself, he secretly sought death in battle so he could be with his loved ones again.

'I like Sir Richard,' Kaja declared, 'and think it is foolish that he does not wear his emblem. He is a good man.'

Conrad looked behind at the round shield dangling from Kaja's saddle, which bore a leering red wolf symbol.

'No such reticence for you, Kaja.'

'It is to honour you, *Susi*,' she replied, 'as leader of the army.'

'He's no longer the Marshal of Estonia,' Anton said, 'just plain Brother Conrad.'

'He was stripped of his office on the orders of King Valdemar of Denmark,' added Hans.

'The man we are riding to save?' said Kaja incredulously.

'That is correct,' replied Conrad.

'It makes no sense,' she scoffed.

Conrad laughed. 'You should go and tell Master Rudolf that.'

But Rudolf was fixed on saving the Danish king and was delighted when the army reached the shoreline of Lääne County to find dozens of boats waiting along the long, white sandy beach that fronted the calm, blue waters of the Gulf of Riga. The spring sun was warming the land and a gentle breeze was blowing in off the sea as the army pitched its tents a short distance from the sand. Gulls drifted on the breeze overhead, the sea shimmered in the sunlight and war seemed a long way off.

As the tents were being pitched and ponies and horses unsaddled Hillar rode to a nearby village and returned with a white-haired man whom he introduced to Conrad. The man was old and slightly stooped, the brother knight estimating his age to be at least seventy. But his blue eyes were clear and alert and his mind keen. He was dressed in a simple woollen tunic, leggings and leather boots. His leather belt was decorated with bronze, to which was fastened a sword in a leather scabbard, indicating that he was a man of some importance.

'*Susi*,' said Hillar, 'this is Koit, the county elder.'

Conrad extended his hand to the old man and was surprised by his iron-hard grip.

'A pleasure to meet you, sir.'

Koit retained his grip on Conrad's hand as he examined him with his piercing eyes.

'So you are the one they call *Susi* and whom I have heard so much about. Hillar has told me much about you.'

He released Conrad's hand. 'You do not appear to be tainted by corruption.'

'I hope not, sir,' replied Conrad, thinking it was a strange thing to say. 'I must thank you for assembling the boats to transport the army to Oesel.'

Koit gave him a sly smile. 'It was easy enough, son of the forest wolf, to persuade the parish elders to convince their villagers to lend you their boats.'

Conrad was about to question him further when a mounted sergeant rode up and saluted.

'Brother Conrad, Master Rudolf requests your immediate presence at his tent.'

Conrad acknowledged him and said he would attend the master immediately.

'Perhaps you would like to accompany me to meet the commander of the army, Koit,' said Conrad.

Out of courtesy he asked Hillar to accompany them, the old man saying nothing as they walked from the Estonian camp to where the Sword Brothers and their mercenaries were erecting their shelters. But his eyes missed nothing as they threaded their way through the round tents, outside of which sat brother knights cleaning their mail and swords, their full-face helms on the ground beside them. Many recognised Conrad and raised their hands in acknowledgement or shouted a greeting. On the tops of the tents pennants bearing the insignia of the order fluttered in the breeze. Sergeants were examining the hooves of horses and banging tent pegs into the soft earth.

'Some men wear helmets that have wide brims while others wear helmets that cover their faces,' said Koit. 'Why is this?'

'The helmets with wide brims are worn by sergeants of my order,' Conrad told him, 'whereas the helmets that cover the face are worn by brother knights.'

'And what is the difference between these two groups?' enquired Koit.

'In my order only those who are lords can become brother knights, sir,' said Conrad, 'though there are exceptions. Sergeants are recruited from those who are not lords and they can go no higher than sergeant.'

'You were a lord before you joined the men of iron?' asked Koit.

Conrad shook his head. 'I was the son of a baker, sir.'

'Uku must have smiled on you, son of the forest wolf.'

Hillar looked uncomfortable as Koit spoke the name of the chief Estonian god in the camp of the Sword Brothers but Conrad merely smiled at the old man. Catholicism was a new religion in this land and Conrad knew that it would take years before the natives accepted the Holy Church and renounced their old gods. At the moment the two religions battled for supremacy in men's hearts and souls, though Conrad believed that the Church of Rome would eventually triumph, though through persuasion, not force of arms.

At Rudolf's tent Koit received a hearty welcome, the deputy commander of the order embracing him and escorting him to a chair where he poured him a cup of the wine from the flask he had been saving for an auspicious occasion.

'Welcome,' said Rudolf, pulling out the chair for Koit to sit in.

'This is Koit, master,' said Conrad, 'the elder of Lääne County who has assembled the boats to take the army to Oesel.'

Rudolf nodded at Hillar and then introduced masters Bertram and Mathias and Sir Richard to Koit, who regarded the bald headed, clean-shaven Sir Richard with curiosity. He then took a sip of the wine as Rudolf ordered Conrad and Hillar to sit at the table.

Rudolf smiled at Koit. 'On behalf of the Bishop of Riga and my order I would like to thank you for your efforts in amassing the boats to enable us to get to Oesel.'

Koit studied the hard faces of the three masters. 'There are many among my people who have fought the Sword Brothers. I myself was at Wolf's Rock by the side of Nigul when Lembit forged an alliance of the Estonian tribes.'

He sipped at his wine again, all eyes on him. 'After our defeat at Wolf's Rock many of my people believed that the gods had deserted them. The Sword Brothers swallowed Saccalia and forged an alliance with Kalju, which interpreted as a sign that if Rotalia wished to remain free then it too should seek a treaty with the Sword Brothers. But then the Danes and Oeselians came and laid waste our land with fire and sword.'

He looked at Hillar 'Many of our men, those who had lost their families, abandoned the charred remains of their villages and sought sanctuary in the forests, there to wage war against the invaders.'

He drank again from his cup. 'And then word reached me that among the Sword Brothers there was one who was talked of as being the spirit of the forest wolf in human form, a warrior who had united the tribes and who had vanquished a great army at Fellin with nothing but a collection of old men and women. They called him *Susi* and flocked to his banner. Hillar told me that the Danish king, the same king that you go to rescue, desired the death of *Susi* and that the wolf spirit had volunteered to give himself up. But such was the love the Sword Brothers and Estonians had for *Susi* that they destroyed the Danes in front of their fortress rather than let him be taken.'

'It is as you say, sir,' said Rudolf solemnly.

Conrad knew that what Koit was saying could be interpreted as blasphemy in the eyes of the Holy Church, which was punishable by death. But Rudolf and the other two masters merely nodded as Koit spoke. They knew that there was more to winning wars than butchering an enemy on the battlefield.

'I have done as Hillar requested of me,' continued Koit, 'because my people believe that *Susi* has been sent to deliver them. But I have to tell you that they are no friends of the Sword Brothers who have killed many Rotalians.'

'You no doubt killed our men at Wolf's Rock also, sir,' replied Rudolf. 'But here we are talking to each other instead of trying to slice open each other's bellies. The Sword Brothers, do not forget those who have aided them.'

'My people desire peace,' said Koit. 'For too long their land has been used as a plaything by barbarians.'

Rudolf seized his chance. 'In recognition of your assistance to the Sword Brothers, sir, I pledge that Rotalia shall have a treaty of friendship with our order.'

Koit finished his wine. 'I cannot speak for the whole of Rotalia.'

Rudolf pressed the matter. 'You said yourself, sir, that Rotalia has been laid waste. Who better to rebuild it than a man who has shed blood for his people, a man who fought by the side of Nigul at Wolf Rock?'

Koit was taken aback. 'I was your enemy that day.'

Rudolf stood and offered his hand to Koit. 'Then let us now be friends, sir. Will you also have the friendship and support of the Sword Brothers, who pledge to stand by *your* side against the Oeselians and Danes?'

Koit turned to Conrad.

'What would you advise, son of the forest wolf?'

'Master Rudolf is a man of honour,' answered Conrad, 'whose fearlessness in battle is matched by his honesty off it.'

Koit smiled to himself and stood before clasping Rudolf's forearm.

'So be it.'

Thus did Rotalia fall to the Sword Brothers, though the conquest was not to be at the point of a sword but by persuasion and goodwill.

Afterwards Rudolf asked Conrad to remain as the others went back to their tents. Wenden's master was in an ebullient mood. He poured Conrad a cup of wine and held his own cup up to toast him.

'You have done damn well, Conrad, and if it was in my power to lavish you with lands and titles I would do so, but alas our vow of poverty forbids it.'

'I have done nothing, master,' replied Conrad, somewhat perplexed.

Rudolf pointed at him. 'On the contrary, the Estonians have taken you to their hearts. Your name and reputation achieves what it would take crusader armies years to achieve.'

Conrad looked into his cup.

'Something bothers you?' asked Rudolf. He saw the troubled look on Conrad's face. 'Speak freely.'

'Rotalia follows the pagan religion, master. If we try to impose the teachings of the Holy Church on its people there will be great resentment.'

'There will be no imposition, Conrad,' Rudolf assured him. 'We will follow the example of Sir Richard in Saccalia and use time and the hand of friendship to achieve our aims. And now, if you will excuse me, I have to consult with Brother Lukas. We take ship tomorrow. And Conrad.'

'Yes, master?'

'We will be leaving some of your men behind to guard the horses. But make sure you bring that Estonian girl along with you.'

'Her name is Kaja, master.'

'Good, it is very important she accompanies us.'

Kaja was delighted when Conrad informed her that she would be among those going to Oesel and after the evening meal spent a long time cleaning her sword, scabbard and helmet. Conrad would have preferred she stay with Sir Richard's Saccalian levies and members of the Army of the Wolf who would remain to guard the horses and ponies. The number of men crossing the sea to Oesel was to be a thousand, plus one woman.

The next morning they assembled on the white sand as the crews of the boats hauled their vessels into the calm Baltic and waited for their passengers to board. There were over a hundred single-masted boats in the water, all clinker-built vessels with planks hand split from green logs and fastened together with leather. The hulls were coated with tar to keep them watertight and the sails were hand woven from hides.

Conrad, Hans and Anton travelled in the company of Kaja, Hillar and Koit, who was most anxious to see how the Sword Brothers would fight without their famed warhorses. As the crew pushed the boat out to sea to begin the journey to Oesel, Hans and Anton began peering to port and starboard.

'If we get caught on the open sea by a fleet of longships we'll be in trouble,' said a worried Hans.

'The Oeselian warships are blockading Matsalu Bay and Reval,' Koit reassured him, staring at the blonde-haired woman sitting on a chest clutching the Sword Brothers' flag. 'We will be on Oesel before they can be alerted. Let us hope we have enough space on the boats to evacuate all the Danes.'

Anton laughed. 'Hopefully all the Danes will be dead by the time we reach them.'

Koit was surprised by the venom in his voice.

'You dislike the Danes?'

'They were responsible for the death of our friend,' said Conrad, who turned the axe in his hand.

'He was killed at the Pala,' said Hans.

'And others among the men of iron think like you?' asked Koit.

Conrad nodded.

'Then why do you go to save them?'

Conrad, Hans and Anton looked at him with blank expressions.

The light breeze and calm waters made for a pleasant trip, the sun turning the early morning sea shiny grey. The boats, which were steered by a single hand-held oar at the rear, gradually formed a long line of vessels as they headed northwest towards Oesel.

'We are heading for the strait between Muhu and Oesel,' Koit informed the brother knights, 'an island adjacent to Oesel. We will sail up the strait between the two islands before landing

97

near where the Danes are besieged. Because of the favourable wind and tides there will be no need to land on Muhu itself.'

He pointed ahead. 'The navigator and scouts are in the lead vessel with Master Rudolf, the leader of the men of iron.'

'He is deputy commander of our order,' said Conrad. 'The leader of the Sword Brothers is at Riga.'

'Why is he not here?' asked Koit.

'There is sickness in Riga,' Hans informed him. 'No one may leave the city.'

'The Danes blockade Riga just as the Oeselians strangle Reval,' said Anton. 'Another reason to hope that they have all perished on Oesel.'

Conrad turned the axe once more. Hopefully Count Henry would also be among those besieged. Then he would have another opportunity to exact revenge on the German lord for the death of Johann.

After the initial concern about Oeselian longships the gently rocking of the boat, the pleasant breeze and the warming sun had a calming effect and soon the brother knights were lying on deck relaxing. Their shields, helmets, swords, maces, axe and crossbows were stacked against the gunwale as the crew went about their business.

'Do you both realise that this is the first time we have been at sea since we arrived in Livonia,' said Hans. 'It seems like yesterday.'

'You were a lot thinner then,' Anton reminded him. 'I thought you would not survive the journey.'

'Perhaps we won't survive this journey,' remarked Hans glumly.

But after an hour the boats reached the strait between Oesel and Muhu, fish eagles swooping overhead as the vessels headed into the passage of water that was around two miles in width. The boats hugged the shoreline of Oesel as they sailed north. The brother knights stirred themselves as the crew prepared a sparse meal of sausage, bread, salted fish and water. Koit sat with the three, Hillar and Kaja as they ate their meal.

'Another hour, perhaps longer,' said Koit, 'and then you will be feasting with the Oeselians.'

'We've beaten them before,' said Conrad.

'Hiller informed me that you fought a single combat with Prince Sigurd,' said Koit, 'eldest son of Olaf.'

Conrad stuffed a piece of salted herring into his mouth and nodded.

'And defeated him,' said Kaja with pride.

'And let him live,' stated Koit.

Conrad nodded again.

'*Susi* is merciful,' added Kaja.

'You may live to regret that decision, son of the forest wolf,' remarked Koit.

'How many can we get on this boat?' asked Conrad, changing the subject.

Like the others it was some forty-five feet in length and had a width of just over eleven feet. It seemed large and accommodating but there were only six of them plus five crewmen.

'Twenty passengers, perhaps one or two more,' answered Koit. 'But no horses or ponies.'

'Valdemar will have to leave his warhorses behind,' said Conrad, prompting him and his two friends to burst out laughing. Koit looked at Hillar in confusion. They did not know that a warhorse was a symbol of a knight's status and to abandon it was both shameful and expensive. Koit thought their behaviour most strange.

It was just before midday when crews in the boats in front used red flags to signal that they had reached their destination. The message was relayed to the boats behind as Conrad and his colleagues strapped on their swords, Anton and Hans tucking their maces into their belts and Conrad likewise his axe. Then they loaded their crossbows and knelt by the gunwale at the prow of the boat, Kaja, now helmeted, kneeling beside them.

The boat swung sharply to port to head towards a long shingle beach and a seemingly unending forest of pine beyond. Conrad scanned the beach and saw no sign of enemy activity.

'That forest could be full of enemy warriors,' hissed Anton, reading Conrad's mind.

They were perhaps two hundred paces from the beach, the other boats now either side of their own in a long line. In each one crossbowmen knelt with loaded weapons ready to shoot at any Oeselians that showed their faces. Conrad rested

100

his crossbow against the gunwale and held out his arm, palm down. Hans and Anton placed their own hands on top of his as Kaja scrambled to form a fourth spoke of the wheel.

'As dust to the wind,' said Conrad.

'As dust to the wind,' the others answered.

They returned to their positions, the brother knights putting on their helms as they rested their fingers against crossbow triggers and waited. There was absolute silence – no wind, no cries of seagulls, nothing – as it took what seemed like an eternity for the boats to reach the shore. Hillar was crouched low against the gunwale, Koit beside him. Then the bottom of the hull scraped the pebbles under the water and a single voice pierced the air.

'God with us!'

Seconds later cheers and shouts answered the rally as men jumped into the water and scrambled ashore. It was a mad rush of warriors, brother knights, sergeants and mercenaries, the latter initially standing to shoot their crossbows over the heads of the invaders if required. Conrad left his crossbow on board, leapt over the gunwale and splashed into the water, losing his footing on loose pebbles and falling head first into the sea. Hans hauled him to his feet and dragged him forward, Conrad regaining his footing as he stepped on to the beach and raced on, sword in hand and shield held before him as a defence against enemy missiles. All along the shingle men raced to the treeline – twenty paces from the water – and rushed into the forest. And then stopped as they realised that there was no enemy among the trees.

Conrad retrieved his crossbow and quickly gathered his warlords around him as Rudolf and Sir Richard organised their respective contingents. As they did so the boat crews pushed their vessels back into the water where they would drop anchor and wait for the army to return. If it returned.

There were no horn calls or trumpet blasts. Everyone knew the plan: land on the beach two miles from the bay where the Danes had landed and march across land to the Danish camp. Speed was of the essence as a thousand men tramping through a forest, many of them dressed in white surcoats and carrying white shields, would make a lot of noise and would be impossible to disguise.

Priests walked up and down the line, voicing encouragement as commanders barked orders at their men to get into position. As agreed at the council of war the day before the Army of the Wolf formed the centre: Harrien, Rotalians and Tonis' wolf shields standing shoulder to shoulder and reinforced by the order's mercenary crossbowmen. On the right, the place of honour, stood the brother knights of Wenden, Segewold and Kremon, together with fifty-five sergeants equipped with crossbows and a hundred and fifty Jerwen warriors led by Andres. To the left of Conrad's warriors were Sir Richard and his knights, Saccalian levies and another fifty-five sergeants shouldering crossbows.

Master Rudolf led his wing forward and the rest of the army followed. Conrad, his crossbow armed, turned to Kaja holding the banner.

'Whatever happens, stay close.'

Leatherface, on the right of Hans, grinned mischievously.

'Don't you worry, Brother Conrad, if you are killed I'll take good care of her.'

Kaja sneered at the lecherous mercenary. 'I can take care of myself.'

At first the going was hard as they moved through the trees, men tripping on bushes and roots and snapping dead branches underfoot. The sounds were accompanied by low grunts and curses and Conrad had no doubt that the enemy would be alerted to their presence long before they came into view. But after half a mile or so of slow progress the pines gave way to a forest of ancient oaks, the trees widely spaced with long grass between them. This made visibility as well as movement easier and the pace picked up. Beautiful yellow and purple orchids were crushed underfoot as the army tramped towards the enemy.

There was a palpable sense of tension in the air that increased with every step taken. Far from the pace increasing it actually slackened as men took care where they placed their feet and peered ahead into the trees to discern any movement. A deer broke cover and darted away, fraying everyone's nerves further. But the mercenaries and sergeants, old hands who had spent years campaigning in Livonia, did not shoot any quarrels.

The advance continued. The crossbowmen, including Conrad and his two friends, were in the second rank, ready to shoot at the enemy when they appeared. The Oeselians fought in a similar fashion to the Livs and Estonians: a shield wall of four to six ranks that locked its horns with the enemy shield wall until one broke. But Master Rudolf had no time for a drawn-out mêlée He wanted to disperse the enemy with missiles, break through to the Danes and then withdraw to the boats.

'Hear that?' whispered Leatherface.

'Woodpeckers?' said Hans.

Leatherface chuckled and winked at Kaja.

'Wood being chopped more like. We are close to the enemy.'

He had been nonchalantly shouldering his crossbow but now he pulled a quarrel from one of the quivers dangling from the shoulder straps and placed it in the groove of the stock, against the drawn-back bowstring.

'Look sharp,' he hissed to his colleagues to his left.

They walked on for another couple of minutes, the sound of chopping getting louder as the widely spaced oaks began to give way to a forest of spruce. But not before the Oeselian party was spotted. There were around a score of them, most engaged in chopping wood for either shelter or firewood. They had posted no guards because they were on their own island and the Danes were closely besieged. So they initially did not spot the blocks of warriors approaching them.

Leatherface loosed the first quarrel, the sharp crack of his crossbow being shot making some of the Oeselians turn and gaze in the direction from where the sound came from. There was a succession of snaps as the other mercenaries released their triggers, followed by yelps and screams as the missiles hit their targets. The relief force was around two hundred paces from the Oeselians, the survivors turning tail and running into the trees as another volley of bolts was directed at them. Knowing that the survivors would alert the besiegers, Rudolf and the other brother knights on the right increased their pace to pursue them. They entered the tall spruce; the rest of the army swarming into the forest as ahead the shouts of the fleeing Oeselians filled the trees.

'I'm getting too old for this,' complained Leatherface as he broke into a trot to keep up with those around him.

Conrad, who had shoved his helmet on top of his head during the advance, again looked behind at Kaja.

'Stay close,' he ordered before pulling his helm down. Hans and Anton did likewise as they entered the spruce trees and forged ahead.

He heard the shrill blast of horns. The enemy was alerted.

They pushed on, a sense of excitement laced with trepidation infusing them. Conrad could hear shouting ahead from a multitude of voices. The enemy would be waiting for them. He said a silent prayer that his courage would not fail as the spruce trees suddenly ended and the relief force entered a large meadow. Actually that was incorrect. It entered a wide and

105

deep area of tree stumps. He raised his crossbow and the signallers nearby blew their horns to order a halt. He commanded five hundred men of the centre – half the army – and he had no intention of letting it get fragmented amidst a forest of stumps.

On the right Rudolf also halted his men, Sir Richard on the left initially leading his knights forward to get to grips with the enemy shield wall that was rapidly forming just beyond where the stumps ended. But his trumpeters blew their instruments and he and his men shuffled back to align themselves with the Army of the Wolf.

Leatherface slapped Conrad on the back. 'Now you'll see why Master Rudolf pays us so well.'

Conrad shoved his helmet up. 'I thought you haven't been paid in months.'

Leatherface hooked the bowstring over the double-pronged metal claw attached to the front of his leather belt, placed a foot in the metal stirrup fitted to the fore-end of his crossbow's stock and forced the stirrup downwards. The bowstring, attached to the claw, was drawn along the stock until it slipped over the catch of the lock. He placed a new bolt in the stock's groove.

'We sorted out that business.'

He leered at Kaja. 'Master Rudolf knows I am too important to let go. Don't worry, sweet thing, I won't let any Oeselian rape you.'

Kaja ignored him.

'Shields!' shouted Conrad, again pulling his helmet down. There was one rank of warriors in front of him, all armed with hand axes to hack at the enemy in front when the shield walls collided. Behind him the other Estonian warriors brought their shields up to form a roof as a defence against Oeselian arrows.

The Oeselian shield wall was thickening by the minute, warriors running to equal the extent of the relief force's line and then outflank it as hundreds of Olaf's men prepared to destroy the new arrivals. Men with spears and axes began hurling abuse at Rudolf's army, banging the hafts of their weapons against their shields to produce a mighty din to both intimidate the enemy and bolster their own courage. The Oeselian shields were all round and painted with a mixture of colours: red and yellow, black and yellow and red and white. The men that held them all wore helmets with nasal guards and mail shirts. They were the best fighters in the Oeselian army and among them would be Olaf himself, though Conrad had no knowledge of what he looked like. A few Oeselians broke ranks and ran forward, big men with no fear who spread their arms to bare their torsos in an act of bravado that brought loud cheers from their comrades. One ran forward and hurled his spear at the ranks of the Army of the Wolf, the point slamming into the earth a few paces from the man in front of Conrad.

'Time to shut them up,' snarled Leatherface.

'Wait for Master Rudolf's signal,' shouted Conrad from within his helmet.

But the brother knight was getting concerned that the enemy shield wall was still thickening and lengthening and they were doing nothing. Soon, notwithstanding the belt of tree stumps in front, it would start inching forward to get to grips with them. Beyond the shield wall he caught glimpses of tents and a long mound of what appeared to be a rampart, on top of which was segments of a low wall. Then he heard a blast of horns and what he had feared was happening: the Oeselians were moving forward.

He did not know how many warriors were in the enemy's shield wall but it overlapped the relief force's line at each end by at least fifty yards. There were perhaps a hundred paces between the two sides when Olaf's men began shuffling forward, his warriors shouting their war cries and promising to send the Christians to their hell. Their confidence was high because although they would have seen the banners and insignia of the Sword Brothers, the men of iron had no warhorses that made the earth tremble when they charged.

Then Rudolf gave his signal.

A sharp trumpet blast came from the ranks of the Sword Brothers, followed by deeper horn blasts among the Army of the Wolf and a trumpet call from Sir Richard's ranks. And then the shooting started. Conrad aimed his crossbow, pulled the trigger and went about reloading his weapon. Master Rudolf had brought two hundred and fifty crossbowmen to Oesel, three more including Conrad, Hans and Anton, and now they methodically went about their business. Loosing missiles from behind the front ranks they shot four hundred and eighty bolts in thirty seconds, delivering the same number in the following thirty seconds.

They continued shooting up to four bolts a minute, the metal-tipped missiles cutting through the air to hit enemy necks and faces. The Oeselian line staggered and then stopped as the shield wall walked into a swarm of iron-tipped quarrels. The shield wall's front rank disintegrated as bolts were aimed at just above the Oeselian shields. Men collapsed, clutched their faces in agony or fell backwards, dead, on to the men behind.

In two minutes over nineteen hundred bolts had been shot at the enemy shield wall, in front of which was a rapidly forming mound of dead and dying men. The crossbowmen continued shooting, reaching into their quivers to extract bolts to shoot at the enemy. There was nothing rushed about their work, just a calm, steady sequence of loading, shooting and reloading. The Estonians, Sword Brothers and Sir Richard's knights remained silent and still as the crossbowmen went about their business.

Opposite was a noisy scene of carnage as warlords tried to establish some sort of order as their men were cut down in front of their eyes.

'Raise shields,' came the cry as someone noticed that the Christian soldiers were shooting at heads and necks.

So the Oeselians raised their shields to hide their faces and bolts began slamming into the leather and wood. But the order's mercenaries and sergeants were canny and simply adjusted their aim. There was a slight pause, a temporary silence and then dozens of high-pitched screams as quarrels began to slam into legs and groins suddenly exposed as the Oeselians raised their shields. If anything the crossbowmen's task was easier as they aimed their bolts at a dense forest of unarmoured legs.

Conrad had shot at least a dozen bolts when what was left of the Oeselian shield wall began to edge back and then dissolved as those who were uninjured could take no more and ran for their lives. For a few seconds Conrad thought that an age-old habit would take hold of his Estonians and they would break ranks and charge to pursue the enemy. But they had been at Wenden for months and in that time had spent many hours training with the brother knights, sergeants and mercenaries.

'Hold your ground, you heathen bastards,' shouted Leatherface, his head and neck covered in sweat. 'I'll kill the first man who breaks ranks.'

Conrad shoved his helmet up on his head.

'Maintain order, wait for the command.'

It came seconds later when Master Rudolf's trumpeters signalled the advance. The three blocks of soldiers began walking forward, skirting the tree trunks easily enough but then having to tread on the piles of dead and dying Oeselians. It was a ghastly sight, men sobbing and whimpering with crossbow bolts embedded in their jaws, cheeks and noses, or staring in horror at their shattered shins and bleeding thighs. The lucky ones had been killed instantly when a sharp-headed bolt had

110

gone into an eye socket and then the brain. Or had pierced their windpipe. But they all ended up dead when they were trampled on and men with axes or maces put them out of their misery.

The enemy had seemingly disappeared as the army pushed on into a mass of empty tents and campfires. The pace picked up as soldiers appeared on the earth rampart ahead, the relief army moving through a line of what appeared to be small, crudely built mangonels, beside each one a pile of stones. Danish soldiers came walking and hobbling from their camp, descending the rampart to stumble into the ditch before cheering their saviours.

Conrad removed his helmet and took gulps of air as Hans and Anton slapped him on the back. He turned to ensure Kaja was still with him. She was, grinning at him from behind the thick nasal guard of her helmet. He uncorked his water bottle and took a swig, resisting the temptation to empty its contents. The Army of the Wolf now descended into loud chatter as the warriors marvelled at their easy victory.

Then Rudolf was standing in front of Conrad, helmetless with sword in hand.

'Get your men inside the camp,' he ordered him, 'and come with me.'

He pointed at Kaja. 'You too.'

Conrad delegated command of the Estonians to Hans and Anton and then hurried after Rudolf, Kaja racing to his side.

'What does Master Rudolf want with me, *Susi?*' she asked.

'I know as much as you, Kaja.'

Chapter 3

Conrad was shocked by the sight that greeted his eyes as he and Kaja tramped after Master Rudolf in the company of Bertram, Mathias, Sir Richard and Brother Lukas, the latter carrying a large leather tube slung over his shoulder. The relief army had swept over the eastern side of the Danish camp, which appeared to be filled with wounded men hobbling around or sitting listlessly round campfires. He could see freshly dug earth covering what he presumed was a burial pit; beside it another pit was being dug. The Danish soldiers looked exhausted, their faces pale, cheeks sunken with black rings around their eyes. They just stood and stared with vacant expressions as the Sword Brothers made their way to the royal pavilion. The stench of human and animal waste and dead flesh made Kaja twist up her face.

'Death has come to gorge itself on this camp, *Susi*.'

Conrad spat on the ground as the odour tickled the back of his throat. 'I fear you are right.'

At Valdemar's pavilion Rudolf spoke to a herald who disappeared inside. After less than a minute he reappeared and ordered guards wearing ripped surcoats bearing the king's insignia of three blue lions surrounded by red hearts on a yellow background to escort the Sword Brothers inside. The aroma under the canvas was only slightly better than that outside. Like most great pavilions it was divided into a number of rooms, the largest of which was the throne area where King

Valdemar sat in a high-backed chair flanked by priests and lords. The churchmen looked deathly pale and jumpy, though a look of utter relief came over them as Rudolf and the others stood in a line in front of Valdemar and bowed their heads.

Conrad was taken aback by the king's appearance. He had seen him only fleetingly on that fateful day in front of Reval. Then he had appeared regal and magnificent, a great warlord in mail on a mighty warhorse surrounded by a host of knights. But now he looked the shadow of that man, his hair greasy and matted, his shoulders slumped, his cheeks sunken and his tired eyes bereft of vigour. He raised a hand to Rudolf.

'Greetings, Master Rudolf. Your arrival is most timely. God has subjected me to a great trial, which I have, with His assistance, passed. And now the Sword Brothers and Danes will unite to rid this island of the pestilence of paganism.'

There were mutterings of agreement from the knights, priests and officials flanking and behind the king, which was acknowledge by Valdemar with a half-hearted lift of a hand.

'Your majesty underestimates the predicament of our situation,' replied Rudolf. 'We have come to expedite the evacuation of what remains of your majesty's army, for my initial observation suggests that it is on its last legs.'

There were gasps from the king's entourage at the Sword Brother's impertinence, though Rudolf and the other two masters remained impassive as the officials and priests whispered among themselves.

'Silence!' snapped the king. He looked at Rudolf.

'You seem to forget, Master Rudolf, that my ships currently blockade Livonia as punishment for the insolence shown to me outside Reval by your own order. Choose your words carefully, Sword Brother, lest my wrath towards your bishop and order increases.'

Rudolf ignored the king and turned to Lukas who removed the top covering of the leather tube, pulled out a large rolled parchment and handed it to Wenden's master. Rudolf held it out to the king.

'This is a document I had drawn up that I would be grateful if your majesty would sign. It is an order from your majesty lifting the blockade of Livonia, ceding all Estonian lands to the Order of Sword Brothers and reinstating Brother Conrad of our order to his position of Marshal of Estonia. If your majesty's chamberlain or justiciar would care to read it I am sure they will find it straightforward and in order.'

Valdemar said nothing at first; in fact none of the Danes responded to Rudolf's words. But then a tall, slim knight wearing a dirty surcoat that bore a white leaf design against a red background began to laugh. The others followed his example and soon the pavilion was filled by Danish laughter. The knight pointed at Rudolf.

'You dare to speak to the king so? You should be on your knees to the monarch who has conquered the Baltic and all of northern Germany.'

Rudolf held the young man's arrogant stare and waited for the laughter to die down. He spoke once more, his voice calm and firm.

'The Oeselians blockade Matsalu Bay and Reval. This camp is surrounded and cut off from its supply base.'

He smiled at Valdemar. 'As the conqueror of the Baltic does not require the services of the Sword Brothers we will depart and leave your majesty to joust with the Oeselians. Please forgive the interruption.'

He handed the document back to Lukas, bowed curtly to Valdemar, turned and strode towards the exit. Conrad saw a portly priest in a mitre and rich attire rush to Valdemar's side.

'Your majesty. I am imploring you to seize the opportunity that the Lord has sent.'

'We are sorely pressed, majesty' remarked a middle-aged knight standing immediately behind the king.

'Wait,' Valdemar ordered Rudolf.

Wenden's master stopped and turned.

'I have heard of the arrogance of the Sword Brothers,' stated Valdemar, 'but now I have seen it with my own eyes. You think that because my position is precarious I will yield to your insolent demands?'

'I do,' replied Rudolf.

'Let me deal with him' said Count Albert, who began to walk forward drawing his sword.

Immediately the three masters, Conrad, Lukas and Sir Richard drew their weapons, as did Kaja.

116

'Stop!' commanded Valdemar. 'Put away your weapons, all of you.'

Rudolf stared unblinking at Count Albert, and then slid his sword back into its scabbard. The other masters and Sir Richard did the same. Conrad also sheathed his sword.

'You too, Kaja.'

She sneered at Count Albert but did as she was told.

'It is death to draw your sword in the presence of a king,' remarked Valdemar casually.

'We serve the King of kings,' said Rudolf, 'and answer to Him only.'

'I do not yield to threats,' stated Valdemar.

'I make no threats, majesty,' replied Rudolf. 'I came here at the head of an army despite your declaration of war on the Bishop of Riga and the Sword Brothers, for how else may your actions be interpreted? As your enemy, therefore, I have extended an olive branch in good faith. But if you refuse my generous terms then I will have no hesitation in leaving this place.'

Valdemar cracked a half-smile. 'Generous terms? You think giving up Estonia and ending the blockade is generous?'

'Of course,' said Rudolf. 'Estonia was never yours in the first place and Lübeck has grown rich from the trade with Riga, which means that your coffers have been filled as you control the city. By maintaining the blockade you cut off your nose to spite your face.'

'That is true, majesty,' said the Bishop of Roskilde.

117

Valdemar angrily waved him away and rose from his chair.

'What will the Sword Brothers give me in return should I decide to accept your terms?'

Rudolf walked forward and bowed his head. 'I would guarantee that my order would not assault Reval, majesty.'

'Is that all?' said Valdemar in exasperation.

'It is an outrage,' fumed Count Albert.

Rudolf turned and pointed at Kaja. 'Take off your helmet.'

She did so and shook her hair free. The Danes looked, astounded, at the blue-eyed beauty who was dressed and armed like a man. Rudolf pointed at the count.

'Any more noise from you and I will order this girl to castrate you, *boy.*'

Mathias and Bertram laughed, though Sir Richard looked uncomfortable. Conrad smirked and rested his hand on the pommel of his sword in case the angry young knight decided to attack Kaja.

Rudolf pointed at him. 'This is Conrad Wolff, Marshal of Estonia, who has brought his army to Oesel. It stands outside this tent. If we withdraw without the king's agreement then I will unleash him and his army against Reval, supported by the siege engines of the Sword Brothers.'

'You would do that?' said the king.

'You declared yourself an enemy of my order, my lord,' said Rudolf. 'Enemies fight each other. I would merely be

118

fulfilling the obligations that you yourself have placed upon me.'

Valdemar stared at Conrad. 'So you are the leader of the army of pagans. Is your army so deficient that you have to include young girls among its ranks?'

Conrad was about to answer but looked at Rudolf first. The master nodded.

'This young girl has just defeated the Oeselians, majesty, which is more than can be said for Denmark's nobles.'

Valdemar's knights were outraged at this and were about to launch themselves at Conrad, who stepped back and adopted a fighting stance, hand gripping the hilt of his sword. But Valdemar stood once more and commanded his knights to control themselves.

'Keeper of the Seal, step forward.'

There were glances between the Danes and then the Bishop of Roskilde approached the king.

'He was killed yesterday, majesty.'

Valdemar closed his eyes. 'Who then has my seal?'

'His deputy, my liege.'

'Whoever has my seal, let him show himself.'

A short, middle-aged man with a ruddy complexion gingerly stepped from behind the Danish lords and prelates. He had a leather bag slung over his shoulder. He bowed deeply to Valdemar.

'Majesty.'

The king pointed at Rudolf. 'I will set my seal to your wretched document so I can be away from this pestilential island. I will end my blockade of Livonia because it harms the interests of Denmark. I will also renounce my claim to Estonia, excepting Reval, as a gesture of friendship to the Bishop of Riga, a prince of the Catholic Church who is engaged upon a holy mission in these parts.'

To the anguish of his knights but the utter relief of his priests hot wax was dripped on to Rudolf's document and stamped with the king's seal. He then signed it. It was handed back to Rudolf who gave it to Lukas for safekeeping.

'But know, Master Rudolf,' said Valdemar, 'that the Sword Brothers, Marshal of Estonia and his heathen army are still my enemies, against which I will strive to exact vengeance for the insult done to me this day.'

Rudolf bowed to Valdemar. 'Majesty.'

Once the agreement had been sealed Rudolf was most urgent for the king and what was left of his army to be away from the death trap that his camp had become. The seriously wounded were left behind to be either killed or taken as slaves by the Oeselians, though as they could not walk they would probably be sacrificed to Taarapita, the islanders' god of war. Any livestock, ponies and horses still alive were similarly abandoned, much to the anger of the knights who killed their own warhorses rather than see them fall into the hands of the enemy.

Valdemar had arrived on Oesel with two thousand fighting men and an entourage of three hundred priests, courtiers and members of the royal household. He left with six hundred soldiers, half of whom were walking wounded and two hundred of his entourage.

Rudolf set a cruel pace to the evacuation beach, eager to be off the island before the day was out. He placed his crossbowmen in the rear and on the flanks and gave orders that they were to shoot at any Oeselians that showed themselves. Fifty wounded Danes expired during the journey, their bodies left behind in the oak forest the army retreated through.

On the beach an ebullient Master Rudolf bellowed at Danes and Sword Brothers alike to board the boats that had come ashore to pick them up. Conrad went over to him as Leatherface and his crossbowmen knelt on the shingle facing the forest, waiting for the Oeselians to pour from the trees. Kaja trailed after him, proudly carrying the flag that now fluttered in a stiffening breeze. Rudolf was watching the portly Bishop of Roskilde clambering aboard the boat where the king stood on the deck. Two of his priests unceremoniously shoved him up and over the gunwale.

'I fear you have made an enemy of King Valdemar, master,' said Conrad.

Rudolf gave a low laugh. 'He was always my enemy, Conrad, and yours. But I have forced him to lift the stranglehold he had over Livonia and accept that he has no claim on Estonia.'

He turned and slapped Conrad on the arm. 'And you have your command back.'

The boat containing the king was pushed off by its crew, the wind filling its sail as it and others left the island.

'He will be back, master.'

'He might,' agreed Rudolf, 'but did you notice that there were no German lords among his followers. I wonder if Valdemar has alienated those whom he had defeated and forced to be his vassals.'

Conrad also wondered if Rudolf had been disappointed that his father had not been present to witness his victory over Valdemar but said nothing. For his part he was disappointed that Count Henry had not been on Oesel.

'So, girl,' Rudolf said to Kaja, 'what did you think of the King of Denmark?'

'He looked tired and defeated, master,' was her reply. 'But will he keep his word?'

'Oh, yes,' said Rudolf. 'He put his seal and signature to a document in front of witnesses and in the sight of God.'

After all the boats had left the beach and formed into a long line of vessels in the strait, Oeselian warriors came from the forest and watched them disappear. When they returned to the mainland Rudolf gave a great feast in honour of King Valdemar's arrival. He gave the king his tent and masters Bertram and Mathias gave their tents to his closest advisers. In the morning he gave the king a horse so he could lead his soldiers and entourage to the Danish ships that were blockaded in Matsalu Bay some ten miles to the north. Hillar provided guides to lead the Danes through the peat bogs and flooded meadows that covered this part of Rotalia. From Matsalu Bay the king could be re-provisioned for the onward journey to Varbola and then Reval.

Rudolf had the whole army paraded as Valdemar and his ragged band trooped north. He made sure that Kaja, minus her helmet, was next to him in the front rank of Sword Brother horsemen as the king rode past, stony faced and staring directly ahead. But Rudolf knew that Valdemar had seen her, the Estonian girl who had rescued the conqueror of north Germany from the Oeselians.

*****

The speed with which the sickness spread through Odenpah was sedate in comparison to the spread of fear and despair that accompanied it. At first men, woman and children were afflicted by a high fever, followed by chills, severe headaches and backaches. Everyone was affected, from Kalju and his wife to the most wretched slaves that lived like pigs in the hovels at the foot of the fort's outer wall. Healers inside the citadel also fell sick and so others were summoned from the surrounding villages. They made medicines from meadow sweet, cranberry and bilberry in an effort to battle the blistered rashes that had appeared first on the victims' faces, hands and feet before covering their whole bodies. They painted pentagrams on the walls and chanted over the pain-racked sufferers. But it was all in vain.

Huge bonfires ringed the fort because everyone knew that the flames had a purifying effect and warded off evil spirits. Leather belts tied with ribbons were fastened around the bodies of Kalju, Eha, Luule, Maarja and Maimu in an effort to enlist the help of the gods and save the royal family. But as the days passed and blood poured from every orifice of their bodies hope faded. Half of those who lived and worked in the fort had died by the time that Kalju passed away, his wife following him two days later. In his lucid moments the chief had given orders that no one was to enter or leave the fort until the pestilence had passed, and that the dead and their clothing, bedding and possessions were to be immediately cremated. So it was that for days black smoke hung over the fort as the bodies were burnt beyond the outer walls. Luule died a day after her mother and Maimu the day after her sister. It was reckoned a miracle that Maarja recovered for everyone believed that Tooni, the God of Death, was resident at Odenpah despite the frantic efforts of the priests and healers to appease him and send him on his way.

The animals were slaughtered first as a sacrifice to the god but people continued to die. So all the surviving slaves were gathered together outside the great hall in the inner stronghold and had their throats slit – fifty women and children – their blood collected in bowls and used by the priests to daub pentagrams on the walls of the hall. And suddenly there was no more sickness.

124

The survivors said it was a miracle but the disease had left a terrible legacy for their bodies were covered with scars. A few were left blinded by the affliction they had suffered. It was reckoned a miracle that Kristjan, the seventeen-year-old son of Kalju and Eha, had been untouched by the plague, despite him having attended his parents and sisters from the beginning of their terrible ordeal. But the boy wept long and hard at the funeral pyres of his family and shed tears of bitterness when he looked at the scarred face of his once beautiful sister.

Kristjan was installed as the new chief of Ungannia and out of politeness he listened to the priests who told him that Tooni was a thirsty god who demanded a great many souls in payment before he departed. But the new chief was not thinking about the gods; only revenge. For he thought it no coincidence that just prior to the outbreak of the pestilence a chest of clothes had arrived, a gift from Kalju's friends at Riga. The chest was full of rich apparel that had delighted Eha and his sisters in particular. But days after they had worn them they had fallen sick. The clothes and chest had been subsequently burnt but Kristjan remembered the logo that had been etched on the chest. He had seen it many times before: a red cross over a red sword. And anger burned within him.

He had no desire to stay at Odenpah so he commanded Indrek, formerly commander of his father's bodyguard and happily also untouched by the pestilence, to issue a summons for the kingdom's warlords to gather at Dorpat. After messengers had been despatched he and Indrek rode north with a small band of warriors. Kristjan vowed never to set foot in Odenpah again or gaze upon its ramparts until he had shed Sword Brother blood.

*****

To ensure Sword Brother control over Rotalia, Hillar and his three hundred warriors were left in the kingdom to support the efforts of Koit to persuade the village and parish elders that Riga's rule would be beneficial and not tyrannical. Hillar's men were delighted that they could return to their villages, those that were still standing after Oeselian and Danish depredations, and see their kinfolk again. In addition, Conrad left behind Andres and his four hundred Jerwen, both to reinforce Hillar if the need arose and to be near their homeland when the time came for the Sword Brothers to seize the whole of Estonia.

'And when will that be, master?' enquired Conrad as the rest of the army was making its way back to Wenden.

'Next year, most likely,' replied Rudolf. 'We still have to convey our good news regarding the lifting of the blockade to Bishop Albert, which will allow him to travel back to Germany to recruit crusaders for next spring.'

'We could have conquered Estonia by ourselves,' muttered Henke. 'We should have left that Danish king on Oesel and marched straight to Reval.'

He was not happy, not least because he had had no chance to split Oeselian skulls on the island, the crossbowmen having achieved victory by themselves.

'If that was my intention, Henke,' said Rudolf, 'then there would have been little point in going to the island in the first place. But now I have Valdemar's signature on a document that pledges to end the blockade of Livonia and cedes Estonia to the Sword Brothers.'

'Minus Reval,' said Walter quick to point out the minutiae of the agreement.

'Quite so,' agreed Rudolf.

Conrad had been asked to ride with the other commanders of the army, the two other masters joining Wenden's castellan and brother knights and Sir Richard and his doughty squire. He had also insisted that Kaja join the group, still delighted with her performance on Oesel. He thought it hilarious that Valdemar had been humiliated in front of his knights and churchmen by realising that a girl had come to rescue him.

'What if he's dead?' Henke said suddenly.

Rudolf turned in the saddle to look at him. 'Who?'

'The Bishop of Riga. For all we know the pox may have killed everyone within the city.'

'Pray God that he still lives,' said Walter earnestly.

But Henke had the bit between his teeth. 'If he is then that little archdeacon runt will be in charge, together with that slimy bastard Nordheim.'

'Your language is intemperate, brother,' Walter scolded him, 'especially as we have a lady present.'

'What lady?' sniffed Henke.

'Kaja,' said Conrad.

'She's a heathen,' scoffed Henke. 'She don't understand what we're saying, do you girl?'

'I understand that you have no manners,' said Kaja in perfect German.

The brother knights burst into laughter though Henke was far from amused. He decided to take out his frustration on Lukas.

'I blame you for all this, Lukas. You taught her how to use a sword and now she thinks she is a lady whereas in fact she is a lowborn Saccalian who should be working in the kitchens.'

But Lukas had heard it all before. 'Just because you were deprived of your quota of slaughter on Oesel there is no need to take your frustration out on all and sundry. As for Kaja, she won her place among the novices on merit.'

'Thank you, Brother Lukas,' she said.

'In any case,' said Rudolf loudly, 'if the worst has happened and Bishop Albert has been taken from us then his Holiness the Pope will appoint a new bishop to take control of matters in Livonia and I can assure you, Henke, that it will not be Archdeacon Stefan.'

'And if you think that piece of parchment will save Livonia from Valdemar's wrath,' muttered Henke, 'then you are mistaken, Rudolf.'

'I am apt to agree with Brother Henke,' said Sir Richard. 'Humiliating a king is no small matter, Rudolf. Something that you and all of us may live to regret.'

But Rudolf was not to be deflated.

'Valdemar made a great mistake invading Oesel, perhaps the greatest of his reign. Before he was Christendom's most feared warlord in northern Europe, the man who had humbled the north German lords and treated the Baltic as his own private lake. But now word will spread that King Valdemar was at the mercy of the pagans and was only saved from death by the Sword Brothers.'

He looked at Kaja. 'Perhaps word will also spread that among those who rescued him was a young girl from Saccalia. How diminished his reputation will be.'

'You seek to provoke rebellion within his domains?' asked Sir Richard.

'My only concern is my order and Livonia, your grace,' Rudolf answered. 'But if Valdemar's attention is focused not on Estonia and Livonia but elsewhere then so much the better for us.'

'Clever,' remarked Squire Paul. 'Bet you wish you had thought of that, your grace.'

'Be quiet,' Sir Richard ordered him.

'I have to say that, notwithstanding the pox that currently ravages Riga,' said Rudolf, 'events are turning to our advantage. Rotalia is under the protection of the Sword Brothers, Ungannia is an ally of the bishop, Saccalia is a close ally of our order,' he tilted his head at Sir Richard. 'And Conrad has been restored to his position as Marshal of Estonia.'

Conrad had to admit that Master Rudolf's plan had been a masterstroke. He prayed that Bishop Albert still lived because the deputy commander of the order he had created had reversed a previously sad state of affairs. Reval could still become a thorn in the side of the Sword Brothers and Jerwen, Wierland and Harrien still had to be subdued. But a small contingent among the men riding ponies in the long column behind him was from Harrien and he had left four hundred Jerwen with Hillar in Rotalia. And just as Hillar had facilitated the absorbing of Rotalia into Sword Brother territory, so he believed that Andres and Riki could achieve the same in Jerwen and Harrien respectively.

The days were getting longer and warmer now, though there was still mist over the bog fields early in the morning. As the guides led the nearly eight hundred men through the forests of pine, birch and fir of southern Rotalia the mood was relaxed, almost carefree. The order's mercenary crossbowmen were particularly happy because the lifting of the blockade on Riga meant a resumption of trade and that meant monies would again be flowing into the Sword Brothers' coffers. And that meant they would be paid. Leatherface was whistling, his crossbow slung over his shoulder, as his pony plodded through a sun-dappled stretch of birch trees with tits singing in the branches.

*****

130

It had been over ten years since the Sword Brothers had taken Fellin during a winter siege. Then the stronghold with its high timber walls and deep moat had been Lembit's second fortress behind Lehola, but now it was the residence of Peeter, Count of Fellin, the Saccalian who had been awarded the title by Pope Honorius himself after the old warrior had accepted baptism. He had fought for Lembit against the Sword Brothers but had been won over to the side of the Christians when a young brother knight had created an army that had relieved Lehola when it had been besieged by barbarians. He had subsequently become a good friend of the Duke of Saccalia, a man who treated him and his people with respect and as equals. Saccalia was at peace and prospered.

It was true that in return for peace and protection the kingdom had to accept Christian priests into its villages. But these men from what Sir Richard had told him were from the Cistercian Order. They had aroused pity when they first appeared with their shaved crowns, and dressed in undyed woollen habits which proclaimed their poverty to the world. They built their own hovels on the edge of villages and lived on a diet of vegetables, herbs and beans. Sir Richard sent food to ensure they did not starve throughout the winter and gave orders that they were not to be molested. At first the people simply ignored them. But gradually the priests' piety and kindness endeared them to the natives, not least because they were the most impoverished inhabitants of each settlement. There were not many of them but they went about their preaching in a quiet, dignified way, so that gradually the seeds of Christianity were planted in Saccalia.

Peeter was in the armoury when a guard reported that a sentry in one of the fort's towers had spotted a column of riders approaching from the east.

'Around a score, lord.'

Peeter gave the order to muster the garrison and strolled outside. Barefooted children ran around Fellin's interior chasing chickens and goats. Slaves fed pigs in pens between the huts. A dozen warriors in leather breastplates, carrying shields bearing wolf insignia formed up in a line in front of the great hall. Most of the wolf shields were with Sir Richard in Rotalia, along with the levies that had been raised from the villages around Fellin and Lehola. Peeter walked over to the open gates in the eastern wall and looked across the wooden bridge over the moat, then peered up at the sentry in the nearest tower.

'Do you see any banners?' he shouted.

'Eagle banner, lord,' came the reply.

Ungannia? Strange, he had received no word from Kalju concerning a delegation. He shrugged. Perhaps it was Kalju himself come to visit his friend Sir Richard. He would have to inform him that he had wasted his journey. He turned and walked back to his hall.

He ordered his steward to tell the kitchen slaves to prepare a feast. The man scurried into the hall's interior as Peeter stood in front of his men and waited to welcome Kalju. It had been too long since he had seen him.

The riders thundered across the bridge and into the fort, children and animals squealing and running for cover as the sweating ponies were brought to a halt and their riders alighted from their saddles. All were wearing helmets and mail shirts with swords at their hips. Aside from the banner man each one was also armed with a spear that they now thrust into the earth. The round shields that dangled from their saddles carried the golden eagle symbol of Ungannia.

The leader took off his helmet to reveal himself not to be Kalju but a powerfully built young man with long fair hair and blue eyes who walked up to Peeter and nodded.

'I am Kristjan, son of Kalju and Lord of Ungannia.'

Fellin's great hall was half empty as Peeter feasted the arrivals that night. Slaves brought great quantities of beer and honey mead for his guests. They served huge portions of roasted boar but Kristjan ate and drank sparingly, as did his men. Peeter's wolf shields, glad to have some excitement after having missed out on the campaign to Oesel, drank and ate to excess, toasting their Ungannian allies and engaging in drinking bouts with their comrades. Peeter sat at the top table with Kristjan, who kept looking at the tonsured priest sitting at a nearby table chatting to a slave and eating even less than him.

'Who is that?' asked the young Ungannian.

'Father Dietmar, sent by Riga to preach in local villages.'

'A Christian?' sneered Kristjan as a slave placed a platter of bloodless white sausages in front of him.

'We are all Christians here, young lord,' said Peeter. 'The world changes and we must change with it. Your own father recognised that when he made an alliance with the Sword Brothers. I trust he and your mother are well.'

Kristjan tore off a small piece of rye bread and nibbled it.

'Has Saccalia abandoned the gods, Lord Peeter? Do men no longer revere and fear Uku, Jumal, Mielikki and Kuu?'

'Men are free to follow their conscience,' answered Peeter as there was a great cheer from his men as one who had drank too much threw up violently.

'Are men free when they are forced to live under the heel of the Sword Brothers?' said Kristjan.

'Why are you here, Kristjan?' queried Peeter, getting annoyed at the surly young man who had arrived unannounced and was enjoying his hospitality with little courtesy.

'I want your aid, Lord Peeter,' said Kristjan. 'Just as Ungannia is a free kingdom so do I desire Saccalia to join me in rejecting the Christian filth that pollutes our lands.'

Peeter was shocked by these words and thought that the young man was deranged.

'These are your father's words?'

Kristjan looked at the older man. 'My father is dead. Murdered by the Sword Brothers. I ask you again: will you join me?'

Peeter was astounded to hear that Kalju was dead.

'I had no idea, Kristjan. Please forgive me.'

Kristjan shrugged. 'You have done nothing wrong, lord. It is the Sword Brothers who are to blame for my parents' and my sisters' deaths. I will avenge them. But will you avenge those Saccalians murdered by the Sword Brothers?'

'That was different, Kristjan, that was war. We have made peace with the Bishop of Riga and Saccalia is free of strife and prospers.'

He placed a hand on the Ungannian's shoulder and looked at him kindly.

'There have been no Sword Brothers in Ungannia, Kristjan. Your grief has blinded you to the truth. How did your parents die?'

Kristjan looked at Father Dietmar. 'The Sword Brothers used Christian magic to kill them, just as it will kill you if you let their wizards practise their black magic here. But you have a chance to throw off the Christian yoke. I have summoned Ungannia's fighting men to my banner so we can wash our swords in Christian blood.'

Peeter shook his head. 'The old ways will not return, Kristjan. Ungannia is free only because it has the protection of the Sword Brothers. In your heart you must know this.'

Kristjan smiled and placed his hand on top of the old man's.

'I knew that would be your answer.'

He held Peeter's gaze as he pushed the point of the dagger into his armpit before whipping it back and thrusting it into the neck of the wolf shield sitting on his other side.

'Now!' he bellowed.

Inebriated Saccalians smiled dumbly as their guests pulled concealed daggers and began a stabbing frenzy. Some Saccalians were slumped at their tables, unconscious from drink, when their throats were slit; others died with confused looks on their faces. A handful tried to resist but were pounced on and had their faces and torsos reduced to bloody pulps. And suddenly it was over.

'Get your weapons,' ordered Kristjan as Peeter slumped in his chair, unable to move as blood pumped from his armpit. As slaves screamed and then fell silent as they too were killed, the Ungannians opened the doors to the hall and attacked the two guards standing outside. They then retrieved their swords, spears and shields that had been stacked on long benches either side of the doors. For it was common custom that guests did not take weapons into a host's hall.

'Secure the rest of the fort,' commanded Kristjan as he strapped on his sword belt. His commander saluted and exited the hall with half a dozen warriors. Of the paltry garrison only a handful still lived and they were in the watchtowers. They would be speedily dealt with.

'Kill the wives and children of these wretches,' ordered Kristjan to another of his men. Another four warriors left the hall. He knew the slaves presented no threat and would already be cowering in some corner, praying to whatever gods they worshipped that their worthless lives would be spared. The other warriors dispersed to stand guard at the entrance to the hall and the doorway that led to the kitchens. Kristjan looked around at the blood-splattered corpses and smiled. His smile disappeared when he heard frantic whispering behind him and turned to see Father Dietmar on his knees clutching in his hands the wooden cross he wore around his neck. His eyes were closed as he recited prayers in a language Kristjan did not understand. He drew his sword, walked over to the priest and smashed the weapon's hilt hard against the side of the priest's face. Dietmar let out a squeal and crumbled to the floor, unconscious.

'Heathen.'

Kristjan sheathed his sword and went back to the top table where the fatally wounded Peeter sat slumped in his chair. One side of his tunic was stained red and his life was slowly leaving him. Kristjan retook his seat and stared at the scene of mayhem in front of him.

'They called my father "the rock" and that was what he was. They say that he was fearless in battle and a giant among men. But when he died he was a festering, diseased husk that barely resembled a person, let alone a man. And it was the same with my mother and sisters, whom I watched decay in front of my eyes.'

He looked at Peeter.

'But do you know the worse thing? It was being helpless, like you are now. Being unable to do anything even though your mind is screaming at you to act. Well, I am going to act.

'I have been told that the greatest gift a Christian can have is to die in the manner that his god, this Christ, met his end. Out of respect for your rank and reputation I grant you this wish. It is the least I can do.'

Kristjan strolled from the hall into the fort's compound, passed the bodies of the women and children his men had butchered, to one of the watchtowers. Before he ascended the ladder to the top of the wall he ordered the gates to be opened. He walked to a tower with a shingle roof as the night was suddenly filled with bright dots that flooded from the forest to the east of the fort. He smiled to himself as the dots became larger and suddenly the area beyond the moat was filled with dozens of warriors carrying torches. His men in the towers began banging their shields against the ancient oak timbers as the warriors outside the fort ran up to the bridge and raised their shields and weapons when they saw their lord standing on the battlements. They then began shouting his name.

'Kristjan, Kristjan,' and he smiled to himself once more.

In the morning he sent men to the surrounding villages to kill any Christian priests and to announce that Kristjan had come to liberate them from the wicked foreign religion and the Sword Brothers. Carpenters from the closest settlement were brought to Fellin and ordered to build two crosses made of oak that were planted by the side of the lake to the south of the fort, but not until Peeter and Father Dietmar were nailed and lashed to them. Kristjan stood at the foot of the cross that Peeter was fixed to and watched the old man pass from this life.

Because of his knife wound he expired after an hour on the cross. It took Father Dietmar longer to die and Kristjan thought his screaming and thrashing around when he was first nailed to the wood was most undignified. But after a while his only sounds were low moans and pathetic cries and after two days he made no noise at all.

The bodies were left to rot as a warning to those who might be tempted to practise black magic.

*****

The now depleted army that had saved Valdemar on Oesel and won Rotalia for the Sword Brothers was in high spirits as it continued its journey back to Wenden. It was traveling among the forests, lakes and meadows of Saccalia, a column of horses, ponies and mules slowly making its way home. The spring days were getting longer and though the sun showed itself, most days the constant breeze kept the temperature pleasant for men wearing mail and leather armour. Soon the army would reach the River Pala, not far from Lehola, where it would bid farewell to Sir Richard and his knights and levies.

'I'm looking forward to seeing Lehola again,' reflected the English lord. 'It is a strange thing to have found peace in a land far from my own country.'

'You will have to forgive the duke,' said Squire Paul, 'he has been at the wine and his tongue rambles.'

'You are lucky you still have yours,' remarked Sir Richard. 'I should have cut it out years ago.'

Their bickering was endless but Conrad thought that they had great admiration for each other, notwithstanding the difference in status between them.

'England is very different from Livonia and Estonia, your grace?' enquired Conrad.

Once again he was riding in the company of the army's commanders, Rudolf informing him it was only proper that as leader of the Army of the Wolf and now restored to his position as Marshal of Estonia he should ride with him, the other two masters and Sir Richard. Kaja, who had taken it upon herself to be a sort of personal standard bearer for Conrad, rode behind him carrying the banner that Rudolf had given him. Walter carried Wenden's banner and the flags of Mathias and Bertram were carried behind the two masters, though Sir Richard still had no standard. They rode in the vanguard of the army, a score of Sir Richard's lesser knights providing a thin outer screen and beyond them Saccalian scouts to guard against the army being attacked by an Oeselian war band or outlaws.

'Different?' said Squire Paul, answering for his lord. 'It's exactly the same. Always raining, winters that send the cold to burrow into your bones – and endless forests.'

'For once my insolent squire speaks the truth,' agreed Sir Richard. 'But here life is less complicated.'

'We make a new land here, your grace,' said Walter solemnly, 'a godlier place.'

'Or god forsaken, depending on your point of view,' mused Paul.

'And you, Conrad,' said Sir Richard, 'what will you and your army do now that the Danes have ceded Estonia?'

'That will be for the bishop to decide,' answered Rudolf.

'If he still lives,' remarked Henke behind Walter.

'The way you keep going on, Henke,' said Rudolf, 'anyone would think that you want the bishop to die.'

'I've seen what the pox can do to a city, that's all,' Henke replied. 'For all we know every citizen of Riga could be dead, which means that you are King of Livonia, Rudolf.'

'*Master* Rudolf to you,' Rudolf scolded him.

'We should have killed that arrogant bastard Valdemar,' stated Henke loudly.

'He is a king anointed by God,' said Walter, appalled that Henke should suggest murdering a sovereign.

'We serve the King of kings,' replied Henke, 'or so Otto is always telling us. So I think that beats a measly king.'

Rudolf laughed and the other two masters smiled.

'I do not think it works like that, Brother Henke,' said Master Bertram.

'Have it your own way,' said Henke. 'But Valdemar won't forget the insults the Sword Brothers have dealt him and he will be back next year with a large army to seek retribution.'

'In that I think you may be right, Brother Henke,' said Master Mathias.

'I did not insult him,' insisted Rudolf, 'I rescued him.'

Henke guffawed. 'Forcing him to sign a document of surrender after telling him that your army was full of heathen girls was not insulting him, more like rubbing his nose in a pile of dung.'

'Why would my presence insult such a great king?' asked Kaja innocently.

'Because he is a great, and you are a low-born heathen girl,' answered Henke.

'As opposed to a low-born mercenary,' remarked Conrad casually.

'Careful, marshal,' said Henke threateningly, 'you don't risk getting yourself mortally wounded in front of your heathen bed warmer.'

Conrad swung in his saddle. 'Who is going to mortally wound me, brother?'

'Why me, of course,' answered Henke.

Conrad laughed. 'You have more chance of sprouting wings.'

'Enough you two,' ordered Rudolf. 'Try to remember you are brother knights of the Sword Brothers.'

'The woodpeckers have stopped tapping.'

They all looked at Kaja after her observation. They were moving through a meadow between two expanses of spruce forest, the passage narrowing ahead as the meadow gave way to an ancient winding track that threaded through the spruce. They were around two miles north of the River Pala. In the spring woodpeckers usually began their drumming in late March and so common was the sound throughout Livonia and Estonia that it became just another daytime noise. Rudolf held up a hand to signal a halt as Conrad looked left and right and turned an ear to the forest.

'She's right,' said Squire Paul. 'No tapping.'

Behind them the contingents of brother knights and sergeants came to a halt and drew their swords. The air tingled with the threat of impending violence even though there were no indications of an enemy presence. But the order's soldiers and mercenaries had spent many years fighting among the forests and lakes of Livonia and Estonia and had developed a sixth sense when it came to pre-empting a hostile attack.

Conrad drew his sword as the others pulled blades from scabbards. He pulled his shield off his back and slid his left forearm through the straps on its inner side.

'Do you think your knights and scouts are dead, Sir Richard?' queried Henke as he peered ahead at the gap between the two forests.

But less than two minutes later Sir Richard's riders cantered from the space between the trees, followed a few moments later by his scouts. They rode over to their lord who probed them about what lay ahead.

'Did you see anything suspicious?'

'No, my lord,' answered a thickset man, an Englishman Conrad assumed, with a straggly beard. 'It's all clear to the river.'

'There are men in the forests,' said Kaja.

The thickset man laughed. 'There is nothing in the trees, girl, aside from the usual forest demons who torment little girls.'

Sir Richard raised his palm. 'Enough. She is Saccalian and has a nose for such things.'

'We will advanced in close order and dismounted,' announced Rudolf. He turned to Walter. 'Inform the mercenaries.'

Walter saluted, turned his horse and trotted away to speak to Leatherface.

'With your permission,' said Conrad.

Rudolf nodded and he and Kaja rode to the rear of the column where the hundred and seventy men of the Army of the Wolf formed the rearguard.

'Why have we stopped?' asked Hans when they reached them.

'Kaja thinks the trees hide an enemy,' said Conrad as he jumped from his horse. 'Master Rudolf has ordered everyone to dismount and form close order for the march through the forest ahead.'

It took around fifteen minutes for the column to reorganise its dispositions, the Sword Brothers' knights forming the vanguard, behind which were Sir Richard's knights and Saccalians, with the Army of the Wolf deployed in the rear. The mules and ponies carrying the supplies were distributed among each formation. The sergeants and mercenaries, all equipped with crossbows, were deployed on the flanks. Every fifth man held the reins of his beast and those of another four horses or ponies; the other four walked with their weapons at the ready.

'Roll up that flag and stash it on your horse,' Conrad told Kaja as she walked along with the banner. 'I don't want you to be a target for an enemy archer.'

She did as she was told and then returned to walk beside Conrad, Hans and Anton trailing after them. Leatherface appeared as the Estonian warriors behind clutched their axes and spears and scanned the treeline for any activity. Conrad sheathed his sword, drew his axe and turned it in his hands as Hans and Anton, their helmets shoved up on their heads like their friend, gripped their maces.

'Master Rudolf got spooked, did he?' grinned Leatherface.

Conrad pointed his axe at Kaja. 'Kaja believes that an unseen enemy is near.'

The leering mercenary stared at the shape of her breasts beneath her mail armour.

'And we have to walk to the river for that?'

'It's only a couple of miles,' said Hans.

They were in the very rear of the Army of the Wolf, Riki commanding the left flank and Tonis the right. They stood around for what seemed like an age until the column moved slowly ahead, towards the gap between the trees.

'Keep your eyes peeled,' shouted Conrad, 'and your shields tight to your bodies.'

The brother knights walked backwards as the army headed towards the Pala, wolf shields on either side of them and Kaja behind. Leatherface strolled nonchalantly along, crossbow armed and at the ready as the trees on either side got nearer. The only noise came from the column: the jangling of horse bits, the snorting of the animals and the shuffling sound of hundreds of men moving slowly. From the forest came only an ominous silence.

'*Susi*,' Kaja whispered as the tension continued to rise by the minute, 'may I ask you a question?'

'What is it?'

'Why do you and brothers Hans and Anton not use your swords?'

'Maces and axes are better for close-quarter fighting,' he told her. 'As you continue to attend Lukas' lessons you will learn that. Swords are expensive. In a one-to-one fight they are the weapons of choice. But when it comes to hacking at many enemy soldiers close up I prefer my axe.'

Kaja looked at the Danish sword she had found lying on the battlefield at Reval.

'I prefer my sword.'

Conrad looked at her. 'Of course you do. It's a nice sword.'

'Probably belonged to a great lord,' said Hans. 'Perhaps the property of a close friend of King Valdemar himself. And you stole it.'

'I did not steal it,' she insisted. 'I found it lying on the ground.'

'Concentrate on the trees,' hissed Conrad as the rear of the column entered the forest and walked along the winding track. The trees and fern-covered forest floor enclosed them on each side. Conrad saw the trunk of a spruce that had been gnawed by an elk and shafts of sunlight lancing through the forest canopy but saw no movement.

They pressed on, seeing and hearing nothing but in their minds imagining an enemy warrior behind every tree. No one spoke now. There were no sarcastic comments or nervous laughter, only deathly quiet and frayed concentration. Sweat trickled down Conrad's face as he searched for the enemy. He wished that an assailant would show himself just to break the tension but none did. And then, after an hour of mental torture, the column left the trees and entered the great expanse of meadow through which the Pala flowed. And there, ahead, was Master Thaddeus' marvel.

It had been built the previous summer: a wooden bridge that spanned the Pala when the snows melted and the river burst its banks in the spring to flood the meadow it ran through. It was positioned next to the track and the ford across the river that disappeared when the spring melt water arrived. Nine hundred feet in length, Master Thaddeus had based his design on the bridge constructed by Julius Caesar in antiquity when the Roman had taken his army across the River Rhine.

The piers supporting the bridge were fashioned from thick logs that were tied together in pairs with a two-foot gap between them. They had been driven into the ground north and south of the river when melt waters had disappeared and the Pala was shallow and slow moving, and also into the riverbed itself. Once two rows of piers had been secured large logs were placed between them, the logs slotting into the spaces formed by the two-foot gaps. Then angled posts were lashed to the piers, which were forty feet apart, to provide additional support. Once the support structure was in place, logs were laid at right angles across the piers and then planking was nailed to them to form a roadway. When it was finished villagers for miles around came to see this engineering wonder, which masters Rudolf, Mathias and Bertram now stepped on to begin the last leg of the journey back to Wenden.

And at that moment warriors flooded out of the trees to attack the rearguard, while the southern end of the bridge was suddenly filled with a seething mass of men with axes and spears.

Kristjan had sprung his trap.

The crusader army had been strung out over a distance of half a mile before Kaja's comments about the woodpeckers had caused Master Rudolf to order it to dismount and close up. It now had a length of around five hundred yards, the Sword Brothers on the bridge in the vanguard, followed by Sir Richard's men, half of whom were on the bridge, and the Army of the Wolf in the rear. As the enemy flooded from the trees

148

Conrad knew his men could not outrun the enemy. For one thing there was already a press of men and animals forming around the bridge's northern end. If he ordered a retreat there would be a mad crush and the enemy would be among them in moments.

'Shield wall!' he shouted.

Horns sounded and his Harrien and wolf shields began to form into line, Riki and Tonis bellowing orders and shoving men into position. Leatherface was also shouting at his crossbowmen to take up position behind the front rank of Estonians. Ponies, horses and mules became skittish and difficult to control as the horde of enemy warriors raced towards them, shouting their war cries at the tops of their voices. There was no time for the pre-battle ritual as Conrad nodded to Hans and Anton and then pulled down his helmet over his face. He manhandled Kaja back to where others were trying to calm the animals and then pushed his way into the shield wall. He caught sight of knights and Saccalians coming forward to reinforce his men but then heard a series of cracks as Leatherface and his colleagues began shooting.

And then the enemy shattered his shield wall.

A hundred and fifty men had formed a thin defence of three ranks in an effort to protect those escaping across the bridge. But they were assaulted by hundreds of enemy warriors, men dressed in brown, grey and green hues and carrying round wooden shields, many of which were painted with a golden eagle design – Ungannians! They wore helmets and those in the

149

front ranks were protected by mail or leather armour and were armed with a mixture of axes, swords and spears. Their intention was to overpower the shield wall and then slaughter those on and about to get on to the bridge. The shield wall's front rank disappeared as the Ungannians hurled themselves at it, thrusting with spears and hacking down with axes to bludgeon their way through the wall of human flesh. The fifty or so crossbowmen that had managed to get in line and loose at least two volleys were either trampled on or had their skulls split open as a pagan wave swept over them.

Conrad was standing between Hans and Anton when the Ungannians struck. The wolf shield in front of Leatherface killed his first opponent before disappearing from view as three or four enemy warriors speared and hacked at him with axes. Leatherface shot one of his killers with his crossbow before a spear was thrust into his guts.

'No!' screamed Conrad, who launched himself forward, split the haft with the downward blow of his axe and then whipped it back viciously to slice into the spearman's neck. He clutched his wound and staggered back, Conrad standing over the prostrate Leatherface and catching an axe blow on his shield. Before his attacker had a chance to recover he turned his axe in his hand and swung it forward to drive the spike on the opposite side of the axe head into the warrior's mail armour. The man gasped before collapsing to the ground, dead.

Conrad yanked the spike free, stepped forward, crouched low with his shield held high and collided with a wild-eyed man

150

with a sword raised above his head, heaving the man up and over him. The warrior hit the ground hard on his back and was killed as Hans reduced his face to a pulp with his mace.

Conrad saw something flash by his side and saw a warrior in front of him slump to the ground with a spear in his groin. It was an excellent throw. He turned and saw the figure of Kaja dragging Leatherface back from the fray. She must have thrown the spear and had also disobeyed his orders. He turned back just in time to avoid a scything sword blow that would have dented his helmet. But as it was he deftly stepped to one side, smashed his shield into the right shoulder of the Ungannian, thereby unbalancing him and sending him sprawling to the ground. Anton killed him by smashing his boot down hard on the back of the man's neck, snapping his spine.

The battle had degenerated into dozens of single combats as the survivors of the Army of the Wolf, surrounded and outnumbered, fought to stay alive. The three brother knights, now having space to dodge and duck their opponents, reaped a grim harvest. Their moves, honed on the training ground over many years under the watchful eye of Lukas, were instinctive. But even as he killed men Conrad could still hear his tutor's words in his mind.

'Keep moving; always keep moving. Don't stand around waiting to be hit. Avoid blows; make your enemy cut air. Your feet are as important as your sword arm. You're not wrestlers but dancers so dodge, duck, feint, weave and deceive.'

151

Conrad started laughing as two men ran at him screaming blood-curdling war cries. But they were gripped by frenzy while he was calm and thinking ahead. He opened his arms to expose his torso to encourage them and they increased their speed. He suddenly leapt to the left to avoid them and tripped the warrior on the left, sending him clattering to the ground. His comrade tried to stop and turn but in the few seconds it took him to halt and change direction Conrad had reached him and split the side of his helmet with his axe. He grunted and collapsed to the ground. The other man had meanwhile risen to his feet and retrieved the spear that he had let go of when he hit the ground, only to have his right wrist smashed by Conrad's axe. He screamed in agony, released the spear, dropped his shield and instinctively cradled his half-severed hand with his left arm. He gave Conrad a pitiful look before the brother knight ended his life with half a dozen axe strikes that staved in the top of his helmet.

Above the din of men swearing and screaming and animals whinnying he heard a sudden blast of trumpets behind him followed by a great roar. He prised his axe from the dead man's twisted, gore-splattered helmet to see a great wedge of warriors and knights charging forward led by a lord in a white surcoat and full-face helmet – Sir Richard.

The Duke of Saccalia's attack was like a battering ram that smashed into the Ungannians, at first stopping them and then driving them steadily back. Conrad removed his helmet and held it aloft.

'Rally, rally Army of the Wolf.'

Horses and ponies were scattering in all directions, those tasked with holding their reins having abandoned them to fight the Ungannians. Some lay on their sides, dead and dying, while injured mules with terrible gashes in their flanks stood calling mournfully. Slowly exhausted wolf shields and Harrien began to gather round their leaders, the wounded Riki and the unharmed Tonis. Hans, his helmet battered and his surcoat and mail shirt ripped, embraced him. As did Anton whose shield had been reduced to splinters. He threw it on the ground as Sir Richard's three hundred men continued to force the Ungannians back towards the trees.

'Kalju is no longer our friend,' said Conrad bitterly.

Hans was looking at his helmet. 'The death of his son must have tipped him over the edge.'

'We gain Rotalia and lose Ungannia as an ally. Master Rudolf will want revenge for this,' said Anton.

As the Army of the Wolf again formed a ragged shield wall to protect the northern end of the bridge, the wounded hobbled to the structure. Sir Richard kept his men under a tight leash, and once the Ungannians had withdrawn he too pulled back his men to reinforce Conrad's warriors. The brother knight had rushed over to where Kaja was kneeling beside Leatherface, holding a water bottle to his mouth. He feared the worst as he knelt by the mercenary's side. Despite his rough nature and coarse manners Conrad had grown very fond of Leatherface over the years.

'That spear thrust knocked the wind out of me,' he complained. He saw the look of concern on Conrad's face. 'Just a glancing blow. Nothing that a well-made gambeson can't deal with.'

Conrad placed a hand on his shoulder. 'Praise God for that.'

Leatherface looked longingly at Kaja. 'Would you grant a dying man a last wish, darling?'

She took the water bottle from his lips and replaced the top.

'I would, if you were dying. But as you are not I suggest you get up and stop play acting.'

Conrad helped him to his feet.

'You are a cruel one, lady,' he complained. 'And I've lost my crossbow.'

'I'm sure we can find you another one,' said Conrad.

But as Sir Richard's men pulled back to join Conrad's warriors to form a semi-circular shield wall around the northern end of the bridge, it became apparent that many supplies had been lost. Mules and ponies loaded with supplies had bolted, many into the trees to where the Ungannians had fled. The Sword Brothers still had all their supplies and Sir Richard had retained about half of his, but the Army of the Wolf was now woefully deficient.

Before darkness fell enemy shields were collected to build campfires as there was no opportunity to gather firewood with the forest beyond the northern end of the bridge occupied by the enemy, as was the ground to the south of the structure. The Army of the Wolf and Sir Richard's soldiers stood guard at the northern end, the Sword Brothers at the southern end as the commanders held a council of war at its mid-point. It had rained at dusk but now the clouds had departed to allow the moon to bathe the land in a pale grey glow. And with the moon came a rapid drop in temperature. Rudolf's breath misted as he spoke.

'So, Conrad, the festering wound of his son's loss has led Kalju to basely betray us.'

Conrad avoided the master's eyes. 'It would seem so, master.'

Rudolf looked at the enemy campfires beyond each end of the bridge.

'Well, he's no tactician that much is certain. He divides his forces, thus inviting us to defeat them separately. Tomorrow we will attack and teach Ungannia a lesson.'

'We will push on through to Lehola?' queried Sir Richard.

The duke's stronghold was only a few miles away to the south. To push through the enemy at the southern end was both sensible and the best way to extricate themselves from the situation they found themselves in.

Rudolf shook his head. 'Hearing your reports it is apparent that the main strength of the enemy lies beyond the northern end of the bridge. That is where we will attack, therefore. Besides, the Sword Brothers do not flee from an enemy.'

155

The order had had a relatively easy time of it defending the southern end of the bridge, the wild charge of the enemy killing two brother knights and fourteen sergeants before the Ungannians were stopped in their tracks by several volleys of crossbow bolts. After that the brother knights and sergeants formed a line of mail and iron that the enemy could not break.

'Tomorrow the crossbowmen will advance on foot with our mounted knights and sergeants. After their missiles have thinned the enemy's ranks the horsemen will attack and scatter them. The task of every man tomorrow is to kill Kalju.'

'Just one problem with that, Master Rudolf,' said Leatherface, who was still nursing a bruised rib.

'What?' snapped Rudolf.

'The lads are down to their last few bolts. We used a lot on Oesel and a fair few today. If you give battle tomorrow then that will be the last of their ammunition.'

'Strip the dead ones,' said Rudolf harshly.

Leatherface wiped his nose on his sleeve. 'Already done that. We lost thirty crossbowmen today but their bolts won't make much of a difference.'

'The plan stands,' stated Rudolf.

'Let us hope that Fellin and Lehola are still loyal,' said Sir Richard. 'If the enemy is south of the Pala then those places might have fallen.'

'The Ungannians have no siege engines, your grace,' said Conrad, trying to sound optimistic.

'One battle at a time,' said Rudolf. 'We will worry about your grace's strongholds once we have dealt with the Ungannians.'

The meeting over, Conrad and Leatherface wandered back to the Army of the Wolf, which had suffered fifty dead preventing the enemy swarming on to the bridge. They stopped when they heard footsteps behind them and saw Rudolf approaching.

'Conrad, convey my gratitude to Kaja. Her intuition meant we suffered less casualties today than we might otherwise have suffered.'

'She's a smart girl,' smiled Leatherface, 'good looking, too.'

Rudolf frowned at him. 'I would think very ill of someone who made improper advances to her.'

'So would I, Master Rudolf,' said the mercenary, 'she is like a daughter to me.'

'I will convey your gratitude, master,' promised Conrad. 'She will be most pleased.'

Kaja was delighted with Master Rudolf's thanks but less pleased when Conrad informed her that she would not be part of the mounted force that was to attack the Ungannians. The Army of the Wolf huddled round the meagre fires of burning enemy shields, Sir Richard's men sharing their food that was cooked over them. The Sword Brothers on the bridge had no fires and ate their food cold. They also could not pitch their tents, though Rudolf insisted that the chapel tent be pitched among the shelters of the Army of the Wolf. Otto said mass at Matins early the next morning, after which Conrad and the other members of the order checked the horses, fed and watered them before saddling them. It was a cold morning, an easterly breeze adding to the bite in the air. Conrad wrapped his cloak around himself. Because they had brought no wagons damaged armour and helmets could not be replaced. Neither could surcoats. So he, Hans and Anton stood by their mounts with ripped surcoats splashed with blood. Hans wore a pagan helmet with a nasal guard.

'Found it lying near a dead Ungannian.'

'Let's hope it brings you better luck than its former owner,' remarked Anton.

A sudden blast of trumpets signalled the beginning of the day's work. Conrad held out his arm, palm down. Hans laid his hand on top and Anton placed his hand on top of Hans'.

'As dust to the wind,' said Conrad.

'As dust to the wind,' came the reply.

They hoisted themselves into their saddles and joined the other two hundred and forty horsemen forming into line.

Sir Richard's Saccalian levies were posted to guard the southern end of the bridge, the Army of the Wolf the other end of it. The one hundred remaining crossbowmen stood behind the horsemen as Rudolf rode up and down the line issuing his orders. The early morning was cool and bright, the swollen river and flooded meadows on either side making the air smell damp. Rudolf had no helmet, a mail coif his only head protection as he went up and down the line. He brought his horse to a halt in front of Walter who carried Wenden's standard.

'We advance, pretend to run away and then kill them when they run after us.'

'What if they don't chase after us?' asked Henke, his helmet resting on the front of his saddle.'

'They are pagans, Henke,' replied Rudolf. 'They have no discipline, or so you are always telling me. We will see if your theory is correct. And Henke?'

'Yes, Rudolf?'

'Try not to kill any of our crossbowmen during your precipitous flight.'

The other brother knights and sergeants burst into laughter as Henke slammed the helmet on his head and drew his sword. The others did likewise and soon all along the line men were pulling swords from their scabbards. The banners of Wenden, Segewold and Kremon hung limply in the wind as Rudolf trotted a few paces in front, raised his sword and shouted the motto of the order.

'God with us!'

The order's soldiers shouted in kind, signallers blew trumpets and the line moved forward. There was a gap of at least three paces between each horseman as they broke into a trot and then a canter, the iron-shod hooves kicking up great clumps of damp earth. The Ungannians were rapidly moving into formation: a lone line of shields locked together around four hundred paces away. The sun glinted off whetted spear and sword points and a few arrows arched into the crystal clear sky, shot from the rear ranks. They fell harmlessly into the earth seconds before the horsemen reached them. The Ungannians were making a racket that threatened to raise the dead, shouting and screaming at the tops of their voices, their rear ranks banging the handles of their axes against the insides of their shields.

The Sword Brothers and Sir Richard's knights raised their swords as they neared the shield wall, but all slowed their horses. The signallers blew their trumpets and suddenly the mounted knights turned and fled, digging their spurs into the flanks of their horses to create the illusion of precipitous flight.

The Ungannians took the bait.

The front ranks of their shield wall raised a great cheer and suddenly swept forward in an attempt to catch the fleeing horsemen. There were frantic horn calls as their chiefs tried to restrain them, to no avail. Their men had given the Sword Brothers a bloody nose the day before and now the vaunted 'men of iron' were running. Running! So they ran after them, thinking only of wanting to catch the Christian knights so they could kill them.

The horsemen galloped towards the thin shield wall of the Army of the Wolf, passing through the line of crossbowmen who now began shooting at the oncoming Ungannians. They loosed two volleys as the Sword Brothers and Sir Richard's knights halted, turned their horses around and charged again towards the pagan warriors.

The Ungannian charge was not halted or even slowed by the crossbow bolts that felled perhaps fifty or sixty men. It just made Kristjan's men more determined to quicken their pace to get to the accursed Christians. But it was stopped dead in its tracks when dozens of horsemen were suddenly among them, hacking and slashing with their swords as they passed. The crossbowmen, now useless and exposed in the open, hurried back to the safety of the Army of the Wolf, Leatherface, his right arm in a sling, bellowing orders and curses for them to get a move on. And ahead the horsemen were cutting down Ungannians like a farmer scythes wheat.

Conrad, the reins positioned behind his saddle's high pommel, let his horse guide itself through the onrushing figures ahead, the animal instinctively heading for any gaps between warriors. This left him free to use his shield to ward off any spear or sword thrusts aimed at his mount's belly but, more importantly, allowed him to slash at passing warriors. Speed and precision were his weapons, using the edge of his sword to cut the backs of necks and shoulders as he rode passed.

He raised his sword to strike a warrior armed with a spear but the man spotted him and raised his shield to parry the blow, at the same time pointing the spear at Conrad. So he ignored the man and rode on as Hans on his right side leaned over and thrust the point of his sword into the warrior's back. He was wearing mail armour but the sharpened point and weight

161

behind the thrust was enough to force the blade through the iron links into his flesh. It did not kill him but wounded him sufficiently to remove him from the battle.

A few brother knights, most notably Henke, preferred to use their maces against the pagans, aiming to split their helmets with a mighty swing as they passed by. It was an effective tactic as the mace was a bludgeoning instrument, much like Henke himself.

The Ungannian chiefs in the shield wall had restored order and stood beyond the front ranks with swords in hand to prevent any more of their men running forward. But now the Ungannians cursed and wept in frustration as they stood and watched the horsemen cut their friends and kinsmen to pieces. As the last were surrounded and killed by mace blows and sword strikes, they fell silent.

Trumpets commanded the horsemen to withdraw as the Army of the Wolf and the crossbowman gave a mighty cheer and raised their weapons in salute as the Sword Brothers and knights walked their horses back to the bridge. Behind them they left a ground covered with Ungannian dead. It had been a short, sharp victory but it still left Rudolf in a dilemma.

He called a council of war after the brother knights, sergeants and Sir Richard's men had been instructed to dismount and stand with the Army of the Wolf to repel an Ungannian attack. But it never came. After half an hour Kristjan's men withdrew back into the forest and everyone was ordered to stand down. The horses were taken on to the bridge, a Saccalian warrior reporting to Sir Richard that there had been no sign of the enemy beyond its southern end.

'We have satisfied honour,' stated Rudolf, 'now we must seek the counsel of reason or our pride will be punished.'

'We should push on to Lehola,' said Sir Richard. 'Our supplies are running low.'

'And my boys are now out of ammunition,' added Leatherface.

'What of the bridge, master?' asked Conrad.

Rudolf shrugged. 'What of it?'

'The Ungannians may burn it.'

'If they do they do,' said Rudolf. 'We will build a new one. Now my priority is to secure Sir Richard's strongholds and return to Wenden to plan the campaign of retribution against Ungannia. Kalju will discover that he has started a fire that it is impossible to extinguish.'

Lehola was only a few miles away but it took most of the day to reach it. Rudolf insisted that the Christian dead be collected and loaded on to mules and ponies so they could be given a proper burial outside the walls of the fort. A number of horses and ponies had been lost the day before, which meant that many had to walk to Lehola. Conrad also insisted that the dead among the Army of the Wolf should be taken back to Lehola, to be cremated there. Otto and several of the priests objected and said they should receive a Christian burial but Conrad said no. Some of his men had been baptised but the majority of the dead had not renounced their pagan beliefs and so in death their wishes would be respected. They took their complaints to Master Rudolf but he told them that Conrad was Marshal of Estonia and as they were in Estonia they had to obey his orders. So an army of dead men made the journey back to Lehola. Once there the sorry tale of Fellin was relayed to Sir Richard.

Lehola was a great stronghold, its outer timber walls being four hundred yards in length and two hundred yards wide. The great hall in the inner stronghold could feast five hundred men and within the fort were storerooms, stables, huts, forges and an armoury. When the army arrived there were a great many women and children in the inner compound, residents of the nearby villages that had provided the levies for Sir Richard's army that had gone to Oesel. There was a happy reunion between warriors and their families but in the hall there was nothing but grim faces as an old warrior with a limp that Sir Richard had left in command of the fort updated his lord and the Sword Brothers on the situation. His hair was pure white and his skin wrinkled and leathery, but he still had fire in his eyes and he spoke with authority.

'The only reason this place was not taken was because one of the garrison of Fellin managed to get here on foot after being knocked out and left for dead. So I shut the gates and sent riders to the villages so the people could either get here or seek sanctuary in the forests.'

'You did well, Harald,' said Sir Richard.

'Kalju has taken Fellin and his army sits in northern Saccalia,' said Rudolf. 'And were it not for a stroke of luck he would be sitting in this hall. It is a most regrettable state of affairs.'

'I must remain here to organise a counterattack against Fellin,' stated Sir Richard. 'I would ask you to send me reinforcements, Rudolf.'

'Then I must get back to Wenden as quickly as possible,' replied Rudolf, 'where I can hopefully muster an army.'

'What army?' asked Mathias. 'Have you forgotten that the pox rages in Livonia?'

'Only in Riga,' said Rudolf. 'I am hopeful that I can persuade Fricis to muster his Livs to aid us.'

Bertram sucked on his teeth. 'He's Bishop Albert's man, Rudolf. He won't do anything without Riga's authority.'

Rudolf looked at Conrad. 'Perhaps your brother, Conrad, may be useful in this instance.'

'Rameke?' said Conrad.

Rudolf nodded. 'Precisely. I am sure he will respond kindly to a personal request for aid.'

'I will ask him,' said Conrad.

Rudolf slammed a fist into his palm. 'Good.'

'I will also leave Tonis and his wolf shields here, your grace,' Conrad said to Sir Richard. 'As Saccalians I think they will wish to stay and aid you in your fight.'

The Army of the Wolf had numbered eight hundred and seventy men when it had departed Wenden. When it returned

165

from Lehola it contained fifty. While Riki and his Harrien rode to the rebuilt village south of the castle and Mathias and Bertram took their men back to Kremon and Segewold, Rudolf scribbled a message for Bishop Albert. Even though all contact with Riga was forbidden he had to inform the bishop that the blockade of Livonia had been lifted but that a new war had broken out in the east against a former ally.

Chapter 4

The mass of never-ending forest groves were green and lush with pine, spruce and birch trees, sweet with spring scents. The alder, bird cherry, hazel and rowan bushes were in full bloom, the latter already being plundered by local villagers who believed that rowan protected them against evil and so placed it above the entrances to their huts. Vsevolod had to admit that Lithuania in spring was not an unattractive place; in fact it was very similar to his homeland of Gerzika that lay north of the Dvina. Though it might as well have been a thousand miles away. After the tedium and biting cold of winter he always liked to leave the confines of the stronghold of Panemunis to fill his lungs with fresh air and get away from the plague of petitioners that always descended on the place once the ice and snow had departed and the tracks became passable again.

He had been persuaded by his wife to undertake a tour of the villages closest to Panemunis so as not to appear a remote, distant ruler, which is precisely what he wanted to be of course. But Rasa, a Lithuanian by birth and the daughter of the late Grand Duke Daugerutis, had pestered him incessantly so he had relented. He knew the people held little affection for him and derisively called him 'the Russian' behind his back, but they loved Rasa, especially her fiery spirit. At every village they passed through the people, stinking imbeciles that they were, greeted her with great affection. Mothers held up their dirty, malnourished babies for her to touch, though Vsevolod was

167

appalled and tried to deter her. But Rasa would have none of it; indeed, she dismounted from her horse and embraced the wretches, which caused Vsevolod even more distress but increased their love for his wife.

They had just left a village where his wife had once again paid no heed to her safety, mingling among the inhabitants freely.

'You should not expose yourself to danger,' Vsevolod rebuked her.

She laughed. 'What danger? These are my people. They love me and I love them.'

Vsevolod grimaced. 'Rulers rule and their subjects are subjugated. That is the natural order of things, my love. It is bad enough having to ride among their filthy hovels without having to actually touch them.'

'You will never win them over with that attitude.'

Vsevolod's mouth curled into a sneer. 'I do not want to win them over. I just want them to do their duty.'

They were riding at the head of a column of fifty other riders, two of whom were carrying Vsevolod's own standard – a silver griffin on a blue background – and the banner of Rasa's father: a black boar on all fours against a red background. The mounted soldiers were all Russians, members of the prince's bodyguard for he went nowhere in Lithuania without sizeable protection. The ravines, hillocks, meadows and forests might possess great beauty but they could also hide an assassin or, worse, a group of assassins.

To protect against such a possibility he always had his guards near. He insisted that they not only be Russian but also natives of Gerzika to ensure their absolute loyalty. Aras, his general, his fixer and the man tasked with keeping his son-in-law Mindaugas safe, thought it highly amusing but had to admit that the prince's bodyguards were impressive. They wore helmets with nasal guards and mail aventails protecting their necks and shoulders. Lamellar armour cuirasses made up of burnished rectangular iron plates protected their torsos. The elongated plates were linked together first in horizontal rows, then vertically by means of leather thongs passed through holes in the plates. Each plate had a number of fixing holes distributed over its entire surface. Once fastened together the rows of lamellae overlapped upwards. In this way the scale cuirass greatly exceeded its mail equivalent in terms of defensive properties. Lamellar armour could protect its wearer from thrusting weapons and arrows. Even bludgeoning weapons such as maces could fail to penetrate the lamellae, the force of their blows being 'scattered' over the plates, though the wearer would be winded from such a blow at the very least.

Aras looked behind at the two files of horsemen in their armour, shields bearing a silver griffin, blue tunics, tan leggings and leather boots. Each rider was armed with a lance, sword and dagger.

'You have brought peace, lord,' he said to Vsevolod, 'and for that you have the people's gratitude at least.'

'Gratitude?' sniffed the prince. 'I doubt they know the meaning of the word.'

'Don't be so stuffy,' said Rasa. 'Lithuania is at peace, the gods ravage Livonia with pestilence and your daughters have good marriages.'

He smiled at his wife. She was right about his daughters. He had engineered the marriage of his eldest daughter Morta to Prince Mindaugas, the son of the late Prince Stecse who had been the chief warlord of Grand Duke Daugerutis. He had plans to make Mindaugas grand duke when the opportunity presented itself. His other daughter Elze had been married to Prince Ykintas, son of Duke Butantas, leader of the Samogitians. By a happy coincidence Ykintas and Mindaugas had become friends as well as relatives. Vsevolod also had the friendship of Kitenis, Duke of the Aukstaitijans, and amicable relations with Viesthard, Duke of the Semgallians, notwithstanding that he had tried to conquer Viesthard's kingdom after forging an alliance with the Northern Kurs. All in all it was a happy state of affairs.

'Mindaugas believes that we should raise an army, cross the Dvina and conquer Livonia,' said Aras, 'considering that it is in a weakened state.'

Vsevolod rolled his eyes. 'And I suppose that Prince Ykintas agrees with this foolish notion?'

Aras nodded. 'Yes, lord, they are itching to give the Bishop of Riga a bloody nose.'

'As we all are, general,' smiled Rasa.

'The princes have taken to heart the call by the *Kriviu Krivaitis* for a holy crusade against Livonia,' added Aras.

The *Kriviu Krivaitis* was the spiritual head of the Lithuanian people, a high priest who lived in a hut near a sacred forest grove surrounded by younger priests and white-robed virgins.

'As a military man, general,' said Vsevolod, 'I hope you impressed upon our young firebrands that marching an army into a plague-infested country is a recipe for disaster.'

'I did mention it, yes,' answered Aras. 'That's the problem with peace, my lord, princes and dukes have too much time on their hands.'

They left the ravine and entered a broad meadow littered with snowdrops and buttercups, and saw a rider approaching at speed.

'Look lively!' shouted Aras as he nudged his horse forward to place himself between the royal couple and the galloping horseman. Half a dozen Russians cantered ahead of him and others flanked the prince and his wife. The rider, seeing the phalanx of horsemen ahead, slowed his horse and raised his right arm.

'State your business,' shouted Aras.

'I bring a message for Prince Vsevolod from the commander of Panemunis, lord,' answered the man, who appeared to be unarmed.

The column halted as the courier walked his horse forward until he was before Aras.

'What message?' demanded Vsevolod.

The courier bowed his head to the prince.

'Torolf, ambassador to Duke Arturus, has arrived at the castle and begs an audience with you, highness. The commander asks what is to be done with him?'

'Tell him to kill him,' joked Aras, smiling.

But Vsevolod was not amused. 'Do no such thing. Return to Panemunis and impress upon the commander that Torolf is an ambassador and may not be harmed. Go!'

The man bowed, turned his horse and galloped away. Vsevolod sighed deeply.

'So Torolf emerges from whatever rock he was hiding under,' remarked Aras. 'I wonder what mischief he is making?'

'Nothing to the advantage of Nalsen and Selonia, I'll warrant,' said Vsevolod glumly.

As they recommenced their journey back to their home a knot tightened in the prince's stomach.

It took an hour to reach Panemunis, Vsevolod giving orders that Torolf was to be given quarters, food and anything he desired while he and his wife changed their clothes and refreshed themselves. Normally he would have deferred an ambassador until the next day but this was Torolf, the voice of Arturus, formerly duke of the Northern Kurs but now the leader of all the Kurs following his defeat of Duke Gedvilas, who had been killed in the battle. Arturus had sent the duke's head to him as a present, and also a not so subtle warning that it was unwise to make Arturus an enemy.

The ambassador was shown into the throne room in the main hall of the fort, the banners of Gerzika and Daugerutis hanging on the wall behind the prince and his wife who were dressed to impress. Rasa had changed from her leggings and boots into a blue dress with wide sleeves, golden belt and a white cloak fastened at the right shoulder with a silver brooch. Black leather shoes completed her appearance. Vsevolod wore a long white tunic that ended just above the knees, with gold edging around the cuffs and neck. He too wore a cloak, his coloured red and adorned with silver griffins and fastened to his right shoulder by means of a silver griffin pin. In the Russian fashion he carried no weapons about his person. Aras, dressed in his thick black leather tunic, black leggings and black boots, stood by his prince's side, with Russian guards behind the throne and along the walls.

Vsevolod gave the signal and the doors opened to allow Torolf to enter. Moments later a gangly man in his early thirties walked into the chamber. He may have been an ambassador but he dressed like a poor farmer: simple black tunic, tan leggings, gaiters and boots. Two things made him stand out: his height and his red hair, which was shaved above the ears and plaited from the crown to the back of his neck. His red beard was neatly trimmed, his brown eyes missing nothing. He halted in front of the thrones and bowed deeply first to the prince and then to Rasa.

'Hail, highnesses. Thank you for seeing me at such short notice. The rivers have been unusually high this spring and movement has been difficult.'

'I hope your quarters are acceptable, Lord Torolf,' smiled Vsevolod.

Torolf smiled back. 'The hospitality of Panemunis is famous throughout all Lithuania, highness.' He bowed his head to Rasa. 'As is the beauty and wisdom of its princess.'

'You are too kind, ambassador,' smiled Rasa.

'How may we help you?' enquired Vsevolod.

Torolf maintained his smile. 'It is some while since my lord has contacted you, highness, and he sends his regrets for being so remiss. He has been preoccupied with matters pertaining to Kurland.'

'Kurland?' queried the prince.

'The name Duke Arturus has given the land that now encompasses all the Kurs following the death of the traitor Gedvilas,' answered Torolf. 'The duke has sent me to ask a favour of your highness.'

Vsevolod's mouth went dry. 'Favour?'

Torolf's smile slowly disappeared. 'As an ally of my lord he believes that it would be better if you approached the other dukes on his behalf, seeing as there has, in the past, been some misunderstandings between them and Duke Arturus.'

Aras laughed. The 'misunderstandings' Torolf referred to related to either attempts by Arturus to assassinate the other dukes or kill them on the battlefield. Vsevolod froze him with a stare.

'Please continue, Lord Torolf.'

'Duke Arturus feels that it is time for all Lithuanians to be united against the heathen Christians north of the Dvina. He believes that the pestilence that now ravages Riga is a sign from Perkunas that we should unite in the face of a common foe and not to bicker among ourselves.'

'A sensible policy,' agreed Vsevolod.

'To which end,' continued Torolf, 'my lord proposes a meeting of all the dukes at a place of your highness' choosing so that he may extend the hand of amity and reconciliation to the other dukes.'

'Those that are still living,' said Aras under his breath.

'Duke Arturus feels,' added Torolf, 'that the words of Prince Vsevolod carry great weight throughout Lithuania and would expedite such a meeting faster than his own approaches to the other dukes, so misunderstood is Duke Arturus within their kingdoms.'

'And if the other dukes refuse to countenance such a meeting?' said Vsevolod casually.

Torolf's bow creased thoughtfully. 'Then my lord will have no option but to continue the war that the other dukes started.'

Vsevolod brought his hands together and rested his chin on his thumbs. Arturus calling for peace was like a fish sprouting legs and walking on land. Ever since he had first heard of the Kur leader he had been embroiled in conflict with someone, be it Riga or the other dukes. And now he desired peace. A happy thought passed through Vsevolod's mind: perhaps the Kurs were exhausted by years of incessant warfare and genuinely desired peace. Perhaps Arturus could be subdued by diplomacy instead of military means.

'You may inform Duke Arturus,' said the prince, 'that I will devote all my energies to bring his proposal to fruition.'

Torolf, clearly delighted, bowed to him again.

'We will continue this conversation tonight, Lord Torolf,' said Vsevolod, gesturing to an official by the doors to come forward, 'when we dine together. Rindas will escort you back to your quarters.'

Torolf bowed to the prince. 'Highness.'

Bowing to Rasa, he retreated from the chamber in the company of Rindas, the doors closing behind them.

'Interesting,' remarked Aras. 'Hard to believe that Arturus wants peace but he definitely wants something.'

'You should have that ambassador's head for his insolence,' hissed Rasa. 'Asking you to be an errand boy for his lord.'

'We do not kill ambassadors, my love,' said Vsevolod calmly. 'Besides, I see an opportunity in his insolence. I wonder if the Kurs are so weakened by years of warfare that they have no option but to beg for peace. If so then Arturus has made a grave mistake by his approach.'

'That is a lot of ifs, my lord,' said Aras. 'An eagle does not voluntarily cut off its talons.'

'General Aras is right, husband,' said Rasa. 'Arturus is not to be trusted.'

'I am in agreement with you both,' replied the prince, 'but you forget that at this moment I have the friendship of the other dukes. What friends does Arturus have? None.'

'I doubt that bothers Arturus, my lord,' commented Aras.

But Vsevolod was too intrigued to let the opportunity slip. The prospect of a meeting with Arturus was also too enticing. He did not inform his wife and general but the chance of actually meeting the duke of the Kurs face to face, the man who was the stuff of children's nightmares, was too irresistible. And the opportunity to out-manoeuvre him diplomatically was even more so.

*****

'Ouch!'

Leatherface's haggard features melted into a grimace as Ilona placed the compress against his injured rib and proceeded to wrap the bandage around his damaged ribcage.

'Don't be a baby,' she admonished him. 'I thought you were supposed to be Livonia's most fearsome mercenary.'

'Fearsome looking, certainly,' said Conrad, sitting on a stool nearby.

The return to Wenden had been uneventful, the column of riders making good time back to the castle. They were greeted by the happy news that the pox had subsided at Riga and Bishop Albert, who still lived, had lifted the quarantine from the city. Rudolf immediately sent a courier pigeon to Grand Master Volquin, informing him of affairs concerning Oesel, Rotalia, Ungannia and Saccalia, and had sent another pigeon to Treiden to enlist the aid of Fricis and Rameke regarding a relief force to go to the aid of Sir Richard. His plan was to send the Livs and what remained of the Army of the Wolf north. He would stay at Wenden to guard against Ungannian incursions into Livonia.

Ilona tied off the bandage. 'I have applied an apple cider vinegar compress to assist the healing of the rib, which appears to be bruised rather than broken.'

'Lucky for me,' smiled Leatherface as Kaja assisted him in putting on his shirt.

Conrad had called to see how the old mercenary was following the return to the castle, Master Rudolf having ordered him to seek the immediate assistance of Ilona. Now in her mid-thirties, everyone loved the raven-haired Liv who had saved Rudolf's life years ago at Holm and who had become a famed healer. The brother knights and sergeants adored her for that act, the mercenaries liked her because she provided cures for their tooth and joint aches and the villagers loved her because she was an accomplished mid-wife who had saved many a young woman's life during the perils of childbirth.

'Right, that's me done.' Leatherface made to rise from his stool but Ilona raised a finger to him.

178

'Your treatment is not yet finished.'

She went to the wooden shelves on the wall of her hut, picked out a small earthenware pot and shook a small amount of what looked like powder into a wooden cup. She then poured water into the cup, stirred it and handed it to the mercenary.

'What is it?' he asked suspiciously, holding his nose over the cup and sniffing the liquid.

Ilona shook her head. 'Tell him, Kaja.'

'It is turmeric, which is derived from an exotic plant called ginger. The plant is grown here at Wenden in a special shed that is kept warm all-year round because it likes humidity and sheltered spots. It cannot be grown outdoors on account of the winter frosts and summer winds.'

'That's told you,' said Conrad.

'It is very rare and expensive, so drink it and stop complaining.'

Leatherface grimaced and downed the liquid in one.

'And no ale for at least four weeks,' she told him.

'Four weeks?'

'Eat yoghurt instead.'

Kaja helped to put on his sling that would keep his arm in place so as not to disturb the injured rib.

'Slit my throat now,' he muttered.

Ilona placed the container back on the shelf.

'So you go to Treiden, Conrad.'

'Yes, lady.'

She smiled. He was now a great warlord yet when he talked to her he was still that nervous young novice who had just arrived from Germany. She looked at Kaja.

'You wait for Fricis and Rameke to arrive at Wenden?'

She was remarkably well informed. No doubt Rudolf had told her his plans. He confided in her in all things, it seemed.

'God willing, lady.'

'You must be disappointed that Kalju has turned against you, Conrad,' she probed.

'Master Rudolf was spitting blood over his betrayal,' interrupted Leatherface. 'I reckon he'll have his head on a spear before the summer's out.'

'Let us hope that Sir Richard does not suffer the same fate beforehand,' was all that Conrad would say on the matter. Kaja could hardly contain her excitement at the prospect of Rameke arriving at Wenden. At least someone was happy.

He walked back to the castle in the company of Leatherface, leaving Ilona and Kaja to their mysterious potions.

'So Kaja is to marry young Rameke,' he said.

'I believe so,' replied Conrad.

'You're a cagey one, you.'

'What do you mean?' Said Conrad.

'You know they've been besotted with each other ever since they met at the Dvina, just before we crossed the river to slaughter a few Lithuanians. Rameke won't be happy that you took her to Oesel.'

Conrad sighed. 'It was Master Rudolf who requested her presence on the expedition.'

'He might live to regret that as well.'

Conrad frowned at him. 'As Kaja has returned safe and sound I don't think Rameke will have angry words with Master Rudolf.'

Leatherface laughed, causing a sharp pain in his side.

'Not Rameke. Valdemar. You think he will crawl back to Denmark all grateful and forgiving? He'll be back; you can count on it. Are you a betting man, Brother Conrad?'

'No.'

The mercenary scratched his nose. 'Pity. I was going to have a wager with you.'

'About what?'

'Who among Kalju, Sir Richard and Master Rudolf will be the first one unfortunate to have his head lopped off and placed on the end of a spear?'

*****

The square was packed with excited citizens, sullen boyars and merchants and grim-faced guards. The white walls and golden domes of Novgorod's St Sophia Cathedral stood stark and harsh against the brilliant blue sky, the church looming over the unpaved square that was already turning into a mud patch. The boyars and merchants were wrapped in cloaks and furs for despite the sun it was still cool and a northerly wind was adding to the overall gloom that possessed the city's nobles and richest citizens. They had been ordered to attend this squalid affair on the orders of Prince Mstislav, the ruler they had appointed but now wanted to be rid of.

The prince's entourage arrived only when all the summoned dignitaries had assembled in the square. Archbishop Mitrofan headed the procession, resplendent in his red and gold vestments and elaborately embroidered mitre. Two young monks swung incense burners in front of him and behind other monks carried flags bearing images of icons of the Orthodox Church. Then came priests dressed in dark brown and dark red mantles. They were followed by Mstislav and his wife, the Cuman Princess Maria. The royal couple were surrounded by guards in lamellar armour, helmets and armed with spears. Among the soldiers were a number wearing green cloaks and carrying shields that were round and carried a strange symbol that resembled the letter 'c' according to the heretical Roman Catholic alphabet. Like their Russian counterparts they were rough-looking bearded men whose eyes darted left and right to search for any suspicious movements among the packed throng of citizenry. Their leader, a clean-shaven man with long black hair who also wore a green cloak, stood beside Mstislav as the prince led his wife into the square, towards a row of seats that had been positioned on a wooden platform in front of the scaffold in the centre of the square.

A group of trumpeters wearing the black boar livery of Mstislav placed their instruments to their lips and blew a sharp blast to announce the entry of the city's ruler, who politely acknowledged the cheers of the citizens and the rather muted applause of the boyars and merchants. He took his seat next to his wife, the man with the clean-shaven face standing behind him.

'You see how the nobles smile at me with gritted teeth, Vetseke?' said the prince. 'After all I have done to increase their wealth they still despise me. If there is one thing that *I* despise it is ingratitude.'

'The people love you, lord,' replied Vetseke.

Vetseke was himself a prince but his straitened circumstances precluded Mstislav from treating him as an equal. He and a band of loyal followers had fled to Novgorod in the aftermath of the defeat and death of Lembit, seeking sanctuary in the Russian kingdom. Once he had been the ruler of the principality of Kokenhusen, but now the castle that had been his home was in the possession of the Sword Brothers and he was a penniless, landless prince. Mstislav used him and his men to collect the squirrel pelts that brought great wealth to the city. Vetseke was desperate to return to Livonia to fight the Sword Brothers but Mstislav, at first enthusiastic about supporting him, had done nothing to encourage his fight against the Bishop of Riga. He thought he would be destined to remain in the forests and marshes of northern Russia but then the gods had sent a miracle.

He had been escorting the prince from the city's kremlin, across the bridge over the Volkhov River, when a would-be assassin came out of nowhere brandishing a knife. Vetseke had managed to wrestle him to the ground and was about to kill him with his sword when Mstislav had ordered him to stop. The prince's guards manhandled the individual away and an angry Mstislav ordered him to be questioned 'closely' to discover if he had acted alone or was part of a plot against him. Ever since the loss of his banner to the Sword Brothers and the failure of the attempts to seize it back the prince had been angry, suspicious and volatile. Angry at what he saw as incompetence and treachery all around him, suspicious of the boyars, suspicious of the merchants, suspicious of the mayor of Pskov and in fact almost everyone. But Vetseke went from being something akin to a favourite pet to a valued adviser.

'The people may love me, simple fools that they are,' said Mstislav, 'but there are others who have elevated the vice of ingratitude to an art form.'

He sneered at the ranks of the boyars and merchants congregated opposite as the prisoner was led into the square, surrounded by four huge executioners dressed in leather aprons. Spearmen stood sentry in front of the crowd to keep order though there was little prospect of that. People loved a good execution and today's spectacle promised to be something special.

'I have heard news from Ungannia, highness,' said Vetseke, smiling politely at Princess Maria who appeared bored by all the proceedings.

The prisoner was led on to the scaffold that had been erected in the centre of the square, the burly executioners forcing him down on his knees before Mstislav. The dagger that he had tried to plunge into Mstislav's heart was chained to his right wrist, though there was no danger of him using it. His 'close questioning' had involved him being beaten severely, his face a mass of bruises. But no bones had been broken and he was still fully conscious so he could more fully 'enjoy' his punishment.

But the prince was staring at the small, middle-aged man with deep-set eyes who had tried to kill him.

'He said nothing to the interrogators, swore he was acting alone but I don't believe him. The boyars were behind it, I would stake my reputation on it.'

'Highness,' interrupted the commander of the guards, 'the executioners are desirous to begin the punishment.'

Mstislav turned away from the condemned. 'What? Oh, very well.'

He turned his wife. 'Perhaps you would like to begin this poetic drama, my dear.'

Maria smiled politely and nodded to the commander, who turned and signalled to the chief executioner to begin proceedings. The scaffold was low – no more than four feet – which was unusual as it allowed only the front section of the crowd to see what was going on. On the wooden boards stood a brazier filled with red-hot coals, a table holding metal pincers, knives, hammers and ropes, and a raised, cross-shaped object made of thick oak in the centre. The prisoner, denied the solace of a priest because Mstislav had decreed that parricide was an offence against God and as such the perpetrator's soul was damned anyway, was stripped naked and tied to the cross by means of leather straps. The contraption had been designed specially so that his right wrist projected beyond the end of the crossbeam, whereupon two of the executioners clasped the brazier with iron tongs and moved it to directly beneath the prisoner's right hand and wrist.

There was an ear-piercing shriek as the blade of the dagger, the chain and then the man's wrist and hand melted in the white heat. The crowd broke into delirious cheering and mothers at the back held their babies aloft so they could see the justice of Novgorod being administered. The prisoner squealed 'Oh God, oh God' as the brazier was moved away to leave a red stump where his hand had been.

'As I was saying, highness,' pressed Vetseke, 'Ungannia has rebelled against the Sword Brothers.'

Mstislav angrily held up a hand to him. 'Do not speak to me of Ungannia. My banner was stolen and my brother-in-law was murdered by the Sword Brothers there.'

The prisoner was thrashing around on the horizontal cross as pain shot through his body, his face contorted with agony. One of the executioners threw a bucket of water over him so he did not fall into unconsciousness and miss the next stage of the entertainment. The others, meanwhile, were heating the pincers in the brazier as the prisoner began frantically reciting prayers.

His next sound was a slow, high-pitched whine that grew in volume as the chief executioner took a knife from the table and slowly sliced off his testicles. This brought giggles and bawdy cheers from the crowd, the executioner slowing his movements and grinning to the people as he cut through the flesh.

Mstislav noticed Archbishop Mitrofan with his eyes closed.

'Archbishop,' he shouted, 'is the Lord's work not to your liking?'

The archbishop, visibly shaken by the horror unfolding a few paces from him, his face pale, tried to smile at the prince.

'Keep your eyes open,' Mstislav growled. 'All of you watch the punishment that awaits those who try to topple me.'

The executioner held up the prisoner's testicles in a bloody hand and then threw them into the crowd. Loud cheering.

'The boyars and merchants grow rich, Vetseke,' continued the prince as the other executioners proceeded to pinch the prisoner's flesh with red-hit pincers.

'Because of the rule of law that I have established in and around this city their trade in musk, sable, ermine, squirrel pelts, flax, jewellery and slaves flourishes. And what thanks do I get? A knife in my guts.'

The prisoner was once again thrashing around on the cross as chunks of his flesh were ripped from his body by the pincers. The scaffold was now awash with the victim's blood and two of the executioners sprawled on the slippery surface, falling heavily on the boards. One screamed as the pincers he was holding seared his leg.

'Amateurs,' sneered Mstislav.

Vegetables were hurled from among the poorer citizens at this display of unprofessionalism and the chief executioner rebuked his subordinates. The condemned, meanwhile, was in the throes of a spasm as his body reacted to being torn, seared and having three appendages sliced or burnt off. The chief executioner raised his hand to Mstislav and bowed his head.

'Ah,' said the prince, turning to his wife, 'the finale is for you, my dear, in recognition of your heritage.'

'You are too kind, my lord,' she purred, her mood having brightened at the display before her.

The prince nodded at the executioner who barked an order to two filthy urchins who had been loitering by the side of the scaffold. They hurried away into the crowd as the prisoner, now fading, was again doused with water.

'If only the boyars had your loyalty, Vetseke,' mused the prince. 'And what are you? A landless prince who relies only on his wits to survive?'

'You are too kind, highness,' said Vetseke through gritted teeth.

'Loyalty and bravery must be rewarded,' continued the prince. 'But how to reward you? That is the question.'

He looked at the prince as four black stallions were brought into the square, through the crowd and next to the

188

scaffold, the stable hands having difficulty controlling the beasts as the smell of gore entered their nostrils and their ears heard the bloodthirsty cheers of the crowd.

'What would you have, Prince of Kokenhusen? A mansion in the city, an estate beyond its walls, or perhaps one of my wife's innumerable sisters as a wife?'

Alarm flashed in Vetseke's eyes. 'You are too generous, highness. But if I may be so bold as to request that I be allowed to leave the city with my men and a few additional reinforcements so I may join the rebellion against the Sword Brothers.'

Mstislav threw up his hands. 'We have been over this a hundred times. I wasted hundreds of lives when Domash besieged Odenpah, and a brother-in-law when Gerceslav invaded Livonia. I see no reason to squander any more of my soldiers' lives in futile expeditions into the west.'

'A hundred Russians, highness, to retrieve your banner, that is all I ask,' pleaded Vetseke.

Mstislav's ears pricked up. 'My banner?'

'It was lost at Dorpat, highness, when Ungannia was the friend of the Sword Brothers. But now that kingdom is an enemy of the heretics. The son of Kalju has blamed the deaths of his parents on the Sword Brothers and has vowed vengeance on them. If your banner is still in his possession my arrival in Ungannia with soldiers to aid his cause would make him amenable to returning it to your highness.'

Mstislav stroked his beard thoughtfully as the prisoner was released from his shackles on the cross and leather straps were fixed around his wrists and ankles. The horses were positioned at each corner of the scaffold and the straps secured to the prisoner were then fixed to the beasts' harnesses. In this way the prisoner was spread-eagled in mid-air above the scaffold as the horses took the strain. But then the strap around the bloody, raw stump at the end of the prisoner's right arm slipped off the limb and he hung awkwardly in the air, moaning and trying to wriggle free.

The executioner waved his arms frantically at the stable hands who then shouted and pulled at the horses to retreat a few feet. They did, the prisoner crashing on to the boards.

'What is the problem now?' bellowed Mstislav, the prince jumping to his feet and pointing to the chief executioner. 'Get over here!'

He may have been a brute with massive forearms and a barrel chest, a man accustomed to ripping, slicing and burning flesh, but he looked distinctly nervous as he jumped from the scaffold and rushed over to stand before the prince, whose eyes were bulging with rage.

'I specifically decreed that the wretch was to have his limbs torn off by four stallions,' he shouted, 'as a special treat for my wife. You are making a fool of me and disappointing my wife.'

190

The man shook his head so hard Vetseke thought it would roll off his shoulders. He laughed; it might be cut off in a few moments.

'No, no, no highness,' the man stammered. 'We are having problems strapping his right wrist. It's not there, you see.'

Mstislav pointed at him. 'Sort it out or I will have your head decorating that scaffold.'

The man gulped, bowed his head and raced back to the scaffold, screaming at his men to get the prisoner's right wrist secured to the horse harness. They did this by strapping a number of belts around the poor wretch's arm and securing them as tightly as possible. Then the prisoner's ordeal entered a fresh phase. Princess Maria clapped her hands together with delight as the stallions were whipped and shouted at to pull as hard as they could. The prisoner screamed, the crowd cheered and hooted and Mstislav smiled as he looked for the first limb to be wrenched from its socket. But nothing happened.

The horses strained, the stable hands wielded their whips and the prisoner shrieked and cried for mercy but his limbs remained in place. The crowd quietened and then began whistling and jeering, more vegetables hurtling through the air to hit executioners and horses. The prince pointed at the chief executioner who, in an act of desperation, took a knife and began slicing at the prisoner's right armpit. The man gave an animal-like yelp as his arm was torn from its socket and the crowd roared its approval. The executioner then went to slice at

191

the prisoner's left leg, using the knife to cut away the sinews at the top of his leg. Once more the limb was yanked from its socket. Mightily relieved, he used the blade to achieve the same for the victim's left arm and right leg. Eventually, his apron covered in blood, he stood and gazed down at the limbless torso of the now dead prisoner.

There was an unseemly squabble when part of the crowd decided that the dead man's left leg would be a good souvenir of the occasion and rushed forward to grab it. Half a dozen of Mstislav's guards used both ends of their spears to crack heads and pierce bellies before order was restored. Princess Maria, delighted that her husband had recreated the execution method frequently employed by her people, but which she had not seen since she was a child of the steppe, kissed him on the cheek.

He smiled at her and then spoke to Vetseke.

'Very well, prince, I will grant your request. You may go west with a hundred of my men and may God go with you.'

'Thank you, highness,' said Vetseke. He closed his eyes and thanked Laima, the Goddess of Fate, for delivering him from his life of miserable exile.

Across the square the boyars and merchants slowly drifted away, saying little to each other, their heads cast down. One of the boyars, of distinguished appearance with a sable-lined cloak around his shoulders, acknowledged his friend Gregori. Yuri Nevsky, patriarch of Novgorod's wealthiest and most powerful boyar family, wore a resigned look.

'It was most kind of the prince to invite us to the execution, do you not think, Gregori?'

His friend, a short, stout man, was agitated. 'His hatred of us intensifies, Yuri. Your son is lucky to be out of this den of madness. I trust he is well.'

'Yaroslav thrives, thank you,' replied Yuri, 'but he is most eager to return to Novgorod, if only to see his mother.'

Gregori laughed under his breath. 'It would be better for your wife, his mother, to visit him in Pskov. Safer too.'

'Do not forget where real power lies in this city, my friend,' said Yuri. 'The *veche* appoints and dismisses Novgorod's princes.'

'Has anyone told Mstislav that?' asked Gregori, not a trace of irony in his voice.

*****

From the battlements of the fort atop Toompea Hill Rolf, Count of Roskilde and Governor of Reval, had a bird's eye view of the town, the perimeter wall and the surrounding terrain. To the north were the blue waters of the Gulf of the Finns, to the south the unending forests of Estonia, though immediately south and ringing the town an army of Oeselians, Harrien and Wierlanders. It had been a month since King Valdemar, gripped by a permanent black mood, had departed Reval with his bishops, bodyguard and the entourage of his court, or what was left of it following the debacle on Oesel. The loss of hundreds of men had not disturbed the king

193

or his knights. What really troubled them was that they had been forced to kill their surviving warhorses. Two weeks after the king's departure the Estonians had attacked the town. A week later the Oeselians had joined them outside the walls.

The king's departing words to him were: 'I leave Estonia in your safe hands, Rolf. I will return next year with an army to exact vengeance on the Oeselians and Sword Brothers'. As he watched the fleet of cogs sail out of Reval harbour, now no longer blockaded by Oeselian longships, he knew that the simmering resentment of the Estonians would flare up into open rebellion with the departure of the king. The Harrien would have seen the triumphant procession of Valdemar and his army through their land before the attack on Oesel. And they would have seen the pathetic remnants of the kings' army limp back to Reval in the aftermath of the abortive campaign. The Danes had been in Estonia for three years and in that time they had treated the indigenous people harshly, not least in using them as forced labour to build Reval's defences.

Rolf turned to Count Albert, who had pleaded with his uncle to be allowed to stay on in Estonia to defend Reval.

'Here is a question for you, Albert. If we had not abused the pagans in order to construct the defences around Reval, do you think that they would have still attacked the town?'

Albert looked at the groups of pagan warriors being marshalled for another assault against the perimeter, in front of which lay many of their dead from previous assaults.

'Pagans have no foresight or intelligence, just a cunning, animal instinct. This siege is a case in point. It makes no sense to hurl men against strong defences but they do it day after day.'

'They probably assumed that with the departure of the king our numbers would be so diminished that we would be unable to hold the perimeter,' replied Rolf.

But even with depleted numbers that perimeter was a strong one. Over the three years that the Danes had occupied Reval they had substantially increased and strengthened its defences. The perimeter now encompassed not only the town but also Toompea Hill, on which the fort that would one day be a mighty stone castle stood. The trees that had surrounded the original settlement had been cut down, not only to provide building material for the perimeter wall but also to create open ground in front of it. In this way an attacker would have no cover against missiles shot from the walls.

Hundreds of Harrien, Jerwen and Wierlanders were rounded up as forced labour to work on the defences. Many died from malnutrition and exhaustion as Rolf's soldiers and engineers set a cruel pace to finish the works, because the governor knew that peace in Danish Estonia was fragile and likely to break down at any time. The labourers first dug a deep ditch, its walls sloping at an angle of forty-five degrees, the earth from which was used to raise a high rampart behind it. Sharpened stakes were placed in the bottom of the ditch. The engineers were careful to ensure that a narrow, horizontal strip of land a yard wide was left between the ditch and the rampart to prevent the latter sliding into the former.

The walls themselves were constructed in the Russian style, which made use of the abundant stocks of timber in Estonia rather than stone and brick that was used in Denmark and Germany. On top of the rampart stood a row of log cells along the perimeter. These cells comprised rows of horizontal logs on three sides, the rear being left open. The front formed the outside face of the perimeter wall, which had a height of sixteen feet. Inside each cell was a fighting platform where crossbowmen could shoot bolts through loopholes in the parapet. In addition, the upper part of the wall projected slightly over the lower part to allow missiles to be shot at the space at the foot of the wall. A shingle roof covered the entire perimeter wall, including the walkway to the rear of the cells that linked them all. It provided protection from the weather and enemy missiles.

An innovation that Rolf had insisted on was a number of square timber towers at regular intervals along the perimeter wall. Forty-five feet in height their fighting platforms were also protected by shingle roofs.

Rolf had seven hundred men under arms to defend the walls, the most important members of which were a hundred and fifty German crossbowmen. He had thanked God when Valdemar had decided to leave them at Reval rather than take them to Oesel because their missiles had inflicted many casualties on the besiegers. Count Albert had returned from

Oesel with just under fifty men, which were used to form the garrison of the fort atop Toompea. He had had to strip Varbola of its garrison but if Reval held out then he could always re-occupy it later.

The first pagan attack had been all along the line, the warriors carrying scaling ladders and bundles of branches tied together as they approached the ditch. Led by their village elders they hurled the bundles into the ditch to form makeshift bridges to allow them to cross the stake-filled moat and scale the rampart. Because the ditch was deep the pagans were forced to group at various spots in order to throw enough bundles into the ditch to cover the stakes sufficiently to allow men to cross it.

So the Estonians slid down the side of the ditch, crossed the bridges of bundles and scrambled up the other side. And then the crossbowmen began shooting. From behind their loopholes they poured volley after volley at the pagans in and around the ditch. Only one in ten Estonians wore mail armour, a higher percentage had helmets and all had shields. The latter, around three feet in diameter and made of fir, offered some protection but only when linked together. But the crossbowmen easily found targets as men exposed their bodies while negotiating the sides of the ditch and crossing the bundle bridges. They lost at least two hundred men in their first attack, another hundred the day after and today's assault looked like being as costly.

The Oeselians showed a marked reluctance to approach the walls, their leaders having learned from painful experience at Odenpah how costly assaulting walls defended by crossbowmen could be. Nevertheless, their numbers added to the size of the besieging army that now surrounded the town and which outnumbered the garrison by at least three to one.

'They are retreating, lord.'

Rolf turned away from viewing a large phalanx of Oeselian warriors grouped close to the perimeter wall protecting the base of Toompea Hill. A Danish knight was pointing to the east to where groups of Estonians were falling back from the wooden bridge across the moat giving access to the town via two gates. It was a tempting target and after their losses attempting to cross the ditch the Estonians had tried to rush the bridge. But Rolf had deliberately not burnt it to entice the enemy. The towers each side of the bridge were filled with crossbowmen who shot the enemy to pieces as they tried to smash down the gates with a crude battering ram fashioned from an oak trunk.

'Now is the time to sally out and disperse them once and for all,' stated Albert.

Rolf shook his head. 'I think not. You have less than fifty horsemen, which will make little impression on the enemy.'

'Then give me foot soldiers as well,' pleaded Albert. 'One attack will scatter them and end this miserable siege.'

Rolf was tempted. He knew that the Harrien, Jerwen and Wierlanders were poorly equipped farmers but the Oeselians were a different matter. He had no intention of suffering the same fate as his liege lord.

'No, Albert. The pagans will lose heart and disperse of their own accord. The king entrusted the safekeeping of Reval to me and I will not disregard his command.'

Albert threw up his hands and stormed off as the Estonians withdrew to their camp, the Oeselians likewise retreating. Rolf smiled with satisfaction. The armouries contained plentiful supplies of crossbow bolts and the town's stores were well stocked with food. He was confident that he could hold Reval with ease.

*****

'Bring him in.'

Sir Richard pointed at one of the guards standing by the doors to the hall, the man saluting and exiting the chamber.

'What he has to say may interest you, Conrad.'

The brother knight, his two friends, Rameke, Kaja and four hundred warriors had arrived that morning, riding out of the pre-dawn gloom to attack and scatter the Ungannians that had been sent to besiege Lehola. Besiege was perhaps too strong a word. Surround would be more accurate. They had set up camp and shot a few arrows at the ancient timber battlements. But mostly they had been content to sit and wait until Sir Richard surrendered. He had attempted a couple of sallies that had inflicted some casualties on the Ungannians and, more importantly, captured some goats, pigs and chickens that the enemy had plundered from nearby villages. But there were at least five hundred Ungannians encamped around the fort with more arriving each day to swell their numbers. They massed outside the main gates to ensure that Sir Richard could not deploy his whole garrison outside the walls.

It was therefore a great shock when hundreds of men on ponies charged out of the nearby woods and infiltrated the enemy camp, cutting down many a bleary-eyed, half-asleep Ungannian. They killed upwards of two hundred before the rest scattered, heading for the sanctuary of the surrounding forest. A few did not panic and managed to reach their own stabling area. But they mounted their beasts and galloped south back to Fellin rather than counterattacking the relief force.

The commanders of the relief army now sat with Sir Richard in Lehola's great hall in the company of the Duke of Saccalia, Tonis and Squire Paul. The women and children that had been living there during the siege had been ejected. Hans looked most unhappy with the meagre portion of bread he had been served, along with a cup of water. Anton nudged Conrad and laughed at their friend's discomfort.

'You should be thankful, Hans,' Conrad told him, 'at least you weren't trapped here on half-rations.'

'Half-rations?' said Sir Richard. 'Another week and we would have been eating rats and dogs.'

The guard reappeared bringing in a prisoner with a thick beard, torn tunic and two black eyes. He was shoved down on the floor in front of the top table where Sir Richard and the others were sitting. His hands and feet were bound with rope.

'We caught this one when I sent a party of horsemen after the Ungannians fleeing into the trees,' said Sir Richard. 'This one was taken alive, the others were killed.'

'They should have killed him as well,' hissed Squire Paul standing behind his lord.

The prisoner, undeterred by his perilous position, gave Sir Richard a contemptuous stare. When he saw the white surcoats and red insignia of Conrad and his friends his contempt turned into visceral hatred.

'Murderers!' he shouted at the Sword Brothers.

Conrad, taken aback, stood and walked around the table to stand in front of the prisoner. The man burned with venom as he stopped in front of him.

He spoke to the prisoner in Estonian. 'Explain yourself.'

The man spat on Conrad's boots.

'I don't think he likes you,' said Hans who shoved aside the stale bread on his plate.

Conrad seized the man's shoulders and hauled him to his feet.

'If I am your enemy then I deserve to know why, seeing as once your lord and his wife regarded me as a friend.'

The man chuckled, blood between his teeth from when he had been beaten earlier. He eyed Conrad for a moment.

'I remember you. You were one of those who came to Dorpat with Lord Kalju, may Uku protect his soul, when Villem was killed.'

Conrad was again surprised. 'What do you mean, Uku protect his soul?'

The prisoner curled up his lip. 'Kalju is dead, as is his wife and two daughters. But you would know that, would you not Sword Brother, seeing as it was your sorcery that killed them?'

'Kalju and Eha are dead?' said a shocked Anton.

'They always showed me kindness,' lamented Kaja.

'Dead? How?' Conrad was confused.

'Killed by the sorcery of the Sword Brothers,' was all that the man would say.

'Tell the Marshal of Estonia who leads the Ungannian people,' ordered Sir Richard.

The man looked defiantly at Conrad. 'The gods spared Kristjan so he could be their avenger in this world.'

'Kristjan?' scoffed Hans. 'He is but a boy.'

'A boy with fangs, Brother Hans,' said Sir Richard. 'He seized Fellin and killed Peeter in short order. And would have taken this place too had it not been for a stroke of luck.'

'He will take this place and kill you all,' spat the prisoner.

Sir Richard sighed and shook his head.

Paul leaned forward. 'Now he has talked, my lord, it's best if he is executed. You don't want a sworn enemy still living.'

202

Conrad spun round as the Duke of Saccalia waved the guard forward.

'I beg for his life, your grace.'

Paul frowned and Rameke looked surprised.

'Sir Richard is right, Conrad, this man would slit your throat if there was a knife in his hands.'

'Let me have him,' said Paul, 'I will have him dangling from the walls in no time.'

'Castrate him,' growled Kaja.

They all looked at her in surprise but she merely smiled at Conrad. 'One of the stable hands at Wenden told me that castrating a wild stallion calms him down.'

'If I were you I would be worried,' Hans whispered to Rameke.

'We don't want to calm him down, girly,' said Paul irritably, 'we want an end to him.'

Sir Richard held up a hand to still the conversation. 'Why do you want his life, Conrad?'

'So he can convey a message to Kristjan, your grace.'

Conrad turned to face the man. 'He is at Fellin?'

'He may be,' the prisoner answered evasively.

Conrad looked at Sir Richard.

'Very well, Marshal of Estonia, I relinquish him to your mercy.'

Paul sighed loudly, earning him a rebuke from Sir Richard.

'Tell Kristjan this,' Conrad told the prisoner. 'He may have won a few easy victories but soon Bishop Albert will turn his vengeful gaze towards Ungannia and when he does he will show no mercy. He will send a great army to conquer Ungannia and lay waste to its villages. The men of iron will crush Kristjan's warriors and machines will reduce his forts to splinters. Tell him that if he does not surrender himself immediately to the mercy of the Bishop of Riga he will bring about the end of Ungannia and the enslavement of its people.'

The man looked disinterested as he was led away.

'I remember Kristjan from the last time we were at Odenpah,' said Anton. 'He was an arrogant pup then and took a dislike to Conrad. Obviously losing his parents has not changed his nature or his opinion of our order.'

'Let us hope that your words cower him, Conrad,' said Sir Richard, 'because if not then he will hold Fellin for the rest of the year.'

'You will not assault it, lord?' asked Rameke.

Sir Richard shook his head. 'I do not have to worry about just Fellin. There are Ungannian bands roving all over Saccalia. This fort is full of those who have fled their villages after they were attacked. Others have fled to the forests. It is difficult to estimate but there may be a thousand Ungannian warriors in Saccalia.'

Hans was astounded. 'That many?'

'This Kristjan has gathered every man to his banner,' said Sir Richard.

'Which makes letting one go so he can fight again little sense,' added Paul.

'Be quiet,' Sir Richard ordered him.

The English lord continued. 'Even with the lifting of the Danish blockade the bishop will not be able to travel to Germany and return to Livonia with an army before the leaves begin to turn brown. And few crusaders will wish to arrive in winter so that means it will be next spring until matters in Saccalia can be addressed.'

Conrad walked back to his seat.

'Rameke and I rode with four hundred men, your grace,' he said, 'plus fifty crossbows and twenty barrels of bolts, a gift from Master Rudolf. He is most desirous that Saccalia remains loyal.'

'We could assault Fellin, lord,' suggested Hans, 'before invading Ungannia.'

'In normal circumstances I would agree with you,' replied Sir Richard, 'but these are not normal circumstances. Tonis, tell our guests what news your scouts have gleaned.'

'The Harrien, Wierlanders and Jerwen are in open rebellion against their Danish overlords,' said Tonis. 'The Oeselians have joined this rebellion I have been told.'

'And the Russians?' asked Conrad.

'No word of them stirring in the east, *Susi*,' answered Tonis.

'Not yet,' said Sir Richard, 'but I would stake my warhorse on them joining in sooner or later, which leads me to my plan for the rest of the summer and winter.'

He looked at the leader of the wolf shields. 'I have talked with Tonis and he is in agreement that we should stand on the defensive here at Lehola until the bishop arrives with an army.'

Sir Richard turned his attention to Conrad. 'But to do so means Lehola becoming a citadel not a refuge. There are over five hundred women, children and elderly currently within its walls. They cannot go back to their villages and I would not see them suffer in the sanctuaries deep in the forests.'

'It is easy enough in the summer but would mean death for most when the snows come,' said Tonis.

'You will understand, Conrad,' continued Sir Richard, 'that as a Christian lord I cannot abandon those who are under my protection to such a fate.'

'Of course not, your grace,' replied Conrad. 'So what is to be done?'

'The village to the south of Wenden, *Susi*,' said Tonis, 'is large enough to provide them with shelter, especially now that Andres and Hillar are in Rotalia.'

'I would ask you and Rameke to take these people back with you to Wenden, Conrad,' said Sir Richard, 'so that Lehola is filled with soldiers only.'

'It took us ten days to get here,' said Anton, 'four hundred armed men in the saddle guided by scouts. It would take us upwards of a month to get back with five hundred young and old travelling on foot.'

'Women, children and the old would slow us down,' agreed Hans. 'And if we were attacked many would die.'

Squire Paul laughed out loud. 'So much for protecting the weak and needy, isn't that what it says in the rules of the Sword Brothers? I do not know, not being able to read.'

'You won't be able to speak if you keep on,' Sir Richard threatened him, 'for your tongue will be cut out.'

'No, he is right,' said Conrad. 'We took a vow to respect and defend the weak, the sick and the needy and that is what we will do.'

He looked at Rameke. 'But my brother took no such vow and it is his warriors who rode to this place.'

Rameke smiled at him. 'We are brothers and share our triumphs and perils.'

He cast a glance at Kaja. 'Besides, Saccalia is dear to my heart.'

Hans peered at the stale piece of bread. 'Well we had better fill our bellies before we set out. It is going to be a long journey.'

The next day Conrad sent Riki and his fifty Harrien west while Sir Richard allowed his knights to stretch their horses' legs by despatching patrols north, east and south to hunt down any straggling Ungannians. The rest of the garrison divided their time between taking part in hunting parties and saying farewell to their families as the latter prepared to make the

207

journey south to Wenden. Conrad stood with his two friends, Sir Richard and Rameke as those too old to walk or ride were assisted onto two-wheeled carts and made comfortable.

'Well,' said Hans, 'God reminds us of our duties for He has provided us with an abundance of the helpless and needy for us to assist.'

Tonis embraced a fair-haired girl who was clearly distressed at having to leave her beloved. She stood with other young women, some clutching the hands of children and others holding babies in their arms.

'I hope we have enough men to fend off any assaults,' said Rameke. 'If we are attacked and enemy warriors get among our column it will be slaughter.'

'Perhaps I could spare Tonis and his wolf shields,' pondered Sir Richard, 'that is *your* wolf shields, Conrad.'

'Tonis,' called Conrad.

The strapping Saccalian commander sauntered over.

'*Susi?*'

'Sir Richard gives you a choice, Tonis,' said Conrad, 'as do I. You can march south with us to protect your beloved and her family, or you can remain here with your wolf shields. The decision is yours to make.'

He looked back at the attractive young woman in her green woollen skirt, her hair falling down her back. He was clearly torn and knew that if he stayed he would not see her again for a year, if he saw her at all. At length he sighed and turned back to Conrad.

'I am Saccalian, *Susi*. If I march south then I will abandon my homeland. My place is here, at Lehola.'

Conrad placed a hand on his shoulder. 'Lehola will never fall with men such as you defending its ramparts, Tonis.'

'The Marshal of Estonia speaks the truth,' said Sir Richard. 'And know, Tonis, that the Duke of Saccalia breathes a huge sigh of relief at your decision.'

Conrad looked at the white clouds and blue sky above. There was an easterly breeze that gave the morning a slight chill but it was now summer and by noon it would be very warm.

'We must be away. I want to get as much distance between here and tonight's camp as possible.'

He looked at Sir Richard. 'I hope, your grace, that Lehola will draw the Ungannians as a flame draws moths to allow us to sneak away unseen.'

Sir Richard smiled. 'Pray God it is so.'

He offered his hand to Conrad. 'God be with you.'

Conrad took it. 'And with you, your grace. Send word to Wenden if you are hard pressed. I have men in Rotalia and they can be joined with forces that Master Rudolf can muster to raise a relief force.'

Sir Richard looked at the imposing walls of Lehola. 'Now I don't have the civilians in the fort it will be a hard nut to crack. I intend to be a thorn in this Kristjan's side.' He looked at the women and children. 'Men fight better if they know that their families are safe.'

'Rameke, will you command the vanguard?' asked Conrad. 'I will bring up the rear with Hans and Anton.'

Rameke nodded, said his farewells to Tonis and Sir Richard and made to leave. But then stopped and turned.

'Conrad, it is dangerous for Kaja to carry your banner. If we are attacked then she will become the enemy's chief target. I would ask you to entrust it to another.'

'I will carry it,' offered Hans, 'if she will surrender it.'

A happy Rameke walked away to organise his men. The Sword Brothers went to the fort's stables to saddle their horses and then led them out of the gates to where the press of civilians waited, a profusion of reds, greens, blues and greys, most of them belonging to skirts and shawls. Conrad shook his head. He had become a nursemaid. He and his two friends looked up at the battlements where Sir Richard and Tonis were standing. He raised a hand to them both and then to Rameke and the great retreat began.

Kaja refused to relinquish her banner.

The pace was slow, the warriors walking beside their ponies holding the reins, a woman or child in the saddle. Some women cradled babies in their arms as they sat in the saddle while some of the children insisted on skipping along beside the beasts. Rameke, at the head of the column, sent out scouts to reconnoitre the route ahead and the forests on either side. Conrad, his shield slung on his back, his helmet and two lances dangling from his saddle, walked beside his horse, a young girl sitting in the saddle. Riding Hans' horse was a sullen teenage boy, the girl's brother, and on Anton's horse the pair's mother, a frightened woman in her twenties whose eyes had seen much misery and death during the past few weeks. The girl, though, perhaps taking refuge in a make-believe world, was cheerful and inquisitive.

'What's his name?'

Conrad, far from happy at the column's lethargic pace, his eyes constantly scanning the trees for signs of an enemy, was not listening.

'Huh?'

'Your horse, what's his name?' pressed the girl.

'He doesn't have one.'

'Then how do you call him?'

Conrad rolled his eyes. 'I don't call him. I go to the stables to collect him.'

'My name is Hele,' she said, 'It means "bright", isn't that right, mother?'

The woman managed a half-smile and nodded. Conrad rolled his eyes to Hans.

'What's your name?'

'Mother of Christ,' said Conrad.

'That's a funny name,' smiled Hele, revealing her two front teeth had yet to sprout.

'What? No, my name is Brother Conrad.'

'You are lucky Father Otto didn't hear you blaspheme, Conrad,' said Anton, 'otherwise it would have been a flogging for you.'

'What's a flogging?' said the girl innocently.

'Hush, Hele,' said her mother, 'this is *Susi*. He has better things to do than amuse you.'

But Hele's eyes lit up. '*Susi*? The wolf of the forest.'

Then she looked confused. 'You do not look like a wolf.'

'Oh, I don't know,' said Hans, 'bedraggled hair, fangs and bad tempered. I would say he is a lot like a wolf.'

'I am not bad tempered,' snapped Conrad.

Hans smiled at Hele. 'See what I mean?'

The first day passed without incident, on the second the column made good progress through meadows filled with bilberries, cloudberries and blueberries. When a campsite was chosen, usually beside a stream or brook, the men pitched the tents while the women would spend time picking edible mushrooms and wild strawberries and raspberries to supplement the cured meat and biscuits that the Sword Brothers had brought with them. The warm weather, pleasant sights and smells and peaceful nature of the terrain they were moving through lessened the fear and anxiety among the civilians. But for Conrad the tension within him increased each day. He saw the enemy everywhere: among the trees, in the tall meadow grass and lying in wait by the sides of fords. He hated being a nursemaid.

On the third night, as he stood guard in the descending gloom of dusk, he saw movement in the trees and then ghost-like figures emerging from the edge of the forest.

'Stand to!' he shouted as the enemy shuffled towards him.

Horn blasts shattered the silence and frightened birds flew from trees as warriors grabbed weapons and shields and rallied to their chiefs. Hans and Anton came bounding over to their friend, followed by Rameke and Kaja, the latter wearing a helmet with sword and shield in hand. Conrad drew his sword and slipped his left forearm through the straps on the inside of his shield. Ahead the enemy continued their advance. Behind them crying children and frightened women huddled together.

'They are not warriors,' said Kaja, 'they are villagers.'

Hans laughed and slapped Conrad on the back.

'You've been listening to too many stories about forest demons, my friend.'

'Stand down,' Conrad shouted, ramming his sword back in its scabbard.

The bedraggled group shuffled forward, their heads bowed and arms raised in the air as an act of submission. They were dirty, tired and their clothes were torn. A middle-aged man with sunken eyes spoke to the Sword Brothers, avoiding their eyes as he spoke.

'We were hiding in the forest when we saw you pass, lords. We beg that you take us with you.'

It was quite pathetic, thought Conrad. They asked for succour even though they did not know where his column was heading. Most of them had probably never left their village, let alone Saccalia. He doubted they knew where Wenden was. But what could he say?

'Warm yourselves by our fires,' he said. 'You are welcome to join us.'

The next day saw two more groups venture from the forests to ask for protection. One contained mostly children, all of them barefooted and gaunt. So the column swelled in numbers as it wound its way south. Hele talked incessantly, about the birds, the sky, the pigs in her village and wolves.

'Did you know that they howl at night, Conrad?'

'Yes, I believe they do.'

'Do you howl at night?'

He looked up at her. 'Of course not.'

'He does snore, though,' said Hans.

'Most loudly,' smiled Anton.

Hele giggled and his two friends laughed. Even the surly brother managed a smirk and the mother looked as though the great burden she carried – the loss of her husband – had lifted a little. The sun was shining, the rain had mostly held off and the spirits of the civilians were slowly improving. The afternoon was again bright and sunny, with a westerly breeze making tramping through meadow grass in full armour bearable. And it was on that breeze that the sounds of men's shouts were brought.

The hairs on the back of Conrad's neck stood up and he swung round to look at Hans and Anton. They had heard them too and knew that horsemen were approaching. Conrad held up his hands to Hele and asked her to ride with her mother for a few moments while he spoke to his friend. She smiled as he passed her over to her mother, who now had alarm in her eyes.

He jumped into the saddle and galloped along the line of ponies and carts.

'Have a care,' he shouted to the warriors.

This had the effect of sending alarm along the column with the speed of a lightning bolt. When he reached Rameke and Kaja the warriors had picked up their pace and the cart drivers urged their beasts on.

'We have company, coming from the east,' Conrad said to them.

'There is a ford ahead,' Rameke told him. 'We should get the people across it so the enemy will be forced to cross the river at the same place and cannot outflank us.'

'How far is it away?'

'The scouts report about a quarter of a mile.'

Conrad wheeled his horse around. 'I will protect the rear. God be with you.'

'I will come with you, *Susi*,' said Kaja.

'No,' he ordered, 'stay with Rameke.'

He dug his spurs into the sides of his horse and galloped back to Hans and Anton. On the way he collected over a score of Rameke's men, all of whom had spears in addition to axes. He jumped down from his horse and lifted Hele back into his saddle. He told three of the warriors to lead Hele and her family towards the ford with all speed, first taking the lances and helmet from his horse.

'Where are you going, Conrad?' Hele called to him.

'To speak to some wolves,' he shouted back.

'An apt analogy,' mused Anton, the sounds of the approaching horsemen getting louder.

Conrad ordered the warriors to form into line, Hans and Anton falling in either side of him.

'Back as quick as you can,' he told them, 'but hold your formation.'

They had gone but a hundred paces when the horsemen appeared, black shapes in the distance that rapidly became larger. Conrad looked behind him. The column of ponies and carts were hurrying to the ford and there was a widening gap between him and it. He looked back at the horsemen, now about four hundred paces away. The meadow was wide and flat and they were right in the middle of it.

'Back,' he shouted.

The warriors needed no second prompting, racing away with the brother knights following. They covered another two hundred paces before Conrad could hear hooves clubbing the earth.

'Stand,' he shouted.

A panting Hans and Anton stood beside him, the other warriors closing up on either side of them. Behind them the ponies and carts were splashing across the ford; in front the horsemen, all wearing black leather cuirasses, helmets and carrying round shields bearing the sign of the moon, deployed into line and levelled their spears at Conrad's thin line.

'Spears,' he called, 'they will not break us if we hold our nerve.'

His heart was pounding in his chest as the riders, who suddenly appeared huge men on even larger beasts, bore down on them. Helmet now pulled down over his face, he gripped the mid-point of the lance with his left hand, the metal end pointing at the horsemen, the other end shoved into the ground and held in place by his right foot. Hans and Anton did the same with their lances while Rameke's men had their spears tucked beneath their right armpit.

The horsemen charged and made a lot of noise and for a moment Conrad thought they would ride right over them. But he was right: they reined in their mounts, slowed them and jabbed their spears forward. Their commander, a clean-shaven man with a green cloak around his shoulders, bellowed an order in Liv and they wheeled their horses away. Rameke now joined his brother, around forty of his men with him to extend the line of spears that defended the ford. Some of the horsemen were attempting to cross the river upstream, guiding their horses down the gently sloping riverbank and into the water.

'Kill the women and children,' shouted the man with the green cloak.

Conrad hoisted the lance to shoulder level and hurled it at him just at the moment another horsemen rode in front of the leader. He arched his back as the point of the lance went into the leather armour and he fell from his saddle. Conrad picked up his other lance as some of the horsemen trotted from the water to attack Rameke's men from the rear. More were jumping from their horses to race at the spearmen and engage them in single combat. And all the time their leader rode up and down shouting orders.

A man on foot came at Conrad, using his axe to shatter the haft of his lance. Conrad let go of the shaft and drew his sword, dodging a swing of the man's axe and pulling his own from his belt. He swung his axe at the man's head and thrust his sword forward. The warrior avoided the axe but failed to see the sword strike until the point pierced his thigh. He groaned in pain and limped back but Conrad had no time to finish him off as another man came at him, swinging his axe and cutting the strap that held his shield in place on his back. It fell to the ground as Hans grabbed the rear of his surcoat and pulled him back.

'Time to get across the river,' he shouted, pointing his sword to dead Livs on the ground. The mounted and dismounted horsemen had attacked the flanks and rear of the line and had done much butchery.

He saw Rameke fighting beside Anton and then heard a horn sound behind him.

'Again,' Hans shouted at the signaller who blew his instrument once more.

Conrad picked up a spear lying beside a dead Liv and hurled it at a horsemen bearing down on him, the point going into the horse's chest. The beast whinnied and crashed to the ground, pinning its rider underneath. Other horsemen splashed through the water, Conrad was helpless to prevent them crossing to the other side. He was losing the battle.

There were dead warriors floating in the water and other bodies around where Rameke and Anton were fighting with a cluster of men. There was a sudden blast of horns from among the enemy warriors still mounted and in seconds those on foot disengaged and withdrew. Conrad and Hans ran over to Rameke and Anton as the man with the green cloak barked orders at his men to mount their horses. Many among them wore lamellar armour, helmets with thick nasal guards and carried shields that were almost shaped. They were certainly not Livs.

'Why are they falling back?' queried Rameke as the enemy suddenly about faced and galloped away.

'That's' why,' said Anton, pointing upstream to a mass of riders approaching.

They were riding ponies and dressed in greens, blues and browns. Most were armed with spears and their shields bore the insignia of Harrien and Jerwen. Riki and Andres had arrived.

The two leaders splashed across the ford and dismounted in front of Conrad, who pulled off his helmet.

'Your timing is most excellent,' he told them.

'We were almost a feast for crows,' added Hans.

'They were Livs,' said Rameke angrily.

'And Russians,' commented Conrad.

'Why are Livs fighting alongside Russians?' asked Anton.

No one had an answer to his question so Conrad ordered the few enemy dead to be stripped of anything useful and the civilians to be moved south of the ford. The day was waning and he wanted to make camp away from the scene of carnage. Rameke embraced Kaja and then the three brother knights. Conrad was searching for his shield when a grim-faced Hans rode to him with a spare horse in tow.

'The strap was cut and I swore it fell hereabouts,' he said to his friend.

'You had better see this, Conrad.'

He shook his head concerning the mystery of the shield and hoisted himself into the saddle. Hans galloped back to the ford, riding across it to where the ponies and carts carrying the civilians stood a couple of hundred yards back from the river.

'What is it?' asked Conrad, halting his horse next to where his friend and Anton stood staring at the ground.

His mouth fell open as he saw Hele and her family lying on the grass. He leapt from the saddle and knelt down beside the young girl who had been killed with a blow to the back of the head. He gently lifted her lifeless body and cradled it in his arms. He closed his eyes and held back his tears with an iron effort.

'Some of the enemy got among the carts,' said Anton, 'they have killed upwards of fifty women and children.'

Conrad said nothing but he made a vow to find and kill the clean-shaven man who wore a green cloak.

Chapter 5

That summer was beautiful in Lithuania. The forests of pine, spruce and birch were full of elk, wild boars, deer and lynx. The glittering blue lakes were brimming with fish and the meadows were home to a multitude of hares and rabbits. Hillocks were covered in snowdrops and buttercups and the air was filled with scent of alder, bird cherry and hazel. Throughout the land herds of wild horses feasted on lush meadow grass, reed and bark, and the trees were teeming with woodpeckers, black terns, corncrakes and kestrels. Peace reigned in Lithuania and while the gods cursed Livonia with pestilence and war, they blessed the land south of the Dvina with prosperity and abundance.

In each of the kingdoms the priests and people tended and left tributes in the *alkas*, the holy places where perpetual sacred fires burned. They included groves that could not be cut, wells that could not be fished and fields that could not be ploughed. The farmers in particular were diligent in their respect of the gods and in the spring had taken their horses to the rivers to be bathed, their stalls and troughs being blessed with the blood of a black rooster. So pleased had Krumine, the Goddess of Agriculture, been with the farmers and their families that she had ordered the *Dvynai Asvieniai*, the twin white stallions that pulled the cart of the sun through the heavens, to work each day to warm the land and grow the crops. And they had done marvellous work for the fields were full of ripening rye, barley, oats, peas, hemp and flax. Of course

221

the farmers helped in ensuring the harvest would be bountiful by observing age-old rituals, such as never going to the fields on an empty stomach, for to do so would make the ears of grain grow empty. Similarly, when preparing to sow barley they had always eaten a pig's tail beforehand, thus ensuring that the barley ears would grow long like the swine's tail.

The people gave homage to the gods; the gods smiled upon Lithuania and worked a miracle. For Duke Arturus, a man both loathed and feared in equal measure, had agreed to sheathe his sword and seek peace with the other dukes. After much negotiation the place assigned to be the venue for the historic meeting was Dobele, a small hill fort on the border with Semgallia and the newly created kingdom of Kurland. The discussions had taken place between Lord Torolf and his subordinates and the *kriviai*, the white-robed priests who were the intermediaries between mortal men and the gods. Normally there would have been no need for Lord Torolf to be involved in such negotiations, but Duke Arturus had killed all the *kriviai* in his domain and so there were none in the land of the Kurs. The chief priest, the *Kriviu Krivaitis*, who lived in a sacred grove near to Panemunis, was now too old and frail to make the journey. But he had sent his chosen successor, a dour young man with skin as white as his robe.

For days beforehand soldiers and officials of Duke Viesthard prepared the ground and requisitioned food from nearby villages. Huntsmen were commissioned to shoot great quantities of wild boar, elk and deer to feed the retinues of the

222

other dukes that would soon be arriving. It had been agreed that each duke should bring no more than a hundred men, in addition to slaves that would attend to duties such as pitching tents, cooking, serving meals and cleaning the campsite.

Duke Viesthard was already in residence when Prince Vsevolod and his entourage arrived, a great procession of the prince's bodyguard carrying huge banners depicting the silver griffin of Gerzika and the black boar of the late Grand Duke Daugerutis. Slaves walked beside carts carrying clothing, tents, horse furniture and shoes, food and spare weapons and armour.

The day after Duke Butantas arrived with his retinue, which included his son Ykintas, the husband of Vsevolod's daughter and good friend of Mindaugas. It had been the intention of Vsevolod to leave the latter at Panemunis but Aras had persuaded him to take the young prince along, believing it would be a good experience in politics to attend what promised to be a most unique occasion. So he and Ykintas embraced each other as the great elk antler banner of Duke Butantas was planted in the ground beside the black boar, the silver griffin and the iron wolf standard of Semgallia. Duke Kitenis of Aukstaitija, having asked permission of Butantas to travel through his kingdom, arrived after the other dukes. His banner of the black axe was placed alongside the others.

'I wonder if we will see the black seagull beside them,' remarked the wiry framed Butantas, looking up at the standards flapping in the wind.

Viesthard shrugged. 'Arturus was the one who suggested the meeting. I see no reason why he should not come.'

'He has the shortest distance to travel,' said Kitenis, 'and yet is the last to arrive. Some might consider that bad manners.'

Aras chuckled. 'Perhaps you could tell him that when he arrives, my lord.'

Vsevolod said nothing but merely observed. As a Russian he would always be considered an outsider by the other dukes, but Aras had made his army a formidable instrument and the marriage of his daughter to Prince Ykintas had strengthened the ties with Samogitia. In addition, Morta was married to Mindaugas, the son of the late Stecse, a man whose memory was still respected throughout all Lithuania. He was determined that one day Mindaugas would be grand duke, to be manipulated to retrieve his lost home of Gerzika. But all that was in the future.

Of more immediate concern was the shape of the pavilion where the meeting would be held. The pale priest sent by the *Kriviu Krivaitis* advised that two rectangular benches should be placed one over the other at right angles to resemble a star cross, the emblem of Ausrine, the Goddess of the Sun. The tent housing such a table should be the same shape to bring the blessing of the goddess. When Viesthard asked him to elucidate on where everyone should sit around this strange-shaped table the priest shrugged and said he would consult the gods. Kitenis suggested a square table inside a square tent but Vsevolod said that there would be four dukes plus himself, so one would have to share one of the sides with another duke, thereby diluting the prestige of both of them. Butantas came up with a satisfactory proposal for a round table inside a round tent.

'In this way no one will be offended or lose face,' stated the Duke of Samogitia.

Butantas said that his son should attend the meeting. He would stand behind his father, Vsevolod stating that as his heir Mindaugas should also be present. The other dukes had not brought their sons but raised no objection to the young princes being in the tent. The pale-faced priest was asked by them all to be the master of ceremonies, subject to the approval of Duke Arturus. But as the days passed the Kur leader was conspicuous by his absence and everyone believed that he was not coming. Vsevolod was disappointed and Viesthard annoyed. But on a crystal-clear summer's morning, the air sweet with the scent of meadow flowers, the dukes' banners hanging limply undisturbed by any wind, horns blew to sound assembly with the news that a column of horsemen was approaching.

The dukes and their commanders gathered on horseback at the perimeter of the camp, their mail-clad soldiers in their brightly coloured tunics and burnished helmets behind them. From their *spisas* hung pennants indicating to which duke they owed allegiance. Aras seated behind Vsevolod and next to Mindaugas looked at the young prince.

'So he came. Take a good look when he arrives. It's not every day that you see a real life demon.'

225

'Duke Arturus comes to secure the peace, general,' replied Mindaugas.

'We'll see,' sniffed Aras.

The horsemen of Kurland rode black beasts, their back and breastplates black leather with additional leather shoulder pieces and long *pteriges* – leather straps – protecting their thighs. On their left sides they carried round wooden shields faced with leather bearing the image of a black seagull, their helmets fitted with black horsehair plumes and a single nasal guard. Their tunics, leggings and boots were black, as were the bridles and saddles on their horses. Two men led the column of riders. Immediately behind them a standard bearer carried a great banner that would have shown a black seagull had there been any wind. Every rider aside from the two at the head of the column carried the long *spisa* favoured by Lithuanian horsemen. And at their hips they carried swords and axes.

The tension began to build as the Kur column slowly wound its way through a small stream and across a broad meadow to reach the campsite. The other dukes and Vsevolod sat in silence on their horses, occasionally glancing behind to reassure themselves that their soldiers were nearby to assist them if the Kurs suddenly attacked. A crow cawed overhead and some of the horses whinnied, bobbing their heads up and down. And still the Kurs came. Mindaugas looked at his friend and now brother-in-law Ykintas and smiled nervously. Ykintas moved his right hand to rest it on the pommel of his sword.

'Steady,' hissed his father, seeing the movement.

The Kurs walked their horses forward until one of the two men at the head of the column raised his hand to signal a halt. His men stopped but he carried on until he was but five paces from the other dukes. In appearance he was no different from his men in his black leather armour and simple iron helmet. But when he removed it he revealed a brooding, thoughtful, menacing face. Duke Arturus, unlike most Lithuanian men, had neatly cropped hair, beard and moustache. His round face was large and distinguished by a long, twisted scar that ran down its right side. His brown eyes scanned the line of horsemen before him and then he spoke.

'Greetings, my lords. I thank you for your attendance.'

Aras raised an eyebrow. He was expecting a loud, brutish bully but instead Arturus was softly spoken. There was no threat in his voice.

'I see that I am the last to arrive,' he continued, 'for which I convey my sincere apologies. The duties of a ruler are sometimes taxing and time consuming.'

'No apology necessary, my lord,' said Viesthard.

Arturus tilted his head at him. 'Duke Viesthard, I am glad we are meeting as friends and not looking across at each other on the field of battle.'

Viesthard, remembering the deprivations his people had suffered at the hands of the Kurs, gave him a curt nod.

'Perhaps you are tired from your journey, Duke Arturus,' said Vsevolod, 'and wish to refresh yourself before we sit down to talk.'

'Prince Vsevolod,' smiled Arturus, 'we meet at long last. I trust the Princess Rasa is well and Morta and Elze.'

'Well, thank you,' replied Vsevolod, slightly discomfited by the duke's knowledge of his family's names.

Arturus shifted his gaze to Mindaugas. 'Prince Mindaugas, your son-in-law and son of Prince Stecse.' He looked at Ykintas. 'Now brother to Prince Ykintas by virtue of his marriage to the youngest daughter of Prince Vsevolod. Thus are the Nalsen and Selonians bound to the Samogitians. How clever you are, Prince Vsevolod.'

The Russian was feeling distinctly uncomfortable and was trying to think of an appropriate reply when Duke Kitenis spoke.

'We are all impressed by your knowledge, Arturus, so let us get seated round a table and get to the kernel of the matter.'

Arturus smiled ruefully. 'Blunt and to the point, like the black axe of Aukstaitija.'

Ten minutes later the dukes and Vsevolod were seated at the round table. Behind Arturus stood a tall, lean man with a square jaw beneath his black beard. He smiled a lot in contrast to his lord. Arturus introduced him as his deputy, Prince Lamekins. Mindaugas stood behind Vsevolod and Ykintas behind Butantas, two selected princes assuming positions behind Kitenis and Viesthard respectively. Those seated were offered beer to drink but Arturus declined and asked for *gira* instead, a non-alcoholic drink made from rye bread. As he brought his lips to the tankard the pale priest entered the tent and raised his arms.

'Great Dievas, who created the world, look upon these...'

Arturus jumped up. 'Who is this who interrupts us?'

The priest stopped his speech and gave Arturus a look of fury.

'This is the chosen heir of the *Kriviu Krivaitis*,' stated Prince Vsevolod solemnly.

'The gods speak through him,' added Kitenis.

Arturus sighed. 'Very well. Call on your gods, priest.'

And so he did, asking Dievas, the chief god, to bless the meeting and guide the tongues of all those present. Vsevolod, being of the Russian Orthodox faith, nodded politely as the pagan's voice thundered and called on his gods. But Arturus made no attempt to hide his boredom and contempt, examining his fingernails as the priest walked around the table imploring the gods to smile on Lithuania. When he had finished he retreated to stand by the tent's entrance flaps, which he proceeded to tie together.

'Now that the priest has finished assaulting our ears,' said Arturus, 'perhaps I may explain why I asked for this meeting.'

Vsevolod leaned forward, his elbows resting on the table, his hands brought together.

'How long has it been now since Grand Duke Daugerutis crossed the Dvina to wage war against the Christians?' asked Arturus.

'Nine years,' answered Butantas.

'You would know, my lord,' said Arturus, 'for you were one who fought alongside the grand duke. Well, it is time that Lithuania had a new grand duke.'

'That is a matter for the gods to decide,' said the priest.

Arturus ignored him. 'I propose that I become the grand duke.'

Kitenis laughed. 'Grand dukes are chosen from among the dukes who rule their kingdoms, Arturus, after which the selected candidate is ratified by the *Kriviu Krivaitis*.'

'What Duke Kitenis says is true,' said Butantas.

'Why would we choose you, you who has waged war against Semgallia and Samogitia?' asked Viesthard.

'My apologies,' said Arturus, 'I did not make myself plain. I do not ask to be made grand duke. I demand it. I have united the Kurs and see no reason why I cannot do the same with all the Lithuanian peoples. Only in unity can we hope to defeat the Christian filth north of the Dvina.'

'By uniting the Kurs you mean defeating and killing Duke Gedvilas,' remarked Kitenis. 'You threaten us with the same fate should we oppose you?'

'I do not need to threaten you, Kitenis,' said Arturus calmly. 'I have stated my demand. It is up to you how to respond to it.'

'Semgallia renounces it,' stated Viesthard flatly.

'As does Aukstaitija,' added Kitenis.

Arturus looked at Vsevolod. 'And what about you, Russian, do you speak for the Nalsen and Selonians or do you have to consult your wife before you decide the fate of those Lithuanians that live under your heel?'

There were gasps around the table and the priest marched forward to harangue Arturus.

'You are a murderer of priests, a blasphemer who defiles this meeting with his presence. I curse you, I…'

His speech was cut short by the blade of a small knife that Arturus whipped out and slashed across his throat in a blur of a movement. The priest made a gurgling sound as a great fountain of blood shot out from his neck onto the table. His eyes rolled back into his head and he collapsed forward, smashing his nose on the edge of the table before falling to the floor, dead. The dukes jumped up and shouted angrily at Arturus, who leaned back in his chair and brought his hands together.

'If you wish to kill me then do it now,' he said to them all. 'Because this is the last chance you will get.'

Lamekins' hand went to his sword as Mindaugas and Ykintas drew their blades and walked forward. Lamekins met their stares with a look that dared them to fight him.

'Ykintas,' shouted Butantas, 'put that weapon away.'

'And that includes you, Mindaugas,' said Vsevolod, alarmed that he would be caught up in any violence.

Arturus stood, staring contemptuously at Vsevolod. 'This meeting is over. Any of you, apart from the Russian, who wishes to change his mind has a month to prostrate themselves before me at my stronghold at Talsi. I piss on all of you.'

He walked to the tent flaps, untied them and walked outside with Lamekins, hand still on the pommel of his sword, covering his lord. After the Kurs had ridden from the campsite Aras sat with Vsevolod and Mindaugas in Vsevolod's great pavilion. Mindaugas was seething.

'We have hundreds of horsemen in this camp. We should hunt Arturus down and kill him for his blasphemy.'

'It will take more than a few hundred horsemen to kill Arturus,' said Aras. 'If we were deep in our own land I would be apt to agree with you.'

He walked over to the pavilion's open entrance and peered west.

'But that is the land of the Kurs and not many who enter return.'

'What now?' was all that Vsevolod could utter.

'Now, my lord,' answered Aras cheerfully, 'we return home.'

Mindaugas, brimming with youthful enthusiasm and naivety, was also cheerful.

'Arturus has declared war on all of Lithuania. He will be defeated and dead by the end of summer.'

*****

Conrad drew the cloak around his shoulders. The heat of summer had gone now and the deciduous trees were turning red and gold as their leaves died and gently drifted to the ground. Today was unusual in that there was a brisk northerly

232

wind; usually the autumns at Wenden were long and pleasant. Soon the farmers in the surrounding villages and the settlement next to the castle would be harvesting their crops. And that included the fields around Thalibald's old village, now rebuilt, expanded and home to those Saccalians he had escorted back from Lehola. Those that had not been killed along the way, that is. He clenched his fists but then shook his head. He was angry with himself for thinking harsh thoughts in this place of peace and calm.

The cemetery at Wenden was a beautiful place, if such a term can be applied to a place of graves and dead bodies. But the gardeners kept the grass and paths well tended and the low white stone wall that surrounded it was always in pristine condition. He looked up at the castle's great round southeast tower that watched over the cemetery, the huge standard bearing the insignia of the Sword Brothers being gently ruffled by the wind. Two flags bearing the same design fluttered from the mighty gatehouse and another banner hung from the southwest tower. No one would be in any doubt as to who occupied Wenden Castle. The shouts and encouragement of Brother Lukas on the training field reached his ears and he smiled. He remembered his time as a novice; it seemed like yesterday.

He looked down at the grave of his wife and child and read the inscription on the gravestone, just as he had done a hundred times before. He saw the fresh flowers before him and said a silent prayer to keep safe Ilona who always ensured a

233

tribute was on their grave. And he asked God to protect Kaja too, who likewise paid her respects to his wife and son even though she had never known them. He looked at the graves of his friends Bruno and Johann, and then at the other brother knights who had been laid to rest here. With each year that passed more of his comrades were buried here and he knew that he would one day be lying with his family. The thought comforted him.

He became aware of a presence behind him and turned to see Master Rudolf.

'I hope I am not disturbing you, Conrad.'

'No, master.'

He walked up to stand beside him and looked at the grave.

'Ilona was very fond of Daina. I think it comforts her to attend to her grave when you are away.'

'It comforts me too, master.'

'The Saccalians seems to have settled into Thalibald's village, Conrad. The elders from the other villages tell me that it is going to be a good harvest this year.'

'Praise God.'

He glanced at Conrad. 'It seems but a short while ago when we were working in the fields outside Thalibald's village helping his people gather in the crops. You were a fresh-faced novice then. How the years pass.'

Conrad looked at the graves of Bruno and Johann. 'Many have fallen since that time.'

'And more will follow, I fear. But not this year, Conrad. This year the Oeselians and those Estonians that have not joined your banner are locked in conflict with the Danes, and as you know Sir Richard stands firm at Lehola.'

'We should mount a campaign in the winter against Ungannia, master,' said Conrad.

'You feel that Kristjan has betrayed you, Conrad?'

He looked at Rudolf. 'No, master. But he has allied himself with the Russians and that presents a direct threat to our order and Livonia.'

'That will be a matter for the bishop to address. But for the moment I have a more immediate task for you.'

Conrad looked at him expectantly. 'Yes, master, of course.'

'I want you to deliver the document that King Valdemar signed to the office of Grand Master Volquin at Riga.'

Conrad's heart sank. 'Riga, master?'

'Yes. Normally I would send it to the bishop's palace but Bishop Albert has taken ship to Germany to raise recruits for next year's campaign and I don't trust that toad Archdeacon Stefan.'

Conrad could barely hide his disappointment. 'Yes, master.'

Rudolf heard the indifference in his voice.

'You do not seem pleased by my decision.'

Conrad shrugged. 'I go where you command, master.

Rudolf laughed. 'I do not command you, Conrad. I ask. You seem to forget that you are Marshal of Estonia and a very famous man in Livonia.'

Now it was Conrad's turn to laugh. 'I am?'

'Of course. The man who saved the bishop's life, killed Lembit, raised an army of pagans that defeated the Cumans and Russians and defied the most powerful king in northern Europe before the gates of Reval. And let's not forget you subsequently humbled said king on the island of Oesel. Your name is well known not only in these parts but throughout Germany as well. An important document should be in the safe keeping of such a famous warrior during its transportation.'

'I think it was you who humbled King Valdemar on Oesel, master.'

Rudolf smiled, a glint in his eye. 'The point is I want you to go to Riga to deliver the document. Take Anton and Hans along with you.'

The next day the three friends set out, Conrad with the document in a leather tube tucked into a saddlebag. Hans and Anton were delighted to be on a new adventure, though Conrad was far from happy, barely speaking as they trotted along the track that followed the course of the Gauja. A packhorse that Anton led carried their food and tent for the journey that would take two days.

'What's the matter with you?' asked Hans after they had travelled an hour in silence.

'He got out of the wrong side of the coffin this morning,' quipped Anton.

Hans laughed but Conrad shook his head.

'I have been reduced to an errand boy,' he complained.

'Next year you will be doing what makes you happy. Killing people, so don't worry,' said Hans.

'I do not take pleasure in killing,' insisted Conrad.

'I do,' stated Anton.

'So do I,' said Hans, 'as does Conrad. He just convinces himself that he doesn't.'

But as they got nearer to Riga their mood brightened with the prospect of seeing the city again. It had been twelve years since they had first landed there after their journey from Lübeck and they were curious to see if the place had changed. And as they neared the city they realised that the countryside around it certainly had. Livonia was covered in forests, lakes and rivers but as they rode south on the morning of the third day, being only around fifteen miles north of Riga, they noticed that areas of woodland had been cleared to make way for villages.

The settlements were small, perhaps a dozen huts in addition to a wooden church in the centre and a few barns and sheds around it. The buildings had been made of wood from the surrounding forests with roofs made of thatch. Surrounding the settlements were fields, grazing land and a mill used to crush crops. The mill could either be a windmill or, more likely because of the abundance of rivers and streams in Livonia, sited near a water source. And so it was that on an overcast autumn day the three brother knights rode into a village populated by German settlers to witness a most distressing scene.

Just outside the simple wooden church, which in truth was nothing more than a square barn with a wooden cross mounted on the roof, a crowd of villagers was gathered in front of their priest. Conrad recognised him instantly as a member of the Cistercian Order in his undyed habit, tonsured head and leather shoes. A large wooden crucifix hung around his neck, much like the one that the mad Abbot Hylas wore at Wenden. As the riders approached Conrad could see a young woman being held between two male villagers, her head cast down. She was dressed in a dirty long skirt that was ripped in several places. She was also bare foot.

'You have been found guilty of witchcraft, girl,' announced the priest loudly to murmurs of agreement from the villagers. 'Have you anything to say before sentence is pronounced?'

The girl looked up, tears and pleading in her eyes. 'No understand,' she muttered in Liv.

Conrad brought his horse to a halt a few paces from the church, the priest turning away from the girl when several of the villagers began pointing at the three brother knights.

'She does not understand what you are saying' Conrad told the priest.

The churchman, annoyed that his work had been interrupted, pointed at the girl.

238

'She understands well enough.'

One of the men holding the girl, an ugly wretch with a sadistic leer on his face, suddenly grabbed her long hair, twisted his hand and yanked her head back.

'Look at Father Arnulf, witch.'

'Let her go,' said Conrad calmly.

Hans sighed. 'We don't have time for this, Conrad.'

'It's not our business,' added Anton.

Conrad passed his reins to Hans and dismounted.

'We protect the weak and helpless, remember.'

He walked over to the priest. 'What crime do you accuse this girl of?'

'I told you, soldier. She is a witch. Now be on your way and leave the matters of God to those who understand His word.'

In a flash Conrad pulled his dagger with his right hand, spun round and drove its pommel into the nose of the man who was holding the girl's hair, breaking it.

'And I told you to let her go.'

The villagers began cursing Conrad as he turned the dagger in his hand and pointed it at the other man.

'Let her go.'

The man with the broken nose was lying on the ground clutching his wounded face, groaning as pain shot through his skull.

'You have no right to interfere in church business, heretic,' shouted the priest. He pointed at Conrad and looked at the villagers.

'Seize him.'

They suddenly stopped shouting and looked at each other nervously, wondering what to do and hoping that someone would try to restrain the tall, strapping knight standing before them. No one did.

'I do not fear you,' said Father Arnulf defiantly.

'I do not want you to fear me, father,' replied Conrad, 'I just want an explanation as to why you accuse this girl of witchcraft.'

The man on the other side of her released his grip and retreated as the girl looked at Conrad. She had the fair hair and blue eyes of her race in stark contrast to the more swarthy features of the German settlers around her. Conrad asked her what she had done to provoke them so and she replied that she lived in a nearby Liv village but had often visited this settlement to administer cures.

'I make ointments and potions from herbs and flowers,' she said in her own language.

'You are a healer?' said Conrad.

She nodded. 'I cured a baby of a fever, that is all. Their headman said that I was a servant of the devil but I do not know him.'

Hans began munching on an apple as Conrad turned back to the priest.

240

'She saves a child's life and you accuse her of witchcraft?'

The man glared at Conrad. 'The child was dying and had been given the last rights. And then suddenly it lived. It was the devil's work.'

The villagers voiced their support for the priest's opinion.

'In addition,' said Father Arnulf loudly, 'we found proof that she is a servant of the Devil. She has a witch's mark.'

A gasp of horror came from the villagers. Father Arnulf held up his hands.

'A mole on her inner thigh,' he announced.

Conrad looked at him with disgust. 'I warrant you had fun searching for that.'

'You mock the Lord's work?' the priest shot back.

'I mock your pious sanctity,' replied Conrad. Behind him Anton looked at Hans, shook his head and rolled his eyes. Hans continued munching on his apple.

'It is written in Exodus,' the priest suddenly shouted, 'thou shalt not suffer a witch to live.'

'Burn her, burn her' shouted the villagers and the girl began to sob. He walked forward, placed an arm around her shoulder and led her away.

'No one is burning anyone today,' he said firmly.

The men in the crowd wanted to stop him but they saw his powerful frame, the dagger now back in its sheath on his hip, the sword on the other side and the axe tucked into the back of his belt. They insulted him and shook their fists but did not move.

'I will take her back to her village,' Conrad announced. 'You had better pray that the chief does not send a war party to exact vengeance.'

'This is our land,' shouted a villager.

'There is no room for pagans in Livonia,' cried another.

'Conrad,' said Hans, tossing away the apple core, 'have you heard of the phrase "biting off more than you can chew" by any chance?'

Conrad led the girl towards his horse. 'Of course.'

Hans pointed ahead. 'Well you are about to learn if there's any truth in it.'

Conrad looked to where he was pointing and saw at least half a dozen riders approaching, men in mail and red surcoats bearing the cross keys insignia of Riga. Father Arnulf suddenly ran towards the horsemen, waving his arms in the air as he did so.

'Save us, good Christian knights. Deliver us from pagans and heretics. They have saved a witch from justice.'

The horsemen spurred their horses forward into the village, passing the priest to halt next to the villagers, who began pointing at Conrad.

'He saved the witch and threatened Father Arnulf. Kill him.'

The girl began shaking as two of the riders, both wearing kettle helmets, dismounted and marched towards Conrad. Hans and Anton left their saddles and drew their swords. The commander of the Rigan horsemen, a square-faced fellow with an open-faced helmet, pointed at Conrad.

'The Sword Brothers have no jurisdiction here. Hand her over and be on your way.'

'I cannot do that,' replied Conrad.

The commander nodded to the two sergeants as the other four horsemen arrived behind him. Conrad noticed that one was dressed in a red mantle and had a mitre on his head but he had other things to worry about as the sergeants drew their swords and came at him. They shifted their shields to cover their torsos as Conrad jumped forward, pulled his sword, ducked to the left, thrust the blade forward and then whipped it back to slice the hamstring of the sergeant on the right of the pair. Both wore mail hauberks but their legs were unprotected and thus an easy target. The man gave a sharp yelp and went down on one knee, his face contorted in pain.

The second sergeant spun to his right to face Conrad who pulled the shield off his back and thrust his left forearm through the straps on its inside. The commander shouted at his other men to dismount as Hans and Anton sprang forward to assist their friend.

The second sergeant attempted a vertical cut to Conrad's head but the brother knight jumped back so the blow sliced only air. He then sprang forward and used his shield like a battering ram to knock the sergeant off his feet. The sergeant stumbled rearwards and fell on his back, Conrad ramming his

243

left foot down onto his groin. The man emitted a high-pitched scream as a voice thundered a command.

'Enough!'

Conrad kept pressing his foot into the man's groin as the individual in the red mantle and mitre jumped from his horse and strode over to him. He was perhaps in his late fifties or early sixties, of solid build with a round face. With his mitre he was well over six foot and appeared to have a solid frame. He pointed at the man groaning at Conrad's feet.

'Release him.'

Conrad did not recognise the individual, though the gold pectoral cross that dangled from a gold chain around his neck indicated that he was a man of some importance in the Holy Church. The other soldiers had now dismounted and drawn their swords but Hans and Anton had likewise unsheathed their blades and were standing beside their friend.

The churchman looked at them and then at the soldiers of the Riga garrison.

'All of you will place your swords back in their scabbards or will face severe punishment. Do not think that because my brother Albert is in Germany I will allow Livonia to become a domain of bandits.'

Conrad removed his foot from the man's genitals. 'You are the brother of the Bishop Albert?'

'I am Bishop Hermann of Buxhoeveden, formerly of Germany but now a resident of Livonia.'

He looked at his guards who slid their swords back in their scabbards. Hans and Anton did the same, leaving Conrad the only one with a weapon in his hand.

'And now,' said Hermann, 'as I have introduced myself to you, brother knight, perhaps you would afford me the same courtesy. Unless you propose to martyr me.'

'Lord bishop?' said Conrad, who suddenly remembered he had a blade in his hand. He hastily put it back in its scabbard. 'I am Brother Conrad of the garrison of Wenden and Marshal of Estonia and I apologise for my ill manners. These are my friends and fellow members of my order: Brother Hans and Brother Anton.'

They both bowed their heads to Hermann.

'So you are Conrad Wolff,' said the bishop. 'My brother has talked much of you, of how you saved his life and killed the pagan leader Lembit. And here you are, standing before me.'

The officer of the open helmet stormed over to the bishop.

'The Sword Brothers should be arrested, sir. They have wounded two of my men.'

Conrad looked at the soldier hobbling back to his horse with a sliced hamstring and the other being helped to his feet.

'They will live.'

The officer glared at him. 'You have shown disrespect to the soldiers of the garrison of Riga, for which you will be punished.'

Conrad laughed. 'Are they soldiers? I thought they were overdressed bodyguards of Archdeacon Stefan, fit only for frightening children or raping young maidens.'

The officer went to draw his sword again.

'Think carefully,' Conrad warned him. 'Draw that sword and only one of us will be alive afterwards.'

The bishop, far from intervening, was watching the unfolding drama with interest. On one side was the angry officer in a fine surcoat but who was already running to fat, on the other the sturdy killing machine that was Conrad Wolff. He did not intervene because he was a good judge of men and knew that the officer treasured his own life above that of the reputation of the garrison of Riga, such as it was. He fumed for a few seconds, gave Conrad a hateful look and then stormed off to assist his man with the sore testicles.

'Take your men back to the city,' the bishop called after him. 'I will make my own way there.'

'It is not safe for you to ride alone, lord bishop,' the officer replied.

'We are travelling to Riga, lord bishop,' said Conrad, 'and would be honoured to be your escort.'

The bishop clapped his hands together. 'The Lord provides. Excellent.'

The officer sniffed and assisted his soldiers into the saddle, then gave the order for the others to mount up. With a curt salute he bid farewell to the bishop and led his men away from the village.

'So,' said Hermann, looking at the Liv girl, 'what is happening here?'

'A familiar tale, lord bishop,' Conrad told him. 'A lecherous priest and a pretty young girl who found his advances repugnant.'

Hermann walked over to Father Arnulf and extended his right hand, on which was his bishop's ring with its large amethyst. Father Arnulf fell to his knees and kissed the stone, his parishioners also kneeling.

'Welcome, lord bishop,' said Father Arnulf.

'I will be taking the girl,' stated Hermann.

The priest looked up. 'She is a witch, lord bishop, and should be burnt for her sins.'

'That will be decided by a church court in Riga,' said Hermann sharply, 'it is not a matter for a lowly priest to decide.'

The bishop looked at the villagers. 'Go back to your work, all of you. Do you not know that the devil makes work for idle hands?'

The villagers sheepishly rose to their feet and shuffled away, some muttering as they did so. Conrad placed his cloak around the girl's shoulders as Hans and Anton regained their saddles. Father Arnulf made to rise.

'Did I tell you to get off your knees?' asked Hermann.

'No, lord bishop,' answered the priest, who resumed his position. 'Forgive me.'

'You have no authority to execute people, Father Arnulf,' stated the bishop, who saw the bruises on the girl's face, 'or torture them. Do you understand?'

'Yes, lord bishop,' came the mumbled reply.

'Well,' smiled Hermann, 'let us be on our way, Conrad.'

He walked back to his horse and regained his saddle. Conrad helped the girl onto his horse so she could sit behind him. She wrapped her arms around his waist and clung on for dear life, not saying a word as they trotted from the village. Behind them Father Arnulf stood up and dusted himself down.

The bishop riding beside Conrad took a cloth from his sleeve and carefully wiped the amethyst.

'Do you know why amethyst is chosen to be the stone of a bishop's ring, Conrad?'

'No, lord bishop.'

'It is because the purplish colour is supposed to prevent drunkenness and bring a sense of peace and devotion. The gem's colour resembles wine, you see, and is a reminder not to succumb to the temptation of drink. It also reminds the wearer not to become drunk with power but to focus on more spiritual matters.'

'Most interesting, lord bishop,' said Conrad, in truth not at all interested.

Hermann noted the indifference in his voice. 'Something troubles you?'

'Forgive me, lord bishop, but is this girl, having been saved from being burnt at the stake, now going to be taken to Riga where she will most likely suffer a similar death?'

Hermann smiled. 'Of course not. I said that to appease Father Arnulf, deluded fool that he is. We will take her to her home, if she has one.'

A relieved Conrad conveyed this happy news to the Liv who gave him a broad smile. They rode to the outskirts of her village that was around three miles from the Christian settlement. He told her that she should avoid it in future and warn the other residents of the settlement to do likewise. They then resumed their journey to Riga.

'Where is your army, Conrad,' enquired the bishop, 'your Army of the Wolf?'

'Part is at Wenden,' answered Conrad, 'the greater part is in Rotalia.'

Hermann, fascinated, asked him questions concerning Wenden, the Oeselians, Danes and affairs in Ungannia.

'So you believe this Kristjan will prove an implacable enemy?' asked Hermann.

'I met him only once, lord bishop,' said Conrad. 'He has an unforgiving nature. Apparently he believes that the Sword Brothers killed his parents and has sworn revenge. He also has the support of the Russians, which means that Saccalia will be very vulnerable, as will be Livonia.'

'What course would you advise, lord marshal?'

Conrad thought for a moment. 'If Kristjan cannot be reasoned with he will have to be defeated and Ungannia conquered. After that the rest of Estonia will have to be subdued, both to rid it of the Oeselians and crush the power of the Danes, which means capturing Reval.'

Hermann's eyes widened. 'The list of the enemies of Livonia grows long.'

'That is why your brother created the Sword Brothers, lord bishop.'

Hermann looked at him and his friends riding behind them, hard men, heavily armed and attired in mail.

'There are some that say that the Sword Brothers are too powerful, that they strive to make Livonia their own kingdom rather than my brother's.'

'I thought it was God's kingdom,' replied Conrad, then realising who he was talking to. 'My apologies, lord bishop, I meant no respect.'

'You are right, Conrad. It is God's kingdom.'

'I must also apologise for insulting your son, lord bishop,' said Conrad.

'My son?'

'Archdeacon Stefan. I had no idea that he was your son.'

A look of horror spread across Hermann's face.

'He is my sister's son, not mine, thank the Lord. So your apology is unnecessary.'

'He will not take kindly to his soldiers being assaulted, Conrad,' said Hans.

'They are not his soldiers,' replied Conrad irritably, 'they are Bishop Albert's.'

'Perhaps you could tell my nephew that,' suggested the bishop.

They arrived at Riga two hours later after a pleasant ride through sweet-smelling meadows and woods teeming with game and birds. The air was fresh, the weather warm and the company most agreeable and Conrad thought Livonia was truly blessed. Until he entered Riga.

An imposing stone wall now surrounded the city, but more impressive were the castle and the cathedral, the latter more massive and magnificent than the former and both dominating the skyline. It had been eleven years since Bishop Albert had laid the foundation stone of the cathedral and, notwithstanding the fire that had severely damaged the structure three years later it had become a powerful statement of the might of the Holy Church in the Baltic. It had been constructed of bricks, stone blocks being used only in the outer corners of the building. The architects had constructed it in the style of ancient Rome so that it displayed a strong sense of proportion and order. It was also solid, like a rock to withstand the assault of paganism, and like the buildings found in ancient Rome its design included numerous rounded arches and vaults. It literally dwarfed the other wooden churches in Riga.

As they drew nearer to one of the gatehouses Conrad's nose was assaulted first by the stench of dung, animal and human, the result of night soil men who were tipping barrels of excrement into the streams that ran to the Dvina. Though the likelihood that the filth would be carried to the great river was minimal. Pigs rooted around in the dung, lifting their muck-covered snouts up to peer with their tiny eyes at the four riders as they passed them to walk their horses into the city.

Now the quarantine had been lifted the road was full of hawkers, carts, Livs and boys with dirty faces and even dirtier clothes running between the horses and carts to beg. The bishop ignored them and Conrad waved them away but Hans threatened to cut off the light-fingered hands of one who tried to interfere with the load carried on the packhorse. Above them spearmen in the livery of the garrison leaned against the battlements, unconcerned by the bustle below.

Fortunately it had not rained earlier so the dirt road was not too badly churned up as they walked their horses passed by town houses of merchants and abbots, servants shovelling animal dung that had been deposited in front of their masters' houses. Conrad was amazed by the noise, the voices of hundreds of people arguing, bartering, chatting and laughing. The raucous revelry of alehouses spilled into the streets to compete with the haranguing of white-robed friars threatening hell and damnation on the drunkards. At Wenden everything was ordered, calm and quiet, aside from when it was at war. But here everything was chaotic and loud. Outside the castle Bishop Hermann said his goodbyes.

'I hope to see you all again,' he said to the three friends. 'A word of caution, Conrad: I would not stay too long in Riga.

My nephew has a malicious aspect to his character and has probably already learned of the incident at the village.'

'I will sleep with one eye open, lord bishop,' said Conrad.

Hermann raised his hand, turned his horse and headed towards the bishop's palace just a short distance away.

'A curious day,' opined Anton. 'We have made a friend of the bishop's brother and an enemy of his nephew.'

'I'm quaking in my boots,' said Conrad, spurring his horse through the gates of the castle.

Grand Master Volquin was chuckling in his boots when Conrad presented him with the document that had been signed by King Valdemar. He showed it to Master Godfrey, the commander of Holm Castle, one of the order's castles a short distance east of Riga.

'I wish I had been on Oesel to see that king grovel to the Sword Brothers.'

Volquin poured wine for Conrad and his two friends into silver flagons.

'So Conrad,' said the grand master, 'do you think that Valdemar will return next year with an army at his back to teach us a lesson?'

Conrad toasted Volquin and Godfrey. 'I fear so, grand master.'

'He's right,' agreed Godfrey.

Volquin nodded thoughtfully. 'So what strategy would you recommend, Marshal of Estonia?'

Conrad saw Hans drain his flagon. 'Seize Reval, grand master. Without it the Danes will have no base from which to launch a campaign against us.'

Godfrey emptied his flagon, refilled Hans' and then his own. He looked out of the window of Volquin's office in the castle.

'We should muster the order, join with Conrad's bastard heathens and take Reval before the winter.'

'You would like that, wouldn't you, Godfrey,' remarked Volquin. 'But may I remind you that we are the servants of Bishop Albert not a band of mercenaries. And we now have Ungannia to worry about.'

Godfrey drained his flagon and belched. 'You think Sir Richard will be able to see out the winter, Conrad?'

'Yes, master,' replied Conrad. 'Lehola will defy Kristjan, of that I have no doubt.'

'You see,' Godfrey said to Volquin. 'We have a God-given opportunity to take Reval and present it as a gift to the bishop when he returns from Germany.'

Volquin smiled but shook his head. 'Saving Valdemar's arse is one thing, even if Rudolf did rub his nose in the manure, but declaring war on him is quite another. However, if he does return with an army next year then I will certainly consider your proposal, Conrad.'

Volquin sighed. 'Besides, the garrison of Riga is in no state to support our order in any ventures this year. The pox killed a quarter of it, another quarter deserted and I doubt we could raise more than a couple of hundred militiamen from the city and surrounding villages.'

'The pox ravaged Riga, grand master?' asked Hans, nodding as Godfrey offered to refill his flagon.

'It killed and scarred enough, Brother Hans,' replied Volquin, 'even took a dozen of my own mercenaries. But cities recover and so will the garrison. That snake Nordheim has taken himself off to Germany to recruit more brigands and cutthroats.'

'Which means Archdeacon Stefan won't tolerate any of his personal bodyguard leaving the city when he returns from Dünamünde.'

'He returned this very morning,' said Volquin.

Godfrey clapped his hands together as in prayer. 'Praise the Lord he still lives.'

'That one would survive the great flood,' joked Volquin. 'Fortunately Bishop Hermann is in charge of the city until his brother returns.'

'We met the bishop on our way here, grand master,' Conrad told him.

He then informed him about the episode with the Liv girl, the altercation with soldiers of the garrison and the intercession of the bishop.

Godfrey pointed at Conrad and his friends. 'You should have killed all those soldiers, and the villagers too. I hope you are not going soft, Brother Conrad.'

Volquin shook his head. 'You speak out of turn, Godfrey. The new settlers are going to turn this land into a new Jerusalem.'

'A new Germany, more like,' retorted Godfrey, 'and that's a den of whores and thieves. I should know, I spent enough years travelling through it as a mercenary.'

Volquin looked at the three brother knights. 'I think it would be prudent if you all took advantage of the hospitality of Holm tonight before your return to Wenden. The archdeacon might take it personally that some of his men have been roughly handled.'

'They will recover, grand master,' said Anton. 'Conrad only nicked one and made the eyes of another water.'

Godfrey, now a little drunk, howled with laughter. 'Allow me to translate the grand master's words. You stay here tonight and chances are that arch-demon Stefan will send some assassins to slit your throats, either that or arrange an ambush a few miles outside the city tomorrow. He's a malicious, vindictive little bastard who never forgets.'

'Not the words I would use,' said Volquin, 'but I think Master Godfrey has succinctly summarised the reasons why you should ride back with him to Holm.'

And so they did, reaching the castle an hour later. It had been one of the order's castles for twenty-six years and in that time it had gone from being a pagan timber stronghold to a mighty citadel of stone. Surrounded on three sides by a wide, deep moat and on the other by the waters of the Dvina, its ten-feet-thick walls surrounded a courtyard a hundred and thirty feet in length and one hundred feet wide. As at Wenden the towers flew the flags of the Sword Brothers and a huge banner of the order hung over the entrance of the large gatehouse.

After they had attended Nones prayers in the large stone chapel the three friends stood on the battlements looking south across the blue waters of the Dvina. There were now boats on the waterway, river vessels carrying goods from Novgorod, Polotsk and the Lithuanian kingdoms for sale in Riga or onward transportation to Lübeck. Most were powered by a combination of oars and sails, though a few of the large, more rounded boats were moving under sail power only. It was a beautiful scene, the blue of the Dvina and the black shapes of the boats set against the greens, reds and gold of the unending forests of Semgallia.

'I wonder what is happening south of the river,' mused Anton.

'Master Godfrey said that peace reigns among the Lithuanian kingdoms,' answered Hans.

'Let us pray it does not last,' said Conrad. 'Now that the pox has passed Livonia might become a tempting target for the Lithuanians.'

*****

Conrad's prayers were answered because the peace that reigned in Lithuania was only the prelude to a holy war. A war declared by the aged *Kriviu Krivaitis* and preached by his priests in every

257

village and stronghold. The August and September harvests were gathered in and then the village elders mustered their levies. They brought their men to the assembly points assigned by the princes whose lands they worked and then marched to where their duke had planted his banner. The place assigned by the head priest to be the location where the dukes would gather was the site where his heir had been brutally murdered by Duke Arturus. This meant that it was the end of October before the holy army had assembled. But such was the size of the force that gathered at the Kur border that it was commonly believed that there would be no battle, just a triumphant march to Arturus' stronghold at Talsi, which would be stormed with ease.

The largest contingent was that of Duke Butantas: two thousand horse and five thousand warriors on foot. Duke Viesthard, whose kingdom had been the target of many Kur raids, would have liked to match these numbers but his people had suffered at the hands of both Arturus and the Christians. He therefore could muster only five hundred horse and two thousand foot. It took much persuasion on Rasa's part to convince her husband that to take the field against Arturus was an honourable thing. In the end Selonia and Nalsen sent a thousand horsemen and three thousand warriors on foot. Vsevolod ensured that his Russian guards surrounded him at all times. He also badgered Aras to impress on the commanders of his horsemen that their first loyalty was to the husband of Princess Rasa. For his part Prince Mindaugas thought the whole campaign akin to a pilgrimage, and he and Prince Ykintas pledged their allegiance to each other and dreamt of glory.

The last to arrive was Prince Kitenis at the head of a thousand mounted Aukstaitijans and three thousand foot soldiers. Thus were four and half thousand horsemen and thirteen thousand foot gathered around the ancient hill fort of Dobele. The army marched west on the last day of October, though the entire morning was spent with dozens of *Kriviai* going among the soldiery blessing every *spisa*, spear and sword. Vsevolod was beside himself with boredom but the warriors loved it. His misery was complete when it began to rain, which quickly turned the ground to mud.

After two days the army had reached the lush valley of the Abava River, a waterway some forty paces wide but shallow enough for a man to wade across with ease. And there, in a large area of open ground, the dukes found the army of Arturus, the left flank of its black ranks anchored on the river. The despatch of scouts revealed it to be numerically inferior to its opponents, especially with regard to the horsemen that made up the Kur right wing. A hurried council of war decided upon the tactics that would win the day. The foot would assault the Kur foot drawn up in the centre while the horsemen, massed on the left flank, would crush their mounted opponents and then sweep around the flank of the Kur foot to envelop Arturus' army. Ykintas pledged to cut off the head of the Kur leader and send it as a present to the *Kriviu Krivaitis*.

Over four thousand horsemen thundered across the damp earth to attack the Kurs' left wing, which promptly turned and fled. Despite being drawn from a number of kingdoms the charging horsemen managed to slow and wheel right to get behind the Kur foot, to find a line of spearmen drawn up behind the Kur centre. The horsemen tried to smash through these warriors but could make no impression upon them as the Lithuanian foot soldiers marched forward to smash the Kur centre.

It was unfortunate that none of the dukes had thought of conducting a more thorough reconnoitre of the ground because if they had done so they would have discovered a large group of horsemen sheltering in the trees that began a few hundred paces from where the Kurs' left flank had ended. Prince Lamekins now led these men from the trees to attack the rear of the dukes' horsemen as the Kur left wing that had fled now reappeared on the battlefield. No one knew if one of the dukes decided that the battle was lost and ordered his soldiers to retreat, many cast Prince Vsevolod's horsemen as the villains. But whatever the truth soon hundreds of horsemen were falling back.

In the centre the advance of thirteen thousand foot soldiers faltered and then stopped with the withdrawal of the horsemen. As the flood to the rear of the latter increased a trickle of foot warriors, most being farmers, also beat a hurried retreat. This turned into a torrent when the Kur foot suddenly charged forward.

Ironically most of the losses suffered by the dukes were not on the battlefield. Butantas, Kitenis, Viesthard and Vsevolod and the majority of their horsemen escaped. But six thousand of their foot soldiers were hunted down and killed by the Kurs, Lamekins' horsemen doing the most carnage as he pursued the enemy east. Only the merciful advent of night halted the butchery. Kur losses were two hundred dead.

It had been a most remarkable day.

Chapter 6

Kristjan stared at the spitting and crackling fire in the centre of the hall and pulled the fur-lined cloak around himself. The slaves had been feeding the flames all morning, heaping logs on to the stone hearth but he still felt cold. He used his hand to scoop more porridge from the bowl and shoved it in his mouth. It was already lukewarm. He hurled the wooden bowl across the straw-covered floor.

'Bring me some that is hot,' he shouted at the slaves.

He rubbed his eyes. The idiot slaves had placed damp wood on the fire that had filled Fellin's hall with smoke. His clothes stank of it and his eyes smarted, which all added to his misery. Perhaps he would have a couple crucified later. It was the only thing that brought him any cheer these days. He sat with a look of thunder on his face and reflected on a year of heartache and disappointment. The death of his parents and sisters had filled him with rage and a desire for vengeance. He had raised the whole of Ungannia and swept into Saccalia, capturing Fellin with ease. But then his attempts to take Lehola had ended in bloody failure, the accursed Sir Richard defending it like a wily bear does its winter lair. And so with the coming of winter he had been forced to abandon the siege. Worse, in the autumn he had sent many of his warriors back to Ungannia to harvest the crops in the fields. He had been delighted when Prince Vetseke had arrived at the head of mounted warriors, including Russians, but he realised that as long as Lehola still held out he would not be able to strike south into Livonia.

'Where is this Sir Richard from?'

'A place called England, I believe,' answered Vetseke sitting on the opposite side of the fire.

Kristjan gave him a blank look. 'Where's that?'

'A place far to the west,' said Vetseke, taking a bowl of hot porridge offered him by a slave. 'He came to Livonia as a crusader and decided to stay.'

Kristjan snatched a bowl of porridge from a slave. 'I hate these crusaders. I do not go around invading other people's kingdoms, forcing them to pray to my gods. This land was at peace before they and the Sword Brothers came.'

Vetseke remembered it differently, especially the years of incessant raiding by the Estonian tribes against the Livs, to say nothing of the depredations of the Russians. But he said nothing. He had learned quickly that Kristjan was volatile and liable to fly into blind, murderous rages at the slightest provocation. But then he was just a boy.

'He has a bald head,' said Kristjan, 'this Sir Richard. Let's hope that he is feeling the cold as I am. Put more wood on the fire,' he shouted at a slave. 'If it is damp I will kill you myself.'

'When the snow melts we should leave this place and march north to join the other Estonian tribes that are fighting the Danes,' suggested Vetseke.

'Abandon Fellin?' Kristjan was appalled.

Vetseke shook his head. 'I did not say abandon it. Just leave a garrison here. You are the last of the free Estonian leaders; indeed you are the only Estonian leader. The others are dead. You could be the new Lembit, uniting the tribes to destroy the Sword Brothers.'

'Will the Russians support me if I join the rebellion in the north?'

'Of course,' Vetseke lied. 'I am but the vanguard of a great army that will be put at your disposal in the summer. Prince Mstislav himself has assured me that he will support your war against the Sword Brothers, the apostates who stole his banner.'

Kristjan appeared pleased by this. 'It was taken to Wenden where it remains, I assume. It can be retrieved easily enough.'

Vetseke raised an eyebrow. The boy obviously inhabited a fantasy world. Taking the timber walls and towers of Lehola had been beyond him and stone castles such as Wenden were even tougher nuts to crack. And yet the fact that he was the son of Kalju, 'the rock', and the last male member of his family alive after the others had been killed made him the figurehead of the fight against the Sword Brothers and the Bishop of Riga.

Vetseke pressed his case. 'The fact is that among the Estonian kingdoms only Ungannia and its people remain free. Saccalia and Rotalia have become playthings of the Sword Brothers, while Wierland, Harrien and Jerwen are swapped between the Oeselians and Danes like an old whore. Go north,

Kristjan, and rekindle the flame of freedom among your people.'

Kristjan looked at the hissing and spitting fire and dreamed of leading the whole of Estonia in a war of liberation. He looked at the Sword Brother shield hanging by the side of the throne he had had made during his stay at Fellin. Vetseke had given it to him as a gift after the Russian prince had won a skirmish with the Christian knights just before he and his men had arrived at Fellin. How he would love to take such a trophy.

'We should move before the snows melt,' Vetseke told him, 'to steal a march on the Sword Brothers. We do not want to be trapped here if they lay siege to Fellin.'

'You think I fear the Sword Brothers and their engines?' snapped Kristjan, his nostrils flaring.

Vetseke masked his contempt. 'You are the son of Kalju so I know that you fear no one. But your father was not only fearless, he was cunning and possessed great foresight. That is why he remained one step ahead of his enemies and that is why Ungannia remained free under his rule.'

Kristjan was soothed by the prince's words.

'You really think that the Harrien, Wierlanders and Jerwen will listen to me?' asked Kristjan.

Vetseke stood and walked around the fire to look at the arrogant young pup.

'I am certain of it. They are crying out for leadership. Unite the tribes, Kristjan, and become the man you are destined to be.'

Kristjan gave him a twisted smile. 'I will give the order this afternoon. We will march north to give heart to those fighting for Estonia's freedom.'

Vetseke smiled but inside he was mightily relieved. The winter had been a long one and he feared for his sanity if forced to remain cooped up any longer in this dismal fort with only the dreary tantrums of this boy for company. He was beginning to regret leaving Novgorod.

And by the frozen lake a short distance from Fellin iced skeletons with nightmarish grins hung from crosses, the skin on their frames having long since been picked clean by the fat ravens that came every day looking for fresh meat.

*****

Hans always suffered in the winter. He felt the cold more than Conrad and Anton and though his body had padded out after the years of nutritious and plentiful food provided by Wenden's kitchens, his face retained a slightly gaunt appearance. All three were wrapped in thick cloaks with fur collars and had fur-lined caps on their heads as protection against the biting cold. The birth of Christ had been celebrated a month ago and the land was in the iron grip of winter. Roofs were covered with frozen snow but the castle's cobbled courtyard was swept clean every day and the battlements were likewise kept tidy. Inside the outer perimeter paths and the main track were similarly kept unblocked, novices, brother knights, sergeants, mercenaries and civilians armed with shovels and brushes working furiously after every snowfall to prevent the passageways becoming stretches of ice. The civilian workers shivered in their wooden huts and burnt peat blocks supplied by Master Rudolf to keep the cold at bay.

Conrad loved Livonia's winter. The vivid blue cloudless skies, the crisp air and the absolute quiet. Hans pulled part of a loaf of bread from under his cloak as they headed towards the armoury.

'I don't,' he complained. 'It makes me feel hungry.'

'You are always hungry,' said Anton.

They had eaten lunch and had been to the chapel afterwards to give thanks for the food and were now preparing to go hunting elk. The garrison, workers and villagers in the settlement below the castle's northern escarpment all needed feeding, to say nothing of the Saccalians in Thalibald's old village. The harvest had been bountiful but the extra bellies that needed to be filled meant hunting parties were being despatched on a daily basis to kill elk, wolves, beaver and deer. The surrounding lakes were also plundered for fish, holes drilled in their frozen surfaces so lines could be dropped into the water to lure fish to the hooks on the end of them.

'You three look like a bunch of slave traders in your fur hats and felt boots. Off to raid a village for some maidens?'

They turned to see the grinning Leatherface ambling towards them. He had recovered from his cracked rib and was, like them, wrapped in a fur-lined cloak and hat, with the flaps pulled down over his ears.

'We are off to hunt elk,' Conrad told him.

'Want some company?' he beamed.

'Not really,' replied Anton.

Leatherface rubbed his hands. 'That's settled, then. You boys could do with someone showing you how to shoot a crossbow.'

Hans rolled his eyes but Conrad smiled. It was good to see the old rogue back to his incorrigible best. So they all went to the armoury to acquire their crossbows and quivers of bolts. Today they would not be riding in chainmail or helmets, not only because they were not going to war but also because the armour was devilishly difficult to keep clean and dry in winter. Novices and brother knights spent hours cleaning it with cloths and coating it with oil. This came from the Mediterranean and was used by the Holy Church in its sacraments. It was prohibitively expensive but nevertheless was supplied to the order by Riga. Conrad saw the hauberks hanging up in rows in the armoury, each one having a gap between it and the others to allow the air to circulate freely to prevent the build-up of moisture.

At the stables they collected their horses, which were kitted out in white caparisons, each one thickly padded and quilted and covering the head for protection against the cold. Two testy mules were also collected, one loaded with a tent and firewood, the other with the crossbows, quivers, spare clothing and food. There was no wind and the sun was already dipping in the west when the four riders exited the outer perimeter gates and trotted across the bridge over the ditch. They then turned left to take them along the castle's eastern ramparts before passing the village and heading north.

'It's going to be cold tonight,' said Hans, sniffing the air.

'Don't you worry, Brother Hans,' smiled Leatherface, 'we'll get a nice fire going to keep you warm.'

In truth they were all well wrapped, with socks, woollen underwear, woollen leg wraps beneath their trousers, woollen shirts, aketons and linen-covered and thickly quilted gambesons that had long sleeves and extended down to their knees. Were it not for the red cross and sword insignia that adorned their horses' caparisons, their cloaks and fronts of their gambesons they would have blended in perfectly against the white terrain.

The snorts of the horses were the only sounds as the party rode through the soft snow among deciduous trees stripped of their leaves and standing black and stark against the sky, the evergreens' low-lying branches heavy with snow.

'So,' said Leatherface, 'how's my girl getting along?'

'If you mean Kaja,' said Conrad, 'then she is doing well. She will be marrying Rameke this spring to become the wife of the Liv's most famous warlord.'

'So I've still got time to persuade her to change her mind and come with me when I buy my alehouse,' said the mercenary.

'What a dilemma,' said Hans, 'marry a famous and handsome warlord or agree to run a dingy back-street drinking den with an old goat who will maul her every night. How will Kaja choose?'

The three brother knights burst out laughing, which startled a bull elk nearby who bolted away. In a deft movement that left them all speechless Leatherface, who had loaded his crossbow and had it rested across the front of his saddle, brought the weapon up to his shoulder, shot it and brought down the elk. The beast groaned in agony and collapsed in the snow. Conrad spurred his horse towards it, dismounted, pulled his dagger and slit its throat, the blood staining the snow red.

Hans and Anton looked in amazement at Leatherface. The old soldier took it in his stride.

'You boys. Too busy picking on an old man instead of studying the ground. I saw the tracks running parallel to our route and knew one was close. I also knew it was a bull because they dribble piss when they are walking.'

They did not get much sleep that night, being forced to stand guard over the carcass as wolves circled their camp. The next day, the carcass having frozen solid during the night, they strapped it to a sled fashioned from fir branches and rode a short distance to pick up a trail of elk tracks. In winter the beasts usually congregated in large herds of males and females that paw through the snow to browse on grass, shrubs, twigs and tree bark.

Despite Leatherface's mockery the day before all three brother knights knew well enough how to hunt elk in winter. The guidelines were simple enough: always keep the wind in your face because if elk become aware they are being hunted they will use the wind to their own advantage. The golden rule was to go slowly when on foot and stop every couple of minutes to look for the slightest ear twitch or flash of horn. And always be aware of any broken tree limbs or pine needles knocked off overhead branches – a sure sign of being brushed by antlers.

It was a good morning's work – six bulls killed, which meant well over a thousand pounds of meat once the carcasses had been butchered properly. As with the first kill the dead animals were lashed to makeshift sleds and hauled back to Wenden. Their faces were pinched by the cold but Hans in particular was delighted to be heading back to the castle and its dining hall that always served plentiful amounts of food.

'Do you think we will be invited to Rameke's wedding?' asked Anton.

'Of course,' answered Conrad. 'We are his brothers and friends. And Kaja would be mortified if we were omitted from the guest list.'

'I think you boys have more pressing things to worry about than wedding invitations,' said Leatherface. 'This year is going to be a bloody one, you mark my words.'

*****

'I want that wretch's head.'

Valdemar had recovered much of his vim following his defeat and humiliation on Oesel. He had been forced to march

271

overland with the remnants of his army from Matsalu Bay to Varbola and then on to Reval. Once at the port he had ordered Count Albert and Count Rolf to hold it at all costs while he returned to Denmark to raise a new army. There had been some concern that the Oeselians might capture the king during his journey across the Baltic. But his flotilla of four cogs had reached Roskilde safely and he had immediately issued a summons to his lords to prepare for a new campaign in Estonia in the new year.

'Henry the Black', Count of Schwerin and the father of Rudolf Kassel, stood impassively before the royal dais as the king ranted. The throne room of Dronningholm Castle was packed with prelates, soldiers, ladies in their finery and their noble husbands, though the throne next to the king's was empty after the death of Queen Berengaria, which had been met with almost universal relief throughout Denmark. Nevertheless, the king had his eldest son, Valdemar the Young, by his side today, the boy having inherited his father's narrow face. He was thirteen years old now and Henry wondered if he had inherited his mother's vindictive character. He hoped not.

'Master Rudolf of Wenden,' continued the king, not knowing that he was talking about Henry's son, 'dictated terms to me. To me! A king appointed by God himself.'

'Shameful,' said Andrew, Archbishop of Lund.

Nicholas, Bishop of Schleswig, and Peter, Bishop of Roskilde, standing next to him nodded like the compliant sheep they were. Henry tried hard not to laugh. His brother Gunzelin beside him made no attempt to hide his feelings and smiled. Valdemar saw it.

'You think that showing disrespect to a king is a matter for mirth, Lord Gunzelin?'

'No, majesty,' sighed Gunzelin.

'I have written to His Holiness the Pope to demand that he disbands the Sword Brothers,' continued Valdemar, 'though after I had sent it I realised that there will be no need for that.'

'Really, your majesty?' queried Archbishop Andrew.

Valdemar looked at him knowingly. 'They will soon not exist now that our brave Count Henry is back with us. Ere long I will take ship with a great army to destroy the Sword Brothers and tear down their heretical castles. What say you, Count Henry, are your men hungry to serve their liege lord? Will you and your men unsheathe the blade of vengeance against the Sword Bothers?'

All eyes turned expectantly towards the count and his brother. But 'Black Henry' was not the same man that had taken thousands of crusaders south two years before. He was still a formidable warlord but his powerful frame seemed diminished and his face bore a world-weary look. His skin had been browned by a bright Mediterranean sun but the fire in his eyes was greatly diminished.

'My men?' he replied at length. 'Let me tell you about my men, your majesty.'

The throne room tingled with anticipation as the lords and ladies expected to hear a tale of heroism about smiting the ungodly.

'When we finally reached what we thought was the Holy Land a third of them had either died of disease or had deserted. We took ship in Italy and landed not in the Holy Land but in Egypt, a godforsaken land inhabited by flies and pestilence. When we finally arrived at the main crusader city, a shit-hole called Damietta that you can smell hours before you actually see it, a few more hundred had died of disease and exhaustion. We were housed in a filthy collection of tents outside the city along with thousands of idiots who had believed the preachings of the church to go on crusade.'

The archbishop and bishops became uncomfortable and then angry as the count continued to lambast the Holy Church.

'For the first few weeks we forgot about soldiering and concentrated on staying alive on the maggot-infested food that the city authorities agreed to feed my men on.'

He scowled at the prelates. 'Of course the bishops, archbishops and other priests lived well off the backs of their Egyptian slaves, none more so than the leader of the crusade, Cardinal-Legate Palagius, the self-appointed commander-in-chief of the army. A man who had become so fat on rich living that he had to be carried around in a golden litter by eight black slaves. No doubt he had one for every day of the week and two on Sundays.'

There were gasps in the throne room. Archbishop Andrew pointed a ring-adorned finger at the count.

'You blaspheme, Count Henry.'

Henry chuckled. 'Indeed I do, archbishop. But then you have not seen good men who have fought beside you for years die before your eyes as their guts turn to liquid and then pour out of every orifice. You have not heard the unceasing moans and pitiful whimpering of men eaten away by maggots and disease, begging for death as they lay in stinking cots in their own filth.'

'Enough,' commanded Valdemar, 'I did not order you here so you could upset the ladies of my court.'

'Upset, majesty?' said Henry mockingly. 'Surely as good Christians they would want to know that men died heroically on crusade, fighting to regain Jerusalem from the Saracens.'

'You recovered Jerusalem?' enquired Bishop Nicholas naively.

Gunzelin laughed mockingly. 'Jerusalem? It might as well have been on the other side of the world.'

'The great Palagius,' interrupted Count Henry, 'marched us into a swamp by a river called the Nile that became flooded when the commander of the Saracen army, a sultan named Al-Malik al-Kamil, opened the sluice gates. The cardinal was forced to crawl on his knees and beg for his and our lives.'

'Shameful,' someone called.

The count spun round. 'Shameful? Perhaps it was, but more so was the cardinal surrendering Damietta and agreeing

275

that the crusader army, what was left of it, would evacuate Egypt.'

The room was silent as the count conveyed this dreadful news.

'But you will be pleased to know,' said Gunzelin loudly, 'that Palagius managed to escape unharmed, along with his black catamites.'

Henry looked at the annoyed Valdemar. 'I returned to my lands with less than a thousand men, most of them shadows of their former selves.'

'God will not forget their sacrifices,' commented Archbishop Andrew, 'and will keep the souls of those who fell in His service safe.'

'A great comfort to their families, I'm sure,' remarked Gunzelin.

'Have a care,' the king warned him. 'You could get your tongue bored for such a comment.'

Gunzelin met the king's iron stare with indifference. Valdemar stood.

'Count Henry, in two months I sail to Reval. You will muster five thousand men and bring them to Roskilde where you and they will board ships to accompany me to Estonia.'

The room broke into applause and Valdemar smiled. His son gave the count and his brother a disdainful glare and smiled at his father. Henry gave the king a lukewarm bow, turned and marched from the room in the company of his brother, the haughty ladies of the court looking down their noses at them.

'I am finished with crusading, be it in the Mediterranean or the Baltic,' remarked Henry to Gunzelin as they left the throne room.

*****

Kristjan and Vetseke did not travel directly to northern Estonia. Instead they journeyed back to Dorpat where Indrek, Kalju's former deputy, was in command. There they waited for the snows to melt and then emptied the armoury of axes, spears, shields, armour, helmets, bows and arrows. It had been six years since the Oeselians, Russians and Estonians had been defeated in the snow before the walls of Odenpah, when the Sword Brothers had aided Kristjan's father. The hundreds of dead had yielded a rich harvest in weapons, helmets and armour, which had been distributed between Odenpah and Dorpat. And now Kristjan plundered the latter.

'Might I ask why, lord?' enquired Indrek as his warriors loaded the weapons and armour on two-wheeled carts.

'I am taking them north as a gift,' replied Kristjan.

'A gift for whom, lord?'

'For our allies,' replied Vetseke, smiling.

Indrek had known the Liv prince for only a short time but already disliked him. He disliked the way he had wormed his way into the affections of Kristjan and disliked the fact that he had the support of Novgorod. From bitter experience he knew that Mstislav was no friend of Ungannia.

Indrek ignored Vetseke. 'We may need all the weapons and armour we can get our hands on, lord, if the Sword Brothers mount an offensive against Ungannia this year.'

Kristjan smiled. 'I have thought of that. The Sword Brothers will not be troubling Ungannia this year, or the next or indeed any year. They will be too busy defending Livonia from invasion.'

He looked at the carts with canvas covers over their cargoes filling the courtyard of Toome hill fort. Below was the bustling town of Dorpat that stretched from the hill to the River Emajogi a quarter of a mile to the north.

'You have arranged the barges?' asked Kristjan.

Indrek nodded. 'Yes, lord.'

'Then we will be away. I want to reach the grove as quickly as possible.'

Kristjan and Vetseke walked towards their horses held by soldiers.

'Your people miss you, lord,' Indrek said to Kristjan.

Kristjan hauled himself into the saddle. 'I miss my parents, brother and sisters, Indrek. What would you have me do? Sit here shedding tears of bitterness or avenging their loss?'

He told Vetseke to escort the carts down the hill to the docks on the riverside where the barges were moored. He turned his horse towards the gate but then wheeled it around and nudged it to where Indrek stood before the entrance to the ancient wooden hall.

'My sister is well?'

'She would prefer her brother to be by her side, lord.'

'I leave her in your care, Indrek, and I leave Ungannia in your care.'

He turned his horse and trotted from the courtyard. At the docks two hundred Ungannian warriors on ponies waited for their lord, as did over a hundred Livs and Russians.

The Emajogi, the great 'Mother of Waters', was swollen with melt water though fortunately its current was not raging. Nevertheless, it took the rest of the day to transport the carts, ponies and horses to the northern bank over two hundred yards from the southern shore. Fisherman in flat-bottomed boats cheered the lord of Ungannia and stared silently at the Russians as the barges were towed across the waterway. Other barges bringing goods from Pskov and Novgorod were moored at jetties and the smell of hot tar drifted across the water from the barge yards dotted along the dockside.

Kristjan closed his eyes and breathed in the cool, fresh air after they had crossed the river. The patchwork of peat bogs, rivers and floodplains interwoven with forests of pine, spruce and fir produced an aroma that was unique to northern Ungannia and southern Jerwen. At once both calming and invigorating. Sometimes he wished that he could close his eyes and keep on riding until the end of time.

'Where are we heading, lord?'

Vetseke's voice snapped him out of his pleasant dream.

'To see someone who can magic up an army,' replied Kristjan.

'I thought we were going to see the leaders of those who have been laying siege to Reval.'

Kristjan smiled. 'I may be young, prince, but I know my race. Ungannia has been no friend of the Jerwen, Harrien and Wierlanders of late. If we appear suddenly and without notice they are likely to slit our throats.'

Vetseke shrugged off his concern. 'Surely not, lord. You are Kalju's son, a man who has…'

'My father did not fight at Wolf Rock, prince,' said Kristjan, cutting him off. 'There are many among the Estonians who still see Ungannia as a friend of the Bishop of Riga. Their memory is long. I therefore need the support of someone whose word they trust without question. Whom many believe to be the embodiment of the soul of Estonia itself.'

'Who?' asked Vetseke.

'Rustic.'

No one knew where he came from or how old he was. Some said that he was the father of Rusticus, the brutal deputy of Lembit who had been killed at Wolf Rock with his master. But others dismissed the theory. He had lived in the sacred grove at Kassinurme for as long as anyone could remember, a fat old man wrapped in rags who had the ear of the gods. Kristjan had grown up hearing stories about Rustic. How he prophesised the future, made barren women fertile and imparted wise words to warlords. He had been a part of the fabric of Jerwen for so long that people presumed him to be immortal, which only added to his mystique.

The sacred grove, actually an oblong mound surrounded by ancient trees, was only twenty miles north of Dorpat as the crow flies, though it took the column of carts and riders two days to reach it, being forcing to thread a path through peat bogs and flooded meadows. They passed through a number of villages along the way, women rushing indoors with children clinging to their skirts. At one settlement the men rushed to the track to bar Kristjan's way, forming a ragged shield wall of old men and young boys. But Kristjan rode forward alone and explained who he was and that he was journeying to see Rustic, whereupon the villagers stood aside and let him and his men pass. Many gave the Russians hostile looks for Jerwen bordered Novgorod and many of the old men remembered times when Russian soldiers had raided their villages for slaves and plunder.

'You had better stay here,' Kristjan advised Vetseke when they had reach a great expanse of pine forest three miles beyond where they had encountered the shield wall. 'Rustic does not like foreigners, or so I am told.'

Vetseke looked around. 'How do you know he lives in this forest?'

'Some among my men have visited him and told me the route we should take before we left Dorpat.' Kristjan pointed at the trees. 'Besides, the numbers of ribbons tied to branches has increased since we left the village.

Vetseke saw the white and red ribbons fastened to branches to honour the gods.

'I have been living among the Russians for too long. I had forgotten.'

Kristjan tugged on his horse's reins and nudged him into the trees, between two pines festooned with ribbons.

'You might as well pitch camp here,' he said to Vetseke. 'I might be a while.'

His horse seemed to know the way as it walked along a path meandering through pines, beech trees, the occasional broad oak, red maple and black cherry. The air was so thick with the scent of pine that it was almost overpowering and after a while Kristjan fell into a pleasant stupor. He did not know how long he had been riding through the forest; it seemed like hours. But eventually he came to a crystal clear lake where a figure sat hunched by the water's edge with his back to him. On the other side of the lake, beyond a thin screen of pines, was a grass mound.

'So you have come.'

The voice startled Kristjan somewhat, so calming and silent were the surroundings.

'What do you want, Kristjan, son of Kalju?'

The voice was deep but not aggressive, though he could not put a face to it as the man whom he assumed was Rustic still had his back to him as he fished the lake.

'I have to come to seek advice.'

The man, around five paces away, slowly placed his rod next to him, resting it on a stand fashioned from a branch with two forks. He rose and turned to face Kristjan. He wore a threadbare long woollen brown tunic and a cloak of the same colour around his shoulders. His shoes were made from single pieces of leather. He was certainly overweight, his huge belly making his tunic bulge. His grubby fingers were chubby and his nose resembled a pig's snout. His eyes, also pig like, were clear and piercing.

'Advice or support?' asked Rustic. 'If you came for advice then you would not be accompanied by a host of warriors and carts full of weapons.'

Kristjan wondered how he knew of such things. Perhaps he was a god in human form. He dismissed the idea. No god would inhabit such a grotesque body.

'Do you intend to sit on your horse and interrogate me like one of your slaves?' asked Rustic.

Kristjan blushed and dismounted. Rustic walked up to him until their two faces, one young and handsome, the other old and foul, were inches apart.

'You have the arrogance of youth, young warlord,' said Rustic, 'and yet I see a burning desire for vengeance in your eyes. You seek to avenge the deaths of your parents?'

'And my brother and sisters,' hissed Kristjan.

'And you wish me to aid you in this task?' said Rustic.

'Yes.'

'So in fact you do not seek my advice but wish to enlist me to your cause, young warlord.'

Kristjan snorted in anger and turned away from him. He walked over to a tall pine that had moss wrapped around its trunk. He made to place a hand against it.

'Do not touch the trees,' snapped Rustic. 'They are holy and may not be soiled by your hands. This is a place where men seek union with nature, themselves and their ancestors. It is not a site for a council of war.'

Kristjan turned. 'I apologise, sir. I meant no offence.'

'Tell me the truth,' demanded Rustic, 'want do you want of me?'

Kristjan swallowed. 'Very well. It is no secret that you hold great sway among the people. I wish to wage war against the Sword Brothers. I intend to march north to rally the warriors of Jerwen, Harrien and Wierland to my banner. The carts are loaded with weapons to arm any who would join me.'

'There are many who object to Russians coming into our lands,' said Rustic.

Kristjan shrugged. 'Prince Vetseke offered me his sword and I accepted. He is a Liv and seeks the same thing as me.'

'Which is?'

'To first rid Estonia of Christians and then destroy the land they call Livonia.'

Rustic twisted his misshapen mouth. 'Ambitious aims indeed. Your father allied himself with the Christians. Why do you now turn against them?'

'My father made a mistake and was deceived by the Sword Brothers. He and my mother were killed by their magic.'

Rustic pointed at him. 'Your father deserted the gods and they were angry. Whose magic is stronger, that of the gods who have lived in this land for thousands of years or the Christian god? Your parents angered Uku and so he sent Surm, the God of Death, to claim their lives. He torments them now in Hiiela, the land of the dead.'

These were hard words for Kristjan to hear.

'My parents were good people,' he stated meekly.

'You do them honour, young Kristjan,' said Rustic. 'You have shown respect to the gods and I will ask them to send me a sign to indicate they think your cause is worthy of their support. I will say no more now. You must go.'

'You will not help me free this land, your land, of the heathen invaders?'

Rustic's huge nostrils flared. 'Did you not hear me? I said I would ask the gods regarding the matter. You must go to the sacred forest hill at Paluküla and there await my answer.'

Paluküla was to the northwest, in Harrien and many miles away. It would take up to two weeks to get there.

'To travel there would show your piety to the gods, young Kristjan.'

Rustic saw the horse ambling over to a birch tree.

'If your horse eats anything in this sacred place I will kill it.'

Kristjan raced over to his horse and grabbed its reins. Rustic waved the back of a hand at him to indicate he and his horse should depart. He walked back to his stool and picked up the rod.

'Go to the sacred forest hill, young warlord, and there await the decision of the gods.'

Bitterly disappointed, Kristjan rode back to find his men pitching their tents. He immediately rode to where the Russians were camped and informed Vetseke of the sage's decision. The Liv saw the disappointment in the young man's eyes.

'Priests and mystics are a law unto themselves. You will return to Dorpat?'

Kristjan looked at him, the dozens of campfires and the warriors joking and preparing their meals.

'No. I must show my men that I have faith.'

'If you go to this place for nothing you will be many miles from Ungannia,' said Vetseke. 'It is spring and the Sword Brothers will be marching to the relief of Fellin. We will not be able to help the garrison if we are in Harrien.'

'We must trust the gods,' said Kristjan with conviction.

'I have learned the hard way,' replied Vetseke, 'that the gods are often slow to repay our trust, Kristjan.'

*****

Conrad, Hans and Anton stood in front of Rudolf's oak desk in the master's office. They had been tilting at the rings in full armour when a novice had arrived with a message that all three were to report to Master Rudolf immediately. As a result they were all sweating profusely as they stood to attention in a line.

They held their helmets in the crook of their arms, their foreheads beaded with sweat. Conrad made to pull down the mail coif that covered his head.

'Leave it,' commanded Rudolf.

The master had been attending to clerical matters all morning and was dressed in non-martial attire. Over his linen shirt and woollen breeches he wore a long, dark tunic that reached to his ankles. It had tight-fitting sleeves and was belted at the waist. Rudolf picked up a document and leaned back in his chair.

'Do you know what this is?' he asked Conrad.

'No, master.'

'It is a letter addressed to me from Archdeacon Stefan at Riga. Now aside from one eminent servant of the Holy Church paying his compliments to another, why should my brother the archdeacon suddenly pick up the quill to contact me?'

His question was met by a row of blank expressions.

'Let me explain,' said Rudolf, tossing the letter on the desk. 'The archdeacon is mightily aggrieved that two of his soldiers were recently attacked by members of the order, specifically,' he picked up the letter and perused it, 'Brother Conrad and two of his knavish accomplices from the garrison of Wenden.'

Rudolf pointed at Hans and Anton. 'I assume he is talking of you two?'

Hans smiled. 'Yes, master.'

Anton nodded.

Rudolf's eyes narrowed. 'The archdeacon demands that I surrender you all to his tender mercy. No doubt he wishes to see your hanged bodies dangling from the walls of Riga.'

Hans' eyes opened wide in shock but Conrad was having none of it.

'I was the one who injured the garrison's soldiers, master, Hans and Anton had no part in it.'

'I know that,' replied Rudolf. 'The archdeacon was quite specific regarding your actions. Hamstringing one man and apparently condemning the other with an inability to have children.'

Anton laughed. 'They got off lightly, master.'

'My congratulations, Conrad, not only have you made an enemy of Commander Nordheim, you have also alienated Archdeacon Stefan, his superior. Your list of enemies grows long and impressive.'

'I have no regrets over my actions, master,' said Conrad defiantly. 'I took a vow to defend the weak and the helpless and could not stand by while a young woman was murdered because she refused to lie with a priest.'

Rudolf smashed a fist on the table. 'You are supposed to be the Marshal of Estonia and commander of your army, not some wandering white knight devoted to helping the wretched of humanity. If the order loses you your army of Estonians will fall apart, which will directly affect the fortunes of Livonia and the Sword Brothers.'

Conrad was not to be moved. 'I await your punishment, master, but reiterate that brothers Hans and Anton had no part in the matter.'

'I stand with Conrad,' stated Hans.

'As do I,' insisted Anton.

'How very noble,' mocked Rudolf. 'Fortunately for you I don't give a damn about Archdeacon Stefan and care less about his miserable garrison. I shall inform the archdeacon that the proper form of communication with masters of the order is to first contact the office of the grand master. I will also inform him that I have no authority over the Marshal of Estonia, which is not strictly true but will nonetheless make the matter of punishing him, that is you, Conrad, not my responsibility.'

He saw the three brother knights looking smug.

'However, as you have brought the good name of Wenden into disrepute all of you will spend the next week on latrine duties and mucking out the stables.'

Their expressions changed to ones of indignation. 'But, master,' said Hans.

Rudolf held up a hand. 'The logic is quite straightforward, Brother Hans. You dropped me in the shit so I am doing the same to you. Now all of you get out.'

Outside novices were sweeping the courtyard and heaping piles of horse dung into wheelbarrows. The brother knights looked at each other.

'Say it,' urged Conrad.

'Say what?' said Hans.

'That I should have left well alone at that village,' replied Conrad.

Anton shrugged. 'It doesn't matter now. At least we didn't get flogged.'

'The garrison of Riga should be disbanded,' said Conrad to no one in particular. 'It is Archdeacon Stefan who should be flogged.'

'That's the Bishop of Riga's nephew you're talking of,' Hans cautioned.

Conrad gave his friend a slight smile. 'You know what they say: you can choose your friends but you have no choice when it comes to family.'

'Imps of Satan!'

The novices stopped what they were doing, as did a file of sergeants marching from the dormitory, when the thunderous voice of Abbot Hylas filled the courtyard. Most days the deranged priest could be found mumbling to himself in the chapel or wandering in the grounds of the castle's outer perimeter. Children and women avoided him and the mercenaries teased him. But mostly he was left to his own devices, wandering into the kitchens to be fed at breakfast, lunch and supper. He adored Ilona, the person who had nursed his body when he had returned from Saccalia after being tortured by Lembit. He saw the raven-haired beauty as the Virgin Mary in human form. For some reason he hated Conrad and his friends, perhaps because it had been they who had found him wandering in the wild after his terrible ordeal. The wooden crucifixes that hung around his neck jangled as he stormed over, his eyes bulging.

'You are all going to die!' he screamed. 'The pit of hell awaits you. Blasphemers!'

He stopped a few feet away from Conrad and pointed a finger at him.

'You are Satan's chief imp, fornicator. The mark of Cain is upon you. I will witness your death and the crows feasting on your flesh, child of a devil's whore.'

That was enough for Conrad. He marched up to Hylas and struck the mad priest across the face with the back of his hand, sending him sprawling on the cobblestones. The novices and sergeants cheered and whistled. Conrad smiled and then had cause to regret his actions when Master Rudolf exited his hall.

'Get back to your work,' Rudolf shouted at the novices as the sergeants quickly carried on marching towards the gatehouse.

Within seconds he was standing before Conrad.

'Are you going to strike me as well?'

Conrad felt himself starting to blush. 'No, master.'

Rudolf assisted the groaning Hylas to his feet and then struck Conrad in the face with the back of his hand.

'Hurts, doesn't it. All of you now have two weeks on latrine duties, starting immediately.'

They sheepishly bowed their heads at Rudolf and began walking towards the stables where their horses waited to be cooled down and brushed. Conrad caught the eye of the mad Hylas, blood at the corner of his mouth.

'Imp,' the lunatic sneered.

*****

It took two weeks for Kristjan's army to reach the sacred forest hill at Paluküla, the highest point in northern Estonia. The land was still wet after the melting of the snows and ice but it was blossoming into life, the desolate white of the winter giving way to hues of greens, red and yellows with the arrival of spring. Vetseke's Livs and Russians grumbled that they were heading in the wrong direction but the young Ungannian leader had the look of a man on a mission and so the prince said nothing. Most days he and his men assisted the carts in travelling along waterlogged tracks and through swollen streams. It was tiresome work but the Ungannians appreciated their help and the mood among the warriors was positive. Everyone had heard of Rustic and they believed that their leader had been given a message from the gods. Vetseke knew otherwise but kept his thoughts to himself. One thing was certain: Kristjan would need more men if he was serious about fighting the Sword Brothers. A lot more men.

The sacred hill itself was larger than he had expected, a great tree-covered mound spread over sixty acres. Surrounded by peat bogs, birch forests and clear sparkling streams, the hill itself was dotted with sacred limes, oaks, alders, birch and lindens. There was a small village on its southern side, a collection of wooden huts that were the lodgings of those who protected the site – the keepers of the sacred hill.

Kristjan rode with Vetseke into the village, in truth nothing more than a dozen huts, a large barn and several piles of firewood. They halted in the centre of the settlement and looked around. There were no people, no animals and no insects. Nothing.

'Looks deserted,' observed Vetseke.

'Perhaps there is another village nearby,' said Kristjan.

'So, you have come.'

The heads of the two horses reared up in alarm as the sharp voice pierced the air. They swung in the saddle to see the source of the voice behind them. It was a tall individual in a loose-fitting white robe with a hood that covered his head. They could only see his clean-shaven chin and lips. Kristjan was slightly unnerved by his sudden appearance and hidden face.

'Welcome, Kristjan, son of Kalju, we have been expecting you.'

'We?' said Vetseke, looking around and seeing no one.

'The friend of the Russians must leave,' commanded the keeper, 'his presence violates this sacred place.'

Vetseke was a Liv and respected the old religion but he was still a prince and used to giving orders, not taking them. He turned his horse to face the keeper and casually drew his sword. He was about to issue a veiled threat when he suddenly shouted and threw his sword to the ground. Kristjan looked at him in confusion. Vetseke, flustered, smiled weakly at him.

'Damnedest thing. For a moment I thought I was holding a hissing snake.'

'Leave your horse here, Kristjan, son of Kalju,' said the keeper, who suddenly turned and began walking towards the hill. 'You will not need it.'

Kristjan shrugged, handed the reins to Vetseke and dismounted.

'Make camp nearby,' he said to Vetseke. 'I will not be long.'

He followed the keeper out of the village to the foot of the hill, which consisted of a number of grass-covered ridges, making the climb easy.

'Do not touch the trees,' commanded the keeper, 'they are sacred.'

The hill could be seen from miles around but in truth it was not particularly high and soon Kristjan found himself on its tree-covered summit threading a path between oaks that could have been as old as the earth itself. Their gnarled trunks were huge, their branches twisted into strange shapes.

The keeper said nothing despite Kristjan's attempts to engage him in conversation. After a while he gave up trying and the pair walked on in silence. He became aware that not only was there an absence of conversation but also of wildlife. No woodpeckers tapping or tits cheeping. No warblers, corncrakes, rose finches. Nothing. He felt the hairs on the back of his neck stand up, had goose bumps on his arms and his mouth became dry. The silence was oppressive, as though nature had fled from this place to get away from the gods that inhabited it. He became aware of the thumping heart in his chest. On they went, past lindens decorated with red ribbons, silver earrings and bronze bracelets – offerings to the gods.

Eventually they came to a copse of lindens, all the trees having dark fissured bark, their trunks covered in lichen. The keeper stopped.

'We are here.'

He pointed to a rather stunted linden, obviously very old, where a large, inverted tear-shaped round grey object nestled in one of the lower branches.

'You want the help of Taara?'

Taara was the God of War and Kristjan knew that lindens were the trees of the deity. He nodded.

The keeper pointed at the round object. 'Then tear that apart and retrieve the silver torc that lies within and you will have Taara's blessing and protection. But before you do know this: Taara will know your true aims and will determine whether they are noble or selfish. You may deceive yourself and your fellow man but you cannot deceive the gods.'

Kristjan was delighted. Rustic had obviously given his blessing to his venture and now all he had to do was break apart some sort of foliage to get a silver token of the God of War. He walked over to the linden tree and stopped when he saw the insects buzzing around. A hornets' nest!

He looked back at the keeper who stood motionless, the hood still covering his face.

'You think Taara gives his help cheaply, Kristjan, son of Kalju? You must prove to him that you are worthy of fighting in his name.'

He looked at the hornet's nest. He had been taught that they were better left alone for to disturb one was to invite the wrath of a thousand stinging demons. He had seen animals and people killed in such attacks, their lifeless bodies swollen and red. He hesitated.

'There is no shame in refusing the task,' said the keeper. 'Only those who are worthy have the courage to attempt what lesser men fear.'

Kristjan remembered the terrible deaths of his parents and sisters, the arrogance and treachery of the Sword Brothers and the dozens of warriors who had marched to this place. He breathed deeply to compose himself and drew himself up.

'Remove your armour,' said the keeper.

Kristjan was shocked. 'My armour?'

'Taara will be your protection, unless you do not believe in his powers.'

This was madness. He knew he would get stung but at least his armour would afford him some protection. He sighed and removed the mail armour, dropping it to the ground.

'Your tunic as well,' commanded the keeper.

Kristjan shook his head. The hornets would be able to sting through the thin material with ease anyway, not to mention his face, neck and hands.

He reflected that he might follow his mother, father, brother and sisters into the afterlife, leaving his disfigured sister as the only surviving member of his family. But, for better or ill, he had come to this place and would not turn back now. He concentrated on the nest, which seemed calm with only a few hornets flying around it. He closed his eyes and asked Taara for protection, then raced forward.

The nest was resting on a branch around five feet off the ground and so he was able to smash his fist into it to knock it to the ground. It fell on the soft earth and he ducked under the branch and drove his boot into the soft, crumbly material. He was elated to see a glint of metal and bent down to retrieve the silver torc, and was then engulfed by a swarm of enraged hornets.

The first thing he experienced were not stings but noise, an angry buzzing that grew in intensity until he thought his ears would burst. The volume of the humming got louder and louder as the insects became more and more enraged. He clutched the torc in his hand and stood. And then pain engulfed him. It was not one or two or even a number of stings but an intense heat that originated in his hands and then crept up his arms as the hornets stung him viciously. It was as if his limbs were being slowly immersed in boiling hot water. It took all his willpower to keep hold of the torc as the insects stung his chest, back, legs, neck and face.

He closed his eyes as searing pain was inflicted on his whole body. He screamed out loud as he staggered away and then tried to run to get away from the hornets. But his efforts were in vain as they kept on stinging him and every part of his body cried out for mercy. He closed his eyes to protect them as his eyelids were repeatedly stung. He tried to swat away his tiny tormentors but this enraged the hornets even more and resulted in more stings. It was as if a thousand red-hot pincers were pulling his body apart. He could no longer scream or even wail, just emit pitiful low moans as his body was tortured beyond endurance. He tried to keep hold of the torc as he fell to his knees and then collapsed face-first on the ground. The last thing he remembered before passing out was the accursed buzzing in his ears.

He could not open his eyes when he regained consciousness, so swollen were his eyelids. His whole body was aflame with itching and pain. Had he been able to see he would have viewed laid out on a bed a naked body that was almost completely red, with a thousand wheals surrounding each tiny puncture denoting a hornet's sting. He could feel the pain that occupied every muscle and bone of his body and tried hard not to cry out in agony. But he was also aware of cool relief being applied on parts of his frame.

The keepers worked fast, applying fresh bandages that had been soaked in vinegar for at least fifteen minutes to the most injured parts of his flesh. He did not know how many of them worked around his bed but their touch was tender and their skill high. They crushed fresh basil leaves to release the herb's natural oils and pressed it gently on to a sting to draw the poison. After a day of intensive treatment, during which he was turned frequently so the wheals on his back could be treated, he began to feel partly alive as opposed to being roasted over a fire.

'The gods are with you, Kristjan,' he heard, the voice female and soothing.

Gentle fingers applied honey to each sting to calm the skin around it and all the time sweet reassuring voices told him that he would live and not be scarred. On the second day he was able to open his eyes, to see four young women in pure white robes attending him. One lifted his head so he could drink water from a cup while the others washed and treated his athletic body. On the third day the pain and swelling had subsided and the crushed basil relieved his itching. He noticed that all the female keepers had blonde hair, blue eyes and flawless skin. They smiled sweetly and touched him with the gentleness of forest nymphs and his body responded. First by healing itself and then being aroused as he observed the shape of their breasts and the curves of their hips and buttocks. They washed every inch of him and giggled when his manhood responded.

'Your strength returns, Kristjan,' said one as she washed his inner thigh with a soft cloth.

He mumbled an apology and redness returned to his cheeks, though it was not the fire of hornet poison but embarrassment as he blushed.

'You should not be ashamed of your body,' she told him, her touch doing nothing to dampen his now throbbing manhood. 'The gods have given you a body that is strong and beautiful. You should be proud of it.'

Nevertheless, the next day he asked for a long tunic to cover his modesty and was given a pair of linen undergarments instead. The keepers informed him that his body needed air to recover and opened the shutters of the hut he was lodged in. Village huts were usually dusty, dim places but this abode was clean, spacious and remarkably airy. The result was that by the sixth day he was able to stand and put on his clothes, minus his old leggings and shirt that had been burnt. He was given fresh breeches and a new shirt and walked into the spring sunshine a man reborn.

Vetseke and two of his senior chiefs came to him, relieved and delighted that he still lived after his ordeal. He noticed that they studied his face and neck for any scars or blemishes.

'Not a mark on you,' admired Vetseke.

'Was it very terrible, lord?' asked one of his bearded chiefs.

'Like being thrown on a raging fire,' he answered.

'This belongs to you, Kristjan, son of Kalju.'

He turned to see the faceless keeper with the hood holding the silver torc that he had nearly died for held in his right hand. The man lifted his arm and held out the prize.

'The torc of Taara is yours, Kristjan, son of Kalju. Your prayers have been answered.'

Kristjan took the silver band and placed it around his neck, expecting the sky to crack with thunder. Nothing happened. Vetseke and the chiefs looked around at the empty village, expecting to see an army of warriors spring from the ground. For that is what they came for. Instead a black cat walked nonchalantly in front of them, turned its head to give them a disapproving stare, before wandering off.

'Your life is over as Kristjan,' said the keeper. 'Just as Taara sent the hornets to cleanse your spirit with their stings so must you now go as poison among your enemies. Henceforth your name is Murk.'

'Venom,' said one of the chiefs.

'Your poison must strike down the wolf,' stated the keeper.

'I do not understand,' said Kristjan.

He detected the semblance of a smile on the keeper's lips. 'You will.'

'Eat well today, young lord,' said the keeper, 'and sleep well tonight. Tomorrow climb the sacred hill once more and turn your eyes to the east. Then you will have your answer.'

'What does that mean?' asked Vetseke as all of them instinctively gazed eastwards. To see nothing except trees and sky. Kristjan turned back to ask the keeper another question but he was not there, having seemingly vanished into thin air.

He hardly slept at all that night and was attired in his armour before the dawn broke. As guards wrapped in cloaks marched up and down to keep themselves warm he walked from his tent towards the sacred forest hill. Ponies were tied to wooden rails and bleary eyed men emerged from their shelters with aching limbs to throw damp firewood on the barely warm embers of campfires. He left the camp and walked across the meadow at the foot of the hill, his boots soaked by the early morning dew. It may have been spring but the land was still damp and so the hill was wrapped in a thick mist that would take a while for the sun that was now emerging in the east to burn away. He ascended the hill, occasionally slipping on the wet grass, being careful not to disturb the sodden branches of the trees as he went. He kept a hand on the hilt of his sword and pulled the woollen hat down over his ears to keep them warm. After half an hour he was at the edge of a thicket of alders and halted. He pulled the cloak around himself and waited, for what he was not sure.

'Murk,' he muttered.

A strange choice of a name, he mused. He touched the torc around his neck. The coolness of the metal reassured him. He wondered if the keepers set such a task for every visitor to the hill. He dismissed the idea. Too many travellers would die from hornet stings. He also wondered about the beautiful female keepers who had restored his health. Were they married? To have one as a wife would be a gift from the gods indeed.

Kristjan filled his head with these thoughts as the sun climbed slowly into the sky and warmed the earth. To the south was his camp where men were cooking porridge over a myriad of fires that were replacing the mist with smoke. To the west were the forests and meadows of Harrien and Rotalia, and beyond those kingdoms the island of Oesel. He looked around for any signs of life but saw only trees, shrubs and flowers. The hill appeared to be empty.

After a while he sat on the ground and used an alder as a back support, first checking that there were no hornet nests in its branches. His stomach rumbled; he should have eaten something before he left camp. He drew his knees up to his chest, rested his chin on them and closed his eyes.

He thought he had been asleep for only a few minutes but the position of the sun indicated that it was mid-morning. He rose to his feet and stretched out his arms and back. Parts of his body were still sensitive and he winced when his scabbard brushed against his left leg. Then all thoughts of pain and hunger left him as he looked east and saw Taara's gift. The tracks and meadows were filled with groups of men on foot and riding ponies, streams of humanity making their way towards the sacred forest hill. He clenched his fists and gave a shout of triumph. The sun glinted off hundreds of whetted spear points and the blades of axes tucked into belts. There were also lines of men who had no weapons. He smiled to himself. They would be furnished from the supplies he had brought from Dorpat. Among the groups of warriors were carts and standards displaying the emblems of the region they had travelled from: the lynx of Harrien, the boar of Wierland and the bear of Jerwen.

Estonia had rallied to his banner.

*****

The brother knights looked at each other and then at the blonde-haired Estonian warrior standing by the side of Conrad. The weekly meeting of the twelve brothers was usually a mundane affair devoted to either financial or administrative matters. But this meeting was different. A rider had arrived from Hillar in Rotalia to inform Conrad that a new army had arisen in Estonia. Worryingly, Hillar reported that a few of his men, mostly Jerwen, had deserted to join Kristjan.

'It's Lembit all over again,' said Henke, unconcerned, 'and we all know what happened to him.'

He smiled at Conrad. 'Looks like you have a rival, Lord Marshal of Estonia.'

'I killed Lembit,' replied Conrad, 'I can do the same to Kristjan.'

'Nevertheless,' said Rudolf, 'this is a dangerous development. He already holds Fellin and another victory might convince all of Estonia to join his cause.'

'Is that likely?' asked Walter

Conrad looked at the warrior. 'Tell them what you have heard.'

The man spoke in his native tongue, which was understood by all those present. Even Hans, who could not read or write, had an intimate knowledge of the Estonian language as well as the Liv tongue, and also knew a smattering of Russian.

'Kristjan marched his army to the holy site at Palukūla.'

Henke sighed. 'Where in the name of all that's holy is that?'

'In Harrien, lord,' replied the warrior.

'He is no lord,' said Conrad.

'I like to think of myself as a lord of war,' retorted Henke, 'first among equals in the order.'

Conrad laughed and shook his head. Henke's brow furrowed.

'I would be more than willing to prove this to you in single combat, *brother*.'

'Enough,' snapped Rudolf. He looked at the warrior. 'Continue.'

'The keepers of the sacred forest hill have given him the name Murk and the rumour is that Taara himself fights alongside him,' the warrior stated.

'Who is Taara?' enquired Walter as Henke yawned.

'The Estonian God of War,' replied Conrad.

'This Kristjan has a large army?' asked Rudolf.

The warrior nodded.

'He will try to take Lehola, master,' said Conrad, 'and after that will invade Livonia.'

'We need to nip this in the bud,' stated Rudolf, 'both to help Sir Richard and to prevent a general conflagration in Estonia.'

Henke was bemused. 'When the bishop arrives with an army we can crush this Kristjan, retake Fellin and conquer Estonia.'

'There are also Russians among Kristjan's forces,' said Conrad.

There were murmurs of concern around the table. If Kristjan had allied himself with Novgorod the consequences for Livonia could be grim.

'That settles it,' said Rudolf. 'We cannot wait for Bishop Albert to arrive. I will contact Kremon and Segewold and order their garrisons here. In addition, I will request that Fricis sends Rameke and a sizeable contingent of warriors to Wenden to join with us. Then we will march north and deal with this Kristjan. Conrad, order your men in Rotalia to march south to join us.'

'Yes, master,' replied Conrad.

'No getting married for Rameke, then,' whispered Hans to his friend.

There was a knock at the door to the main chamber of the master's hall.

'Come,' ordered Rudolf.

A sergeant entered, marched up to Rudolf and saluted.

'Forgive the interruption, master, but there is a contingent of the garrison of Riga at the outer gates requesting entry.'

A circle of confused faces looked at each other.

'The garrison of Riga?' smirked Henke. 'Perhaps they have come to support your new campaign, Rudolf.'

'What business are they on?' Rudolf asked the sergeant.

'I do not know, master. Their commander is insistent that he speaks to you on a matter of some urgency.'

'Must be important to march all the way here,' said Walter.

'Perhaps Archdeacon Stefan has run out of young boys and wants to know if Wenden has any to spare,' opined Henke.

The brother knights laughed but Rudolf was not amused.

'Quiet. This is no laughing matter. Allow them in,' he told the sergeant.

The man saluted and left, closing the door behind him.

Conrad thought it unusual but gave it no more thought as Rudolf dismissed them and he, Hans and Anton left the master's hall and made their way to the armoury. Their two-week punishment had been completed and now they could concentrate on preparing for the march north to relieve Lehola and deal with Kristjan.

'Who would have thought that bad-tempered boy at Odenpah would turn out to be a threat to Livonia,' remarked Hans.

'Who indeed,' replied Conrad.

He stopped when the party from Riga marched across the drawbridge, through the gatehouse and into the courtyard. There were five riders followed by half a dozen crossbowmen and ten spearman, all wearing red, their surcoats and gambesons sporting the gold cross keys emblem of Riga.

'Halt' called their commander who wore an open-faced helmet.

'I recognise him,' said Anton.

'As do I,' added Conrad.

It was the man who had been escorting Bishop Hermann on the day they had rescued the Liv girl from the villagers.

'I have a bad feeling about this,' said Hans.

Rudolf, Walter and the other brother knights had also exited the master's hall and observed the soldiers as they stood behind their commander.

'What business brings you to Wenden?' called Rudolf.

The commander, who had registered Conrad's presence, nudged his horse forward.

'I am Captain Clausse here on official business of Archdeacon Stefan, Governor of Riga, Keeper of the Official Seal and Lord of all Livonia in Bishop Albert's absence.'

Laughter echoed around the courtyard as the brother knights, except Walter who was a sticker for correct procedure, heaped derision on Stefan's ludicrous claim to be ruler of Livonia.

'Surely you missed out Lord High Warden of the Privy,' mocked Henke, which was followed by more laughter.

Captain Clausse was not laughing as he reached into a saddlebag and pulled out a document with a wax seal.

'This is for Master Rudolf,' he said firmly.

'Get off your horse, captain,' replied Rudolf menacingly as the laughter died down.

Clausse stared at the tall, athletic Rudolf. 'You are Master Rudolf?'

Rudolf folded his arms across his chest. 'It is considered good manners for guests to dismount when they are invited into my castle.'

Clausse took a deep breath and got off his horse. He walked over to Rudolf, saluted and handed him the document.

'This an arrest warrant for one Conrad Wolff, a brother knight of this garrison. We are to take him back to Riga immediately.'

The brother knights began laughing again but Rudolf told them to be silent. Walter was appalled by the warrant.

'Archdeacon Stefan has no jurisdiction over the Sword Brothers. They are answerable to Bishop Albert only.'

Rudolf tilted his head at Walter.

'My deputy, Brother Walter, is a keen student of the law. Your warrant has no authority here.'

Conrad and his two friends had ambled over to where Clausse faced Rudolf. The captain pointed the document at him.

'He injured two of my men and interfered in a legally sanctioned execution. I will not be leaving without him.'

Rudolf held out his hand so Clausse could give him the document, which he duly did. The master ripped it in two and threw the parts to the ground.

'Turn around, get back on your horse, leave this castle with your men and do not look back.'

Clausse issued a haughty laugh. 'Do you not see the armed men at my back, Master Rudolf? I will only be leaving when that criminal,' he pointed at Conrad, 'is bound and being dragged along by my horse.'

The brother knights slowly began to move apart to give themselves space to manoeuvre. Henke stepped forward and offered Clausse his hand.

'Conrad Wolff is not worth fighting over, captain. Will you take my hand by way of an apology?'

Clausse, reassured by the friendly gesture, took Henke's hand. Henke smiled and tightened his grip on the captain's hand. Clausse looked discomfited, confused and then angry as Henke held his gaze, suddenly lurching forward to begin chewing off the captain's nose. Clausse screamed in pain as Henke bit deep into the captain's now bloody nose.

The brother knights drew their swords and raced forward, Conrad plunging his sword into the horse of one of the garrison. There was a series of wicked snaps and hisses as the crossbowmen on the battlements of the gatehouse shot at their Rigan counterparts. The latter tried to load their crossbows to shoot back but three had been felled before loosing a single bolt. The alarm bell began to ring and sergeants sprinted from the dormitory and armoury. One threw a spear that struck one of the horses, which reared up and threw its rider. Hans was on him in an instant, plunging the point of his sword into his throat.

Conrad pulled his dagger as the soldier that he had unhorsed sprang to his feet and directed an overhead strike with his sword. Conrad stepped back to avoid the blow and leapt to the left to attack the man's unguarded right side. He whipped his sword from left to right to make a diagonal cut to the soldier's arm, the edge of his blade slicing open the chainmail at the top of his arm. The soldier thrust his sword forward to plunge the point into Conrad's belly but the brother knight used his dagger to sweep the blade away and then launched his own thrust. This attack was devastatingly effective, the point of his sword striking the man's neck in a blur of a movement. The strike did not have his full bodyweight behind it but the point was razor sharp and it pierced flesh with ease. Nor did it kill, but within seconds blood was spurting from the wound like a tiny fountain.

Conrad moved around him as the soldier tucked his shield tight to his body and attempted to match the brother knight's movements. But he was losing a lot of blood and Conrad was like an angry hornet, darting in and out to slice his hamstring, calf and thigh. When the latter was cut he yelped and went down on one knee. He was beaten and threw his sword on the cobbles to surrender, just at the moment Conrad stepped forward and slashed his sword diagonally across his opponent's neck, severing the windpipe. The man gurgled as a huge red fountain shot from his neck and he pitched forward on to the stones.

The courtyard was the scene of a plethora of individual combats, with spearmen battling brother knights and the occasional crossbow bolt hissing through the air. The shooters on the battlements had desisted their activities now that brother knights and sergeants were weaving around their targets. More sergeants came from the dormitory in answer to the alarm bell but their addition was not needed. The Rigan spearmen, trained to fight as part of a unit of soldiers, were being cut down by the better-trained and motivated brother knights.

Conrad turned when he heard footsteps on the cobbles behind him and saw Abbot Hylas coming towards him, clutching one of the crucifixes that hung around his neck in front of him.

'Imp of Satan, I curse you.'

'Get back to the chapel, abbot,' Conrad told him.

But Hylas had fire in his eyes and carried on advancing. Conrad had no time for him as a spearman thrust his lance at him, the brother knight leaping back to take his belly beyond the reach of the spear point.

'Kill him, avenging angel!' screamed Hylas at the spearman as Conrad feinted left and then right as the soldier jabbed his spear at him. He held his almond-shaped shield on his left side and so Conrad swung his sword at the man's head to allow him to dart right. The spearman swivelled and thrust his weapon forward – straight into Abbot Hylas' guts. The abbot gasped in surprise, the soldier froze and Conrad struck. He jumped forward, twisted his sword and drove one of its cross guards into the soldier's eye socket. The man shrieked in agony, dropped his spear and died when Conrad plunged his dagger into his other eye socket.

He sprang back and grabbed the faltering Hylas, just at the moment a crossbow bolt slammed into the churchman's side. He groaned and became a dead weight as his life seeped away.

'Kill him,' Conrad screamed at Hans, pointing his sword at the crossbowman who was frantically reloading.

Hans rushed forward just as the crossbowman placed a bolt in the stock of his weapon. He looked up to see Hans swing the sword he was holding with both hands horizontally at him. The blade flashed, the metal cut deep into his neck and his head was detached from its body. Conrad looked around and saw that the fight was over. All but one of the men from Riga were dead, along with one sergeant who had been shot by a crossbowman. Two brother knights had been injured, though not seriously, and three horses had been cut down.

Henke stepped back and spat part of Clausse's nose from his mouth. His face and surcoat were smeared with blood, none of it his own. The captain staggered back and fell on to his back groaning loudly, clutching at what remained of his nose.

Rudolf, bloody sword in hand, walked over to Henke.

'Look at the state of you. Get that mess cleaned off your face and go to the laundry to collect a new surcoat. You are supposed to be a Sword Brother.'

Henke grinned to reveal teeth coated with blood. 'What about him?'

He nodded at Clausse.

Rudolf sighed. 'Lukas.'

Brother Lukas, expert swordsman that he was, had amused himself against the Rigans by fighting with a mace in one hand and an axe in another. He now tossed the latter to Rudolf. The master stood astride the prostrate Clausse, gripped the axe with both hands and brought it down hard on the captain's neck, decapitating him.

Rudolf threw the axe back to Lukas. 'What about him?'

The master looked around as Conrad, Hans and Anton shook hands and grinned at each other. Walter was kneeling by the body of Abbot Hylas, deep in prayer. Conrad walked over to Rudolf.

'Thank you, master, for defending me.'

Rudolf slapped him on the arm. 'Like I said, Conrad, the Governor of Riga has no authority over the Sword Brothers. Arrogant little toad. He dares to send an armed gang to my castle to demand that I surrender one of my men. I am within my rights to go to Riga and disembowel him. Lucky for him that I am a reasonable man.'

Conrad looked at the red-clothed corpses that were being hurled into carts brought into the courtyard from the wagon park below the castle.

'Most reasonable,' agreed Conrad.

Chapter 7

Schwerin Castle had originally been a pagan timber fort on an island in Lake Schwerin, twenty-five miles east of Lübeck. But the pagans had been defeated and their fort destroyed by the great crusader Henry the Lion, who had founded not only a stone castle on the site but also a city nearby. The island the castle stood on was reached by a narrow causeway, which often flooded in the winter. Over time the causeway was raised and reinforced so the castle could be accessed all year round. But at the same time the castle itself was strengthened and enlarged so that it became a formidable fortress. The causeway ended at a stone barbican, which was entered via a drawbridge, a moat having been dug in front of it. The barbican in turn led to the castle's gatehouse, the latter also having a drawbridge. In this way an attacker would have to cross two moats before reaching the castle's thick walls.

Count Henry of Schwerin had often considered King Valdemar to be lucky that he did not have to assault his mighty fortress during the time when he had been his enemy. The count and his brother had been forced to retreat south following a defeat at the hands of the Danes. His castle had been denuded of its garrison and had surrendered without a fight. Valdemar had allowed 'Henry the Black' to return to his home in return for his fealty and the promise that henceforth he would serve the Danish king. But it had been an uneasy alliance. On one side arrogance and overbearance, on the other resentment and a barely concealed desire for vengeance.

'I have to say, count,' remarked Valdemar, 'that your table never ceases to amaze me with its varieties of meat and fish dishes.'

It had been some time since the yellow griffin banner of Schwerin had flown beside that bearing the three blue lions of Denmark above the castle's mighty square keep. But today the two flags fluttered in the May wind against the blue backdrop of the lake.

'The lake is rich in pike, bream, perch and eels, majesty,' smiled the count, 'and the surrounding woods are home to many wild boar and deer.'

Valdemar nodded approvingly at the fare heaped on the great table that was raised on a dais. A small army of pages and servants were serving the king, his eldest son Valdemar the Young, the count's brother Gunzelin, Archbishop Andrew of Lund, Bishop Nicholas of Schleswig and Bishop Peter of Roskilde. No women were present out of respect for the fact that the king's wife had died two years earlier and he had yet to choose a replacement.

'A lavish feast indeed,' said Archbishop Andrew. 'The Lord has been bountiful.'

The count could barely hide his contempt as the churchmen gorged themselves to fill their fat bellies. But he had to admit that his cooks had surpassed themselves. The first course had comprised a civet of hare, a quarter of stag, a stuffed chicken and a loin of veal. Next came silver platters holding roasted roe deer, capons, chickens, pigeons and hard-boiled eggs. He ate a small portion of each out of politeness but the prelates shoved food into their mouths as though it was their last meal. How he would like to make that a reality.

'So,' said the king, washing his hands in a brass bowl filled with warm water held by a page, 'how goes the assembly of my German vassals, Count Henry? I am eager to get back to Estonia to wash my sword in pagan blood. I have already despatched reinforcements to the garrison of Reval that will suffice to hold the pagans at bay until I arrive with my army.'

The prelates were nodding and drinking greedily from their silver chalices. The wine the pages were serving was among the finest in all Europe, a white wine produced by the monks at the Cistercian Abbey at Eberbach. It was supposed to be sipped so it could be appreciated more fully. But the churchmen drank it like thirsty men guzzle water.

Beeswax candles mounted on candelabra hanging from the vaulted ceiling cast the great hall in a pale light. Valdemar's face looked unusually long in the candle glow, and it was about to become very glum.

'There is no assembly of German vassals, majesty,' replied Count Henry.

Valdemar stopped eating the pie with a filling of cooked starlings. Bishop Nicholas belched and apologised.

'No German vassals?' said the king. 'Explain yourself.'

Henry sniffed his white wine and then took a sip. Delicious.

'Interesting word: vassal,' the count mused. 'The subordination of one to another.'

One by one the churchmen stopped eating and drinking and looked at Count Henry. Gunzelin continued picking at his roast pigeon.

'How long has it been now,' asked Henry, 'since the lords of northern Germany have been forced to bend their knees to you, majesty?'

'Your tone is impertinent, Count Henry,' snarled the king.

'He should be whipped for his insolence,' said the king's son who in physical appearance resembled his father.

The count ignored the boy. 'To answer your question, majesty, concerning your vassals. They have decided to be vassals no more, being tired of shedding their blood in Danish service.'

The bishops' mouths dropped open at these words.

Valdemar jumped to his feet. 'Guards!'

Gunzelin, his mouth full, looked at his brother and shook his head. The king stood and looked smugly at Count Henry as a file of soldiers marched into the room.

'You will pay a heavy price for your insolence, count,' snapped the king.

Henry gently dabbed his lips with a cloth offered him by a page.

319

'You may be right. But not today.'

Valdemar turned to order the guards to take the count and his brother to the cells but saw that they wore not the livery of Denmark but the yellow griffin of Schwerin.

'Your guards have been disarmed and locked in the cells, majesty,' stated Henry calmly. 'Along with the members of your entourage.'

The guards stood around the table, their swords in their scabbards. The prelates looked at each other nervously as Gunzelin smiled at Archbishop Andrew and took a large gulp of his wine.

Valdemar continued to stand as Henry leaned back in his chair.

'I did consider reasoning with you, majesty,' continued the count, 'but then remembered that reason is not a quality that you possess.'

'You will die for this, Count Henry,' threatened Valdemar.

'Everyone dies,' said Gunzelin, 'even kings.'

'Count Henry,' said Archbishop Andrew nervously, 'what you say is treason.'

'I am aware of the gravity of what is coming out of my mouth, archbishop,' replied the count, 'but necessity gives me no choice.'

'What necessity?' mocked Valdemar.

'The necessity of saving northern Germany from the endless wars that you embroil it in,' replied Henry. 'I give you a choice, Valdemar of Denmark. Renounce your claims on northern Germany and you may return to your domains.'

'I will never renounce the lands that God has bequeathed me,' seethed Valdemar.

'In that case you and your son will be conveyed to Dannenberg Castle, a comfortable residence provided by my ally the Duke of Saxony, where you will remain until you see sense.'

'You would not dare,' said the king.

Gunzelin rose, pointed at the commander of the guards who ordered his men to 'escort' the king and his son from the hall.

'You are an arse,' spat the boy as two guards seized his arms and hauled him away. Bishop Peter was ashen faced as the king and his son were manhandled away.

'You have done a terrible thing,' Archbishop Andrew told Henry.

'Perhaps, archbishop,' retorted Henry, 'but I have the support of Saxony, Pomerania, Lusatia and Meissen.'

'If northern Germany is fatally weakened the nobles of the south will bring their armies here and plunder it,' said Gunzelin. 'We cannot allow that.'

'Bishop Albert is already raising men to take the cross in Livonia,' said Count Henry. 'Someone has to remain behind to protect the towns and villages from mercenary bands.'

'You use that to justify violating the body of a king?' said Archbishop Andrew.

'Believe me, archbishop,' said Gunzelin, 'if we had wanted to violate his body we would have killed him while out hunting today.'

The wine had obviously fortified the churchman because he now stood and gave Count Henry a stare of steel.

'And what do you propose to do with us?'

'You are free to go back to Denmark,' Count Henry told him, 'along with the king's disarmed guards and his entourage.'

Bishop Nicholas closed his eyes and sighed with relief.

'But before you go,' said Gunzelin, 'we have presents for you.'

He pointed at one of the guards. The man walked forward with three wooden clubs held in his arms. He walked up to Archbishop Andrew and offered the clubs.

'Take one,' ordered Gunzelin.

The archbishop, confused, took one of the clubs. The guard then offered one each to Bishop Peter and Bishop Nicholas, who were likewise told to take one.

'Now, your eminences,' smiled Count Henry, 'I know that the Holy Church forbids its priests from spilling blood, so should you feel the need to take the cross in Estonia, you can do so with those clubs without fear of shedding pagan blood.'

Archbishop Andrew threw his club onto the rush mats that covered the floor.

'You blaspheme.'

'And you are a hypocrite,' said Henry. 'Now get out, all of you.'

'But Count Henry,' pleaded Bishop Peter, 'what of Reval and the crusade in Estonia?'

Henry shrugged. 'What of them?'

*****

There was no time to reflect on the gravity of what had happened at Wenden because riders sent by Hillar in Rotalia brought grim news.

'Kristjan is marching south.'

'Marching south?' Rudolf leaned back in his chair. 'I thought he would go to Lehola and lay siege to it, thus giving us time to march to its relief.'

He pointed at the chair on the other side of his desk.

'Take the weight off your feet, Conrad.'

The brother knight sat. 'The rumour is that Kristjan has raised a great army, master.'

'An army of Estonians?' queried Rudolf. Conrad nodded.

'And how does this sit with your Estonians?'

'The majority will remain loyal, master, especially the Rotalians who now have their homeland back.'

'What we need is to inflict a defeat on Kristjan to show Estonia that he is not some sort of liberator,' said Rudolf. 'So in that respect his marching towards us serves our purpose, to a degree. However, should he prevail then I fear his stature will rise markedly. As soon as Rameke arrives with his men we will march north.'

323

'Masters Bertram and Mathias will be joining us?' asked Conrad, thinking of the reportedly high numbers that had rallied to Kristjan.

Rudolf nodded. 'Let's see how this Kristjan stands up against armoured horsemen. What is he like?'

Conrad paused to recollect his memories of the time when he had been at Odenpah and had saved the life of a slave girl from Kristjan's vindictiveness.

'Young and hot-headed, master. Cruel as well.'

'Excellent,' said Rudolf, 'in battle rashness can often lead to defeat.'

Outside the master's office the courtyard of Wenden was again scrupulously clean and tidy. Life at the castle continued as normal and the garrison and the residents of the village were buoyant regarding the return of Bishop Albert and a crusading army. But Conrad was troubled.

'I regret what occurred concerning the soldiers from Riga, master.'

Rudolf pinched his nose. 'Regret? Why?'

'The incident may have severe repercussions for the order.'

'You have no need to concern yourself with that, Conrad. I have written to the grand master informing him of Archdeacon Stefan's gross breach of protocol.'

'Even so,' sighed Conrad, 'the archdeacon will take the insult personally.'

Rudolf laughed. 'I hope so for that was my intention. You are an important man, Conrad, not some base villain to be taken away and hanged on the whim of a fat churchman. But I'm afraid you will no longer be able to travel to Riga again, at least not without an armed escort.'

Conrad thought of the noise, the ramshackle crowded streets and the stench that filled them.

'I can live with that, master.'

Rameke arrived the next day at the head of two hundred bearded, hardy warriors on hale ponies, an additional twenty men driving carts loaded with the Livs' tents, food and spare weapons and armour. The ponies looked slightly ridiculous with their low legs, long bodies and wide and swinging trots, their colours a collection of blacks, greys, chestnuts and creams. But they had amazing stamina and could withstand inclement weather that would kill the horses imported from Germany. The Livs made camp on the meadow outside the outer perimeter while their leader went to pay his respects to Master Rudolf.

He had gone not twenty paces before a delighted Kaja accosted him by jumping into his arms, nearly knocking him over. Conrad, Hans and Anton had also walked down to the outer gates to welcome their friend, who wore a broad smile as his beloved linked an arm in his. Rameke embraced the three brother knights before the party began walking along the track that led to the castle.

'I heard about what happened with the soldiers from Riga,' said Rameke, 'Fricis sends his compliments to all three of you for saving the life of a Liv.'

'We would have done the same if it had been anyone,' said Conrad, 'I despise bullies.'

'Alas we have heard of many outrages committed against our people,' lamented Rameke. 'Many who come from overseas see us as not worthy of sharing this land with them.'

'Encouraged by Archdeacon Stefan, no doubt,' said Anton.

Hans nodded. 'He's no friend of the Livs.'

'Or the Sword Brothers,' added Conrad.

'It is hard to believe that he is related Bishop Albert,' said Rameke.

'It is hard to believe Conrad is related to you, my friend,' said Anton, 'what with you being such a warlord and Conrad being such a poor specimen.'

Rameke laughed but Conrad had to agree that the Liv was very different from the first time he had seen him all those years ago. Then they had been boys but now Rameke was Fricis' deputy and a warlord of great repute. His position was reflected in his appearance: fine quality mail shirt, gilded helmet and a fine sword in an expensive scabbard. He had inherited his father's stocky build and with his thick, shoulder-length hair and full beard he presented a formidable appearance. Conrad thought that he and Kaja would have handsome children.

'I am happy that you are marching north with us,' Kaja said to Rameke, planting a kiss on his cheek.

Rameke looked at Conrad as Hans and Anton looked straight ahead.

'You cannot come this time, Kaja,' said Conrad.

Kaja stopped and placed her hands on her hips, eyes full of fire and nostrils flared to produce a vision of savage beauty.

'Why not?'

'Because they are my orders, Kaja,' replied Conrad.

He thought that would suffice but she stood there, rock like, as the brother knights and Rameke looked at each awkwardly.

'Who will carry your banner, *Susi?*' she asked.

'I will find someone else, do not worry about that.'

Kaja regarded him coolly. 'Then I will ride with Rameke.'

Rameke faced his future bride and took her hands in his.

'I asked Conrad not to take you on campaign with him again, my love. I cannot fight with my mind full of visions of you being cut down by our enemies.'

'It is true, Kaja,' said Conrad, 'and in truth I too have feared for your life on numerous occasions.'

Hans and Anton mumbled their agreement but Kaja was not so easily swayed.

'So I am to be kept here like a bird in a cage until I am married? And afterwards, will I be kept as a virtual prisoner at Treiden?'

Rameke was appalled. 'I would never compel you to do anything.'

Kaja replaced her steely demeanour with a sultry look. 'Then let me go with you, my love.'

But Rameke would not be persuaded. 'I cannot.'

He brought up her hands and kissed them.

'Let us not argue, my sweet. We are soon to be married. When I come back from this next campaign we will be united forever at Treiden.'

'If you come back,' she said.

'We'll make sure he comes back, Kaja,' promised Conrad. 'Have no fear.'

She was only partly pacified but Conrad assured her that the campaign would be short.

'Very short if Kristjan gets here before we leave,' mused Hans.

'I remember him from when we visited Odenpah,' said Kaja. 'He seemed like an angry boy.'

'Now he's an angry man with an army behind him,' Anton told her.

Kaja's ire was partly appeased when she was given responsibility for organising those women from among the Saccalian refugees who could handle a spear or shoot a bow. Rudolf had given orders that the village where the Army of the Wolf had made its base should be abandoned until the threat of Kristjan had been dealt with. Therefore Riki's warriors escorted all the women, children and elderly to Wenden where they were quartered within the outer perimeter. Master Thaddeus was promoted to garrison commander in the absence of Walter and Rudolf. He and his clerks fussed around like mother hens but Conrad had to admit that the new arrivals were accommodated with little trouble, tents being issued from stores to house them.

'It is fortunate that it is early summer,' remarked Thaddeus as he stood with Conrad on the track that led from the castle's gatehouse down the hill to the gates in the outer perimeter wall. 'Tents are not as comfortable as huts.'

'Not if they are attacked by enemy warriors,' said Conrad.

'This Kristjan seems to have sprung from nowhere, Brother Conrad. I thought you were Marshal of Estonia. Cannot you order him to lay down his arms?'

'I could, sir,' laughed Conrad, 'but he would send the courier's head back to me as an answer.'

Thaddeus observed Kaja speaking in front of a group of around thirty women of a similar age to her. Though he could not hear what she was saying she was jabbing the air with an arm as she walked up and down in front of them, sword in scabbard dangling at her hip.

'Kaja is a remarkable young women,' observed Thaddeus. 'Full of fire and enthusiasm.'

'She is a formidable swordswoman,' said Conrad proudly, 'and will make a fine wife for Rameke.'

Thaddeus turned and walked back towards the castle.

'Let us hope that this Kristjan's army does not contain others like her, Conrad, for if so he will surely cause much mischief.'

There was no time to reflect on an army of Kajas with the arrival of the garrisons of Segewold and Kremon the same day. Masters Bertram and Mathias rode to the castle while their men pitched their tents outside the outer perimeter. Conrad was summoned to the master's hall. When he arrived he found a warm welcome from Bertram and Mathias.

'I cannot believe that little bastard Stefan tried to arrest you,' said Bertram.

'He should have his throat slit and his fat corpse thrown in the Dvina,' suggested Mathias.

'Agreed,' said Rudolf, 'but we have more urgent matters to attend to. Conrad's scouts have brought news that Kristjan is marching south at speed. Tomorrow we march north to intercept him.'

'We brought only horsemen, as instructed Rudolf,' relayed Bertram.

'Like the trip to Oesel,' beamed Mathias.

But it was not quite like the expedition to Oesel in that this time the warhorses would be accompanying the brother knights and the sergeants would be fighting as armoured horsemen and not crossbowmen. But the latter, all mounted on ponies, would include the doughty Leatherface who had recovered fully from his wounds. And the novices, all eager to take part in a campaign, would also be riding north. A dozen crossbowmen and all the spearmen, plus Kaja's women warriors, would defend the castle. In addition, Wenden's village also had its own militia – forty men capable of bearing arms raised from the more than two hundred people that now lived there.

Everyone worked until dusk in the wagon park to load the two- and four-wheeled vehicles that would haul the tents, food, tools, spare clothing, weapons and armour, saddles and ammunition that would be needed. Fortunately Livonia's abundance of grassland, rivers and lakes meant that the horses and ponies would have adequate grazing and water each day. Mules pulled the two-wheeled carts while packhorses hauled the four-wheeled wagons. The sergeants drove the carts and wagons, their horses tied to the vehicles. The novices rode their own horses and were responsible for the brother knights' warhorses, the pampered beasts that were valued more highly than the brother knights.

Once the women and children had been settled in the castle grounds Conrad sent Riki and his Harrien warriors north to scout for Kristjan's forces. Once they had been located Riki and his men were to fall back immediately to join the main force.

The castle's chapel was packed when Prime Mass was given on the morning of departure, with sergeants and novices standing outside as the priests of Kremon and Segewold repeated the words of the mass and cast vicious glances at the mercenaries who stood in the courtyard checking their equipment rather than hanging their heads in prayer. Then Rudolf ordered the march north to begin, much to the chagrin of Hans.

'We should have breakfast first. Not a good strategy to march on an empty stomach.'

'We will be eating at lunch,' said Anton, 'and you won't be marching, you'll be sitting on a horse.'

'That's not the point,' Hans rebuked him. 'I need some ballast in my stomach to be in fighting trim.'

Conrad laughed. 'Poor Hans. Just think, the horse he will be riding will have been fed and watered whereas he will be close to passing out due to lack of food.'

He slapped his friend on the back. 'Only through suffering will you reach heaven, my friend.'

'Levity and blasphemy are not the attributes of a Sword Brother, Brother Conrad.'

Conrad rolled his eyes as he heard the deep voice of Otto behind him, before turning to see the extremely tall, thin priest two paces away glaring at him with those cold, black eyes. Conrad was tall but Otto towered over him, his bald head a mass of battle scars, the deepest being the deep gash above his right eye. He resembled a hideous gargoyle that decorated Riga's cathedral.

'Just keeping the mood light, Father Otto,' smiled Conrad.

'Smiting the heathen is not a matter for joviality, Brother Conrad. We embark on God's business.'

Otto wore the simple undyed habit of the Cistercian Order, with the addition of a sword and dagger strapped to his broad leather belt.

'I thought it against the rules of the church for a priest to spill blood, father.'

Otto grinned maliciously. 'Heathen blood does not count, Brother Conrad.'

Rameke, who had been in the chapel with the three masters, saw Conrad and walked over. He carried his round, leather-faced shield that carried the sign of the moon motif, its central metal boss highly burnished. He smiled at the three brother knights and nodded at Otto.

'Father.'

Otto looked down his nose at the design on his shield, which resembled a large 'c'.

'You carry a pagan symbol on your shield, Lord Rameke.'

'The Sign of the Moon, father. It is the symbol of Meness, God of War, who has been worshipped by my people for generations. Legend tells that he wielded a sword of diamonds and wore clothes woven from the stars.'

'Such talk is heresy, Lord Rameke,' fumed Otto, 'you should not indulge it.'

Rameke pointed to his fifty strong bodyguard that waited in the courtyard beside their ponies. Each man also carried a shield that bore the sign of the moon.

'Men fight better when they believe luck is on their side, father.'

'Men do not need luck when they have God on their side, Lord Rameke.'

He gave Conrad a disparaging frown and marched off.

'I'm going to the kitchens to beg for some scraps,' said Hans, embracing Rameke then walking briskly to the kitchens.

'Don't be late,' Conrad told him.

'Yes, lord marshal,' came the sarcastic reply.

Conrad embraced his brother. 'God be with you.'

'And you,' replied Rameke.

Then he embraced Anton before walking back to his bodyguard. There was a touching scene when Kaja, all blonde hair and mail armour, wrapped her arms around her future husband, to the hoots and whistles of his bodyguard. It was a picture that put a deeper frown on Otto's battered forehead. A blast of trumpets signalled that the time for farewells was over as Rameke led his men out of the courtyard and horses and mules were brought from the stables.

The courtyard was expansive but there was suddenly hardly room to swing a sword as beasts were arrayed and inspected before being led over the drawbridge to the wagon park. Then the palfreys were brought into the courtyard. These were riding horses with a smooth gait that would be the mode of transport for the brother knights and sergeants on the march. In battle the former would switch to the warhorses that were brought into the courtyard last.

Aggressive, hot-headed and weighing up to twelve hundred pounds each, the destriers were the pride of the Sword

Brothers. They were well bred, highly trained horses that had been purchased in Germany and shipped over to Livonia at great expense. Conrad thought that it was just as well that each garrison of the order had a maximum of twelve brother knights – the number of apostles that Christ had gathered around him – otherwise the Sword Brothers would have faced bankruptcy.

He and Anton carefully inspected the straps, hooves and saddles of their palfreys before moving on to their warhorses and inspecting them. A stable hand held the reins of a warhorse that was not being checked over by one of Wenden's brother knights.

Rudolf looked up and down the line. 'Where is Brother Hans?'

'Call of nature, master,' replied Anton.

A smiling Hans appeared a couple of minutes later, sack slung over his shoulder. He quickly fastened it to the saddle of his palfrey before Rudolf saw it.

'One day you'll be caught out and get a flogging,' Anton told him.

Hans winked. 'But not today, my friend.'

In one corner of the courtyard Leatherface was shouting obscenities at the one hundred and twenty crossbowmen from Kremon, Wenden and Segewold that he had been given command of. For good measure he was also abusing two armourers who had ventured from their stone and iron citadel in the southeast corner of the courtyard. He stood beside his packhorse and told them in no uncertain terms that they should furnish him and his men with adequate ammunition because there was an inexhaustible supply of pagans. The armourers scuttled back to the massive armoury to satisfy his demands.

'My boys need plenty of bolts to shoot the heathens down.'

This brought a great cheer from the crossbowmen, who waved their weapons in the air. The brother knights released the warhorses to the charge of the novices and walked back to their palfreys.

'I wish I was coming with you, *Susi*.'

He laid a hand on Kaja's arm. 'It is a comfort to me that you are safe here. But remember that you are also responsible for defending this place. So take heed of what Master Thaddeus tells you.'

'Yes, *Susi*.'

He hauled himself into the saddle and wheeled his horse right following another blast of trumpets. Hans and Anton raised their hands to Kaja as Rudolf led eleven brother knights, thirty sergeants, twenty novices and one hundred and twenty crossbowmen from the courtyard. They trotted across the courtyard and down the track to the outer perimeter gates, children waving and running alongside them as they did so. Another twenty sergeants sat on loaded wagons and carts waiting to follow the horsemen, and outside the gates were the garrisons of Segewold and Kremon and Rameke's Livs. Nearly five hundred men began the journey north to halt the advance of Kristjan, while ahead of them Riki's fifty Harrien were scouting the land to insure against any nasty surprises.

*****

Despite it being the beginning of summer the days could still be cool and rainy, the tracks quickly turning to rivers of mud when pounded by hundreds of hooves and feet. The forests and meadows had sprung to life and brimmed with game and birds. The days were long, which meant that Kristjan made good progress as his army headed south. His Ungannians and Vetseke's Russians were all mounted, which meant they could endure the long days easily enough, but those on foot were soon complaining.

'You think that Taara is interested in the bleatings of the common folk?' asked Kristjan.

The sun lanced through gaps in the forest canopy and the air was heavy with the scent of pine. Vetseke riding beside him thought the young man's recovery from the hornet stings had been remarkable, but believed that his youthful enthusiasm was now laced with a dangerous dose of arrogance.

'I think that men driven to the limits of their exhaustion will not be much use in battle, young lord,' replied Vetseke.

'Don't call me young,' snapped Kristjan. 'I am the appointed servant of Taara. My age is irrelevant.'

'We should make camp soon,' suggested Vetseke. 'To give the men and beasts an opportunity to rest.'

'Rest?' scoffed Kristjan. 'They can rest when they are dead.'

He turned in the saddle and shouted at the long, winding column behind.

'On, on. Taara points the way to victory!'

Vetseke decided to broach a topic he had thus far avoided.

'Where are we headed, Kristjan?'

The Ungannian smiled. 'To Livonia, prince. To butcher Livs and burn their villages, to entice the Sword Brothers out of their stone castles so we can destroy them.'

Vetseke, who had personal experience of fighting and losing to the men of iron, was taken aback.

'They are tenacious foes, Kristjan.'

'I agree.'

'You do?'

Kristjan smiled once more. 'Of course. My father taught me that it is a gross error to underestimate an enemy. But if I cut a swathe of destruction through Livonia then I will show how weak the Bishop of Riga is. As a result Novgorod and Polotsk will not be able to resist invading Livonia. This is the message that Taara sent me when my body was filled with poison.'

Vetseke did not reply but pondered over whether being stung by hornets could make the victim insane.

Two scouts who knew the area well were leading the column through a largely uninhabited strip of land between what had been the realm of the Livs and Estonia. The two races had raided each other for generations in search of slaves, livestock or just the pleasure of burning and killing. Vetseke did not trust them but Kristjan seemed content to be flattered by the pair. The scouts rode out of the trees into a meadow of long grass and white and yellow flowers, and pulled up their ponies. On the far side of the meadow, around two hundred paces away, sat three men on ponies. They wore helmets and carried spears and shields.

'Don't like the look of them, lord,' said one of the scouts to Kristjan.

Vetseke turned to his deputy. 'Ride them down.'

Moments later half a dozen Russians were galloping across the meadow, spears levelled as they rode towards the unidentified warriors. But the latter immediately scattered as they turned their horses and disappeared into a forest of birch. Kristjan and Vetseke continued forward, the two scouts urging their mangy beasts on as the army flooded into the meadow.

'Who were they?' asked Kristjan as the Russian horsemen followed the mysterious riders into the dark green forest.

'Livs, most likely, lord,' replied the second scout, 'it's too far south to be our people.'

'You mean Estonians,' said Vetseke.

The other scout spat. 'The Livs used to be lambs ripe for raping and killing before the men of iron arrived. See how they ran without their friends the Sword Brothers to back them up.'

Behind Vetseke his deputy, like him a Liv, bristled at the insult directed at his people.

'You have killed many Livs?' asked Vetseke casually.

'Oh, yes,' replied the other scout. 'We used to call this land the happy hunting ground.'

'There was a tidy profit to be made from capturing slaves as well,' said the other scout, 'before the men of iron came.'

'Do not worry about them,' interrupted Kristjan, 'they will be only a temporary presence in this land.'

Vetseke stared ahead and said nothing. Behind him hundreds of Estonian warriors continued their journey south to Livonia. He too had once led an army against the Sword Brothers that had reached the gates of Riga before being destroyed. He had been captured but Bishop Albert had freed him on condition that he never set foot in Livonia again. But here he was, part of an army led by a boy who was beloved of the gods.

*****

The force from Wenden covered ten miles on the first day and fifteen on the second, a splendid achievement given that it rained every day and the tracks quickly turned to mud. But men got off their horses and ponies and helped the progress of the carts and wagons and everyone was hopeful that they would reach Lehola in a week. At the end of each day Rudolf, as commander of the expedition, would ride up and down the column and issue the order that was given at the end of a day's march on all Sword Brother campaigns: 'Make camp, lord brothers, on God's behalf.'

Pitching the tents was a straightforward and speedy affair, each garrison of the order having practised it so many times that the men could do it in their sleep. The chapel tent was set up first, then those of the masters and the tents of the brother knights and sergeants that circled them. The vehicles were placed in a wagon park and the order's horses, ponies and mules were housed in a temporary stabling area. By the time this had been done and the beasts had been watered, fed, groomed and examined for injuries the sun was dipping in the west.

The Livs had their own camping arrangements that were simpler, their two-man felt tents being pitched around their chiefs' and their ponies tethered either to low-lying branches or carts after being allowed to graze on the lush meadow grass.

After Vespers in the chapel tent evening meals were cooked. Rudolf had insisted on tight camp security so there were no hunting parties, which meant that meals comprised cured meat and porridge. It was customary on campaign to duplicate the eating arrangements that were observed at Wenden. Thus there was a tent where meals were taken and where the brother knights ate first followed by the sergeants. However, because he was Marshal of Estonia Conrad was allowed to take his meals separately, as were Hans and Anton who were his allotted deputies. So, as on many other occasions, they sat outside their tent watching their food being prepared.

341

'I miss Kaja,' said Hans as he watched a novice stirring the pot of porridge hanging over the fire.

'Rameke was most insistent that she no longer accompany us on campaign,' replied Conrad.

'It is the end of an era,' opined Anton as the novice began serving the porridge into wooden bowls.

He handed one to Conrad, then Hans and Anton and went back to his stirring. Conrad estimated his age at around fifteen. He was gangly and had yet to grow into his frame. His name was Manfred.

Hans gulped down his porridge and then called to him.

'Fill it up, Manfred.'

The novice scurried over and took Hans' bowl to refill it. He handed it back to the brother knight. Moments later a familiar figure made an appearance.

'Now then, boys, any chance of a spare morsel for a penniless dog of war?'

Leatherface smiled mischievously at Manfred before sitting on the ground beside Conrad. Manfred picked up a spare bowl and began filling it with porridge.

'Have you eaten, Manfred?' asked Conrad.

'Not yet, Brother Conrad.'

'Then sit down and eat that bowl of porridge.'

Leatherface looked aghast. 'Nothing for me? I preferred it when young Kaja was the cook. She had a soft spot for me.'

Hans finished his bowl and held it out. 'Manfred.'

'You have had enough, Hans,' Conrad told him. 'Manfred has cooked your meal so let the boy eat.'

'There is some left, Brother Hans,' said Manfred in between shovelling the porridge into his mouth at speed.

'You finish it off, Manfred,' Conrad told him.

'None for me?' said Leatherface in a miserable tone.

Conrad finished his porridge and placed his bowl on the ground.

'As the commander of crossbowmen I'm sure you have had more than your fill among your own men, to say nothing of the food you have scrounged on the way here.'

'I'm not into poverty and piety like you are, Brother Conrad,' he protested. 'I thought generosity is supposed to be one of the virtues of the Sword Brothers.'

'Towards those who are desperate and helpless,' said Anton, 'which doesn't apply to you.'

Manfred refilled his own bowl as ordered and emptied the cooking pot, but then scooped some porridge into a fresh bowl and took it over to Leatherface.

'Thank you, boy,' he beamed. 'Now that's what I call Christian charity.'

'So,' he continued, porridge spilling from his mouth, 'what do you reckon about this Kristjan and his army?'

Conrad shrugged. 'I'm more concerned that there are Russians among his men. If he has the support of Novgorod then his threat is greater than if he had been operating alone.'

343

'He's caused all Estonia to rise up, I've heard,' said Leatherface.

'That is the rumour,' said Hans.

'And rumours can turn out to be false,' added Anton.

'That's what I like about you boys,' grinned the old mercenary, 'you always look on the bright side.'

He scooped out the bowl with his fingers, shoved the last morsels into his mouth and stood up. He tossed the empty bowl to Manfred.

'What about you, young pup, what do you think?'

'The Sword Brothers will prevail, lord,' came the answer.

Leatherface looked at Conrad and back at Manfred. 'So you think that King Conrad here will defeat King Kristjan.'

Manfred looked confused and unsure how to reply.

'Be off with you,' Conrad told the mercenary, 'and allow us time to pray for your soul.'

Leatherface turned and walked off. 'Don't you bother yourself with my soul, Brother Conrad, I sold it years ago.'

'That I can believe,' said Hans.

Later, when night had come and there was a chill in the air, Conrad and his friends sat on stools close to the fire and cleaned their weapons. Manfred threw more wood on the fire and sat expectantly on a stool.

'Would you like me to clean your sword, Brother Conrad?'

'A brother knight should always clean his own sword, Manfred, but thank you for the offer.'

He could see that the novice was entranced by the weapon, its blade now bathed in the red glow of the fire. Conrad ran a cloth over the black leather grip and then over the cross-guard, each of its arms being 'waisted' and flared back to their original width at the ends.

'It is a fine weapon, Brother Conrad.'

Conrad looked at the broad and evenly tempered blade, the outer third of which curved gradually to a point. He saw the disc-shaped pommel with its chamfered edges and unicorns carved into both sides.

'It is,' he agreed.

'It was given to Conrad,' said Hans, 'as a present.'

'It was bequeathed to me by Sir Frederick of Tangermünde, a Saxon knight,' said Conrad, 'after he had been mortally wounded at Fellin.'

'I have seen his grave in the cemetery,' said Manfred.

'That was twelve years ago,' reflected Anton. 'How the years pass.'

'And how history repeats itself,' mused Hans. 'For we shall have to assault Fellin again soon.'

'First we have to find Kristjan,' stated Conrad.

That mystery was solved the next day, an hour after dawn when the camp was being disassembled, when Riki and his Harrien arrived. Their leader reported immediately to Conrad who, alarmed, went with the blonde-haired Estonian to find Master Rudolf. The latter was assisting four novices throw his tent into the back of a wagon when he spotted Conrad.

'You look like you have seen a ghost.'

He then saw Riki's concerned look. 'I take it this is not a social visit?'

Conrad nodded at Riki.

'Kristjan is ten miles away, maybe less, lord, and will be at the River Sedde before midday.'

Rudolf's eyes filled with concern. 'The Sedde? Are you sure, that is less than five miles away?'

'Some of my men ran into his army yesterday, lord, and reported back to me after giving the slip to some Russians. Kristjan pushes his army hard.'

He turned to the novices. 'Take that tent out of the wagon and put it up again.'

Ten minutes later he had convened a council of war beside the wagon as the brother knights and sergeants re-erected their tents around them. Rudolf sent a novice to find Rameke, the boy returning with the Liv a few minutes later.

'Kristjan approaches the Sedde,' Rudolf stated bluntly.

'That is forty miles south of Fellin,' said a surprised Rameke.

'And around five miles from this spot,' added Riki, his pale cheeks still flushed with colour from the urgent ride through the pre-dawn dark.

'If we can get to the Sedde first,' said Rudolf, 'then we can hold the river line and Kristjan will have to attack us. We have enough crossbowmen to inflict heavy losses on his army. The foot will provide cover for the crossbowmen. After they have softened up the enemy the horsemen will charge and scatter them.'

He looked at those present. 'Any objections?'

Mathias and Bertram shook their heads and Conrad was nodding.

'It is a good plan,' agreed Rameke, 'and plays to our strengths.'

'Then let us make haste,' said Rudolf.

The Sedde flowed west into Lake Burtnieks and, like many other waterways in Livonia and Estonia, broke its banks at the beginning of spring when filled with melt water. But now it was shallow and slow moving, being no more than three or four feet deep and shallower in some places. It was also narrow – around thirty feet – making it passable along almost all its length. It thus presented no great barrier but would stiffen a defence made up of a shield wall supported by crossbowmen.

It took less than half an hour for the brother knights and sergeants to don their armour and fit their horses with caparisons, the thickly padded and quilted garments that were made in two halves that met at the saddle and also covered each horse's neck and head.

Conrad ordered Riki to stay with the sixty novices who were to guard the camp. He told the Harrien leader that he and his men needed rest after their exertions, but the real reason was that he did not want his Estonians fighting other Estonians. If Kristjan could be defeated, even better killed, then his insurrection would be at an end. Riki was unhappy but

Conrad told him that should the army be defeated then he would be responsible for getting the novices back to Wenden.

The forests were filled with the sound of chaffinches, blackbirds and cuckoos as the thirty-six brother knights and one hundred and ten sergeants, all in mail armour and carrying lances, trotted from camp followed by Rameke's warriors and Leatherface's one hundred and twenty crossbowmen, all riding ponies and all weighed down with full quivers. The day was overcast and there was a gentle breeze but at least the rain had so far held off. The banners of Wenden, Segewold and Kremon fluttered in the breeze, the white caparisons of the Sword Brothers in stark contrast to the lush green scenery they rode through.

They had travelled for less than half an hour, threading their way between expanses of tall birch, when they encountered a group of warriors on ponies and horsemen carrying almond-shaped shields and lances – Russians. The meadow the two sides occupied was suddenly filled with the sound of horns and trumpets as the Sword Brothers deployed into line and the enemy about turned and withdrew.

'Kristjan is over the Sedde, then,' said Hans to Conrad.

'Conrad,' shouted Rudolf a short distance away, 'get over here.'

The brother knight rode over to where Rudolf sat on his horse next to Walter holding Wenden's banner. Mathias, Bertram and Rameke galloped to the impromptu gathering.

Ahead the enemy soldiers were becoming smaller as they fell back. Leatherface trotted up on his unkempt pony.

'Glad you could grace us with your presence,' Rudolf berated him.

'Never rush to a battle, Master Rudolf,' he replied, 'otherwise you might find yourself fleeing from it twice as fast.'

'The plan still holds,' Rudolf told them, helmet shoved back on top of his head. 'As soon as we sight the main enemy force Rameke's men will dismount while we cover them. The crossbowmen will also dismount and advance under cover of the shield wall.'

He looked at Leatherface.

'Think you can manage that?'

'Don't you worry about me, Master Rudolf, you just make sure you don't fall off your horse.'

Mathias and Bertram thought the exchange of words hilarious though Rameke was not amused. Conrad just shook his head and smiled.

'Well, then,' said Rudolf, 'let's put this Kristjan to the sword. God be with you all.'

The brother knights formed into a line, men riding knee to knee, the sergeants in kettle helmets behind them in two ranks, then spurred their horses forward in pursuit of the enemy. Behind them the Livs and crossbowmen followed. Conrad's body tingled with excitement at the prospect of impending violence. His instincts and reflexes were suddenly invigorated, his senses heightened.

349

The meadow narrowed to around two hundred paces as the horsemen rode from it into a wide area of grassland that bordered the river. And there, standing perhaps fifty paces from the Sedde itself, was Kristjan's army.

Rudolf signalled a halt and then rode forward to scout the enemy shield wall. Conrad pushed up his helmet and thrust the end of his lance into the earth. He reached over and offered his hand to Hans.

'As dust to the wind.'

Hans shook his hand and smiled.

'As dust to the wind.'

He repeated the ritual with Anton and then waited as Rameke and his Livs dismounted, every tenth man leading the ponies to the rear, as the crossbowmen loaded their weapons. Then they took up position within the Liv shield wall, directly behind the front rank, and waited. Conrad looked left to see Walter with his eyes closed, deep in prayer. Henke toyed with his mace and Lukas was scanning the enemy army.

The Estonians were deployed in a long line, round shields locked together and the spears of the front rank levelled to form a row of whetted points. Every man had a helmet though Conrad wondered how many had any armour. It was customary to place the best-armed and armoured men in the front ranks of a shield wall, those behind often having no armour apart from a helmet. On the opposite side of the river a forest of birch began a short distance from the Sedde. Just in front of the trees stood a group of horsemen, some armed with lances. There was also a large banner that carried a golden eagle design.

'Kristjan,' muttered Conrad.

It was impossible to determine the size of the enemy shield wall but if the Estonians were in four or five ranks then there were at least five hundred men facing the Sword Brothers.

Rudolf galloped back, a broad grin on his face.

'This will not take long and then we march to the relief of Lehola.'

He rode through the Sword Brothers to request Rameke to bring his warriors forward. The Liv shook the hand of Conrad as he walked forward, his men forming into line in front of the horsemen. Then they waited until Leatherface's men deployed behind their first rank. To match the extent of the enemy shield wall Rameke's men were forced to form into two ranks, the crossbowmen between them. If the two sides came to blows the Estonians would cut Rameke's men to pieces, but that was not the plan as the Livs advanced. Three hundred paces in front of them the Estonian shield wall suddenly erupted in noise.

The Estonians had seen the Livs form up and knew that their numbers were few. They might have spotted the crossbowmen but their numbers were also on the small side and so their confidence grew. They banged their spear shafts against the rims of their shields and roared their war cries, hurling insults at the Livs, their ancient enemies. They would have seen the men of iron on their warhorses, of course, but the Livs stood between them and the Sword Brothers. The cacophony filled the air and rose to a crescendo as Rameke's signallers blew their horns and the Livs walked forward.

Rudolf signalled to the trumpeters to blow their instruments to indicate that the horsemen should follow their allies, Conrad pulling his lance from the earth and holding it upright. He spurred his horse forward; keeping a tight grip on the reins with his left hand so ensure it did not break formation. The Estonians were still shouting and hurling abuse when he heard a succession of thwacks followed by high-pitched screams as the first volley of crossbow bolts struck flesh and bone. Leatherface's men knew that the Estonian shields presented a large target but they ignored them and aimed for the faces above them. Some quarrels missed and shot over the heads of the densely packed warriors, but the majority of the iron-tipped missiles embedded themselves in eye sockets, necks and cheekbones.

Conrad had a magnificent view of the unfolding scene of horror as the Estonian front rank was shredded and then vanished altogether as a second volley of bolts was unleashed. The crossbowmen were shooting methodically, averaging four bolts a minute and whittling down the enemy shield wall like a carpenter planes a piece of wood. Rudolf signalled to the trumpeters who blew their instruments and the brother knights and sergeants moved forward.

Leatherface barked a command and the crossbowmen ceased shooting and formed up in files as Rameke's men bunched together in front of them to create corridors through which the horsemen could pass. Rudolf shoved up his helmet and shouted the orders' war cry.

'God with us!'

Every brother knight and sergeant repeated the cry as the iron-shod hooves of the horses tore up great clumps of soil as they broke into a canter. The line slowed and then temporarily splintered as the horses headed through the gaps created by the Livs and crossbowmen, then reformed when they had ridden past the foot soldiers. Ahead the shattered enemy shield wall was in disarray as chiefs desperately tried to rally their men. But the earth shook as dozens of armoured horsemen thundered towards them.

Conrad released the reins and grasped the strap on the inner side of his shield, bringing it across his torso. His body was braced against the saddle bow as he gripped his lance firmly and kept it clamped under his right arm. The horses broke into a gallop and the distance between the riders and Estonians disappeared in the blink of an eye as the Sword Brothers charged into the enemy shield wall. Except that the shield wall had disintegrated.

It takes men of discipline and with nerves of steel to stand firm against a wall of armoured horsemen charging at them, and the Estonians had neither. The chiefs failed to rally their men who began running back to the river, traversing the sandy riverbank before splashing into the water. Seconds later the horsemen entered the river, splashing through the water to

353

spear the fleeing enemy. Conrad's long years of training took over as he focused on his victim. Just as he had been taught he did not look at the lance tip, instead focusing on the target. The warriors had heard the thundering sound of the horses' hooves and then the splashing behind them and now many turned to face their pursuers. Conrad saw the man turn, move his shield across his body and level his spear. But he had no chance to use his weapon as the point of the lance pierced the wood of his shield, went through his mail shirt and ribcage and burst out of his back.

Conrad could hear Lukas' voice as the man grunted and collapsed in the water.

'One you've speared an opponent let go of the lance like it is a venomous snake, draw your secondary weapon and begin raining blows with it. Strike and press on, don't turn round as this wastes time and is tiring. On, on, always on.'

His horse slowed now it was in the water. He reached down and extracted his axe from the specially designed leather holder attached to his saddle. He pushed his right hand through the leather strap attached to its base and gripped the shaft, swinging its edge against enemy helmets left and right. All the horsemen were now in the water, using their maces and axes to cut down the enemy to fill the river with corpses and turn the Sedde red. His stallion was a rock beneath him, keeping its footing, totally unconcerned about the yelps and screams coming from men having their heads split open and arms shattered.

Conrad's warhorse suddenly shifted left as a warrior swung an axe against his right leg but missed to gash the material of the caparison. He brought his own axe up and swung it sideways to smash the weapon's blade into the man's face, crushing his nose and cheekbones. The warrior screamed, dropped his weapon and staggered a few feet before collapsing on the sandy riverbank. Conrad saw Hans and Anton coming from the water and smiled. It had been another easy victory for the Sword Brothers. But his smile disappeared when a great noise erupted from the trees in front and hundreds of warriors charged out of the forest.

Rudolf immediately gave the order to withdraw. The sergeants who were Wenden's signallers always stayed close to the master and his deputy, blew their instruments to command the horsemen to retire. Conrad and his friends wheeled their horses about and dug their spurs into their flanks. The beasts grunted in complaint but waded through the water again and exited the Sedde on its southern side as the Estonian mob entered the water. The riders galloped back to where Rameke stood with his men.

*****

'You see how they run, prince,' said Kristjan to Vetseke. 'The Sword Brothers are not gods, they are men like us.'

Vetseke was pleased to see the Sword Brothers withdraw and heard the cheers of the horsemen arrayed behind him. But he was sceptical that Kristjan's plan would work and worried

355

that even if it did, the unity of his army would be irrevocably fractured. Recruits from Wierland, Harrien and Jerwen had flocked to his banner and he had distributed the weapons and armour he had brought from Dorpat. But Kristjan saw the warriors from the other kingdoms as inferior to his own Ungannians. To him they were men who were expendable in battle. And it was so now as the Wierlanders charged from the forest into the Sedde to pursue the retreating Sword Brothers. Kristjan had used the Harrien as bait for his trap and they had suffered heavily, first being shot at by crossbowmen before being ridden down by horsemen. Vetseke doubted if more than a third were left alive. Still, if the Wierlanders defeated the Sword Brothers then Kristjan's fame would spread throughout the whole of Estonia.

One of his deputies rode forward as the last Wierlanders left the river.

'Beg pardon, lord, but do you wish to commit your Ungannians?'

Kristjan spun in the saddle. 'Certainly not. I will need fresh men to hunt down the remnants of the enemy army.'

Kristjan smiled at Vetseke. 'And Prince Vetseke's horsemen will ride to the gates of Wenden to demand its surrender.'

Vetseke smiled politely in reply as Kristjan waved his subordinate away. And on the other side of the river the Wierlander assault crashed into a wall of flesh and iron.

*****

'Dismount, dismount.'

A helmetless Master Rudolf slid off his horse, mace in hand, and stood beside Walter holding Wenden's banner. Brother knights and sergeants dismounted to rally to their masters. In front of them the crossbowmen began shooting at the charging warriors. These, initially gripped by the euphoria of victory, literally ran into a swarm of crossbow bolts that felled at least fifty. Because they were widely spaced the Wierlanders' charge was not interrupted as men dodged falling figures in front of them to get to grips with the Livs. But fifteen seconds after the first volley of bolts another one hundred and twenty missiles flew into their ranks, to be followed fifteen seconds later by a third volley.

Conrad stood with Hans and Anton behind the crossbowmen as they went about their work with quiet efficiency, loading, shooting and reloading their weapons as the Estonians ran towards them. By the time the first enemy warriors reached the Liv line at least two hundred of their comrades had been felled by missiles.

There was a succession of cracks as axes and swords struck shields to signal the beginning of the mêlée. The crossbowmen, their task done, immediately fell back and the Sword Brothers raced to support Rameke's men. A few were hit by thrown spears but the majority rushed forward before the Estonians hit them to give themselves some momentum rather than waiting to be struck by charging warriors.

Conrad kept his shield tight to his body as he swung his axe forward over the right shoulder of the Liv in front of him to strike the helmet of the man he was fighting. He missed but the blade sliced down onto his shoulder, severing the chain mail and biting into the material beneath. He withdrew the axe and swung it again at the same spot, this time drawing blood. But then a spear glanced off the side of his helm, sparking ringing in his ears. He was disorientated as the Liv in front hacked down the warrior he had been attacking and stepped forward. He tried to follow but tripped over the body and his legs buckled beneath him. Hans hauled him to his feet.

'Are you hurt?' his friend shouted.

Conrad shook his head as the ringing subsided. The vision slits of the helm gave him limited visibility and he did not see the spear that was suddenly thrust at him and lodged itself in his shield. He saw the metal point protruding through its inner side, just above his left forearm and immediately hacked down his axe on the shaft, splintering it. He threw his shield away, drew his sword and transferred the axe to his left hand. The warrior who had just lost his spear, who was wearing some sort of pointed helmet like the Russians favoured, pulled his hand axe from his belt but dropped it when Anton caved in his helmet with his mace.

And then the enemy was gone.

Conrad looked around and saw panting and exhausted Livs reforming into a ragged line. He saw Rameke, battered and bleeding but still alive, walking up and down the line, shouting encouragement to his men. Hans and Anton, their surcoats spotted with blood, were by his side as the crossbowmen came forward again to shoot at what was left of the enemy. There was a tidemark of dead and dying where the two sides had collided and a meadow littered with enemy dead that stretched back to the river where the crossbowmen had reaped their grim harvest. He heard Master Rudolf's commanding voice.

'Sword Brothers will advance to the river.'

The white-clothed brother knights and sergeants walked through the Livs with the crossbowmen immediately behind them. The garrisons of Wenden, Segewold and Kremon rallied to their banners and advanced in three groups towards the Sedde, each group covered by Leatherface's men.

Conrad's mouth was dry, he was sweating profusely but he was mercifully unharmed. He had no idea how many casualties the order had suffered but he had seen only one or two white shapes on the ground. The crossbowmen searched for targets but there were none, only dead bodies pierced by their quarrels. When they reached the riverbank he saw fleeting figures among the trees and then nothing. The horsemen grouped around the eagle banner had also gone. Kristjan had fled.

*****

The young Ungannian had refused all pleadings by Vetseke to commit his own men to the attack, despite promising that he would also lead his horsemen in support. Instead Kristjan stated that his army needed more training before it could conquer Livonia and ordered a withdrawal. The fact that he had lost many men did not concern him. In anything it confirmed the opinion he held towards the other Estonian tribes.

'Do you know why, alone of all the Estonian kingdoms, only Ungannia has been able to remain free and unconquered?' he asked Vetseke as they rode north.

'No, Kristjan.'

'Because the average Ungannian is superior to a Wierlander, Harrien, Jerwen, Saccalian or Rotalian. It is not coincidence that Taara has given me the task of fighting the foes of Estonia because the leaders of the other tribes have proved themselves unequal to the task.'

Vetseke said nothing as he debated with himself whether he should abandon Kristjan and lead his men back to Novgorod. But then he remembered that he had left some in Fellin to stiffen the garrison.

'Where are we going?' he asked tersely.

'To Lehola, of course,' replied Kristjan. 'It has defied me for too long. I will give the Wierlanders, Harrien and Jerwen a chance to redeem themselves.'

But the attack on Lehola failed and Kristjan lost another one hundred dead before returning to Dorpat to celebrate the mid-summer festival of Ligo.

Chapter 8

Novgorod's merchants grew rich from the trade in grey squirrel pelts, which were transported to either Riga or Reval and then across the sea to Lübeck. It was true that others made a decent profit by trading the pelts of sable, black foxes, polar foxes, marten and white wolves with Constantinople, where the slave markets also did a brisk trade in young Estonian and Liv women and boys with fair skins and blue eyes. But it was the lush, grey-white northern squirrel fur that was in the highest demand and which made those Novgorodians who traded in it very wealthy. And while trade was good the merchants and boyars of the city were content enough. But the Danish blockade on Livonia had severed one of the arteries of commerce and King Valdemar's reverse on Oesel and subsequent imprisonment in Germany had effectively closed all commerce through Reval. The port was now besieged by a motley collection of Estonians and Oeselians, which had resulted in the merchants and boyars becoming fractious.

The interruption in trade not only affected Novgorod's nobles and merchants; it also impinged on royal finances. The city treasury found that tax revenues dropped dramatically, which meant Mstislav had difficulty maintaining his household. And to add to his problems Archbishop Mitrofan began bending his ear about the dismal state of church finances. Novgorod had grown wealthy on commerce but now business was in a dire state and the matter had to be addressed.

The prince hated the *veche*, the city council that appointed and dismissed administrators, was empowered to declare war and peace, levy taxes, adopt laws and approve treaties. It was also empowered to hire and dismiss princes and had once approached Mstislav to be the city's ruler, though he knew it was because he was married to a Cuman princess and could thus prevent her people raiding Novgorod's territory. From the beginning, therefore, it was an uneasy relationship between a *veche* dominated by clans of boyars and wealthy merchants and the prince. Mstislav thought the *veche* irksome at best and a nest of traitors at worst. He also believed that a prince asserted his power through war whereas the *veche* believed that conflict interfered with trade and was to be resorted to only as a last resort.

But Mstislav was no fool and recognised that the *veche*, the members of which believed themselves to be the guardians of law and justice, could be manipulated by employing the right language and arguments. He also knew that it was better to meet with members of the *veche*'s Council of Lords, a sort of inner circle, rather than the whole assembly. The *veche* met in the ancient city hall near the bridge that spanned the Volkhov River. In earlier times the council could be convened by anyone who rang the great *veche* bell that hung above the hall, whereupon different factions would come to blows on the bridge spanning the river to resolve differences. Today, though, only the six members of the Council of Lords were requested at the kremlin.

Mstislav met them not in the imposing throne room but a more intimate setting: a small office beside the main hall. The middle-aged, bearded individuals were shown into the room where soft chairs had been placed in a circle. Mstislav stood as they entered and welcomed each in turn, only taking his seat when they had all sat. Servants brought trays of silver cups filled with *stavlenniy myod*, the strong, honey based alcoholic beverage favoured by the Russians.

Mstislav was dressed in a woollen outer garment called a *svita* made of expensive Byzantine material that extended down to his knees. As was the custom neither he nor his guests wore any weapons inside the palace.

'Thank you for coming,' said Mstislav.

The head of the Council of Lords, Yuri Nevsky, tilted his head politely.

'We are honoured to be here, highness.'

'Tell me, Yuri,' said the prince, 'how is your grandson, Alexander I believe his name is?'

Yuri nearly choked on his drink. His son had been banished to Pskov before his grandson had been born. The exile still rankled with the Nevsky clan, one of Novgorod's most ancient and powerful boyar families.

'He is well, highness, I believe,' replied Yuri, 'not that I have had much opportunity to see him of late.'

Mstislav nodded thoughtfully. 'I would like to see young Alexander. Ask your son to bring his family back to the city. He and they have been away too long.'

Yuri smiled. 'Thank you, highness, you are most generous.'

Mstislav sipped his drink. 'Excellent, family is important. That's settled, then.'

He smiled at the other members of the council who smiled back. To an observer it could have been a gathering of old friends, though Mstislav had up until now treated the members of the *veche* as dangerous dogs. It was most strange. Eventually, Mikhail Vsevolodovich, a close friend of Yuri Nevsky and the *veche*'s appointed *tysiatskii*, the 'thousandman' or military commander, broke the silence.

'Forgive me, highness, but might we know the reason you summoned us here?'

Mstislav looked confused. 'Mm? Oh, yes. Forgive me, it was such a pleasant meeting I had clean forgot. In truth the interruption in trade troubles me greatly. Novgorod is a centre of commerce and without commerce it cannot thrive.'

'We are all troubled by events in the west, highness,' remarked a boyar with a steel-grey beard.

Mstislav placed his cup on the table and spread his hands.

'What to do, what to do?'

He brought his hands together. 'For years now our merchants have had to pay taxes to the apostates in Riga for the privilege of transporting their goods to markets overseas. And when the servants of the corrupt Pope of Rome fall out who suffers? We do.'

'It is most regrettable,' agreed one of the boyars.

'And more than regrettable it is expensive,' added Gregori, friend of Yuri.

Mstislav nodded his agreement. 'To which end I propose taking measures to ensure that Novgorod's trade is not interrupted by the petty disputes of the crusaders. I intend to capture Reval.'

The boyars looked at him in disbelief.

'I realise that the prospect of conflict fills many members of the *veche* with dread,' continued Mstislav, 'but we must take action to secure our western border.'

'How does seizing Reval add to the security of Novgorod, highness?' queried Yuri.

'I will tell you,' replied Mstislav. 'Not only will it provide a secure port from which Novgorod's goods can be shipped to northern Germany without having to pay taxes to the Bishop of Riga. It will also remove the threat of Estonian bandits raiding Novgorod's territory. Chaos rules west of Lake Peipus and the longer it continues the danger increases of armies of bandits flourishing where no law exists.'

'Such a move would provoke a war with the Danes,' warned Mikhail.

Mstislav shook his head. 'Danish power is broken, my friend. Their king was humiliated on Oesel last year and had to crawl back to his homeland, his army destroyed.'

'If, and I stress if,' said Yuri slowly, 'the *veche* was to support your venture, highness, and Reval was seized,

Novgorod is not a seafaring power. We have no ships to transport our goods across the Baltic.'

'That's true,' said one of the boyars, the rest nodding their heads.

'Ships would come to Reval,' Mstislav reassured them, 'just as they go to Riga.'

'And what about the Oeselians?' asked Mikhail. 'They would prey on those ships like wolves among a flock of sheep.'

'Not if we had a treaty with Olaf,' replied Mstislav.

'A treaty, with pagans?' said an appalled Gregori.

'Why not?' replied Mstislav. 'Olaf may be an old pirate but he is no fool. His ships may be the scourges of the Baltic but Oesel is not a thousand miles away. Just as the Sword Brothers invaded the island last year so could we land soldiers on Oesel if Olaf proves uncooperative.'

'What would be the size of the force required to take Reval?' asked Yuri.

'Novgorod and Pskov between them would need to furnish ten thousand soldiers,' stated Mstislav. 'In addition, it may fortify you to know that my cousin, Grand Prince George of Suzdal, has agreed to provide an additional ten thousand men should I march against Reval.'

Yuri smiled politely. Mstislav had clearly given the venture a lot of thought. He had no love for the prince but what he said about Reval was true. If Novgorod and Pskov could ship their goods through the port, which had been enlarged and strengthened by the Danes, then not only would profits increase but, more importantly, commerce would no longer be subjected to the vagaries of Riga's politics. Reval was certainly closer and if an agreement could be reached with the Oeselians then trade with north Germany would certainly flourish.

'We would have to consult with other members of the *veche*, highness,' announced Yuri.

'Naturally,' said Mstislav. 'But may I ask what will be the advice of the Council of Lords?'

The boyars looked at each other before Yuri spoke.

'That your highness' proposal has merit.'

Afterwards the boyars walked from the kremlin, their personal guards escorting them back to their mansions in the city.

'I am glad that you will soon be reunited with your son, Yuri,' said Mikhail.

'That was a surprise, I agree,' replied Yuri.

'As was his idea to attack Reval,' offered Gregori behind them.

'It has merit,' said the boyar with the steel grey beard. 'Riga has proved itself unreliable. If we have our own port, and an agreement with the Oeselians, then trade will not only be secured, it will increase markedly.'

'Mstislav has embroiled us in wars before, Vasily,' warned Yuri, 'that proved not to Novgorod's advantage.'

'Reval is a prize worth fighting for, Yuri,' replied Vasily, 'especially now that Danish power is weak. We might not have another chance.'

At the city hall two days later the *veche* agreed to support the venture against Reval, the deciding factor being the guarantee of aid from Grand Prince George and Mstislav's pledge that Suzdal would not share in the profits once Reval had become a Novgorodian port.

*****

During his more than twenty years of ruling over his people the thing that Olaf took the greatest pleasure in was not the raiding, pillaging and slaughtering of his foes, though these were pleasant enough activities. No, the thing that brought him great joy was visiting the longhouses of his earls, the farms of his freemen and the shops and smiths of his villagers. It was a source of great pride that the blessed island of Oesel, surrounded by a warm sea, a land of kind summers and light breezes, was free from the never-ending warfare that plagued the mainland. In his youth there was incessant strife between the Estonian tribes, between the Estonians and Livs and between the Russians and Estonians and Livs. Now in his sixties, the mainland was the plaything of Danes, Russians and crusaders. The gods had cursed the land across the sea but they had blessed Oesel. His people had been delighted when the Danish king had been surrounded and defeated, even if the Sword Brothers had managed to spirit him away from certain death. They had walked from Kuressaare and the surrounding villages to marvel at the many Danish corpses that had been stripped and laid out on the ground for their viewing, before being consigned to great pyres. It was said that such was the booty taken from dead Danes that every man on the island had a coat of mail and a sword with which to go to war. His people were delighted and in high spirits but Olaf had been saddened.

He knew that Sigurd was thoughtful and cunning, possessed of a keen, enquiring mind unlike Stark and Kalf, who were brave and hot-headed like their dead brother Eric. He had trusted Sigurd when his eldest son had recommended allowing the Danes to land on Oesel where they could be surrounded and destroyed. And though the Danes had left many dead on the island and their king reduced to a laughing stock, he regretted the fact that for the first time a foreign invader had landed on Oesel. He feared it was a foretaste of things to come.

Olaf's hair and beard were now completely white and thinning, though his eyes were still clear and alert and his squat frame did not have an ounce of fat on it. Unlike his father Sigurd kept his face clean-shaven but he had the blonde hair and blue eyes of the majority of his people. They had spent the morning with a friend of his father, a barrel-chested old brawler who had taken them boar hunting. Olaf had been in his element, reminiscing about the old days in between skewering squealing boar, but now he rode at the head of his bodyguard in silence, the only sound the jangling of the ponies' bits and the occasional eagle taking flight from a nearby branch. They were riding by the side of a forest of oak and juniper on the way back to Kuressaare.

'It was good to see Klun again, father,' said Sigurd in an attempt to break the silence that was becoming oppressive.

Olaf snapped out of his daydream. 'Yes, good man Klun. The sort of man you want beside you in a shield wall.'

Because it was summer both had dispensed with mail shirts, wearing only linen tunics and leggings and nothing on their heads. The men of the bodyguard behind them sweated in mail corselets and helmets, their beards either plaited or forked as symbols of their masculinity.

'Stark and Kalf are eager to fight in the shield wall this year, father,' said Sigurd.

His two brothers were on the mainland, part of the garrison of Varbola that had been captured in the aftermath of King Valdemar's ignominious flight from Reval following his defeat on Oesel.

Olaf sighed. 'We will not retain Varbola beyond the end of the year.'

Sigurd was surprised. 'Oh?'

'Danish ships no longer patrol the sea outside the mouth of the Dvina, which means that more crusaders will soon be arriving at Riga. We will need every warrior on Oesel to defend our island.'

'You think the Danish king will return, father?'

Olaf shrugged. 'He may, he may not. But what I do know is that the Sword Brothers will be back once they have settled affairs on the mainland. It is only a matter of time.'

He suddenly pulled up his pony and looked at his son. The leading pair of his bodyguard nearly collided into him and Sigurd as they too pulled up their mounts.

'When you are ruler, Sigurd, you must above all safeguard the people.'

'That time is many years away.'

Olaf waved away his reassuring words. The older man's blue eyes bored into those of his son.

'Save the people, Sigurd, that is my command to you. Forget about glory and bravado. When the time comes your duty will be to safeguard the lives of those you rule over. Do you understand?'

Sigurd matched his father's iron stare. 'I understand, father.'

Olaf nudged his pony with his knees to prompt the beast to resume walking, Sigurd doing the same. The latter attempted to make more conversations with his father but gave up when the old man gave either one-word answers to his questions or merely grunted in response to statements. As a light rain began to fall they rode on towards Kuressaare in silence.

*****

'Cattle?'

Hans was scratching his head, wondering if Conrad was having a joke at his expense.

'That is what Master Rudolf ordered,' replied his friend. 'Two hundred head of cattle.'

'Why?'

Conrad shook his head. 'You know as much as I do.'

'It makes no sense,' said Anton on the other side of Conrad.

'Perhaps Master Rudolf wants to supplement Wenden's food supplies,' suggested Riki riding behind the three brother knights.

'Wenden has enough supplies of food,' Hans told him.

'And Hans takes a keen interest in the castle's food supplies, Riki,' grinned Conrad.

Following the battle at the Sedde Rudolf had ordered Conrad to take Riki's fifty Harrien, plus Leatherface and ten crossbowmen and the same number of sergeants from Wenden, and strike east to the south of Lake Vortsjarv. Meanwhile he would take the main force and chase Kristjan north, both to relieve Sir Richard at Lehola and ensure that the enemy would not have a chance to rest.

'Remember,' Rudolf had told Conrad on the eve of his departure, 'the majority of Ungannia's warriors will be under Kristjan's command, leaving southern Ungannia undefended. Ride hard and fast, seize the cattle and retreat back to Wenden.'

Rudolf would say no more on the matter and so Conrad and his ad hoc force left the next day, along with half a dozen packhorses loaded with tents, crossbow bolts and food. The land was now bathed in summer sunshine and the column of riders made good progress as it headed east.

'Did Master Rudolf say anything about burning villages?' asked Leatherface casually.

Conrad spun in the saddle. 'There is to be no burning, no looting and no raping.'

'Are they Rudolf's orders or yours?' teased Leatherface.

'Mine,' snapped Conrad.

'You've got a lot to learn,' replied Leatherface. 'You can't beat an enemy with soft words and good intentions. In Germany after a victory we would always make sure the enemy's territory suffered accordingly. I remember a time...'

'We are not in Germany,' said Conrad sternly. 'Once Kristjan has been defeated Ungannia will be under my control. I want the people to be loyal, not rebellious.'

But Leatherface would not have it. 'You see that's where you are going wrong, Brother Conrad.'

'Conrad is right,' said Hans. 'If you burn villages the inhabitants will be resentful.'

'We solved that problem in Germany easily enough,' replied Leatherface.

'How?' asked Anton.

'We killed all the inhabitants of the villages we plundered.'

Southern Ungannia was a carpet of green and blue, the thick forests of pine, birch and fir interwoven with crystal-clear

373

lakes and slow-moving rivers. The trees were alive with birds and the forests were filled with game as the riders moved stealthily along ancient forest tracks and by the sides of meadows and rivers to position themselves within sight of settlements. At first Conrad and his two friends would charge out of the trees around mid-morning to carry off grazing cattle. At night the beasts were kept in barns to keep them safe from wolves but during the day it was easy enough to steal them away from under the noses of young boys or old men who were watching over them. The problem was that each village usually possessed only half a dozen cows at most, and so after two days Conrad split his command into four groups to speed things up. He commanded one group, Hans a second, Anton a third and Riki the fourth. Conrad stressed again the necessity of avoiding plunder, rape and bloodshed and arranged to rendezvous in a week on the southern shore of Lake Vortsjarv where the Cumans had been defeated. To reduce the likelihood of violence he ordered Leatherface to be a member of his group.

The first few days were easy enough and soon Conrad was the proud owner of thirty stolen cattle, which only slowed down the raiders but also required guarding night and day.

'You don't want some cattle rustlers stealing them from under your nose, do you?'

Leatherface was having the time of his life, constantly reminding an increasingly irritable Conrad that he was no better than a thief.

'Though a thief with a nice horse, I'll grant you that,' smirked the mercenary.

'Shut up.'

'Strictly speaking, of course, you aren't really a thief.'

'I'm not?'

'Seeing as you are Marshal of Estonia and all, you can requisition what you want.'

Conrad was leading a small party of Leatherface, another crossbowman and two sergeants through wheatgrass at the edge of a forest of pine on their way to raid a village they had scouted the night before. Like dozens of other villages in Ungannia it was a collection of huts adjoining a couple of barns surrounded by pasture and slash and burn land. The abundance of land in Estonia made slash and burn a sensible policy for farmers who planted crops in a field for one or two seasons, thereafter letting the field lie fallow for several subsequent seasons. The farmers moved on to a field that had lain fallow for several years removing the vegetation and burning it, hence slash and burn. The ash produced by the burning added nutrients to the soil to aid the growing of crops. But Conrad was not here for crops and urged his horse on to seize half a dozen cattle grazing in a field nearby the settlement.

'No violence,' he shouted to Leatherface as a young boy, having seen the approaching riders, sprinted towards the huts.

They slowed when they reached the cows so as not to stampede them, the sergeants circling them and using the blunt ends of their lances to move them towards the forest so they could be taken back to camp.

'Here's trouble,' said Leatherface from on his horse behind Conrad. 'Look lively,' he said to the crossbowman beside him, both of them taking a foot out of a stirrup and shoving it in the metal stirrup fitted to the fore-ends of their weapons to load them.

Conrad saw four figures advancing from the village towards them, all carrying round shields and wearing helmets. Three were armed with spears, the other with a sword.

'This should be easy,' remarked Leatherface as he brought up his weapon to aim it.

'No violence,' ordered Conrad.

'Don't be an idiot,' the mercenary told him, 'in case you hadn't noticed they are all armed.'

Conrad spurred his horse forward to intercept the group, which as he got nearer saw was comprised two old men and two young boys, the helmets of the latter too large for their heads. They stopped when he neared them, the old man with a sword taking a few steps forward. He pointed the blade at Conrad who slowed his horse.

'Return those cattle, thief, and I will let you live.'

Conrad halted his horse and dismounted, pulling his mail coif off his head and keeping his sword in its scabbard. He walked towards the old man, who must have been seventy if he was a day. His beard was white, his skin leathery as befitting his age but his eyes burned with defiance.

376

'I cannot do that, sir,' sighed Conrad.

Leatherface and his subordinate were now behind Conrad pointing their crossbows at the old man.

'I have seen many summers and killed many bandits,' sneered the old man. 'They are all the same no matter what robes they wear. Cowards and bullies who only come out of the shadows when the menfolk are away.'

'And why are they away?' said Conrad. 'Because they are fighting beside Kristjan who makes war on Livonia.'

'Do the Sword Brothers make war on women and children?' scoffed the old man.

'The Sword Brothers obey orders,' answered Conrad vaguely. 'I wish you no harm but I must take your cattle. For that I apologise.'

The old man laughed. 'A thief with manners, now that is a first.'

One of the boys suddenly ran at Conrad, his spear levelled at the brother knight's belly.

'Do not shoot!' Conrad shouted at the crossbowmen as the boy neared him.

At the last second Conrad leapt to the left to cause the spear point to pass by his right side, clenching his right fist and smashing it on the back of the boy's neck as he stumbled past, knocking him to the ground. The boy was agile and tried to get up as soon as he had fallen, but Conrad had whipped out his sword and held the point at his neck before he could rise. The brother knight looked at the old man.

'Do you want this boy's life on your conscience?'

The youth was now terrified, fear in his eyes, as Conrad held the sword at his throat. He looked pleadingly at the old man. For the first time the latter looked unsure, hesitant.

'What is this place?' asked Conrad.

'Restu,' replied the old man.

Conrad withdrew his sword from the boy's throat.

'Get up.'

Looking utterly relieved, he sprang to his feet and ran back to the old man's side.

'Forgive me, grandfather,' he said to him.

The old man looked kindly at him.

'I make you this promise. I, Conrad Wolff, Marshal of Estonia, will replace your cattle after the war is over. This I vow to God and to you, and a Sword Brother does not break his vow.'

He picked up the helmet and threw it to the boy.

'Remember,' he said to the youth, 'an enemy never stands still so you can spear him. Think before you attack, never let your rage master you.'

He walked back to his horse and regained the saddle. In the distance the sergeants were herding the cows out of sight. He tugged on the reins to turn the beast around.

'Sword Brother,' called the old man. 'What if you lose the war, what then?'

Conrad smiled. 'The Sword Brothers never lose a war, sir. You will get your cattle back, have no fear.'

He dug his spurs into his horse's side and cantered away, the crossbowmen following.

'Fine words,' agreed Leatherface. 'You should have let us kill them, saves lots of trouble later.'

'When I return their cattle to them I will have earned their loyalty,' replied Conrad. 'Why make enemies when you can make friends with a bit of effort.'

Leatherface sighed. 'That's not really the mercenary way of thinking, Brother Conrad.'

Conrad had been in Livonia for thirteen years. During that time he had learned to use a wide variety of weapons, both on foot and in the saddle. He had taken part in battles against the Estonians, Oeselians, Cumans, Lithuanians and Russians. He had taken part in sieges and been besieged himself. He was a skilled veteran, a man at home on the battlefield. But nothing had prepared him for the stress and frustration associated with herding cattle.

Moving a few beasts was easy enough, but when his raids had collected just over fifty the nightmare began. He and the sergeants made a lot of noise in an attempt to get the herd moving, Riki's warriors trying vainly to dissuade him. The cattle refused to move at first, but when he, the sergeants and crossbowmen attempted to frighten them into moving they scattered in all directions, into the woods, into thickets and into the waters of a river. It took half a day to re-assemble them. Afterwards one of Riki's men, a thickset warrior with a huge beard, berated the Marshal of Estonia.

'You should never shout or whistle when herding cattle, *Susi*. They are not warriors to be barked at. If the cattle start running you have lost.'

'Perhaps we should tie them together,' suggested Conrad.

'Or shoot them,' added Leatherface.

The warrior shook his head. 'All you need is a drover to walk behind them to move them along and calm them.'

'We are in your hands,' Conrad told him, 'just get them moving.'

The next day the warrior began his work, having told Conrad and the others that they should not make any sudden movements or noises that would stampede the herd. He let the cattle form themselves into a loose herd before walking back and forth behind the beasts, to stimulate predator 'stalking' behaviour. This caused anxiety in the cattle and made them want to bunch together. When they had done so the warrior continued to walk back and forth to the rear of the herd but then moved closer to the animals. In response they began walking away from him and in the direction he wanted them to go. Conrad spurred his horse towards two cattle that were apart from the herd.

'Leave them, *Susi*,' said the drover. 'They will join the rest soon enough.'

And they did, walking to the herd that was miraculously moving in the general direction of Lake Vortsjarv.

'A drover replicates the movements of a predator,' the drover told him, 'so for safety cattle will bunch together.'

It was still a frustrating process though, and slow. To ease the boredom Conrad and Leatherface went hunting most days, bringing back the carcasses of at least two roe deer each afternoon that were gutted and cooked in the evening. It took five days to reach the rendezvous point and another week to reach Wenden, by which time Conrad was heartily sick of cows and staring at their rumps. When they reached the castle a beaming Rudolf met Conrad at the outer perimeter gates and watched as the cattle were herded into a fenced-off area near the wagon park.

'How many cattle?' he asked Conrad.

'Two hundred and twenty, master.'

Rudolf rubbed his hands together. 'Excellent, well done.'

'What news of Lehola, master?' asked Anton.

'You can ask Sir Richard yourself, he is here at Wenden,' answered Rudolf, 'but suffice to say that Lehola is safe and well provisioned, though Fellin is still occupied by troops loyal to Kristjan. However, they will be dealt with once Bishop Albert lands at Riga and marches north to join us.'

Conrad was surprised. 'Sir Richard is at Wenden?'

'Of course,' replied Rudolf, 'he is here for Kaja's wedding and will accompany us to Treiden. Rameke has already departed with my note that will be fixed to the church door where they will be married.'

Conrad was even more confused. 'Note?'

Rudolf rolled his eyes. 'Don't you know anything about the marriage ceremony, Conrad?'

'No, master.'

'He don't know anything about herding cattle either, Master Rudolf,' remarked Leatherface who had strolled over for no reason in particular. 'Good job he's useful with a sword, ain't it?'

'After a marriage has been arranged,' Rudolf told him, ignoring the mercenary, 'a wedding notice must be posted to the door of the church where the ceremony is to take place. It states who is to be married, in this case Prince Rameke to Princess Kaja.'

Conrad, now more confused than ever, looked at Hans and Anton who wore similar bewildered looks.

'Kaja is not a princess,' he said to Rudolf.

'She is a farmer's daughter, or was,' added Hans.

Rudolf spread his arms. 'If that is the case then how can her family afford such a large dowry?'

'Dowry, master?' said Conrad.

Rudolf pointed at the cattle. 'Over two hundred head of cattle, a dowry fit for a princess, I think.'

Leatherface bowed his head to Rudolf. 'And here was I thinking that you were a gruff old mercenary like me. I forgot you are a lord's son.'

Rudolf shook his head at the three brother knights who were perplexed.

'Rameke is the second most important Liv in this land after Fricis. There are many Livs who want to see him marry a woman of his own race rather than a Saccalian, much less a penniless, landless Saccalian. But if they are convinced that Kaja is a woman of wealth then they will warm to the union more quickly. And the fact that the Marshal of Estonia and the Duke of Saccalia will be attending the wedding only adds credence to the notion of Kaja's high position. Grand Master Volquin will also be in attendance, as will I.'

Conrad was impressed. He had thought Rameke's wedding would be a small affair in the wooden church in the middle of the village next to the hill fort at Treiden. But Master Rudolf had obviously been thinking ahead.

'The Duke of Saccalia will be giving Kaja away,' continued Rudolf. 'I assume that you will be Rameke's best man, Conrad?'

'Yes, master.'

Couriers were sent north to request the attendance of Hillar and Andres at Wenden, though Tonis remained at Lehola with his wolf shields to hold the stronghold should Kristjan attempt to storm it in Sir Richard's absence. Rudolf also thought it politic not to have the wedding feast at Treiden attended by warriors carrying the symbol of Lembit, who had inflicted much misery on Livonia. But despite the attention being lavished on her wedding Kaja was in a glum mood when Conrad went to see her. She shared Ilona's hut in the outer perimeter, among the simple lodgings of the castle workers and their families. After she had spent a morning on the training field assisting Lukas teaching novices the art of fighting with a sword in one hand and a dagger in the other, he found her sitting outside the hut cleaning her sword. Ilona came from the interior with a small jar filled with one of her herbal concoctions, which she gave to a waiting woman.

'Brother Conrad,' she smiled, 'come to see how the blushing bride is getting along?'

Kaja stopped running the cloth along the length of the blade and looked up. She gave Conrad a weak smile.

'Why so sad?' he asked. 'Has one of the novices got the better of you?'

She smiled more convincingly. 'Not yet, *Susi*.'

'Kaja is annoyed that Father Otto will not be marrying her to Rameke,' said Ilona.

'Oh?'

'Rudolf informed us that a priest cannot marry a couple if he has killed someone,' explained Ilona, 'it is a rule of the Holy Church.'

'Ah, I see.'

Kaja stood and slashed the air with the sword. 'It is a stupid rule.'

'Rudolf told me that Bishop Bernhard will officiate instead,' said Ilona.

Conrad was astounded. 'An honour indeed.'

'I've never heard of him,' stated Kaja dismissively.

'He is the Bishop of Semgallia,' Conrad told her, 'and one of the most important churchmen in Livonia.'

Kaja slashed the air again. 'I prefer Father Otto.'

Ilona frowned at her. 'You will soon be a princess, Kaja, and must learn to act like one. You are very lucky.'

Conrad looked at the handsome Ilona, her hair still as black as night. He wondered if she ever regretted meeting Master Rudolf. She had saved his life and nursed him back to health after his body had been burned at Holm. Everyone knew that she was in love with him and Conrad believed that he was devoted to her. But the vows Rudolf had taken on becoming a Sword Brother meant the two could never marry. And so Ilona chose to remain single and not bear children so she could be near Rudolf.

Kaja's dowry was sent on ahead, guarded by a score of sergeants and the same number of spearmen, with drovers ensuring that the cattle made decent progress after being driven across one of the Gauja's fords north of Wenden and then south along the northern riverbank to Treiden. Master Rudolf also sent heralds ahead to announce in every village the herd passed that it was the dowry of Princess Kaja of Saccalia. The 'princess' herself was accompanied to Treiden by Rudolf as Master of Wenden, Lukas who had taught her how to use a sword, Ilona her Maid of Honour, Conrad as Marshal of Estonia and Hans and Anton because they were her friends. Rudolf had decreed that he and his brother knights should travel to Treiden in full armour, riding warhorses, Hans being entrusted with carrying Wenden's banner as Walter had been left behind to command the garrison. Then came the commanders of the Army of the Wolf, each one in helmet and mail armour and riding well-groomed ponies. Conrad hated the journey because Rudolf decided that he and his men should wear their full-face helms to impress the villages they passed through. Mid-summer's day had recently passed – it was hot and windless so the brother knights roasted in their armour. As did the Duke of Saccalia.

Sir Richard Bruffingham had come to Livonia a crusader in search of redemption, a clean-shaven man with a bald head who wore no coat of arms on his surcoat or shield. But Pope Honorius himself had created him Duke of Saccalia so Bishop Albert directed Riga's College of Arms to create a fitting coat of arms for his position. The college had sent a surcoat, banner and legal document verifying the heraldic device that Sir Richard was now authorised to wear: a white boar's head with golden tusks on a blue background. The boar had been chosen because it was a symbol of endurance, courage and a willingness to fight to the death. The six knights who had accompanied Sir Richard also wore duplicate surcoats that had been made at Lehola and Squire Paul carried the new banner of his lord.

Rudolf's plan had the desired effect. When the party reached Treiden the settlement was surrounded by dozens of tents to accommodate those Livs who had come to see their prince marry. All witnessed the Princess Kaja's procession. Grand Master Volquin was accommodated in the great hall of the hill fort, though Fricis sent a courier to Rudolf and Sir Richard apologising for the fact that there was no room for them or their knights. So they too pitched their tents outside the settlement, the great herd of cattle sent on ahead was in an enclosure to the north of the hill fort.

The settlement was thronged with people on the day of the wedding. Bishop Bernhard in his plain white woollen mantle and habit stood in front of the couple. The simple church with its thatched roof was their background. A sea of faces looked on as Bernhard conducted the ceremony in the open, Kaja wearing a blue dress, the traditional colour of purity. Rameke wore a plain green tunic, brown leggings and leather boots.

Despite its rustic appearance the marriage ceremony was conducted according to strict rules. The aged Bernhard read from his bible with Rameke standing on the right side of Kaja. She stood on the left because God had created woman from a rib in the left side of Adam. Her long blonde hair shone in the sun and Conrad thought they made a handsome couple. He passed a silver ring to Rameke and Sir Richard handed a silver band to Kaja, the items of jewellery were given to Bishop Bernhard who blessed them. They were then exchanged and placed on the bride's and groom's fourth fingers.

When the ceremony in front of the church doors had been concluded they and a select few, he included, went inside the austere building. The couple stood beneath a white linen sheet held aloft by gangly, deathly pale choirboys as the bishop conducted a mass in Latin. After which Bernhard gave the kiss of peace to Rameke, which was passed to his new wife. Thus did Kaja, an orphaned Saccalian girl, become a Livonian princess.

The newly married couple beamed smiles from the top table in the hill fort's great hall beside Bernhard, Fricis, Volquin, Sir Richard and Rudolf. But Conrad thought that the happiest person in the hall was Hans, whose eyes lit up when an endless stream of food was brought from the kitchens for the dozens of guests. Servants brought huge platters heaped with sizzling strips of deer, wild boar, duck, goose and chicken, the meats seasoned with caraway seeds, onions, garlic and white mustard. Strong honey beer – *medalus* – served alongside a non-alcoholic drink made from rye bread and flavoured with fruit and herbs. The Livs called it *kvass*.

Young girls scattered rose petals on the floor among the rushes as the hall filled with the sounds of boasting, laughter and raucous cheering. Soon drunk warriors were trying to grope shapely female servants or grappled with bearded brutes on the opposite side of the table in bouts of arm wrestling. The feasting went on long into the night, after the newlyweds had retreated to their private quarters. Eventually most of the men in the hall fell into a drunken slumber, some staggered outside to collapse when the fresh night air entered their lungs, and a few, sober, took time to reflect. One of the latter was Conrad who left Hans and Anton sleeping on the floor of the hall to wander outside to stare up at the clear night sky.

He walked to the gates of the fort, which had been left open so the guests could wander back to their tents. Few did, either passing out in the compound or preferring to sleep on the floor of the hall. Nevertheless the gates remained open and an unusually large number of guards stood sentry in the fort's towers, outside the gates and in the compound itself.

The fort was on a hill half a mile west of a bend in the Gauja. Two miles to the south, on the other side of the river, was the order's castle at Segewold. Kremon Castle was nearer and on the same side of the river as Treiden. Conrad nodded to the guards at the gates and walked a few paces down the hill, the settlement at the foot of the hill a mass of black shapes. The fort was now eerily quiet after the unending din earlier that had made his voice hoarse as he tried to make himself heard conversing with guests.

He stopped a few paces from the gates and looked at the silver ring on his hand. He thought of Daina and his son Dietmar, both of whom had been wrenched cruelly from him. That dreadful night seemed like only yesterday and though the searing pain that had gripped him in the aftermath of their deaths no longer possessed him, a dull ache still remained. He turned the ring on his finger but became aware of faint footsteps behind him. He swivelled around, hand on the hilt of his sword. He may have been in Treiden but Livonia was not paradise and had its fair share of robbers whose friend was the night.

Bishop Bernhard threw up his hands. 'My mistake to creep up on Livonia's finest swordsman.'

Conrad took his hand away from his sword. 'Hardly that, lord bishop.'

Bernhard was eighty if he was a day yet his frame was still lean and his reflexes sharp. Conrad smiled when he noticed a sword strapped to his waist.

'You were the best man at the wedding, were you not?'

'Yes, lord bishop.'

'There you are, then. The best man is exactly that: the best swordsman that can be found to ensure that a wedding is not interrupted. I think Prince Rameke made a good choice.'

Bernhard looked back at the fort. 'Many men will have sore heads in the morning. But not you, Conrad, eh.'

'Drinking myself into a stupor is not for me, lord bishop. And you?'

'When I was a soldier I liked nothing better than drinking myself into oblivion after a battle. Fighting, drinking, whoring; it was a way of life for a young Bernhard of Lippe. But no longer.'

'You are respected throughout Livonia for your military record and abstemious nature, lord bishop.' Conrad looked away to the settlement at the foot of the hill. 'If only others that hold high positions in the Holy Church in Livonia displayed the same qualities.'

'You speak of Archbishop Stefan,' said Bernhard.

'I do.'

'I heard about the unfortunate incident at Wenden.'

Conrad looked back at the bishop. 'Unfortunate, lord bishop? The garrison of Riga should be disbanded; it is nothing more than a plaything of the archdeacon. I have yet to see it fight on the battlefield.'

'I fear you are right, Conrad,' agreed Bernhard, 'but the good people of Riga are very fond of the soldiers that watch over them while they sleep.'

'When Bishop Albert returns from Germany I hope he will address his nephew's outrageous behaviour.'

Bernhard took Conrad's elbow. 'Walk with me a little further.'

They ambled down the track, the hoots of owls in the nearby forest the only sound in the darkness.

'The bishop will not be returning to Livonia this year, Conrad. I told the grand master and Rudolf earlier and you might as well hear it as you are Marshal of Estonia.'

'The bishop is not ill, is he?' enquired Conrad with concern.

'No, nothing like that,' Bernhard reassured him, 'but King Valdemar has been taken hostage by one of his former vassals, Henry Count of Schwerin.'

'Master Rudolf's father,' said Conrad.

'Indeed. Anyway the king and his eldest son currently reside in one of the Duke of Saxony's castles and Danish power has been gravely wounded, some say fatally.'

'The Count of Schwerin was eager enough to do King Valdemar's bidding when he was in Livonia,' said Conrad bitterly, remembering the death of Johann at the Pala.

'I do not know the reason for the schism between the two,' remarked Bernhard, 'but Count Henry has gathered many north German lords to his side and they are determined to resist any attempts by the Danes to subjugate them again.'

'What does this mean for Livonia, lord bishop?'

'That Bishop Albert's task of recruiting crusaders for Livonia has been made harder, as the north German lords are reluctant to leave their lands if there is a chance the Danes might try to rescue their king by force. However, he has managed to recruit two thousand men for service here this year, mostly from Lübeck and the surrounding towns. Commander Nordheim will be taking ship with them soon.'

'Commander Nordheim will not be leading these soldiers?' asked Conrad, appalled by the idea.

'Have no fear, Conrad, I will be leading the troops from Germany.'

'To where, lord bishop?'

'Fellin,' stated Bernhard, 'we must retake the fort to show this Kristjan that his war against Livonia will lead only to his defeat. And after that Ungannia will be conquered.'

'And what of the Danes in northern Estonia?' queried Conrad.

'Consider this, Conrad,' answered the bishop, 'the Danes cannot fight a campaign in northern Germany and another in

Estonia. We, and specifically you, may benefit from Count Henry's rebellion.'

'Me, lord bishop?'

Bernhard chuckled. 'The Marshal of Estonia should be based in the country's most important stronghold, I think.'

'Dorpat?' proffered Conrad.

'Reval, Conrad.'

*****

Vsevolod thought that the Battle of Abava was bad enough, and reckoned himself lucky to have escaped with his life. But as Aras and his senior commanders stood before him and Rasa in Panemunis' main hall he believed that the terror he had experienced that day was nothing compared to the dread that enveloped the chamber as he listened to a report. Mindaugas, now fully recovered from the bout of flu that had possessed his body during the winter, stood with Morta, ashen faced, as the tale of woe was relayed to them by a short, stout Selonian prince with a deep voice. Even Aras, normally unflappable, bit his bottom lip as the man spoke. His boots and leggings were smeared with mud and his cheeks flushed with the exertion of riding for many miles to get to the stronghold. Normally he would have been compelled to tidy up his appearance before being granted an audience with the royal couple, but such was the gravity of the news he carried that protocol had to be cast aside.

'I have ridden from Mesoten, highness,' the prince stated.

Vsevolod looked at Rasa. 'Mesoten? I thought that was a ruin following the crusader campaign against it.'

The man nodded. 'It is, highness, but your army has taken refuge there following the clash with Duke Arturus.'

'I have been there,' said Mindaugas, 'there is not room on the summit to accommodate two thousand men, let alone their horses and wagons.'

The man looked at Aras, unsure whether to proceed.

'Continue,' ordered Aras.

The man swallowed. 'There are only three hundred men on Mesoten's summit, highness.'

Vsevolod rose from his throne as Rasa and Morta gasped. 'Three hundred! Where are the rest?'

'Dead, highness,' replied the prince, beads of sweat appearing on his forehead. 'We had rendezvoused with Duke Viesthard's warriors and a force of two thousand Samogitians under Prince Skiras, having heard of the approach of an army of Kurs. We took up a very strong position on a piece of rising ground five miles west of Viethard's stronghold of Tervete, but...'

'But?' shouted Vsevolod.

The man was now sweating profusely. 'But when the Kurs attacked and then fell back in precipitous retreat the Samogitians and Semgallians pursued, highness.'

'Let me guess,' said Aras, 'it was feint to lure you away from the high ground.'

'Yes, lord,' replied the prince. 'The Kurs fell back just far enough to split our army before they turned and attacked. They had hidden a mounted reserve behind a hill that cut our foot soldiers to pieces.'

Vsevolod, stunned, flopped down on his throne. 'Only three hundred are left out of an army of, what, seven thousand?'

'Yes, highness, but Duke Viesthard and his Semgallians, what is left of them, fled to Tervete. Most of the Samogitians are dead. Prince Skiras is…'

'Is what?' snapped Mindaugas.

'Also dead, lord,' answered the prince.

'Get out,' Vsevolod growled.

The prince bowed, about faced and rapidly departed from the chamber.

'What does this mean?' said a pale-faced Rasa.

'That Arturus controls most of Semgallia and a large portion of Samogitia if he chooses to strike south.'

'How can this be?' said a distraught Mindaugas. He placed an arm around the shoulder of his wife. 'It is time to show this Arturus the might of Nalsen and Selonia. We must muster every man and send this demon back to hell.'

Morta smiled with pride at her husband's bravado but Vsevolod buried his head in his hands.

'It would make more sense to deprive Arturus of the one thing that he seems to acquire with ease,' suggested Aras.

Vsevolod looked up. 'Which is?'

'Victory, highness,' replied Aras.

'Explain yourself,' demanded Vsevolod.

Aras, now more relaxed, began pacing the chamber.

'Duke Arturus and his deputy Lamekins have proved adept battlefield commanders to put it mildly. It is time to see if they are as accomplished at siege warfare. Fortify the hill forts on the border and let the Kurs try to reduce them without siege engines.'

Vsevolod stroked his beard. 'It would be better if Arturus spent his time reducing strongholds not in Selonia or Nalsen. Go and tell that idiot who brought news of our latest defeat that he is to return to Mesoten and hold it until we organise a relief force.'

'I will lead the relief force,' offered Mindaugas.

Vsevolod looked at Aras and smiled slyly. They were thinking the same.

'There will be no relief force,' said the former. 'If Arturus is amusing himself at Mesoten then we have more time to organise our defences.'

'You would sacrifice three hundred of our men for nothing?' said Mindaugas incredulously.

Vsevolod spun to look at his son-in-law. 'I would sacrifice three thousand if it kept the Kurs out of our lands. The crops still have to be gathered in and if they are not then the people will starve in the winter. Better Semgallia is ravaged than Selonia or Nalsen. See to it, General Aras.'

Aras saluted and pointed at the other commanders in the chamber to follow him. After the doors to the hall had been closed Vsevolod rested his chin in his hands.

'I have greatly underestimated Duke Arturus. I will not make the same mistake again.'

'It is dishonourable to abandon Duke Viesthard,' snapped Mindaugas.

'If you are to become a great warlord, Mindaugas,' said Vsevolod calmly, 'you must realise not only that honour is an expensive commodity but also that allies readily desert each other in favour of their own interests. You think Duke Viesthard would not do the same if the roles were reversed?'

'I would like to think not,' said Mindaugas firmly.

'Your faith in human nature is most touching,' replied Vsevolod, 'but until all men think like you we must keep our wits sharp.'

*****

The land around Pskov was bathed in glorious sunshine that summer, which ripened the crops in the fertile agricultural lands ringing the city. Set amid rolling hills and blessed by a moderate climate, Pskov may have been the so-called 'younger brother' of Novgorod but it was fast becoming its economic rival. The long humid days of early summer were ideal for growing the long-stemmed flax used to make clothing, bedding, fishing nets, ropes and candle wicks. So abundant was the crop that thousands of bales of flax were exported to Livonia every year, in the years that the crusader state and Novgorod were not at war, that is.

To the north of the city were great forests of fir, birch and pine and also stretches of ash, linden, maple, elm and oak. It was no coincidence that timber was also a major industry in Pskov. The forests were also filled with animals that provided the city's furriers with an unending supply of bear, sable, marten, wolf, fox and squirrel hides. The villagers of the ancient hilltop settlements supplemented their income from farming with hunting and trapping, the city's tax collectors gathering a rich tribute in crops and pelts for the city's mayor, or *posadnik*, who was appointed by the prince of Novgorod. Domash Tverdislavich had held the post for many years and had used it to his personal advantage as well as that of Novgorod. He ruled Pskov like it was his own personal kingdom and was usually of a jovial disposition. But today his handsome face wore a scowl.

Ordered by Mstislav to muster an army and lead it to a rendezvous point on the northern shore of Lake Peipus, he knew that once more the prince was taking Pskov and Novgorod to war. There was a time when he led raiding parties far into the west, to the Dvina and even across the river to plunder Lithuanian villages. He had even burned the wooden fort of the Sword Brothers at Holm, before taking many of the Livs who lived in the nearby village as slaves. They were good days and the sight of his banner struck terror into the Livs and Estonians alike. The victories were easy and achieved with little cost. But then more and more Sword Brothers came and built castles of stone to guard their new crusader state. And after them came crusaders and the fighting became hard, costly and far from enjoyable. Of late Pskov had lost many sons to the Sword Brothers and Novgorod even more. The merchants and boyars of those two ancient cities wanted peace and prosperity, not war and destitution. He thought he must be getting old because he was of the same opinion.

'Another glorious campaign to water the soil with Russian blood,' said Gleb bitterly. 'How many of the men behind us will not be returning to their homes, to their families?'

Normally Domash would have silenced his impish *Skomorokh*, one of the ancient strolling performers who were followers of the old religion and who entertained, charmed and seduced the common folk with their songs and tales about the world before the coming of the Orthodox religion. The *Skomorokhs*, despite being condemned by the church as the 'devil's servants', still had great influence, even among the boyars and merchants, and Gleb, whose name meant 'heir of god,' was among the most influential. It was no coincidence that Domash kept him by his side for it smoothed his rule over the Pskovians, though Gleb's tongue could be cutting. Today Domash was glad that it was so.

'How short is the memory of Prince Mstislav,' continued Gleb. 'It was not so long ago that half his army was cut to pieces by the Estonians on the frozen surface of Lake Peipus. And then hundreds more were lost trying to take Odenpah, which had been reinforced by the accursed Sword Brothers. One wonders why Novgorod tolerates such a demented leader.'

The commanders of the *Druzhina*, the élite horsemen of the boyars who were lavishly armed and armoured, looked at Domash but the mayor said nothing. There was a slight breeze that ruffled the great banner of Pskov showing a golden snow leopard on a blue background.

'I am certain the prince knows what he is doing,' said Yaroslav Nevsky, now restored to Mstislav's favour. He had sent his wife and child ahead to Novgorod but elected to stay with Domash out of loyalty, the mayor having offered his family a house in Pskov when they had been exiled.

'Does he?' scoffed Gleb. 'I would have thought that you of all people would have cause to welcome the removal of the oaf who sits in Novgorod's kremlin. By the way, what happened to the oaf's banner that got you exiled?'

Yaroslav blushed and the *Druzhina* commanders tut-tutted but Gleb did not care.

'Thank you, Gleb,' said Domash, 'perhaps you would afford us the courtesy of riding in peace so we can enjoy the verdant countryside.'

'Verdant countryside?' mocked Gleb, 'have you swallowed a book?'

'I will say this and then we will proceed in silence,' said Domash firmly. 'When we get to the rendezvous point watch your mouth. Prince Mstislav has no love for the *Skomorokhs* and will have your head on the slightest pretext.'

'I didn't know you cared,' smiled Gleb, his stringed instrument, a *gusli*, slung over his shoulder.

'I don't,' replied Domash, 'but the prince may have my head as well and I care very much about that.'

'Do not worry,' Gleb whispered to Yaroslav, 'when the Nevsky family rules in Novgorod things will be much better.'

'Silence!' commanded Domash.

The army marched first along Lake Pskov and then Lake Peipus, the great inland waterways that delineated the border between Novgorod and Estonia. The freshwater, blue and warm, was bordered by great stretches of sandy beaches and dunes. Inland the terrain became hillier and covered with pine forests. Dotted along the eastern shore of the lake were fishing villages, mostly a collection of no more than a dozen ramshackle huts with flat-bottomed boats in front of them on the sand. But the people, though poor and threadbare, looked healthy enough for the lake had an abundance of perch, bream and roach to fill their bellies. When the army passed by their settlements young and old alike came to wave and smile at Gleb in his distinctive bright blue tunic.

Domash had been able to muster two hundred *Druzhina* from among Pskov's boyars, along with five hundred of the city's militia. The latter were all foot soldiers equipped with spears and axes and wearing *kuyak* armour – leather shirts with rectangular metal plates attached. The largest contingent and the most poorly armed and equipped was the *Voi*, the soldiers raised from the villages around the city. They numbered a thousand but none wore armour on their bodies, though the city armouries had at least furnished them with helmets to give them a semblance of military bearing. Most carried only a spear and an axe tucked into their belts. All of them held wooden shields that had no leather facings. On their feet they wore shoes fashioned from birch bark. The *Voi* marched alongside the dozens of wagons that carried the army's supplies. A small mounted rearguard followed.

The *Voi* invariably suffered terribly on campaign, being viewed as expendable by army commanders. And yet the men who staffed it were happy enough to answer the call to arms. For one thing the city authorities of Pskov and Novgorod fed them on campaign, though the supply system was known to collapse from time to time. More importantly, the city authorities distributed food to the villages where the men had come from to compensate them for the loss of manpower while they were serving in the *Voi*. In this way the men knew that their families would not starve, which was a great incentive, especially during a winter campaign.

But it was now the height of summer and when the Pskov contingent reached the rendezvous point it was greeted by a great stench produced by a camp holding thousands of men and horses. Mstislav himself had mustered five thousand of the *Voi*, three thousand of Novgorod's militia, all equipped and supplied by the city's *veche*, in addition to eight hundred *Druzhina*, the sons and retainers of the *veche*'s wealthiest families.

402

Mstislav also brought his mounted bodyguard – two hundred lance-armed horsemen in helmets and lamellar armour.

But it was the troops of Grand Prince George of Suzdal that made the greatest impression. The soldiers of Mstislav wore a mixture of green and brown hues for leggings and tunics, but the men of Suzdal sported a dazzlingly array of bright green, red and purple clothing.

The grand prince's élite troops were his two thousand *Druzhina*, all mounted on magnificent horses whose bridles were decorated with silver discs. Each man wore a pointed iron helmet called a *shishak* that had an immoveable brass nasal guard. Officers were identified by metal half masks attached to their helmets – *zabralom* – which protected the eyes and nose. Each rider also wore a *barmitsa*: chainmail that was attached to the bottom edge of the helmet to hang down the shoulders and back. It was wrapped under the chin to closely protect the neck and throat.

Beneath their lamellar armour they wore a *kal'chuga*, a mail hauberk with short sleeves that ended just above the elbow. Like the horsemen of Novgorod and Pskov they carried almond-shaped shields some four feet in length. Carried point down, they protected a horsemen from the chin to the knees. They were light, being made of wood, covered with hide and bound with iron on the edges as a defence against blows. To reinforce them metal strips were fixed to the shield, crosswise, with a semi-circular metal cover plate fastened over the centre of the shield at the intersection. Every shield was coloured red.

403

Like all *Druzhina* their primary weapon was a lance, though many of those from Suzdal also carried javelins called *sulitsa*. These had light, thin shafts some five feet in length and were carried in a small quiver called a *dzhid* that was attached to the belt on the left side. Also attached to the belt was a short, double-bladed knife known as a *poyasnie*, and a sword in an iron scabbard bound with leather and decorated with silver inlay. It was hung on the belt by two rings at the mouth of the scabbard.

The grand prince had also brought with him eight thousand horse archers, missile troops equipped with recurve bows made from sinew, horn and wood similar to the weapons employed by the heathen Tartars. The horse archers were used to mount raids and conduct reconnaissance and had the army been carrying out a mobile campaign into enemy territory they would have been most effective. As it was, of the over twenty thousand men that gathered on the northern shore of Lake Peipus, only nine and half thousand were foot soldiers more suited to assaulting strongholds.

But Mstislav was in a buoyant mood, embracing Yaroslav warmly when he and Domash visited him in the prince's huge pavilion pitched in a fenced-off area half a mile from the stench and dung of the main camp. He invited both of them to a sumptuous feast to be held that evening to cement the fraternal bonds between Novgorod and Suzdal.

The small city of tents, wagons, ponies and horses was swathed in a permanent cloud of smoke as hundreds of

404

campfires were lit. Large swathes of a nearby forest were felled for firewood and to construct rudimentary shelters for those members of the *Voi* that had no tents. Quartermasters visited villages near the lake to purchase fish and boyars and their retainers went into the forests in search of game. And on the western perimeter of the camp sentries halted a small party of horsemen intent on seeing Prince Mstislav.

In camp black-robed monks engaged brightly attired *Skomorokhs* in fierce arguments, while in the prince's pavilion great quantities of beer and *stavlenniy myod* were consumed as the leaders of Novgorod and Suzdal toasted their coming victory. Mstislav promised that every Dane captured at Reval would be given to Grand Prince George as a gift to take back to his city. George thanked the prince but stated that he would also empty northern Estonia of the fair-skinned, blue-eyed women and children that were highly prized as slaves in the Asiatic lands to the south. Mstislav readily agreed – a land devoid of pagans would make his rule in Reval much easier.

Mstislav stripped a chicken thigh with his teeth and tossed the bones onto the floor in front of the table. He started to gulp down a large cup of beer while his eyes watched a guard enter the pavilion and make his way around the walls towards the top table. He stopped drinking, belched and listened as the guard stooped and whispered into his ear. He gave a raucous laugh.

'Show him in.'

The loud chatter began to ebb as two figures were escorted into the pavilion, the lords of Suzdal looking quizzically as the men, both tall and wearing mail armour, walked between the spear-armed guards. One was young with long fair hair, the other older, clean-shaven whose hair was as black as night.

'Well, Vetseke,' said Mstislav to the dark-haired individual, 'I did not think to see you again.'

Vetseke bowed to the prince. 'I bring aid, highness.'

Mstislav wiped his mouth on his sleeve and peered at the angry looking young man beside him.

'Who's this?'

'This is Lord Kristjan, highness, son of the late Kalju,' said Vetseke in Russian, 'and appointed Lord of all Estonia.'

'Appointed by whom?' asked the prince.

'By the gods, apparently, highness.'

Those within hearing distance laughed at Kristjan who gave them a murderous stare.

'Why do they laugh?' he said to Vetseke.

The Liv shrugged. 'I do not know, Kristjan, these Russians have a curious sense of humour.'

Kristjan pointed at Mstislav. 'He is the leader here?'

Vetseke looked at the large, bearded man next to Mstislav who was dressed in a rich red shirt and wore gold rings on his fingers.

'He asks if you are commander here, highness,' Vetseke said to Mstislav.

The prince smiled at Grand Prince George. 'We are joint commanders of this great campaign. But so this pagan simpleton may understand, tell him to speak to me.'

George roared with laughter, as did his commanders, which did nothing to appease the rising temper of Kristjan.

'Tell him I am beloved of Taara and bring three thousand men to assist him take Reval,' he snapped to Vetseke.

The latter nodded. 'Kristjan offers the three thousand men he leads to your service, highness.'

Mstislav was impressed. 'Three thousand? How can a boy muster such a number?'

'The mystics and priests who govern the minds of the Estonians believe he is chosen by the gods to be the liberator of their lands from foreigners,' replied Vetseke.

'Does he know that we go to take Reval and then northern Estonia, to make it Russian?' asked Mstislav.

Vetseke shook his head. 'No, highness, he believes that you have come to assist him free Estonia from the Danes.'

Mstislav pointed at two of his men sitting at a table at right angles to the top table.

'Get up and let our two guests take the weight off their feet and enjoy our hospitality.'

He smiled at Kristjan. 'He will prove a useful idiot.'

'What did he say?' demanded Kristjan.

'He is honoured to have a man chosen by the gods to free his people as an ally,' Vetseke told him.

*****

The strong jaw of Rolf, Count of Roskilde and Governor of Reval, looked like it had been set in stone as he gripped the timber ramparts of Toompea Castle and looked down on the army that ringed the town. He had been given prior warning of the approach of the Russians, who had conducted a leisurely march through Wierland, no doubt looting along the way. He was slightly surprised to see a sizeable Estonian contingent as part of the Russian army and did not know why this should be. He shrugged. In the great scheme of things it did not matter. The enemy had appeared mid-morning and began a slow and methodical encirclement of Reval: to the west the Estonians mustered into their tribal groups. He recognised the boar standard of Wierland, the golden eagle of Ungannia, the lynx of Harrien and the bear of Jerwen. They took up position on the western side of the town's defences, between Toompea Hill and the coast – a relatively short section of the perimeter wall.

The Russians, who comprised the overwhelming majority of the enemy army, were drawn up in front of the southern wall and the eastern ramparts. Two things struck Rolf as odd: there was a disproportionate number of horsemen among the enemy and there were no siege engines.

'How many do you think they have?' he asked the young Count Albert who stood beside him.

Albert's eyes narrowed as he scanned the enemy from left to right.

'At least fifteen thousand, probably more, not counting the Estonians.'

Rolf raised an eyebrow. 'Not counting the Estonians?'

'Ill-armed pagans do not count,' Albert replied loudly enough for others on the battlements to hear him. They laughed at his disparaging of the pagans. Rolf also smiled. His deputy was hot-headed and could be reckless, but he was just the type of commander to hold the hill against this Russian horde. He turned to face the younger man.

'Hold the castle as long as you can. If the enemy breach the defences then fall back with your men. Do not sacrifice yourself needlessly.'

He offered the Count of Orlamunde and Holstein his hand. Albert took it.

'I will not fail you.'

Rolf turned and walked to the wooden steps that led down to the ground. He would direct the defence of the town itself while Valdemar's nephew and his knights, squires and lesser knights – fifty-four men and youths – would hold the castle. It was a paltry number but Rolf had given him fifty crossbowmen to stiffen the garrison. And before the enemy could scale the hill to assault the castle they would have to breach the ramparts around the foot of the hill. To man those defences and the perimeter wall that defended Reval he had seven hundred men. A hundred sergeants, two hundred spearmen and a hundred of his own foot knights would give a good account of themselves if the enemy broke through his defences. But the fate of Reval would rest on the three hundred crossbowmen that occupied the twelve towers along the wall and the parapets between them.

One of the last acts of King Valdemar before he had been basely betrayed had been to despatch an additional two hundred mercenary crossbowmen to Reval to stiffen the defences. Rolf had vowed in the wooden church that had been built in the middle of the town that he would not let the port fall. Valdemar had also sent him a small number of engineers, men who had travelled throughout Europe designing and building castle defences. They were mostly Italian, though one olive-skinned individual said that he had been the personal adviser of the ruler of Constantinople. Aside from constantly complaining about northern Estonia's climate he had been instrumental in laying out the defences beyond the walls.

'Invite the enemy into killing grounds, lord,' he had said to Rolf.

'Invite them into ground where they can be killed? What sort of enemy would do that?'

The man had tapped his nose and smiled, his teeth flawlessly white against his tanned skin.

'The type that has no choice, lord.'

He had the town's smiths produce thousands of caltrops that were laid around the rampart at the base of Toompea Hill in a thick belt that would cripple any horse that ventured too near them. In front of the ditch before the rampart there was a row of trenches five feet deep, in the bottom of which were rows of sharpened stakes with fire-hardened points. Beyond the trenches were three rows of round pits, each one three feet deep and tapering towards the bottom. In each pit was a sharpened stake that was fixed in a clay base so it could not be easily pulled out. Beyond the trenches and pits were rows of round holes some two feet in depth. They were designed to break the leg of a man or horse that fell in them.

The track leading to the town's gates had been altered so that now it approached the entrance in a zigzag fashion. This was designed to not only slow the approach of an attacking force but also expose its flanks to missiles shot from the walls and towers. The rows of round holes dug each side of the track would deter attackers from straying from the road. And if an attacker had any time between negotiating the holes, pits, trenches and caltrops he would also notice the white-painted stones arranged in front of the walls denoting ranges of one hundred yards, two hundred yards and three hundred yards from where crossbowmen would shoot from the parapets. When they were finished the extensive defences that ringed Reval were nicknamed the 'Devil's garden' by the garrison.

It took the rest of the morning and most of the afternoon before the Russian army and Kristjan's forces were ready to mount their assault. Not because it took an excessive amount of time for the troops to be marshalled into position but because of the positioning of the viewing platform. So sure were Mstislav and Grand Prince George that the town would fall easily they had decided to watch the spectacle from a specially constructed platform. They decided that the best

411

position was directly opposite the town gates, so a small army of men were detached from Novgorod's *Voi* to fell trees so a platform could be erected. During the hours it took to fashion a structure raised off the ground three times the height of a man Russians and Estonians stood and sweated in the summer heat. From the brooding walls came no hint of life: no movement, no sun glinting off whetted spear points or burnished helmets. Nothing. The banners above the gates and on the battlements of Toompea Castle hung limply in the still air. It was as if Reval had been deserted.

The attackers were disabused of that fantasy when the attack finally got under way, a hundred trumpets blaring, accompanied by hundreds more drums being banged to signal the great assault. Six thousand *Voi* approached the southern and eastern walls of Reval, while in the west Kristjan's warriors swarmed forward to traverse the 'Devil's garden', cross the ditch and get to grips with the town's timber walls. As the attackers had no siege engines the front ranks carried bundles of branches tied together to fill the ditch to create makeshift bridges. Behind them were warriors hauling ropes and grappling hooks, which would be used to pull down parts of the wall, Suzdal's horse archers riding forward so the ropes could be attached to the saddles of their mounts to make the task easier. On the track that led to the town's gates, meanwhile, a battering ram fashioned from the trunk of an oak tree and mounted on two four-wheeled wagons was pushed forward.

Suzdal's horse archers had unleashed a hail of arrows against the walls, loosing volley after volley which did little save give the foot soldiers some heart as they rushed ahead and then slowed almost to a halt as they encountered the belt of holes. Some of the horse archers got too close to the walls, their mounts stepping into the holes and breaking their legs. Men also stepped into them, twisting ankles and also breaking limbs.

The pits filled with single stakes were easier to spot and avoid but it slowed the advance down to a crawl. And then the crossbowmen began shooting. Among the pits it was impossible for the *Voi* and Estonians to lock their shields to their front or above their heads as a defence against the iron-tipped bolts that hissed through the air. The crossbowmen took their time, shooting no more than two bolts a minute, but after five minutes they had loosed three thousand missiles. The *Voi* never reached the ditch in front of the ramparts, losing heart as hundreds of their comrades were killed or wounded. They fell back more quickly than they had advanced.

To the west Kristjan sent a thousand Wierlanders to assault the walls. Bolts killed three hundred before the rest limped back out of range. Murk was not amused.

'You see how easily their courage fails,' he said to Vetseke as both watched the Wierlanders recoil from the walls. Behind them the prince's Russians and Livs sat on their horses, a mounted body of Ungannians acting as Kristjan's bodyguard.

'Men thrown against well-planned defences will always suffer high casualties,' replied Vetseke.

413

'Not if they truly believed in the gods,' Kristjan corrected him, touching his silver torc. 'Yet another example of why only Ungannia among the Estonian kingdoms remains free. The other tribes have forsaken the gods and so the gods have forsaken them.'

Vetseke saw injured warriors, crossbow bolts lodged in their shoulders or limbs, hobbling back to their camp, or being assisted by their comrades if their wounds were serious. At that moment he also became aware of Kristjan's total indifference to the suffering around him.

'There is one thing that needs addressing,' the prince said as the crossbowmen on the walls ceased their shooting, the low moans of injured men lying among the 'Devil's garden' drifting into his ears.

'Mm?'

'Fellin, Kristjan. It should be reinforced.'

'Fellin is adequately garrisoned,' Kristjan told him. 'After Reval has fallen I intend to march south and resume my conquest of Livonia.'

'The Sword Brothers will attempt to recapture it this summer,' said Vetseke.

Kristjan waved a hand at him as a Wierlander, bleeding profusely from his neck that had a crossbow bolt embedded in it, pitched forward to hit the earth face first.

'After the losses they suffered at the Sedde, Prince Vetseke, I doubt the Sword Brothers will venture from their castles for the foreseeable future.'

Vetseke stared at him in disbelief. He may have recovered physically from the hornet stings but the poison had obviously affected his senses. Perhaps it was time to think about shifting for himself.

Chapter 9

Conrad stared in disbelief at the cluster of crosses and the rotting corpses and skeletons fixed to them. The copse of death was sited on the eastern side of the lake just south of the hill fort of Fellin, which was being closely invested.

'How many do you think there are?' queried Rudolf.

'Forty, maybe more,' replied Henke, swatting away a fly, one of the hundreds buzzing around the grisly scene. 'Someone has been busy.'

Grand Master Volquin wore a look that was as black as his beard.

'I want an example made of the garrison. In all my time in Livonia I have never seen such an outrage.'

'What about in Germany, grand master?' smiled Henke.

'That was different,' reflected Volquin, tilting his head as he remembered the many atrocities he had seen in northern Europe and perhaps had himself committed.

Walter's face registered horror and distress in equal measure.

'We should cut them down, give the bodies a Christian burial and then dismantle this modern Golgotha.'

With that he jumped down from his horse and went down on his knees in prayer.

'Your words encapsulate what we all think, Brother Walter,' said Volquin solemnly. 'It shall be done immediately.'

'Is that a good idea, grand master?' said Henke.

They all looked at him in puzzlement. Henke swatted a fly on his arm.

'If you want to make an example of the garrison then you could always nail a few to these crosses after they have surrendered.'

He looked very pleased with himself but Volquin sighed and wheeled his horse away.

'Take the bodies down and burn the crosses,' he ordered.

'He's going soft,' muttered Henke, turning on Conrad.

'I thought you were supposed to be Marshal of Estonia and ruler of all those that live in it. Looks like Bishop Albert made a mistake in appointing you, baker's boy.'

'One day, Henke,' growled Conrad, 'that tongue of yours will talk your head off its shoulders. Perhaps today.'

Henke smiled. 'If that is a challenge, Lord Marshal, I accept.'

'Enough!' snapped Rudolf. 'Henke, you will arrange for these bodies to be taken down and organise burial parties. After which you will burn the crosses. Get on with it.'

That afternoon Sir Richard arrived from Lehola with a party of horsemen. The Duke of Saccalia stood with Conrad and Rudolf as his friend and deputy Peeter, Count of Fellin, together with the others who had met cruel deaths, was given a decent burial. Afterwards he said little as he retreated to his pavilion that had been erected during the funeral service. Grand Master Volquin ordered that the garrison would not be given the option of surrendering.

The core of the army that set up camp to the south of the fort comprised the brother knights, sergeants, spearmen and crossbowmen drawn from the garrisons of Wenden, Segewold, Kremon, Holm, Uexkull, Lennewarden, Kokenhusen and Gerzika. Those castles had not been denuded of their garrisons, as the reduction of Fellin was not considered a task worthy of mustering all of the order's soldiers. Nevertheless, ninety-six brother knights, a hundred and fifty sergeants, two hundred crossbowmen and the same number of spearmen had marched north behind the grand master's banner.

The largest contingent was the crusaders enlisted in Germany by Bishop Albert and now under the command of Bishop Bernhard. They numbered two thousand and were all foot soldiers, almost all recruited from towns and the city of Lübeck and mostly spearmen wearing either mail armour or gambesons or no armour at all. The best among them were the two hundred mercenary crossbowmen that had been hired in Saxony.

Sir Richard had brought with him from Lehola forty knights, the same number of squires, fifty lesser knights and two hundred loyal Saccalians. The defence of the fort was left in the hands of Tonis and over a hundred wolf shields.

Nearly three thousand fighting men surrounded Fellin with dozens more non-combatants and support personnel. These included priests, monks, the order's novices, surgeons, farriers, blacksmiths, wagon drivers, engineers, stable hands, cooks, armourers, servants and shoe makers. For ease of administration they were all placed under the command of Master Thaddeus, now reprising his position as quartermaster general of all Livonia.

He was now in his seventies and his thin build and deathly pale skin gave him the appearance of a man that could be snapped in two like a twig. But his mental capacity still towered over those around him, his voice calm and assured as he did not so much inform those gathered in Sir Richard's pavilion what should be their strategy as instruct them. The Duke of Saccalia sat at a bench covered with a white cloth to make it into a table, brooding over the loss of his friend Peeter, whose body now lay in the newly established cemetery south of the fort. Conrad kept glancing at him as Thaddeus stood and gave his opinion to the assembled grand master, masters, Sir Richard and Bishop Bernhard. Outside three thousand men and more than that number of horses, mules, oxen and ponies churned up the earth to create a giant ring of mud that encircled Fellin.

'I assume that,' said Thaddeus, smiling at Sir Richard, 'your grace does not wish the fort reduced to ashes?'

Sir Richard raised his eyes and gave a slight nod.

'I thought as much,' continued Thaddeus, 'that is why I did not bring the mangonels or trebuchets.'

'You took a bit of a risk there, Thaddeus,' joked Master Mathias.

Thaddeus raised an eyebrow. 'Risk, Master Mathias? I am not in the habit of taking risks. My calculations are based on probability and mathematics. I remember a period during the siege of Acre…'

'Thank you, Master Thaddeus,' interrupted Volquin, 'perhaps you could enlighten us on how we are to take Fellin without knocking down its walls.'

'A siege tower,' replied Thaddeus, 'the dimensions of which I took the liberty of working out before I left Wenden.'

He held out a bony hand to one of his engineers who held a rolled piece of vellum. He handed it to Thaddeus who placed it on the table and unrolled it. He placed small lead weights on each corner to hold it in place. Everyone stood to examine his handiwork.

'It is six storeys high to take into account not only the height of the timber walls but also the mound the fort is sited on,' said Thaddeus with satisfaction.

'Very thorough,' admitted Volquin. 'How long will it take to build?'

'A week,' stated Thaddeus.

'That long?' said Master Friedhelm.

'I take it you do not want it to collapse while you and your men are inside it?' asked Thaddeus irritably. 'It is a feat of engineering, Master Friedhelm, not something dreamed up after a night in an alehouse.'

'You can use the soldiers that arrived from Germany,' Bernhard told him. 'I want them to be occupied in the days ahead rather than indulging in drinking, gambling and robbing.'

'You should hang a few for good measure, bishop,' Rudolf suggested, 'just to keep the rest in line.'

'It may come to that, Rudolf,' sighed Bernhard, 'they are a rough bunch.'

'I will also require them to fashion scaling ladders and cats,' said Thaddeus.

'Cats?' asked Conrad.

'Wooden sheds mounted on wheels that have sloped sides covered in hides so that missiles will bounce off them,' explained Thaddeus, 'and they will be fireproof. The men inside them can work filling the moat to allow the tower to be moved against the walls. The mound will also have to be dug away as well.'

'I congratulate you, Master Thaddeus,' said Volquin. 'Your calculations and preparations are as thorough as ever.'

The grand master looked at the unhappy Sir Richard.

'We will soon have your stronghold back, Sir Richard, and after that Ungannia will pay for its treachery. That I swear.'

The others mumbled their agreement. Volquin turned to Conrad.

'Lord Marshal, what can you inform us of events in the north?'

They had all sat back in their chairs so Conrad immediately stood and cleared his throat.

'Sit down Conrad,' Rudolf told him, 'you are Marshal of Estonia not some errant novice.'

Sir Richard managed a smile at this and nodded at Conrad who had sent Riki north with his Harrien to liaise with Hillar and send back news of the location of Kristjan and the moves of the Oeselians. A party of Rotalians had returned to him two days ago with the information he desired.

'The Oeselians have occupied the hill fort of Varbola, grand master, but aside from that my men inform me that all is quiet in southern Harrien and along the coast of Rotalia. Kristjan has joined the Russian army under Prince Mstislav that is besieging Reval. Rumours have reached the Harrien and Jerwen among my men that the besiegers have lost many men in attacks on the walls.'

'That suits us,' said Rudolf. 'If the Russians and Kristjan are amusing themselves banging their heads against Reval's walls then we have a free hand here.'

'Have any more of your men deserted your army, Conrad?' asked Sir Richard bluntly.

'No, your grace,' answered Conrad, 'though a few have deserted Murk.'

Master Arnold of Lennewarden was confused. 'Who?'

'The name that Kristjan has taken for himself,' said Conrad. 'Apparently it is the name that Taara, the Estonian God of War, has bestowed on him. In this way Kristjan portrays himself as the one the gods have chosen to liberate Estonia from foreign rule.'

'Another Lembit,' said Master Jacob.

Conrad nodded. 'It would seem so.'

'And what do your Estonians think of this, Conrad,' queried Master Griswold.

'They are loyal to me, master,' stated Conrad.

'Besides,' said Rudolf, 'after getting a bloody nose at the Sedde, Kristjan's credibility will have taken a blow. And it will be reduced further when we take Fellin.'

'To which end, gentlemen,' said Volquin, rising from his chair, 'I suggest we all become servants of Master Thaddeus' engineers.'

Those men who had agreed to take the cross in Livonia may have fancied themselves as heroes battling armies of pagans. Even the basest and most impoverished among them – and there were many – would have at least hoped that they would have spent their days defeating pagans and their nights feasting in celebration of their victories. What they did not bargain on were days filled with back-breaking work swinging picks, digging earth or felling trees. But in the July heat that is what they did, they and the soldiers of the order as Thaddeus' siege tower took shape in front of the fort's southern wall.

The forests were filled with the sounds of branches being chopped and trunks being felled, along with men's curses and shouts as trees crashed to the ground. The warriors of the garrison had filled the walls and towers of the fort when the crusader army had first appeared. Archers had loosed a few arrows that had fallen harmlessly short, whereupon they had desisted their shooting. Thereafter the walls were largely deserted, the only warriors being posted in the towers as a ring of siege works was established around Fellin. Mantlets were first constructed and placed in front of the walls, from which crossbowmen could take shots at those in the towers. After a few of the garrison were killed with bolts in eye sockets the rest learned to keep their heads down. Archers shot a few arrows at the crossbowmen sheltering behind the mantlets in reply, to no effect. However, they did manage to kill a dozen careless crusaders that wandered too close to the walls. But most days there was a distinct lack of activity in and around the fort.

Sir Richard sent his Saccalians north and east to give prior warning of the approach of any relief force. They sent back daily reports noting no enemy activity. Conrad, Hans and Anton spent most days hunting deer, not only for their meat but also to provide hides to cover the surface of the siege tower and the cats. Most of the order's brother knights did the same, both to relieve the boredom and escape the smell of the camp, which began to resemble a slaughterhouse as the horsemen returned with dead animals to be skinned and gutted.

Fifteen days after the crusader army had arrived before Fellin the moat had been filled in and the siege tower finished. The latter had elicited much interest among the garrison when the base and first two storeys had been built. Grand Master Volquin had been worried that the Ungannians might sally forth from the gates in the fort's eastern wall in an effort to destroy it. He therefore ordered the crusaders and order's crossbowmen to deploy in front of the gates, reinforced by a thousand spearmen. But no sally came and so the men were stood down, though their tents were moved to be near the fort's entrance so they could muster at a moment's notice.

As the tower took shape Conrad wondered why the garrison had been content to sit and watch the obvious preparations for an assault.

'Most strange,' he said as he and his two friends walked their horses back to Wenden's stabling area.

'They must believe that Kristjan will attempt to relieve them,' suggested Anton.

'Or perhaps they believe that they can defeat all attempts to storm the fort,' said Hans.

'More likely they believe that we will offer terms if they surrender,' mused Conrad.

Anton stopped and looked at the fort, smoke arching into the sky from campfires inside the compound. In the summer sun it looked peaceful, even serene, its garrison unaware of the horror that was about to engulf it. They led their horses past smiths hammering horseshoes on anvils and armourers mending swords and armour. The pleasing smell of field kitchens aroused Hans' interest and the not-so-pleasing aroma of field stables filled their nostrils as they arrived at their destination. Each castle of the order had its own stable block made up of rows of stables with wooden cross bars dividing the individual stalls and fitted with mangers for feed. The roofing above the stables comprised thick canvas. They led the horses into the stalls, unsaddled them and then proceeded to rub them down, the beasts having cooled down by being walked through the camp. The pampered destriers were being checked over by farriers and novices were mucking out the stalls and shovelling dung into wheelbarrows.

Hans stopped brushing and looked at them.

'That was us twelve years ago, do you remember?'

'I remember the ground was covered with snow then,' said Anton.

'And Bruno and Johann were with us,' added Conrad.

Hans was in a reflective mood. 'Twelve years. Where does the time go?'

'Fighting enemies,' replied Anton.

'Brother Conrad.'

He turned to see young Manfred holding the handles of a wheelbarrow piled high with horse dung.

'Enjoying your first siege, Manfred?'

The novice put down the wheelbarrow, his eyes afire with enthusiasm.

'Yes, Brother Conrad. The siege tower is almost ready. Some say that the novices will be allowed to take part in the assault.'

Conrad knew that they would not.

'Your time will come, Manfred, have no fear.'

The boy's face suddenly became a mask of disappointment.

'What if I am still a novice when the war has ended, though?'

Hans laughed. 'You don't need to worry about that, Manfred. The Sword Brothers have a long list of enemies.'

Manfred's eyes sparkled with relish. 'Excellent. One day I hope to fight beside the three of you if I am worthy.'

Anton laughed. 'We also had to shovel dung, Manfred, so don't trouble yourself about being worthy.'

'You had better attend to your duties, Manfred,' Conrad told him, 'else you will incur Brother Lukas' wrath.'

'Yes, brother,' said Manfred, who gripped the wheelbarrow and pushed it away.

'I'm glad he won't be taking part in the attack on the fort,' said Conrad. 'It will be a messy business.'

Fellin was an ancient and solid stronghold built on a great earth mound. Massive tree trunks sunk in the ground provided vertical support for the framework of interlocking horizontal timbers that comprised the walls and towers. The latter, positioned at each corner of the fort and along the walls, had shingle roofs for protection against missiles and the weather. And from those towers flew banners sporting the golden eagle of Ungannia.

Master Thaddeus and his engineers had finished the siege tower on the eve of the feast of the Assumption of the Virgin Mary in mid-August. The heat had steadily risen and from inside the fort came a stench that overpowered the strong aroma produced by the crusader army. And as the heat of the days increased the wind dropped so the two stinks competed with each other over the fort and siege works.

The day of the attack dawned dry and bright, men sating their thirsts in preparation for the long day ahead. Prime Mass was held in the chapel tent as the eastern skyline changed from orange to yellow, the sergeants kneeling outside the tent as priests went among them. Afterwards Conrad and his friends took breakfast in the eating tent as the Army of the Wolf was not present, Hans taking the opportunity to eat as much bread, porridge, cheese and fruit as possible.

'Fighting is hungry work,' he told his friends.

'You don't want to go to heaven on an empty stomach,' Anton told him.

'Funny you should say that,' said Conrad. 'This is Assumption Day when the Virgin Mary was accepted into heaven by God after her death. I wonder how many others will be dying today.'

Anton shoved a piece of cheese into his mouth and stood. 'Not us.'

Around them the brother knights were hastily finishing their meals to allow the sergeants to be fed in the second sitting. Conrad and Anton grabbed Hans by the arms and hauled him to his feet.

'Come on,' said Conrad, 'leave some food for others.'

They assembled behind the siege tower that was around two hundred paces from the log-filled ditch and cut-away section of the mound beyond. The crusaders had done their job well thanks to the cats that Thaddeus had built for them. The brother knights and sergeants gathered in their respective garrisons, the mood being relaxed as men chatted to each other. Around them commanders barked orders at the crusader foot soldiers to get organised into their companies, scaling ladders resting on the ground beside them. Their assault would be made against three sides of the fort, a covering force being positioned opposite the gates in the eastern wall, which was heavily defended by additional towers either side of the gates.

Crusaders, attired in a wide variety of colours ranging from yellow and red to black and green, marched to their starting positions, priests and monks carrying wooden crosses shouting encouragement and damning the occupants of the fort. Sir Richard came from his pavilion in the company of his knights, squires and lesser knights, all wearing surcoats emblazoned with his newly acquired boar's head symbol. Like the soldiers of the order they carried weapons ideally suited to close-quarter bludgeoning work: axes and maces.

'Well, Conrad,' said Sir Richard, 'today I get my fort back.'

He nodded to Hans and Anton. 'God be with you both today.'

'And you, your grace,' they replied.

'As I have the honour of leading the assault,' Sir Richard said to them, 'I would like you three beside me. Men should fight beside those they like and trust.'

He turned to his men. 'What do you say, boys, shall we have Conrad, Hans and Anton with us this day?'

They gave a hearty cheer and raised their weapons in the air.

'That's settled, then,' barked Sir Richard.

He walked off to inform Rudolf, who smiled and offered his hand to the English knight and Livonian lord. Sir Richard, his followers and the three brother knights walked forward to stand immediately behind the siege tower looming above them. Beside it, looking very pleased with himself, stood Master Thaddeus.

Sir Richard stared up at the wooden structure, its sides and front covered with hides that had been immersed in water until they had been nailed to the boards the night before.

'I hope it is not going to topple over.'

Thaddeus was not amused. 'Topple over?' This tower has been constructed according to mathematical principles, your grace. The chances of it toppling over, as you quaintly put it, are remote to non-existent.'

Sir Richard was about to reply when Father Otto's thunderous voice rang out.

'Kneel, soldiers of the Sword Brothers, so Bishop Bernhard may bless this holy enterprise.'

As one the brother knights, sergeants and followers of Sir Richard knelt and bowed their heads. Bishop Bernhard, ex-soldier and now a prince of the Holy Church and eighty-three years old, raised his arms. His voice was firm and deep.

'Lord, give us the strength on this auspicious day, the Assumption of the Virgin Mary, to smite the heathens and avenge those Thy servants who were basely murdered by those inside the fort. Make our armour invincible and our weapons instruments of Your wrath. Grant us Victory, Lord, so we can honour the Blessed Virgin Mary on this holy day. Amen.'

The kneeling soldiers said 'amen' and then rose to their feet. Volquin drew his sword and raised it aloft.

'God with us!'

The Sword Brothers shouted the war cry of the order and then the grand master signalled the trumpeters to sound their instruments. The oxen hitched to the ropes that would move the tower forward bellowed in annoyance as the high-pitched sound reverberated through the camp. Then the drummers began banging their instruments as the crusaders lifted their scaling ladders and walked forward. In response to the commotion the walls were now rapidly filling with warriors.

Conrad held out his right arm, palm down, and nodded to Hans and Anton. His friends placed their hands on top of his.

'Give us strength, Lord, to scatter our enemies like dust to the wind.'

Anton and Hans answered 'as dust to the wind' and the three friends grinned at each other and gripped their weapons.

'Make way, make way.'

They turned to see Leatherface and five of his men walking towards them, each man carrying three quivers of crossbow bolts.

'I was getting concerned,' said Thaddeus.

Sir Richard looked at Conrad, both of them confused.

Leatherface grinned. 'Now because Master Thaddeus is like a father to you all he has kindly built a platform above the fighting level.'

He pointed up at the top of the tower. 'Up there, right on top, see.'

'Its correct name is a crenelated roof,' said Thaddeus.

'That's right,' smiled Leatherface, pushing his way past Conrad and Sir Richard, 'so we can shoot at the heathens. So when the drawbridge drops you can just walk into the fort and capture it without using your weapons.'

'If that happens then I will make you a lord of Saccalia,' said Sir Richard.

Leatherface winked and grinned. 'I will hold you to that, my lord.'

Ropes were attached to the front of the tower that ran forward to pulleys fastened to thick stumps sunk in the earth dug away so the tower could get close to the walls. The ropes went through the pulleys and away from the walls, being hitched to the four oxen that would be used to move the tower. Once the oxen began pulling they would be moving away from the walls and out of range of any arrows. These began to be shot from the fort as the foot soldiers with scaling ladders moved into position. Crossbowmen using the cover of mantlets also began shooting and soon the air was filled with deadly missiles criss-crossing each other.

The brother knights and sergeants huddled behind the siege tower as archers began targeting the huge structure. Conrad, helm on his head and shield slung on his back, began climbing the ladders inside that led up to the fighting platform. There were two sets of ladders between each level to facilitate the rapid movement of men within the tower. As he climbed Conrad heard the dull taps on the hides nailed to the outside of the tower – enemy arrows. He reached the cramped fighting platform that had a drawbridge in the front that would be lowered when the tower reached the walls. There were two vision slits cut in the drawbridge to allow those behind to pick the right moment to drop it by the simple expedient of cutting the two ropes that held it in place. Leatherface grumbled and cursed as he led the way up the single ladder that gave access to the crenelated roof section.

Sir Richard pulled off his helmet as the tower shuddered slightly and began to inch forward.

'Just make sure you shoot accurately,' he called to the crossbowmen above.

'Don't you alarm yourself,' Leatherface called back, 'we are the finest shots in all Livonia.'

Conrad took off his helmet as Rudolf and Walter came on to the platform behind Hans and Anton. The rest of the men from Wenden and Sir Richard's soldiers waited on the ladders and the levels below. Those men who could not fit inside the tower walked directly behind it, being careful to stay out of the vision of enemy archers. The taps on the tower

433

became more frequent as it moved forward, like the patter of raindrops. Deadly raindrops.

Conrad peered through a slit. Around a hundred and fifty paces to go to reach the fort. He saw a line of helmets on the wall and more in the towers that flanked it. The sun reflected off spear and sword points and axe blades.

'Remember,' said Rudolf, 'Grand Master Volquin wants an example made of the garrison. Take no prisoners.'

The four massive solid wheels, fashioned from the trunk of an oak tree, trundled forward as the oxen pulled on the ropes. Conrad put on his helmet and removed the shield slung on his back, thrusting his left forearm through the inner straps. Sir Richard, armed with a mace, turned and ordered Squire Paul behind him to use his axe to cut the rope when he gave the command. He then nodded at Conrad to do the same when the time came.

Conrad controlled his breathing as the tower neared the wall. He was already sweating, his body encased in an aketon, gambeson and mail armour, the temperature rising in the crowded space at the top of the tower. The structure suddenly lurched to the right as one of the wheels sank into a slight depression in the ground, but such was the technical genius of Master Thaddeus that the tower, now filled with the cream of the Sword Brother's soldiers, did not topple but continued its agonisingly slow advance to the wall.

Conrad peered again through the slit in the ramp cum drawbridge and saw the wall was only a few feet away. Sir Richard saw it too.

'Ready,' the duke shouted, an order that was relayed down the steps and lower levels.

Conrad's heart was pounding in his chest as the tower suddenly stopped and Paul swung his axe to sever one of the ropes. Conrad did the same and the ramp slammed down on top of the timber ramparts. There was a sudden brightness as light flooded into the chamber. A bearded warrior armed with an axe clambered on to the ramp directly in front of Conrad. He toppled backwards when a crossbow bolt slammed into his chest, shot from the roof, as Conrad raced forward. He swung his axe at a warrior's head but cut only air as another crossbow bolt pierced the man in the eye, sending him toppling over the walkway behind the wall.

Conrad jumped off the ramp, Hans and Anton following, and attacked a terrified youth armed with a spear who stood in his way. The boy tried to turn and flee but others behind him blocked his way and so it was easy for Conrad to crush the back of his neck with his axe. The body collapsed on the walkway, Conrad stepping over it to tackle a spearman holding a shield in front of him. Like most pagan shields it was round and had a central metal boss that protected the hand grip. The warrior jabbed both shield and spear forward, Conrad using his axe to sweep the latter away as he raced forward. Hans behind pushed into his friend's back and then swung the mace over Conrad's

435

right shoulder and into the face of the spearman. The warrior screamed then fell silent as Conrad reduced his face to mush with two strikes of his axe.

On he went, Hans and Anton behind swinging their maces at any targets that became available. An arrow glanced off Conrad's helmet, another embedded itself in his shield and all around the shrieks, cries and shouts of men fighting and dying filled the air. Suddenly he was pressed up against a bearded brute who stank of sweat, both of them being shoved forward by their comrades behind. He could not swing his axe or move his shield and neither could his opponent. He saw the ugly features of the Ungannian through the vision slits of his helmet and smelt his foul breath as the warrior grimaced in frustration. He was so close to a Sword Brother but could do nothing; neither could Conrad. The walkway was no wider than a yard, making it impossible for anyone to get by them. But out of the corner of his eye Conrad saw a warrior clamber on to the timber wall, axe raised high above his head, ready to bring it down on the top of his helmet. Anton must have seen him too because the warrior had his legs swept from under him by a swing of his friend's mace. But instead of falling backwards, over the wall, the man pitched forward and fell on Conrad and his stinking opponent, knocking them off the walkway.

He fell on to the roof of a hut, the straw breaking his fall but not halting it as he tumbled through the thatch and into the interior. He fell on his back and had the wind knocked out of him but managed to clamber to his feet, a woman and children

436

screaming in alarm around him. The warrior he had been pressed against on the rampart had also fallen into the hut and now he attacked Conrad, swinging his axe. Conrad instinctively ducked, the blade missing his neck and slicing deep into the cheekbone of the woman behind. She screamed and collapsed as Conrad turned his own axe in his hand and brought the spiked end down on the foot on the warrior. The warrior released his axe. The man groaned in pain as Conrad pulled his sword and rammed it hard through the man's mail shirt and into his guts. He yanked the blade back and then thrust it forward again, this time into the man's neck.

He sheathed his sword, retrieved his axe and rushed outside into the fort's interior. He looked up to see Sword Brothers battling on the walls and Sir Richard leading his men down wooden steps into the compound. He also saw crusaders coming over the walls after ascending their scaling ladders. Around him Ungannians were running to the foot of the steps to the ramparts to battle the Christian tide that was engulfing the fort. Others were forming up in front of the hall, including what looked like Russians with their almond-shaped shields, to form a reserve, ready to launch a counterattack. He saw an archer aiming at the Sword Brothers on the ramparts, ready to shoot. He ran forward and threw his axe at the man, who saw his approach and moved aside to miss the flying weapon. But then Conrad was on him, hacking at his bow with his sword and then slashing at the man's face when the weapon had been split in two. He sensed movement behind him, turned and slashed sideways with his sword, to disembowel a young girl no older than ten who had been in the wrong place at the wrong time.

He cursed himself but had no time to think of his actions when the pagan reserve in front of the hall charged forward as Sir Richard and Sword Brothers ran from the steps to battle them. Another arrow struck his shield, which he now tossed aside as he picked up his axe with his left hand and stood ready to fight a Russian armed with a sword. The man paced towards Conrad but then collapsed on the ground, a crossbow bolt in his shoulder. More and more Russians were hit by the order's crossbowmen who had followed the crusaders up their scaling ladders and were now taking shots from the ramparts. The enemy reserve fell back towards the hall.

'Rally, Sword Brothers.'

He looked behind to see Rudolf, bare headed, holding his sword aloft with Walter standing next to him. He also saw Hans and Anton and ran over to them as a small phalanx of brother knights and sergeants took shape in the compound. Around it there was no discipline or order as men grappled and fought personal battles, crusaders and Ungannians locked in combat, oblivious to what was happening around them. Pigs and goats, freed from their pens, were running around in terror. Some lay dead alongside human corpses and some of the huts were now on fire. But still men kept coming over the ramparts to join the fight. Then the enemy reserve charged again.

'God with us!' screamed Rudolf who raced forward.

438

He was followed by the order's brother knights and sergeants in a wild charge, smashing into the Ungannians and Russians to stop them dead in their tracks. A great, swirling mêlée ensued, the compound echoing to the sound of hundreds of weapons clashing. The soldiers of the garrison, trained to fight in compact shield walls, were soon being isolated and cut down by the Sword Brothers' superior fighting skills. Conrad used his axe to force a Russian spear down towards the ground, thrusting his sword forward so the point pierced the right shoulder of his enemy. The Russian yelped and dropped his weapon, whereupon Conrad ducked left and slashed the man's right calf with a sideways swing of his sword. Hans finished him off with two blows from his mace.

Sir Richard had kept his men under tight control, leading them to the doors of the hall behind the enemy reserve that was now being whittled down by the Sword Brothers. He ordered a score of his men to secure the hall then led the rest against the rear of the enemy. Within minutes, surrounded and suffering serious casualties, the remnants of the Ungannians threw down their weapons and gave themselves up. The dozen or so Russians did the same.

One or two individual fights carried on for a while but soon ended with the cessation of hostilities in the central area of the compound. Conrad and his friends removed their helmets and stood gulping in air, their heads covered in sweat. The burning huts were the first to be dealt with, after which the women and children, those still alive, were ordered from their hiding places into the compound. The male prisoners – just over a hundred – were locked in the stables until their fate was decided, the ponies that had been held in them being taken from the fort to be watered in the lake as they appeared to be on their last legs. The women and children were confined to huts and placed under guard.

It had been a relatively swift victory but not a cheap one. Over two hundred crusaders had been killed in the assault and a further hundred wounded, fifty seriously. Ten brother knights had been killed along with twenty-five sergeants, a further fifteen wounded. That night Sir Richard and Grand Master Volquin held a council of war in Fellin's great hall. Neither was in a merciful mood.

'The prisoners must die,' announced Sir Richard, 'to send a signal to Kristjan.'

'Agreed,' said Volquin, 'but let one live so he can convey a message to his fellow Ungannians that they make war upon us at their peril.'

'And the women and children?' enquired Bernhard.

'I have given the women to your crusaders, lord bishop,' said Sir Richard, 'they deserve some amusement after today. Afterwards they and the children will be released to go where they will.'

'We should organise a raiding party to lay waste Ungannia,' said Volquin. 'We are too weak to lay siege to Dorpat but need to make a gesture.'

'May I make a suggestion, grand master?' asked Conrad.

440

They all looked at him, tired, angry men sitting at a table in a great hall ill-lit by a few candles. Volquin nodded.

'That we do not raid Ungannia.'

Sir Richard ran a hand over his crown. 'That is all very noble, Conrad, but you seem to have forgotten the many atrocities committed by the Ungannians in Saccalia. I must have revenge.'

'And you shall have it, your grace,' replied Conrad, 'but burning and looting will only alienate the Ungannians.'

'So what?' said Volquin.

'May I speak freely, grand master?' asked Conrad.

'You are Marshal of Estonia,' replied Volquin, 'so you may speak as you find in Estonia.'

Conrad nodded in thanks. 'Matters are coming to a head in these parts. Denmark is weakened and next year Bishop Albert will return with more crusaders. We will march into Ungannia and take Dorpat, and after that I hope Jerwen, Wierland and Harrien. The latter three kingdoms have suffered greatly at the hands of King Valdemar's soldiers. I am hopeful that they will join our cause if we treat Ungannia differently to how the Danes have treated them.'

'I am apt to agree with the lord marshal,' said Bernhard. 'It is mid-August now. I suggest we let the Danes and Ungannians bleed themselves dry before Reval and keep the army in Saccalia to deter any Russian incursions south and also allow the Saccalians to gather in the harvest.'

He looked at Sir Richard. 'Unless you have any objections, your grace.'

The Duke of Saccalia suddenly looked very tired.

'Very well, Conrad, we will allow the Ungannians the privilege of gathering in their harvest. But next year Kristjan's kingdom will know my wrath.'

'And that of the Sword Brothers,' added Rudolf.

Conrad thought he would suffer a sleepless night after killing the girl during the battle but he slept like the dead. He and his two friends found a hut in the compound and fell into slumber as soon as their heads hit the straw. He awoke feeling dirty and aching, his surcoat splattered with blood and his helmet dented. He and the other two walked to the chapel tent to attend Prime Mass and then headed to the eating tent for breakfast. Bodies still littered the compound and ground outside the castle and no one was showing any inclination to bury them.

After eating they left their helmets and shields, what remained of them, with the armourers to weave their magic. Bishop Bernhard, possessed of an energy that mocked his great age, went among the captains of the crusaders and ordered them to organise burial details to inter the bodies of the slain. Conrad went to see the prelate as he was haranguing a circle of commanders who resembled a party of thieves with their shifty looks and surly attitudes.

'I've heard the pagans burn their dead, bishop,' said one. 'Don't see why we can't build a big bonfire and throw them on top.'

'Because that is not the Christian practice,' replied Bernhard. 'We bury our dead.'

'But they aren't Christian, bishop,' said a second captain, a man with a black eye patch.

'Once mass is said over their bodies their souls will belong to God,' Bernhard informed them. 'Now see to it.'

They nodded half-heartedly and grumbled as they ambled away, shuffling their feet as they did so.

'The scrapings of northern Germany,' muttered Bernhard with contempt. 'How they contrast with the brother knights of your order, Conrad, especially you, a man who fights with honour and godliness.'

Conrad saw the agonised expression of the girl he had disembowelled the day before in his mind.

'I am just a baker's son, lord bishop, not born into nobility.'

'Ah, Conrad, have you not yet learned the riddle of nobility? The accepted wisdom is that it is inherited, passed down from one generation to the next.'

'God has decreed it so, lord bishop.'

Bernhard laughed. '*Man* has decreed it so, Conrad, so the nobles and their sons may enjoy unrivalled power. But they forget that nobility is not something that can readily be passed from a father to a son. It has to be earned, renewed so it burns

443

like a beacon in the dark. You are possessed of nobility, Conrad, of that I am convinced.'

'You flatter me, lord bishop.'

'You think that saving Bishop Albert's life, killing Lembit and becoming Marshal of Estonia were pure chance?'

'I do not know, lord bishop.'

'They are the will of God,' Bernhard said sternly, 'of that I am convinced.'

'I have a favour to ask, lord bishop.'

Bernhard shook his head as one of the crusaders bent over and threw up on the ground.

'A soldier of God in all his glory. What favour?'

'A couple of carts and some ponies so the women and children may have a less arduous journey back to their homes.'

Bernhard seemed unconcerned. 'If you wish. But why do you take an interest in them? They have their lives, after all.'

'It is not right that they should bear witness to the execution of the prisoners, lord bishop.'

In truth Conrad hated all forms of public execution as it transported him back to the death of his own father that he had witnessed all those years ago. Bernhard gave his assent and the women, their clothes torn and their faces and bodies covered in bruises, and children were loaded on to the carts and escorted from camp. Conrad, Hans and Anton provided the escort, the latter two not knowing why they had been dragged away from witnessing the execution.

'Squire Paul used to be an executioner before he was a squire,' Hans told them, 'so it should be carried out without any problems.'

'I would have thought, Hans,' said Conrad, 'that having nearly been hanged yourself you would be averse to seeing others suffering the same fate.'

'Hans is not a deep thinker like you, Conrad,' joked Anton, 'as long as he has food to fill his belly anything else is irrelevant.'

'You were brought up in a rich household,' said Hans. 'If you had been a beggar you would not treat food so lightly.'

While the three friends laughed and talked the women and children on the carts said nothing, merely staring ahead with blank expressions and eyes devoid of emotion. The women had been raped the night before and the children were gripped by terror, but at least they were alive. When they reached the western shore of Lake Vortsjarv Conrad told them to follow the shoreline south and then east. He had managed to scrounge a couple of tents from the quartermasters and food for their journey. He watched them head south along the water's edge.

'The first village they reach will doubtless take them in for the night,' opined Anton.

'Or rob and kill them,' said Hans. 'Let's hope they don't run into Kristjan and his men.'

'Kristjan is helping the Russians besiege Reval,' Conrad corrected him, 'so that is one less thing for them to worry about.'

*****

But Kristjan was not besieging Reval. He had grown bored of watching men being shot down by Danish crossbowmen or injured by the devious devices the defenders had planted in front of the walls. After two weeks of failed assaults, during which four siege towers had been set alight and damaged by stones and barrels of burning pitch before they even got close to the ramparts, thrown by machines just inside the walls, the besieging army had adopted a strategy of starving the defenders out. No one thought to inform Prince Mstislav and Grand Prince George that the Danes had access to the sea via Reval Bay, which meant fishing vessels could fill their nets to feed the garrison. Kristjan found it all very tedious, the more so when the two Russian commanders began bickering and fights broke out between the soldiers of Novgorod and Suzdal. So he left Vetseke and the bulk of his army camped opposite Reval's western wall and decided to plunder the kingdom of Harrien. This did nothing to endear him to the warriors of that kingdom who were in his army. Then again, what were petty rivalries to one who had been selected by the gods to carry out their divine mission?

Kristjan sat on his horse in the middle of the miserable settlement as his men searched the huts, barns and animal pens.

It was the third village they had raided in two days and each one had been empty.

'Well?' he snapped to his subordinate.

'Empty, lord, just like the rest.'

'Bring that miserable Harrien scout to me,' Kristjan ordered. His men returned from their fruitless search and regained the saddles of their ponies. Kristjan and his bodyguard now rode fine Russian horses, a gift from Prince Mstislav before his temper had turned sour with every day that Reval defied him.

The scout, a former member of Alva's professional war band, his shield carrying the lynx symbol of his former lord, bowed his head to Kristjan.

'Where are your people?'

'Fled, lord, most likely. Either to the caves on the coast or into the forest; or perhaps they are long dead. Some may have been taken by the Oeselians to Varbola.'

'The great Harrien fortress?' said Kristjan. The man nodded. 'I would like to see it.'

'I would advise caution, lord,' said the commander of his bodyguard.

Kristjan waved a hand at him. 'I think two hundred Ungannians and fifty Harrien are more than enough to deal with a few sea raiders.'

The Harrien warrior raised an eyebrow but held his tongue. The Ungannian leader spoke as a man who had never fought an Oeselian shield wall. Kristjan leaned forward and looked at him.

'You know the way?'

'Yes, lord.'

'Then let us be away.'

*****

The kingdom of Harrien may have become the plaything of foreign people but it was still a beautiful land, filled with tall pines, sandstone outcrops, high hills, lakes, rivers and bogs. The springs were as clear as crystal and the forests were teeming with wildlife. The summer heat had dried up many of the smaller rivers and streams but the land was still green and fertile. Olaf had landed in Matsalu Bay and now rode northeast towards Varbola, the mighty hill fort that had been seized by Sigurd and was now staffed by three hundred Oeselian warriors commanded by his other two sons, Kalf and Stark. Despite there being a sizeable number of warriors in Rotalia, members of the so-called Army of the Wolf led by the Sword Brother who had fought a personal duel with Sigurd a few years ago, they had made no aggressive moves against Oesel. Olaf was tempted to land a fleet of longships on Rotalia's shores to avenge the Sword Brother invasion of his island, but for the moment he was more interested in evacuating Varbola.

'It serves no purpose,' he told Swein riding beside him, 'besides allowing my two sons to play at being kings.'

448

Even sitting on the fine horse Swein looked too large for his mount, his great paws clutching the black leather reins as a man who is uncomfortable in the saddle does.

'And you will abandon Leal too, lord?'

Olaf nodded. Leal had been a pagan fort that had briefly been held by the Swedes. But Olaf and Sigurd had combined to destroy the Swedish garrison and since that time it had been held by the Oeselians. It was where he and his friend and the fifty warriors behind him had collected their horses for the ride to Varbola. From the ramparts of Leal, which had been rebuilt after the Oeselians had torched the original stronghold, Olaf's warriors could see the nearest hill fort of the Army of the Wolf. But the two sides had been content to observe each other, each side expecting the other to attack but no hostilities actually breaking out. Thus far.

'Garrisons left on the mainland will be targets for the Sword Brothers, Danes or Russians,' replied Olaf. 'I prefer those powers to fight each other rather than Oeselians.'

'They might combine to fight us, lord,' remarked Swein glumly.

'The Danes and Sword Brothers worship the same god,' said Olaf, 'but have little affection for each other. Both regard the Russians as the followers of a false religion, so the chances of them combining to attack us is remote.'

'What of this Sword Brother, this marshal who fought Sigurd according to the rules of *Holmganga*?' queried Swein.

'He has been made Lord of all Estonia,' replied Olaf, 'so will have his hands full convincing the Danes and Russians that this land is his.'

Swein looked around at the grassland covered with widely spaced pines they were riding through, an endless expanse of greenery and serenity.

'It's gone quiet all of a sudden.'

Olaf held up a hand to halt the column. 'You're right.'

They both saw a group of horsemen ahead, perhaps a score or more around three hundred paces away. Then there were more and among them a great banner.

'Dismount,' shouted Swein as more and more riders suddenly filled the trees ahead.

Olaf slid off his horse and gripped his shield as his men did the same and clustered around him. Swein walked forward to take a closer look at the mysterious riders who had stopped and were also dismounting. He strode back to his lord.

'I could make out shields painted with eagles and lynx.'

'Harrien and Ungannians,' remarked Olaf.

'We give battle, then?' asked Swein, already knowing the answer.

There was a glint on Olaf's eye. 'Just like the old days, my friend.'

They could have stayed on their horses and made a dash for Varbola, which was less than five miles away. But this was Olaf, the leader of the feared Oeselians, a man who would never allow his body to be discovered with wounds in its back.

He led fifty warriors, each one as unconcerned as he by being outnumbered three of four to one by the enemy that was now forming into a shield wall in front of them.

They didn't bother to form into a shield wall; their numbers were far too few. So they stood alongside their lord and king, each man carrying a shield and wearing mail armour and iron helmet. They carried no spears, preferring either a one-handed or two-handed axe. Every man was also equipped with a sword and knife.

'Leave some for me,' Swein shouted, the men laughing and cheering his bravado.

None feared mortality for from infancy every Oeselian had been taught that death was predestined by the gods. If the immortals had decreed that they should die here, in Harrien, then there was nothing to be done about it. They accepted their fate with open arms, determined to take as many of the enemy with them as they could. And that enemy was shuffling forward on foot, shields held in front and overlapping, the front rank holding levelled spears and those behind ready with axes. The best-armed and armoured men were in the front ranks, those without helmets and mail shirts bringing up the rear. They overlapped the Oeselians on each flank and as the shield wall advanced its two wings, facing no enemy, began to outpace the middle so the whole formation resembled a crab's claw, ready to crush the Oeselians in its embrace.

Olaf led his men forward. Some, like Swein, had their lime wood shields faced with hide with iron rims, on their backs as they gripped their two-handed axes with their vicious curved blades. The Oeselians' mood was relaxed, almost nonchalant, which compared starkly to the palpable aroma of nervousness coming from their opponents.

Swein lifted the six-foot-long haft of his axe, bellowed a war cry and sprinted forward, a mountain of muscle and iron propelled by two long legs. Olaf roared with laughter and followed his friend into the iron-tipped teeth of the shield wall. Fifty screaming warriors followed their lords into the embrace of certain death.

Swein took a mighty swing with his axe and literally swept the Harrien in front of him away like an old maid clears leaves with a brush. Seconds later a spear was thrust through his mail corselet into his side but he merely swung his axe at its owner and split the warrior's helmet, killing him instantly. Olaf followed his friend into the maelstrom, swinging his axe forward and holding his shield at an angle in front of him to deflect attacks before they reached his body.

The wings of Kristjan's shield wall turned inwards to envelop the Oeselians, cutting down at least a dozen as the sea raiders were attacked on all sides. Olaf killed two men in quick succession, both wearing only leather caps on their head, before his axe got stuck fast in an enemy shield. The owner reacted quickly and twisted the shield to wrench it loose from Olaf's hand. So the king let it go, drew his sword and thrust it below his opponent's shield into the man's groin. He screamed in pain as his genitals were skewered and he toppled backwards. Olaf walked forward to finish him off but stopped when a spear was thrust into his back. He grunted in pain and arched his back, spinning round and instinctively slashing with his sword to cut his assailant's neck.

'Defend the king,' screamed Swein, grabbing his friend and lord as the bodyguard fought ferociously to reach their liege lord.

Olaf shook himself free. 'I've suffered worse on a boar hunt.'

Swein swung his axe up and then down to halve the helmet of an Ungannian, the blade splitting the man's skull as it descended down to his neck. There was a fountain of blood but the axe blade was buried so deeply Swein could not budge it. He let go of the shaft and drew his sword, pulling his shield off his back at the moment an enemy warrior gashed his shoulder with an axe. He grimaced in pain, hacked down on the man's wrist with his sword and severed the hand still holding the axe.

Half of Olaf's men were dead now, the rest standing with their king as Kristjan screamed at his men to finish the bleeding and battered Oeselians. Olaf gripped his sword with both hands, his leggings stained red with blood. A Harrien stepped over the bodies of two of his comrades to get to grips with the white-bearded warrior in front of him. He too was injured, his leggings torn where an axe blade had cut his left thigh. He was panting heavily as he swung his own axe at the Oeselian, keeping his shield held in front of him. Olaf dodged back, raised his sword high to deliver an overhead strike but in a blur whipped his blade back to swing it from left to right to slice open the Harrien's right thigh. The man yelped and went down on one knee as his right leg gave way beneath him. Olaf was on him instantly, hacking at his neck with his sword until he was dead.

Swein was killed under a plethora of axe and sword strikes as he protected his king's back, taking two of his assailants with him before he groaned, keeled over and collapsed on top of a dead Ungannian. The last men standing of the king's bodyguards – ten injured and fatigued warriors – closed around their lord as Kristjan's men, themselves on the edge of exhaustion, summoned up their last reserves and attacked.

Both sides swung their weapons with difficulty, their movements laboured as if their arms and legs were made of lead. When one fell he did not get up, his wounds, fatigue and weight of armour making it impossible for him to rise. All he could do was wait for an enemy blade or spear to finish him off.

Olaf was the last Oeselian to fall, standing in the middle of a ring of his fallen men, mail corselet ripped in at least a dozen places, his shoulder covered in blood and his left arm hanging by his side, broken and useless. He raised his sword above his head, summoned up his last reserves of strength to roar a war cry and stepped over his fallen warriors to get to grips with the deranged young man with fair hair who had been screaming at his men to kill the king. He got five paces before a dozen of Kristjan's bodyguard cut him down with their swords.

The mortal son of Taara stared wide-eyed in disbelief at the spectacle of horror around him when the bloodletting had ceased. He had thrown his men, of which two hundred were his own Ungannians, against fifty enemy warriors. It was impossible to count the number of dead and wounded among his men because those still alive had collapsed, exhausted, when the fighting had ceased. So he stood among the dead, sword in hand and mouth open, shocked that he could lose so many men against so few enemy warriors. Ever since the trial at Paluküla he had felt invincible, possessed of an unshakeable conviction that he was doing Taara's work. But now he felt alone and afraid and though he managed to regain some of his composure as the light faded and his men recovered from their ordeal, when dusk came he was filled with trepidation once more.

A roll call had revealed that one hundred and forty of his men had been killed and a further forty wounded. All but five Harrien were dead. The enemy were revealed to be Oeselians, believed to have been part of the garrison of nearby Varbola. Kristjan ordered an immediate retreat back to Reval the next morning, angering his men when he told them that there would be no time to cremate their dead comrades. He wanted to be far away from Varbola before the garrison sent out another patrol. They began to wonder if he truly was beloved of Taara.

A patrol from Varbola found the grisly battle site and immediately sent word to the stronghold that Olaf and Swein were among the dead. Kalf and Stark had the bodies of the king, his friend and the royal bodyguard taken back to Varbola where they were washed and dressed in fresh clothes. The next day they were transported to Matsalu Bay guarded by the entire garrison, which abandoned the fort according to the king's wishes. A longship was sent ahead to Kuressaare to report Olaf's death.

When the fleet carrying the bodies rowed into Kuressaare Bay the shore was lined with Oeselians, word having been sent to every part of the island that Olaf was dead. Women wept but the men were proud that their king had fallen in battle and would be assured a place in the great feasting hall in the afterlife. They stood gripping their spears and shields in silent salute as the longship carrying Olaf's body ran gently ashore on the sandy beach and Kalf and Stark jumped down to embrace their mother who waited for her husband. Dalla shed no tears though her handsome face showed great pain. Her fair hair was now streaked with grey but she still resembled the fierce and proud woman that Olaf had married nearly forty years before. She kissed her sons perfunctorily on the cheek and then they clasped the forearm of Sigurd, now ruler of Oesel.

It took the rest of the day and all of the following morning to prepare the pyres outside the town, on which the bodies would be cremated. While this was being done and the women dressed the dead in their finest clothes, Sigurd

456

summoned the earls and leading freemen to the king's hall, the huge building located at the centre of Kuressaare. Bearded warriors with thick forearms and broad shoulders crowded the tiered side benches either side of the centre of the hall. Slaves served honey mead to the assembly as the temperature inside the oak building began to rise markedly.

Sweat ran down Sigurd's neck as he stood in the centre of the hall. He felt short of breath, though whether it was due to the airless interior of the hall or his nervousness he did not know. Guards hurried the slaves away and then closed the doors at either end of the hall. Thin shafts of sunlight came through the ports at each end of the steeply pitched roof and slits cut high in the walls. Torches, fixed to the massive oak posts that supported the roof, burned to provide extra illumination and also added to the hot, stuffy air and the smell of sweat and leather.

Sigurd raised his arms. The hall fell silent.

'I Sigurd, son of Olaf, am here to ask if there are any among you who wish to dispute my claim to be rightful king of the Oeselians?'

A loud belch made Sigurd jump but the laughter that filled the hall in response put him at ease. He looked at the brawny Bothvar who gave him a reassuring nod. There was no one that disputed Sigurd's claim to the throne.

'Very well,' the new king said. 'Today we bury a great king, one who kept Oesel and its people free. And that will be the purpose of my reign – to preserve the freedom of my people.'

The earls and freemen stamped their feet in approval and Sigurd smiled. He had passed his first test. Afterwards the doors to the hall were opened and he left in the company of Kalf and Stark, neither of whom were particularly happy.

'You said nothing of avenging father's death,' complained Stark.

'We should burn Harrien,' said Kalf, 'and after that Ungannia. Kill them all.'

Sigurd stopped and faced his brothers. Stark, like him, was tall and slim, though Kalf had inherited his father's stocky, shorter frame.

'I will decide if and when there is any retaliation. You forget yourselves.'

'We are princes of Oesel,' snapped Stark.

Sigurd walked on. 'Then act like you are.'

At dusk they cremated the bodies of the slain on huge pyres that turned the bodies to ash. As the flames roared and spat, smoke rose high into the sky to carry the souls of the dead men to their rightful destination in the afterlife. As was the custom everyone remained until the pyres were nothing but piles of ash, which were then carefully collected and placed in small wooden chests. Sigurd, Stark, Kalf and the chief earls then each carried a chest to the waterfront where a longship with a black sail waited in the bay.

It had been built by the island's most accomplished shipwrights who had selected the finest oaks to be used in its construction. It had not been specifically built to be Olaf's funeral ship but the king had commissioned it some months before and it had recently been completed. The only thing that had been changed regarding its appearance was the black sail. Fashioned by a small army of woodworkers using broad axes, they had split the oak tree trunks, which had been specially chosen by the shipwrights, into long, thin planks. The boards had been fastened to a single sturdy keel with iron nails and then to each other, each one overlapping the next in the so-called 'clinker' method of construction.

The shipwrights then affixed evenly spaced floor timbers to the keel to ensure resilience and flexibility. Crossbeams were afterwards added to provide a deck and a massive beam along the keel to support the mast. There was a shield rack outboard of the ship where leather-covered shields painted black were arranged in an overlapping fashion. Sigurd and his brothers placed the box containing the ashes of Swein at the rear where the steering oar was positioned. The ashes of their father were placed at the prow near the carved dragon head. The ashes of the king's bodyguard were positioned at the ship's rowing stations – a dead crew to row their fallen lord to the afterlife.

Like all the island's fighting ships it was constructed wholly from oak, not only because of the great strength of the timber but also because it was sacred to Taarapita, God of War. And because the tree was sacred to the god nothing was wasted from the trees that had been felled to build it. So the bark went to tan hides, the bast fibres just below the bark were used to make rope, the twigs were chopped up and added to sawdust and chippings to be used to smoke fish, meat and cheese, and the smaller off-cuts were saved to make charcoal.

Another *drekar*, a dragon-headed longship, was used to tow the funeral ship from the bay as the population of Oesel stood on the sands to watch the last journey of King Olaf. Sigurd stood at the stern with his brothers as the crew pulled on their oars to tow the funeral ship out to sea. Bothvar steered the vessel through a calm water, a light breeze just enough to fill the black sail behind them. After an hour, when Oesel was no longer on the horizon, the *drekar* was turned to take it alongside the funeral ship. Then a single archer lit a flaming arrow and shot it across the water to land among the pitch-covered firewood that had been stacked on the deck of the funeral ship. The rowers dipped their oars gently in the now totally flat sea to take the *drekar* away from the funeral ship as the pitch caught alight and fire roared along the deck. The flames turned from red to yellow as the heat increased and the ship was suddenly engulfed in a raging inferno.

Sigurd stared at the burning vessel as the mast and sail were suddenly enveloped and then disappeared. The ship burned like a huge signal torch for around half an hour before suddenly sinking in an angry hissing sound. He sighed and closed his eyes.

'Farewell, father, until we meet again.'

460

Chapter 10

It took Archbishop Mitrofan nearly an hour to travel from the Cathedral of Saint Sophia, the Holy Wisdom of God, in the kremlin district across the Volkhov River to the Yaroslav Court, the magnificent palace near St Nicholas' Cathedral where the *veche* met. Novgorod's citizens were in an ugly mood after having received news of the heavy losses suffered by Prince Mstislav's army at Reval and they vented their fury on any they associated with the prince. That included Mitrofan, the fawning head of the Orthodox Church in the realm who had always been the first to endorse Mstislav's disastrous wars. He was visibly shaking when he and four of his red-dressed bishops reached the sanctuary of the Yaroslav Court. The guards had had to use their spear shafts to clear a way through the angry mob, which had pelted the churchmen with dirt and rotten vegetables. When Mitrofan had complained to the commander of the guards the man had shrugged his shoulders and told him that it could have been far worse. They could have thrown the archbishop in the river.

The main hall of the palace was packed with the city's boyars and merchants, all standing and mingling freely according to the principle that every man was equal in the *veche*. The animated chatter died instantly when Mitrofan and his priests entered the frescoed hall, the archbishop looking even more nervous as he observed a sea of angry faces. He looked around for allies but found none. Like a group of frightened children the priests huddled together for security.

'Your eminence.'

The words of Yuri Nevsky cut through the tension as eyes turned away from Mitrofan to the leader of the *veche*. The head of the Nevsky clan came forward, a reassuring smile on his face.

'Make way for the archbishop,' he commanded, coming to Mitrofan's side and leading him to the steps up to the raised area at the far end of the hall. The bishops followed like chicks scuttling after a mother hen.

'My thanks in attending, your eminence,' said Yuri, 'but dire news dictates that we must act quickly.'

At the top of the steps Yuri turned to face the dozens of his friends and colleagues who had gathered in the hall.

'Esteemed members of the *veche*,' he began, 'today I have received news of events at Reval. My friends, the news is not good. Hundreds have died in abortive assaults against the walls and hundreds more have been wounded. Far from falling easily Reval stands firm like a rock.'

Angry mumbling spread among the *veche*'s members as fathers thought of their sons who were serving with the *Druzhina*. Yuri raised his hands and asked for quiet.

'My friends,' he let his hands drop to his side, 'for too long the sons of Novgorod have been sacrificed needlessly in fruitless wars to satisfy the vanity of Prince Mstislav.'

His words were met by nods and mutterings of agreement. Mitrofan's look of alarm returned to his face.

'We have fought the Sword Brothers and lost,' continued Yuri, 'and now it would appear that we have made enemies of the Danes, whose ships control the Baltic. What price will Novgorod now have to pay to be able to sell its goods to the people of northern Germany?'

'An exorbitant one,' someone shouted.

'Indeed,' agreed Yuri. 'My friends, it is time that this august body resolved to put an end to these ruinous wars before the Sword Brothers or Danes are besieging the walls of this very city.'

Rapturous applause filled the cavernous chamber. Yuri pointed to the windows.

'This morning I had heralds relay the news that many Novgorodians will not be returning home. You will have noticed the reaction of the citizens on your way here.'

The applause was replaced by laughter as Yuri turned to Archbishop Mitrofan.

'Your eminence, it is the duty of your priests to spread the word among the villages that many of their men folk lie dead before the walls of Reval.'

Yuri looked at Mitrofan, as did the rest of the *veche* and his bishops. He must have felt like a cornered stag as his eyes darted left and right.

'You might also ask your priests to provide comfort to the families of those who have died at Reval,' said Yuri.

'Their families?' stammered the archbishop.

'Yes, your eminence,' replied Yuri, 'for without their men they will most likely starve during the coming winter because there were not enough hands to gather in the harvest. And the city granaries are also greatly depleted.'

The hall fell deathly quiet as Yuri stared at the archbishop.

'Well, I will ask them to relay the sad news from Reval, of course. Yet God might be merciful and still grant us victory.'

'There will be no victory, your eminence,' hissed Yuri. 'There is division and demoralisation in the army. That being the case, your eminence will also instruct your priests to convey a decision that has been taken within the walls of this ancient palace.'

Mitrofan gulped. 'Decision, Lord Nevsky?'

'That Mstislav has been deposed as Prince of Novgorod,' announced Yuri loudly, 'and will be denied entry into the city when he returns from Reval.'

Mitrofan's eyes nearly popped out of their sockets. 'Deposed?'

'Deposed,' shouted one of the *veche*, 'and good riddance.'

Loud applause and cheers followed the words as Yuri Nevsky regarded the archbishop with a satisfied expression. The boyar raised his hand and called for quiet once more.

'Where shall he go?' asked Mitrofan.

'Wherever he wants,' answered Yuri, 'in the company of those who still support him. Your eminence will be staying in the city?'

Mitrofan was a man who liked good living and high station, which is why he had supported Mstislav. He had no desire to be reduced to a wandering beggar, homeless and penniless. On the other hand he did not want to be thrown in the Volkhov or lynched by an angry mob.

'The church takes no interest in politics,' said Mitrofan quietly. 'My only purpose is to serve God.'

'Then in the name of Saint Sophia, the Holy Wisdom of God,' said Yuri, 'I ask you to support the *veche* in this weighty matter as our spiritual leader. Can we rely on the church's support regarding the removal of Prince Mstislav?'

'What of Princess Maria?' asked Mitrofan. 'I will not condone murder.'

Yuri was horrified. 'We are boyars and men of commerce, your eminence, not thieves in the night. The princess will be accorded the proper respect and dignity commensurate with her rank. Our primary concern is the wellbeing of Novgorod and its trading interests. Had Prince Mstislav been mindful of those things we would not standing here discussing his removal and successor.'

Mitrofan's ears pricked up. 'May I assume that I am addressing the prince's successor?'

'You may not,' replied Yuri tersely. 'That is to be decided by this assembly.'

466

'We will be sending a letter signed by the representatives of the *veche*,' Yuri told him, 'informing Prince Mstislav of our decision. I trust said document will carry your eminence's signature?'

Every pair of eyes in the hall was looking at Mitrofan, daring him to say no. He did not.

'In the interests of peace and the security of Novgorod I will be happy to sign,' replied Mitrofan.

The *veche* broke into polite applause and the archbishop looked like a man reprieved on the scaffold.

'Captain,' shouted Yuri as Mitrofan's bishops congratulated their superior, no doubt as relieved as he to have retained their positions, prestige and comfortable lodgings.

The commander of the Yaroslav Court's guard came forward and saluted.

'Please escort his eminence and his bishops back to the kremlin, and make sure they are not molested on the way. They are servants of the church and should be treated with respect. Tell your men to use their weapons if they have to.'

Mitrofan signed the letter that was despatched the next day. At the same time as the courier galloped west the archbishop instructed that his priests were to inform their congregations that Prince Mstislav had proved unworthy to rule in Novgorod and the *veche*, under the direction of God himself, was in the process of choosing his successor. Princess Maria and her servants were quietly removed to St George's Monastery, a short distance south of the city, a beautiful white

467

stone building on the shores of Lake Ilmen. There the monks treated them with great civility.

*****

The tent of Arturus was a simple affair: a round structure with a single entrance flap. It was open as the tired and hungry warrior was escorted towards it, his face deathly pale and his steps faltering. He had been left in command of over three hundred warriors who had taken refuge in the remains of Mesoten hill fort in the aftermath of their army's defeat at the hands of the Kurs. General Aras had promised that a relief force would be sent to rescue them but that had been a month ago. Since then the Kurs had established siege lines around the hill of Mesoten and had amused themselves ravaging the countryside. The pillars of smoke around the fort had been testimony to the torching of villages by Arturus' men. But the Kurs had made no moves to storm the hill, being content to send envoys to request that the warriors surrender themselves, promising them their lives if they did. At first they had refused as they waited for their relief. But as the days passed it became apparent that no rescue force was going to arrive. It was autumn and the days were growing cooler. Their food ran out and so, when Arturus sent another courier requesting that the commander of Mesoten should at least hear what the duke had to say, he accepted. Now, surrounded by a host of black-uniformed soldiers, he was certain that these were his last moments on earth. He began to say a silent prayer to the gods that his death would not be too painful when the commander of his escort stopped him. One of the soldiers ducked inside the tent, reappearing moments later to nod to the leader. He was then roughly searched for any concealed weapons and bundled into the tent.

His eyes took a few moments to adjust to the dim interior of the tent, which contained a simple cot and a table, behind which sat a swarthy individual with a scarred face whose eyes studied him with a hint of menace. Behind stood two huge warriors holding two-handed axes and wearing sleeveless, knee-length hide armour with shields slung on their backs. Two more similarly equipped brutes flanked the inside entrance to the tent. Standing to the right was a lean individual with a thick beard who, to his great surprise, smiled at him.

'I am Arturus,' said the man behind the table, 'and am glad that you accepted my invitation to talk.'

The guest gulped and opened his mouth to say something but no words would come out. Eventually he managed to say 'thank you, lord'.

Arturus looked at one of the guards standing by the open flap.

'Fetch something to drink.'

He looked back at the slightly less alarmed man from the hill.

'And you are?'

'Ringaudas, lord.'

Arturus leaned closer. 'You are a Semgallian?'

'No, lord, Selonian.'

The guard returned with a tray of wooden cups. He offered one to Arturus, another to the tall, lean man who had smiled at him and the third to Ringaudas. Arturus held up his cup.

'To Selonia, home to brave warriors.'

Ringaudas drank the strong mead sparingly. He would have liked to drain the cup in one gulp but his shrunken stomach, for many days not having eaten anything, would have rebelled on ingesting such a rich mixture. Throwing up in the presence of Duke Arturus would surely cost him his head.

Arturus pointed his cup at the lean individual.

'This is Prince Lamekins, my general and the architect of the last, great victory over your people, the Samogitians and the Semgallians.'

Lamekins grinned. 'You give me too much credit, lord.'

Arturus suddenly stood and walked round the table. Ringaudas' heart began to beat faster as the most feared man in Lithuania approached. To his great relief and surprise Arturus placed an arm around his shoulders.

'Do you know why my armies are victorious, even in the face of superior odds, Ringaudas?'

'N, no, no, lord,' stammered the Selonian.

'It is because I have utmost faith in my lieutenants, Prince Lamekins above all. Contrast that with Prince Vsevolod who trusts no one. How can he triumph when he distrusts even his closest advisers?

Ringaudas looked into his cup.

'No relief is coming to save you and your men, Ringaudas. I have scouts on the Selonian border and they report back that there is no activity. You have been abandoned. But I offer you salvation.'

'Lord?'

'Go back to your men and tell them that I, Duke Arturus, offer them freedom and employment, should they wish it. You and your men are welcome to join me. Or you can go back to the summit of the hill and wait for Vsevolod to send a relief army. By the look of you I think you will starve to death before you see that army. You have a day to decide.'

Arturus walked back to his seat. Ringaudas saluted and was escorted from the tent. Lamekins walked over to the flap and watched him go.

'You think he will accept your offer, lord?'

Arturus smirked. 'Oh, yes. Such will be their gratitude that they will probably run down that hill to thank me.'

Lamekins turned away from the flap. 'Why waste time on three hundred half-starving men? We could have wiped them out any time.'

'We could,' agreed Arturus. 'But it is time to turn our attention to the Samogitians. It will not have been lost on Ringaudas and his men that Vsevolod has abandoned them and I have embraced them. I give them their lives and fill their bellies and I may, just may, win their allegiance. And if they lead then others will follow.'

471

Lamekins was sceptical. 'Can we convince Selonian to fight Selonian, my lord?'

Arturus drained his cup. 'Why not? Men who feel they have been betrayed desire vengeance.'

He stood and walked to his subordinate's side, both of them looking at the ruins of Mesoten hill fort.

'We will leave a force here to ensure that the Selonians don't get lonely. Oh, and send orders that the local villagers are not to be plundered. My men have amused themselves enough.'

'What of Tervete, lord?' asked Lamekins.

'We will keep a force near it to watch Viesthard, but I have no wish to see Kurs freeze to death conducting useless sieges. Semgallia is finished.'

'We could organise a strike into Selonia, lord,' suggested Lamekins, 'perhaps even threaten Panemunis itself.'

'We could,' agreed Arturus. 'But I want Vsevolod to spend the coming winter besieged by thoughts that a Kur army may appear before his walls without warning. It is the least I can do.'

*****

'You're sure this is the place?'

Manfred Nordheim peered through the branches to scan the Liv village nestled at the foot of a small hill and surrounded by woods and freshly harvested fields.

472

Gunter nodded. Now a captain of the Riga garrison, his normal disposition was dour but today he was more miserable than usual. Nordheim noted his surly manner.

'My apologies, Gunter, I did not hear you,'

'Yes, commander, this is the place,' replied Gunter curtly, 'Father Arnulf was most precise about its location. He said we must be careful of witchcraft.'

Nordheim laughed. 'Priests. They wrap themselves in cloaks of superiority and frighten their flocks with tales of magic and superstition so the poor will follow them blindly. I'm certain that there's more devilry in the deviant mind of Father Arnulf than there is in that village. Still, the church pays our wages and we have a job to do.'

Gunter shifted uneasily in his saddle. 'I heard that the girl was accused falsely, commander, that is why the Sword Brothers intervened.'

Nordheim nodded. 'I have no doubt she was. You know how the world works, Gunter. A lonely priest takes a liking to a young girl with shapely hips and large breasts and seduces her, or rapes her depending on your interpretation. Better for her and her people if she had closed her eyes and opened her legs.'

Gunter sat in the saddle and stared at the forest floor. The two had ridden ahead to reconnoitre the ground, leaving behind thirty soldiers of the garrison in a camp around a quarter of a mile away, well hidden among the birch trees.

'Tell me, Gunter,' said Nordheim, 'are your quarters in the city adequate?'

Gunter looked up. 'Yes, commander, very adequate.'

He and his wife had been given spacious accommodation near the bishop's palace, away from the packed, foetid streets where plague and sickness were a constant danger.

'And your wife, she is happy?' enquired Nordheim.

Gunter managed a smile. 'Yes, commander, very happy.'

She was heavily pregnant with their first child and he thought himself lucky to be living in a fine, airy house in a good quarter of Riga. It was a good place to bring up a child.

'Just remember, Gunter, that the uniform you wear, the house you live in and the food that feeds you and your family are all provided by Archdeacon Stefan. Men of the garrison, your comrades, were attacked and killed by the Sword Brothers because of a stupid Liv girl who lives in that village. The archdeacon is unhappy, very unhappy. He feels his honour has been besmirched. And if he is unhappy then I am unhappy and that is a most undesirable state of affairs. You understand?'

'I understand, commander.'

Nordheim nodded. 'Consider yourself lucky that you weren't sent to Wenden to arrest Conrad Wolff. Had I have been here I would have petitioned against it. But as it was I was in Germany.'

He spread his hands as a sign of his helplessness.

'Conrad Wolff is a formidable soldier,' said Gunter.

Nordheim noted the admiring tone in his voice. 'I forgot. You served with his army of pagans in Lithuania, did you not?'

'I did, commander.'

474

'Mm. He has certainly made a name for himself in Livonia,' admitted Nordheim. 'Unfortunately he has also made a number of enemies, including the archdeacon. That will be his undoing.'

Gunter was full of doubts. He knew he led a somewhat privileged life as an officer of the garrison of Riga. His duties consisted of little more than inspecting his men, occasionally dealing with trouble in the city's taverns, especially on market days when crowds gathered, men drank too much and fights broke out, and providing a bodyguard for the Bishop of Riga and Archdeacon Stefan. But the bishop was often away for long periods recruiting crusaders and the archdeacon rarely left the city. So all in all it was a most agreeable existence, notwithstanding the occasional unsavoury task. He had been lost in his thoughts but as his mind returned to the present he became aware of a child, a girl no more than seven or eight years of age, standing a few feet away. She was holding a rag doll in her arms and was staring at the two men in their red surcoats on their well-groomed horses.

'Commander,' said Gunter quietly.

Nordheim saw the girl and smiled at her. He slid off his horse and walked towards her.

'Hello, what is your name?'

'Agnija,' she replied, smiling back.

Nordheim pointed at the village in the distance. 'Do you live in that village?'

She giggled. 'Yes.'

475

Nordheim wagged a finger at her. 'Your parents will be worried about you, straying so far from the village.'

'I often come here,' she beamed. 'Are you visiting the village?'

Nordheim grinned at her. 'We are. Why don't you run ahead and tell your parents that we are coming to see them.'

She swayed to and fro excitedly. 'Do you know my parents?'

'We are old friends, Agnija. Now off you go as quickly as you can.'

The girl spun round, her long fair hair splaying as she did so. Nordheim whipped the dagger from the sheath hanging from his belt, grabbed her hair and drew the blade across her throat in a lightning-fast movement. He released her locks and wiped the blade on the moss at his feet as the dead girl crumpled to the ground.

'Ride back and get the others,' he ordered Gunter, who was staring, wide-eyed at the dead child.

'Now!' shouted Nordheim.

Gunter tugged violently on his reins that made his horse cry in pain, turning the beast and digging his spurs into its sides to cause it to rear up and gallop away. Nordheim calmly walked back to his own horse, stroked its head to calm it before retaking his saddle. He shook his head. This was all so unnecessary. In future he would send someone else to Germany when the garrison needed new recruits, perhaps Gunter. Then he could provide solace to his pretty young wife.

Gunter returned with his mounted party of fifteen crossbowmen and fifteen horsemen, the latter being instructed to circle the village while he and the crossbowmen went about their business.

'And do not fire the buildings,' he ordered, 'smoke will be seen for miles.'

He led the crossbowmen as Gunter and the other horsemen cantered across the field to circle the huts and barn, spearing three men on the edge of the village as they did so.

'Move,' shouted Nordheim at the crossbowmen as he drew his sword and spurred his horse forward. He recognised the tell-tale noises that he had heard a hundred times before in Germany when he had taken part in assaults on settlements: women and children screaming, men shouting, dogs barking and pigs squealing.

Driving civilians from villages was easy enough – make a lot of noise during an approach that would prompt the inhabitants to flee their homes in an attempt to escape death. Killing everyone inside a settlement was more difficult and entailed first surrounding the village before butchering everyone inside. But desperate, cornered people often find the strength and determination to fight back and that is what now happened. Seven men, all armed with spears, shields and axes, suddenly appeared around a hundred paces in front of Nordheim, levelling their weapons and huddling together so their shields overlapped.

'Form a line,' he commanded as he pulled up his horse.

The crossbowmen ran left and right pointing their weapons at the Livs, who began walking forward. There was a hiss and an arrow flashed by Nordheim to hit a crossbowman, who groaned and fell to the ground. The commander spurred his horse to the right before giving the command to shoot. There was a loud thwacking sound as triggers were released and bolts flew through the air. The more satisfying sound of high-pitched screams filled the air as iron-tipped bolts went through thin shields to pierce unarmoured flesh. Out of the corner of his eye Nordheim saw one of his horsemen spear a woman who was attempting to flee the village.

The crossbowmen reloaded and shot another volley that killed the rest of the Liv men. Another arrow hit a crossbowman, this time in the leg, the man limping away in pain.

'Into the village,' commanded Nordheim as he searched for the archer.

He saw him standing next to the barn doors, loosing another arrow that knocked one of his horsemen from the saddle. He pointed at the barn where the old, women and children were seeking sanctuary.

'Kill that archer,' he screamed at the crossbowmen.

Moments later a volley of bolts hissed through the air to hit the barn doors that were slammed shut.

'I want that damned archer,' shouted Nordheim as he rode up and down in front of the barn in the centre of the village. Gunter rode to his side.

'No one has escaped the village, commander.'

'Maintain the cordon,' he told him.

His deputy rode away as the crossbowmen took up position around the barn, taking shelter near walls in case the archer shot another arrow from within.

'You inside,' called Nordheim. 'Your men are dead and you are surrounded. Give up the archer and I swear that you will be allowed to live.'

He dismounted and wrapped his horse's reins around a wheelbarrow. He drew his sword, walked up to the barn doors and banged the sword's cross-guard on them.

'You are surrounded and alone and if you do not give up the archer then I will burn this barn to the ground.'

He walked back a few paces and waited. Sure enough, a couple of minutes later one of the doors creaked open.

'I am coming out,' came a voice from inside.

'The bow first,' said Nordheim.

Seconds later the bow was thrown onto the ground and a figure wearing a tunic with a hood walked out of the barn with arms raised. The crossbowmen instinctively raised their weapons as the slightly built figure walked towards Nordheim.

'That's far enough,' he said. 'Take off the hood.'

The archer did so to reveal an attractive fair-haired woman in her early twenties. The crossbowmen leered at each other and lowered their crossbows. Nordheim also relaxed. He waved the girl forward.

'Who taught you to use a bow so skilfully?'

479

'My father,' she answered.

She was a fair maiden, he had to admit, with piercing green eyes, high cheekbones and a slim figure. Her leggings hugged her thighs and he had a mind to keep her as a slave. But he remembered that he was a professional. He rammed his sword point into her belly and upwards to pierce her heart. She made no sound as he pushed hard on the blade until the point exited her upper back, before whipping it back and kicking the corpse to the ground.

'He should have taught you to run.'

He pointed the bloody blade at the crossbowmen.

'Fill your boots, boys.'

They gave a cheer and ran into the barn to begin the killing, first using their crossbows and then going to work with their knives. They murdered the males first, boys and old men, before raping the females of all ages and then either slitting their throats or strangling them, sometimes choking them as they raped them. The infants had their heads dashed against the walls of the barn to silence them.

While this was going on Nordheim ordered the horsemen to collect the Rigan dead, which were loaded on the back of each dead rider's horse. After the crossbowmen had finished their revelry he told them to use their daggers to dig out the bolts from Liv bodies and any that had embedded themselves in the walls of the barn or huts. He wanted no trace that the garrison of Riga had been in this place.

As Gunter led the soldiers from the village back to camp Nordheim went among the dead to examine them personally, in particular the three women in their twenties, one of whom he assumed was the woman who had been accused of being a witch by the lecherous priest. He knew how sloppy soldiers could be. As the light faded he gathered the reins of his horse and hauled himself into the saddle. He looked at the corpse of the female archer and felt a pang of regret. She would have provided many nights of entertainment. He inhaled deeply and remembered that he was, above all, a professional.

*****

The birth of Christ was celebrated at Wenden as the snow lay deep and thick all around the castle. The village at the foot of the stronghold's northern escarpment had increased in size after the Danish blockade had lifted and new settlers had arrived. They usually had only the clothes they stood up in and were invariably gaunt and generally miserable looking when they arrived, the outcasts of northern Germany who had been dealt a harsh hand by fate. So they readily accepted the Holy Church's offer of a new life in Livonia, being promised a plot of land, seeds and a few animals. They were also told that they would be allowed to keep everything they caught hunting. In return they and the other villagers they would live among were to pay a percentage of their crops to the Holy Church and the Sword Brothers. The men were also expected to train as part-time soldiers to augment the army of Grand Master Volquin in times of war.

But there had been no war at Wenden for a number of years. The crops grew, the civilian settlement grew and everyone agreed that God smiled on Livonia. During the Christmas festivities the brother knights had served the food at the feast organised by Master Rudolf. The chiefs of all the nearby Liv villages had been invited along with the leader of Wenden's village and its priest, a monk of the Cistercian Order who had been appointed by Riga. Ilona was also invited, both because she was included in the castle's affairs by Rudolf but also because she was loved by both Liv and Christian villagers for her healing arts.

Rudolf had at first refused Conrad's request to serve at the meal.

'You are Marshal of Estonia, Conrad,' the master had told him as they walked back from the snow-covered training field after a bout of lance practice, both men and horses sweating and their breath misting in the freezing morning air.

'I am a brother knight of Wenden, master,' replied Conrad defiantly, 'and it is a tradition that all the brother knights serve our guests at Christmas.'

Rudolf shook his head. 'I have had Henke begging me to send him on an extended patrol in order to miss it and here you are pestering me to let you be a servant for a day.'

'I am not Henke, master.'

Rudolf laughed. 'That much is true. Very well, have it your own way.'

He stopped when they had reached the top of the escarpment the castle was built on, with the drawbridge directly in front of them. Rudolf looked around at the unending white landscape.

'It is a curious thing, Conrad. Wenden is one of the strongest castles in Livonia, perhaps the strongest. And yet, now it stands complete and awesome, ready to withstand anything our enemies can throw at it, it appears unnecessary.'

'Master?'

He sighed. 'When we first took this hill we beat off attacks by the Livs. Then the Livs became our friends and allies and Wenden was assaulted by Lembit's Estonians.'

'I remember,' said Conrad.

'And after Lembit came the Lithuanians, Russians and Cumans, who all banged their heads against these walls in vain. But now the war has moved on and it appears increasingly unlikely that Wenden will face a serious siege in the foreseeable future. Ironic, do you not think?'

'We live in changing times, master,' agreed Conrad.

They walked across the drawbridge and under the two huge iron portcullises that were positioned in the gatehouse. Rudolf was right, thought Conrad; such a mighty fortress would probably not see any war for a long time. And he intended to make the prospect less likely.

'With your permission, master, I intend to take the Harrien in the village south of Wenden north to link up with Hillar in Rotalia.'

Hillar had kept them fully abreast of developments in the aftermath of the fall of Fellin and the evacuation of Varbola by the Oeselians. It was general knowledge that the Russians had abandoned the siege of Reval after suffering substantial losses. Traders in Riga had subsequently revealed that Novgorod had overthrown Mstislav, who had travelled to Suzdal with a small retinue in the company of Grand Duke George. News from Ungannia told of Kristjan being back in Dorpat with Prince Vetseke, the former having left a garrison in Varbola.

'To what end?' asked Rudolf.

'To take Varbola, master.'

'To conduct a siege in mid-winter, without engines, will undoubtedly end in failure,' Rudolf told him.

'I do not intend to conduct a siege, master,' Conrad replied.

'Even the Army of the Wolf will struggle assaulting such a mighty stronghold,' cautioned Rudolf.

'I do not intend to assault or lay siege to Varbola, master,' replied Conrad. 'It will be surrounded and isolated and those inside, abandoned by Kristjan, will give themselves up to the rightful leader of the Harrien.'

'You?' suggested Rudolf.

Conrad shook his head. 'Riki, master. I intend to make him the leader of all the Harrien people.'

Conrad once more requested that Hans and Anton be allowed to leave with him, along with a small number of crossbowmen from the garrison. Rudolf assigned him Leatherface and a score of his men. They joined Riki and his fifty men in Wenden's courtyard on a numbingly cold January day, the sky blue and cloudless and the sun fiercely bright. Leatherface was wrapped in a thick wolf skin cloak, his head encased in a fur-lined cap with large earflaps. He was not happy.

'A man of my age should be sitting inside by a roaring fire, not tramping through snow to God knows where.'

'To Rotalia,' Conrad told him. 'And I heard that Master Rudolf has promised you and your men large bonuses for conducting a winter campaign.'

'You don't think I do this for free, do you?' he grumbled. 'You won't find a mercenary taking an oath of poverty.'

'Or chastity,' smiled Hans mounted on the horse next to Conrad's.

'Or obedience,' added Anton on the other side of the Marshal of Estonia.

Leatherface flicked a mitten-covered hand at them.

'Are we going or not? My feet are already numb.'

The three brother knights were all riding palfreys but everyone else was mounted on hardy local ponies. Conrad gave the signal for the column to leave the courtyard, Hans and Anton leading the riders as Conrad walked his horse over to the master's hall where Rudolf and Walter stood outside the doors. Conrad saluted them both.

'You travel to Fellin?' asked Rudolf.

'Yes, master. I will collect Tonis and his wolf shields and then march west to Leal, which Hillar has made his headquarters after it was abandoned by the Oeselians.'

'Don't do anything stupid, Conrad,' said Rudolf. 'We will need you and your men in the summer when we campaign in Ungannia.'

'God go with you, Conrad,' said Walter.

'And with you,' replied Conrad, saluting and wheeling his horse away to trot from the courtyard.

The Sword Brothers were experts in fighting in the snow and ice of Livonia but they never let their expertise become arrogance. The white landscape was both beautiful and deadly, a winter terrain of breath-taking views with a multitude of pitfalls. Each man pulled two ponies loaded with food and supplies, for the exertions of moving through waist-deep snowdrifts and across open land buffeted by freezing winds and heavy snowfalls required frequent rest and food stops. The horses were equipped with caparisons and nose bags to protect them from wind chill, and when the snow fell and was blown around by an icy wind the column halted among the nearest trees and made camp. Boughs were cut from the lower branches for bedding and to make lean-tos that were supported at an angle of forty-five degrees by two long uprights. Green timber was cut and used as a base for fires inside the lean-tos to cook food – the first priority when establishing a camp.

Shelters were also created for the horses and ponies and sentries allocated to their temporary stables to inspect the animals at regular intervals. Even though the ponies were hardy beasts they too were draped in clean, dry blankets and fed warmed fodder at the end of every day.

Camp was always sited and set up before the light began to fade. In this way men and beasts were not exhausted and there was time to lay out the camp correctly. Parties to collect timber and water were organised and sentries posted. It meant that progress was slow but ensured that everyone arrived at Fellin in good health and without having been surprised by an enemy.

Conrad was delighted to discover that the scaffold that had been erected to hang the garrison that had been left by Kristjan had been dismantled, the bodies that had hung from it presumably having been buried. Sir Richard had left a small garrison of Saccalians in the fort because the stronghold also housed some of the crusaders that had voyaged from Germany in the company of Bishop Bernhard. The commander of the fort, a chubby individual with a jovial nature, informed the brother knights that five hundred had returned to Riga, having elected to return to Germany before the Dvina froze over, so demoralised were they.

'The majority of the rest are at Lehola, *Susi*,' he told Conrad. 'We have a hundred here, though whether they will all make it through the winter is doubtful. I've never seen men so weak of limb and spirit. God knows where the bishop got them from.'

'The streets of Lübeck and other towns and cities,' Conrad told him. 'What do you hear of Kristjan?'

The man tore off a chunk of the roasted boar on the table in front of him.

'Just rumours, of how he has become a god, or at least the son of a god.'

'What god, I forget?' asked Hans, stuffing a chunk of cheese into his mouth.

'Taara, our god of war,' replied the commander.

'Do the people believe this?' asked Conrad, who knew that a number of Jerwen had deserted Andres to side with Kristjan.

'Not in Saccalia they don't, *Susi*,' answered the commander. 'But they remember Kristjan's soldiers and his Russian allies burning and plundering their villages. The men who returned to those villages before the snows fell wish to repay the Ungannians for their deprivations.'

After the feast the three brother knights bedded down in the warm hall that smelt of roast meat and leather, the warriors and crossbowmen snoring, belching and breaking wind as they slept. Hans, having filled his belly, was sleeping with a smile on his face and Anton beside him was snoring loudly. Conrad got up and tiptoed through the maze of bodies, arms and legs that covered the floor. He left the hall, one of the guards outside eyeing him suspiciously for a second before recognising him and nodding. He walked outside into the night air. Guards were pacing up and down in the fort's towers to stay warm and keep themselves awake, but in the compound itself there was no movement. He looked at one of the carvings of a wolf's head that decorated the eves of the hall. The inside was also adorned with carvings of the same animal, and from beyond the walls of the fort he heard the howl of real wolves. Then he heard a pattering sound and turned to see Leatherface taking a piss against the hall's wall. After he had finished he turned and saw Conrad.

'Brother Conrad. Don't tell me your bladder leaks and doesn't hold very much as well.'

'Just taking the night air, it is more agreeable than the odour in the hall.'

Leatherface grinned. 'Nice and warm in there, though. Much better than shivering in a tent, I think. So, tomorrow we travel to Lehola and then on to Varbola.'

'We go to Leal first to link up with Hillar,' said Conrad.

'Mm. Tell me, how are you going to take Varbola without any siege engines or storming the place?'

Conrad raised an eyebrow at him. 'Master Rudolf has kept you well informed, I see.'

'Me and Rudolf go back many years,' said the mercenary. 'He sleeps better at night knowing that I'm keeping an eye on you. He's very fond of you, you know.'

'I have a plan regarding Varbola,' replied Conrad, 'which will be revealed when it is appropriate.'

Leatherface nodded approvingly. 'I remember a young brother knight sent to raise a rabble of Saccalians so he could relieve Lehola. You remember?'

'I remember,' said Conrad.

'You've come a long way since then, Brother Conrad, and your ambition has grown.'

'My ambition?'

Leatherface wagged a finger at him. 'Nothing wrong with ambition, keeps a man on his toes. I reckon that you're already thinking beyond Varbola and looking further north.'

'You think too much.'

It took a forced march the day after to reach Lehola, the column pushing its way through deep snowdrifts and the men dismounting to lead their animals across frozen streams and lakes. The last part of the march was particularly arduous, snow falling and a wind kicking up to assault soldiers and animals with an icy blast laced with large flakes. The light began to fade as they trod north in the whiteout, Conrad fearing that exhausted men and beasts would have to spend a night in the adverse conditions. But as the last vestiges of day left the land the mighty southern ramparts of Lehola came into view. They extended for a length of two hundred yards and in the centre were the great oak gates that were firmly shut.

A barely audible voice shouted down from one of the towers that flanked the gates.

'Who comes to Lehola?'

'Brother Conrad of the Sword Brothers, the Marshal of Estonia, who asks for entry for himself and the men with him.'

'Stay there,' came the reply.

Hans, Anton and Leatherface behind looked like statues being buffeted by snowflakes as the wind picked up and darkness came. It would be an inhospitable night. Conrad could only see the first few files of the column of riders behind his friends; the rest had been obliterated by the whiteout. For what seemed like an eternity they remained immobile, feeling slowly leaving their fingers. But then one of the gates creaked open and a group came out of the fort, led by Sir Richard who offered a hand to Conrad.

'Good to see you, marshal, get your men inside the fort and out of this snowstorm.'

The other gate opened and Conrad led his horse forward. He was surprised to see the elderly Bishop Bernhard in his white tunic bare headed.

'You should take care, lord bishop, not to catch a chill.'

'Don't you worry about me, young Conrad,' he replied, 'I'm not the one wandering around a frozen Saccalia in the dark.'

Two hours later, after the men had been billeted in some of the huts inside Lehola's outer compound and the horses and mules had been unsaddled, rubbed down, fed and stabled, Conrad's men were feasted in the hall. The great chamber could seat five hundred people but it was half empty, the crusaders that had taken part in the assault on Fellin sitting along benches in one corner. Tonis' wolf shields sat on the opposite side while Sir Richard's knights, or at least some of them, the rest being in the villages they now headed, occupied the benches at tables in front of the top table where their lord sat with his guests. His white boar's head banner hung on the wall behind him.

'So, you go to Leal and then to make war in Harrien,' Sir Richard said to him as he chewed on a boar's rib.

'Yes, your grace,' said Conrad. He looked at Riki sitting at the end of the top table talking to Tonis. 'Harrien has for too long been the plaything of foreign powers.'

'This Varbola,' said Bishop Bernhard, 'it is strongly fortified?'

'The strongest in all Estonia, lord bishop,' answered Conrad.

Bernhard looked in confusion at Sir Richard, who shrugged. The prelate pointed at the fifty Harrien and crossbowmen stuffing their faces.

'And these are all the men you brought with you?'

Conrad nodded. 'Hillar has many more men under his command in Rotalia, lord bishop.'

'And he has siege engines?'

'No, lord bishop.'

Bernhard looked even more perturbed. 'And yet you still believe that Varbola will fall to you?'

Conrad took a swig of his *medalus*. 'Oh, yes.'

'Then I'm coming with you, Conrad,' announced the bishop. 'Your venture intrigues me.'

Conrad looked alarmed, as did Hans sitting next to him.

'You, lord bishop? Surely you are needed here.'

'Nonsense,' said Bernhard loudly, 'the duke has more than enough men to secure his border with Ungannia and all I and my men do is eat up his stores.'

'I am glad to have you here, lord bishop,' said Sir Richard.

Conrad looked at the men in shabby clothing eating at the tables. They had not made a great impression on him at Fellin and that had been in summer. To take them on a five-day journey across a frozen landscape to Leal might be beyond the endurance of many of them. Then there was the matter of the bishop's great age. He did not want the Bishop of Semgallia's death on his conscience.

'You will wish to bring your crusaders with you, lord bishop?' said Conrad.

'What's left of them,' replied Bernhard. 'Many went back to Germany, two hundred were killed at Fellin and another one hundred and fifty succumbed to their wounds in the aftermath. With further deaths, desertions and those men who are staffing Sir Richard's hill forts I can muster two hundred men to accompany you, Conrad.'

'It is very cold in Livonia and Estonia during the winter, lord bishop,' began Conrad.

493

'Especially for one so old,' interrupted Hans, who had obviously drunk too much *medalus*.

Bernhard leaned forward and glared at him. 'Old, Brother Hans? I hope you are not casting aspersions on my ability to take part in a winter march.'

Bernhard was a veteran of many campaigns, a hard-bitten soldier who as the Lord of Lippe had fought in many wars. But it had been twenty-three years since he had entered the monastery of Marienfeld as a simple monk, and at the age of sixty.

'May I be blunt, lord bishop?' asked Conrad.

'Why not,' said Bernhard. 'Tact and subtlety have never been the hallmarks of the Sword Brothers.'

Conrad took a large gulp of his drink. 'Your men will suffer greatly on the march to Leal, and when we get there I wonder if they will become a hindrance rather than a help. I fear the former. I also worry about you, lord bishop. Notwithstanding your achievements in war this land can be unforgiving and makes no allowances for reputation or age.'

'He has a point, lord bishop,' said Sir Richard as a servant laid a large wooden bowl filled with cooked meat on the table, another placing freshly baked bread either side of it. Hans' arm shot out faster than a crossbow bolt to grab a piece of bread.

'It touches me greatly that the Duke of Saccalia and the Marshal of Estonia are so concerned about my welfare and that of my men. God will decide when and where I die, so until that time I intend to remain as active as possible. You two can fret about my age; I will concentrate on more martial matters. As for my men, they volunteered to take the cross and so their lives, like yours, are in the hands of God. I think the Almighty is more than capable of looking after their welfare without your help. Besides, one overriding consideration dictates my actions.'

'Which is, lord bishop?' queried Sir Richard.

'That a prince of the Holy Church out-ranks a duke and a marshal.'

So two hundred men of Bishop Bernhard's contingent set out for the winter campaign against Varbola. Conrad was far from happy and Hans and Anton thought half would be dead before they reached Leal. But Sir Richard furnished them with thick felt capes and winter clothing, in addition to leather boots and warm headgear. Bernhard himself, invigorated by the prospect of returning to his campaigning days, went among them to fortify their spirits. Conrad stood with his two friends, Riki and Tonis in Lehola's outer compound as the bishop rallied his men.

'We go to do God's work, my brothers. After your great victory at Fellin no enemy will be able to withstand your courage and fortitude. The Marshal of Estonia, a man blessed by the Lord who is undefeated in battle, leads us against the heathens. He is Livonia's King David who smote the Hittites with his courage.'

The men, all wrapped in cloaks, gave a mighty cheer and raised their spears in acclamation.

'Who is this King David, *Susi*?' asked Riki.

'The man who united the Israelites,' answered Anton for his friend, 'just as Conrad will unite the Estonian tribes.'

'There is a hard march ahead first,' said Conrad. He looked at his two friends. 'I want you two to keep an eye on the bishop to ensure he does not freeze to death on the way.'

Though the bishop's soldiers were all on foot Sir Richard had supplied them with a number of sleds pulled by ponies to transport their supplies. As Riki and Tonis led their men from Lehola, Leatherface's crossbowmen following, Conrad gathered the commanders of the crusaders to him. Only two wore mail armour, the other four being attired in knee-length gambesons. Split at the front from the crotch down, the garments were put on over the head and fastened by two buttons at the neck. The padding that covered the body comprised cotton and wool between two outer layers of linen, all quilted vertically; the padding on the arms being two layers only. Gambesons offered some protection against sword, axe and spear strikes, though decreasing the penetration of weapons, not preventing them altogether. But at least they were comfortable and warm and offered good protection against the cold and bitter winds the men would experience on the march.

Most of the six were older than Conrad, but his position, reputation and membership of the Sword Brothers earned him their respect, albeit grudging.

'Keep an eye on your men,' he told them. 'It may be sunny but marching through snow is strength sapping. They will be tempted to stop and get their breath; don't let them, especially if there is any wind.

'Our pace will be slow to conserve our stamina and there will be frequent rest stops. When we do stop get your men out of the wind.'

'What wind?' said one in a gambeson, looking up into the cloudless sky.

'The weather can change drastically in a very short time,' Conrad told him. 'And when the wind does pick up make sure those marching against the wind, those in the front ranks, are relieved frequently. One last thing, don't let your men sing or make loud noises when the wind has dropped. In clear, frosty weather sounds carry to great distances and I don't want any enemy patrols learning of our existence unnecessarily.'

They nodded sullenly, grumbled among themselves and wandered back to their men lined up near the gates.

'Miserable bastards,' muttered Conrad.

'Bishop Bernhard's bastards,' said Anton, shaking his head.

'I like it,' said Hans, 'we should have a banner made up with those words in Latin written on it.'

Conrad gave him a shove. 'You can't read Hans so the motto would be wasted on you.'

'How many do you think will reach Leal?' asked Anton.

'All of them,' insisted Conrad, 'and it's our job to make sure they do.'

'Bishop Bernhard's bastards,' said Hans loudly with a grin on his face. 'I love it.'

'As far as I know, Brother Hans,' came a voice behind them, 'my mother and father were married when they conceived me, though I have to confess that I never did question them closely on the matter.'

Hans turned, mortified, to see Bishop Bernhard wrapped in a huge bearskin cloak, his head encased in a fur-lined cap that covered his ears and the back of his neck.

'So I take great exception to you calling me a bastard.'

Hans went pale. 'Lord bishop, forgive me, I did not mean to imply that you are illegitimate. I would never seek to dishonour your name, I...'

Bernhard creased over with laughter. 'It's a good job I don't take offence easily, Brother Hans, so stop your fawning.'

He rubbed his hands together and nodded towards the two hundred men who were beginning to file out of the fort's gates.

'So, what do think of north Germany's finest soldiers?'

Hans stared at the ground, Anton began examining the ends of his mittens and Conrad wore a dumb smile.

'Frost got your tongues?' snapped the bishop. 'Speak freely.'

'They would be better off back in Germany, lord bishop,' said Conrad.

'Well they aren't, so as commander of this expedition it is your job to make sure they all get to Leal in one piece.'

498

'You flatter me, lord bishop,' said Conrad caustically, 'in believing that I can work miracles.'

'Don't be a smart arse,' replied the bishop. 'You are stuck with them and me and that's the end of it. So get used to it.'

Conrad turned and waved a man forward leading a team of ponies hauling a sled.

'In that case, lord bishop, you will do me the honour of alighting your transport for the journey to Leal.'

Bernhard was mortified. 'A sled? Do you think I am a bag of fodder? Where's my horse?'

'In the stables, lord bishop,' said Sir Richard who had exited his hall in the company of Squire Paul. 'Conrad believed that a sled was a more appropriate method of transport for a prince of the church.'

Bernhard's eyes narrowed with suspicion. 'Did he indeed.'

'As you said, lord bishop,' said Conrad, 'I am commander of this expedition so my decision is final.'

Like his commanders Bernhard grumbled and mumbled but did as he was told. Three more horses, all encased in white caparisons bearing the insignia of the Sword Brothers, were brought from the stables. Bernhard said farewell to Sir Richard and Paul and took his seat in the sled, the leader of the ponies wrapping him in a thick blanket once he was ensconced. He led the ponies toward the gates and Hans and Anton, after saying farewell to Sir Richard and Paul, hauled themselves into their saddles and walked their horses beside the sled.

'Your bodyguards, lord bishop,' Conrad called after the prelate, 'to ensure nothing untoward happens to you.'

'He's hardier than he looks,' said Sir Richard.

'That's good because I have cut down corpses from the gallows who have looked healthier,' remarked Paul.

'You think you stand a chance of taking Varbola, Conrad?' asked Sir Richard, ignoring his squire.

Conrad shook his hand and then Paul's. 'I am certain of it, which is more than can be said for getting the bishop and his men safely to Leal.'

Leal was around fifty miles directly west from Lehola, a hill fort sited on the largely flat inland plain of western Rotalia. When the land was in the icy grip of winter there were only six hours of daylight each day, which meant that only four could be spent on the move. The best that could be achieved in such conditions was five miles each day. Those days were some of the most exhausting that Conrad had spent in the whole of his time in Livonia. He did not concern himself with the welfare of his Harrien or Saccalians, and knew that Hans and Anton would keep a watchful eye over the bishop, so he spent all his time among the crusaders, becoming akin to their nursemaid.

He remembered the sage words of Master Rudolf when the Sword Brothers had been conducting a winter campaign.

'Cold produces lethargy in men and their reactions become clumsy and slow, made worse by the bulky clothing they are wearing. The more time they spend outside in the freezing cold the more discouraged they become, even among those, such as the Sword Brothers, who are accustomed

500

to living and fighting in such conditions. This foments an idea in their minds that they are doing more than their fair share of the work. The only way to deter this poisonous idea is to ensure all the work is shared and get hot food into their bellies twice a day.'

Conrad appointed Hans master cook, responsible for ensuring the 'Bishop's bastards' ate two cooked meals a day, invariably thick vegetable broth with strips of cured meat. He knew his friend was a stickler for maintaining meal times and so took to his task with gusto. Conrad himself slept a maximum of three hours a night. Once a campsite had been selected he called all the commanders to his tent to issue orders for the hours of darkness, which included sentry rotas, organising parties to collect firewood – the wood of dead pines, fir and birch – and other parties to cut fresh boughs for lean-tos and bedding. He gave all present the opportunity to report and air any grievances. As the commander of the crusaders, a former soldier with black hair, eyes and beard, was from Saxony and could not speak Estonian, it meant Conrad had to act as translator.

After the nightly meeting he undertook an inspection of the camp. In the Harrien and Saccalian sections it was more a matter of shaking hands and sharing jokes with old comrades of the Army of the Wolf. Their tents were well sited, their stabling areas well-built and their fires well-tended. The crusaders needed close supervision when it came to building and maintain fires. The first night the whole camp was engulfed in thick, choking smoke as the Germans heaped freshly cut evergreen branches on the flames. Conrad, his two friends, Riki and Tonis, the latter two now fluent in German, went among the crusaders to advise them where they had gone wrong. But the fires were not extinguished so as to not demoralise the recruits.

Conrad stood in the middle of a group of tired and cold men, their eyes smarting from the smoke. He arranged some logs in a circular formation, resembling the spokes of a wheel. Where they crossed at the centre he placed some kindling and used a flint and stone to light it.

'This is called the hunter's fire,' he told them. The kindling caught alight and began to burn. He placed several twigs on the flames and the ends of the logs began to hiss.

'Once the fire catches in the centre you can keep pushing the logs into the fire as the ends burn away. With a good supply of firewood this fire burns slowly and warms well.'

Surprisingly, none of the crusaders died that first night. Nevertheless, Conrad issued orders that there would be no movement on the second day. When the bishop queried this he replied that the crusaders would spend the day making snowshoes. Supple green boughs were cut and bent into three hoops, one outer, one central and one inner. The ends of each hoop were tied together and then the three hoops were tied together and a foot holder made from birch bark sheets. These greatly facilitated not only movement over the landscape but also prevented the men's boots from becoming soaked.

The most useful members of the expedition turned out to be Leatherface's score of crossbowmen, all of them hard-bitten, usually reticent individuals who had lived in Livonia for many years. They had been recruited in Germany and their commander made sure they marched with the crusaders. In this way they gradually began to warm to their fellow Germans, giving them tips concerning camp craft, preserving stamina and how to find things to eat even in the barren white landscape they were trudging through. They learned that edible red bilberries grow in pinewoods beneath the snow and that fir and pine cones, when held over a fire, will open and yield nourishing seeds. They told them to keep their hair short as a protection against lice and to brush their hair every morning and evening and shave to prevent moisture caught in beards from freezing.

'Thank you for using your men as guardians of the crusaders,' said Conrad. 'I wish I had thought of it.'

'You've had a full platter to deal with,' replied Leatherface, his cheeks pinched by the cold. 'We'll get to Leal in one piece but you're taking a big risk attacking Varbola in this weather.'

The day was bitterly cold, the sun brilliant and brutal in making the whiteness twice as bright. They were both leading their mounts, Conrad's horse wearing a nosebag to prevent ice forming in its nostrils. Leatherface's Estonian pony, being more squat and hairy, did not require one.

'You should wait till the summer,' continued Leatherface, 'the bishop will be returning from Germany with an army at his back and Grand Master Volquin will be mobilising all the Sword Brothers to march beside him.'

'The bishop will be marching east into Ungannia,' replied Conrad, 'not north into Harrien.'

'So?'

'So there are many among the men I command who want their homelands freed, and I am apt to agree with them.'

Leatherface wiped his running nose on his sleeve.

'What's so special about Varbola, anyway?'

'It is the strongest hill fort in northern Estonia. Its capture will be of huge symbolic value. In addition, I intend to strike a blow against the prestige of Kristjan. If he loses Varbola then he loses northern Estonia.'

'Mm. And the Danes? What about them?'

'What about them?' replied Conrad. 'They can hold Reval but that is all. Their king is in prison and their north German lords are in rebellion. They may be safe behind Reval's walls but they have no power beyond them.'

'You have it all worked out,' said Leatherface, 'I'm impressed.'

Conrad gave him a wry smile. 'The time to be impressed is when it has all come to fruition. Until then it is merely a dream.'

The column reached Leal, which had been strengthened by Hillar's men, with all its complement of crusaders. Admittedly a dozen were suffering from frostbite and a further score were exhausted but Conrad reckoned he had achieved a great triumph. They spent a week at Leal enjoying the hospitality of the Rotalians, the men being warmed, well fed and rested while the Army of the Wolf was mustered. With Bishop Bernhard's crusaders Conrad could gather an army of just over a thousand men in total, but he decided that those Hillar had posted to small forts along the coast as a defence against Oeselian raids should stay put. In addition, a hundred of Andres' Jerwen were left at their posts to defend the eastern border of Rotalia from any incursions from the east. Andres had lost fifty men who had rallied to Kristjan when the Ungannian had first raised his banner, but since then there had been no more desertions.

'I know you must be disappointed that we are not marching to free your homeland,' Conrad had said to Andres the day after the latter had arrived at Leal. 'But when Bishop Albert returns to Livonia in the spring he will conquer Ungannia and then Jerwen will fall to us.'

'It will be good to return home, *Susi*,' admitted Andres, who looked as though he had lost weight since the last time Conrad had seen him.

'Only a few more months, my friend, and then you and your men can return home.'

But until then Andres and two hundred and fifty of his men would march north to Varbola, along with Tonis' one hundred wolf shields, Riki's fifty Harrien, Hillar and two hundred Rotalians and the score of Leatherface's crossbowmen. Six hundred and twenty men riding ponies and leading nearly as many more loaded with tents and supplies. Bishop Bernhard's men were left at Leal but the churchman himself insisted on coming.

'I didn't leave one hill fort just to sit in another,' he told Conrad, 'and I'm not travelling in a sled, either.'

'I cannot guarantee your safety, lord bishop,' Conrad told him.

'I did not ask you to. This expedition has reminded me of my days as a soldier. Even though I entered the church many years ago it has been good to rekindle old memories. You would not deprive an old man of a slither of enjoyment would you, Brother Conrad?'

So the bishop was given a horse and he rode at the head of the column with Conrad, his two friends and the irreverent Leatherface. Most days were crisp and bright, a long column of black figures threading their way through a deserted winter wilderness.

'So,' said Leatherface, 'how are you going to take this stronghold with no siege engines and in the depths of winter?'

It was midday and the kingdom of Harrien was an endless expanse of white in all directions. The sun shone from a cloudless sky, there was no wind and the air was pure and invigorating.

'You must forgive the commander of my crossbowmen, lord bishop,' said Conrad, 'he forgets his place from time to time.'

'He has a point, though,' remarked Bernhard, 'I have been talking to some of your men and this Varbola sounds a most impressive stronghold.'

'It is built on the north side of a knoll in the shadow of a great forest,' stated Conrad. 'It comprises a timber palisade built on an earth rampart fronted by limestone rocks. The perimeter wall is around two thousand feet in extent and has wooden towers along its length. In addition, the fort is surrounded by a thirty-foot wide dry moat. The fort contains a great hall, stables, storerooms, armouries and ninety stone huts to accommodate the substantial garrison. Even Master Thaddeus would struggle to reduce such a fortress.'

Hans and Anton looked at their friend who was wearing a knowing smile.

'Long odds, Conrad,' said Bernhard.

'It's a good job we have you with us, bishop,' remarked Leatherface. 'Because by my reckoning the only chance of taking that fort is if the Lord himself breaks down its walls.'

'What say you, Conrad?' asked Bernhard, 'are you relying on a miracle to take Varbola?'

'Not a miracle, lord bishop,' replied Conrad, 'just a belief in the weakness of men.'

Five days later the bishop was standing on the edge of a forest of pine, with Conrad and his commanders staring at the great hill fort of Varbola. Aside from one day when the Army of the Wolf had been forced to halt due to a snowstorm, this day was like the rest: bright, windless and limb-numbingly cold.

The army had been camped among a cluster of ancient oak trees near the village of Lumandu, approximately three miles southwest of the hill fort. It had once been a thriving settlement with many huts, barns, a central hall belonging to the village chief and animal pens. But that was before Harrien had become a plaything of the Oeselians and Danes. Now it was deserted, its inhabitants having fled, been killed or captured as slaves. It was just one of dozens of villages throughout Estonia that had suffered a similar fate.

'It looks even more formidable close up,' said Leatherface, who placed a thumb on one nostril and blew phlegm out of the other.

Conrad grimaced as he caught the eye of Bishop Bernhard, who merely smiled. He had been deep in conversation into the early hours with Riki who had mysteriously left camp before dawn. No one knew why but now Conrad shed light on the mystery.

'Riki should be in the fort by now, or at least I hope he is. I also hope that he is sitting with the fort's commander telling him of a great prize that is within snatching distance.'

'What prize, *Susi?*' asked Hillar.

'Me,' replied Conrad.

Hillar looked confusedly at Andres and Tonis. Hans screwed up his face and Anton looked bemused.

'I do not understand,' said Tonis.

'Me neither,' added Leatherface.

'My guess is that the fort is garrisoned by Ungannians,' said Conrad, looking at the banners hanging limply from flagpoles atop the snow-capped towers. 'If the commander discovers that the Marshal of Estonia is travelling to Reval to meet with the Danes, and that his route will take him near Varbola, which he thinks is unoccupied, then he will be tempted to sally out to kill or capture him.'

Leatherface laughed. 'Who concocted that ludicrous plan?'

Conrad frowned at him. 'How little you know of our enemies, my friend. Kristjan is motivated by hate: hatred of the Danes but above all hatred of the Sword Brothers. In his eyes we are responsible for the death of his older brother, correctly as it transpires, as well as his parents and sisters, which is incorrect. By now he will have learnt of the fall of Fellin after his ignominious retreat from Reval.'

He pointed towards the fort. 'If the commander of that stronghold has even half a brain he will be organising a force to ride out to attack the village where I am staying.'

'You might have sent one of your leaders to his death, Conrad,' said Bernhard.

'He volunteered to go after I had explained my plan to him,' replied Conrad guardedly.

'That's all right, then,' remarked Leatherface.

'Perhaps I should have sent you,' snapped Conrad. 'You forget that Riki is Harrien. This is his land. Furthermore, before he joined us he was one of Alva's men, a member of the

509

garrison of Varbola. He fought at Wolf Rock against the Sword Brothers. He is a man worthy of respect and trust.'

'And yet you ask him to betray his own people,' probed Bernhard.

Conrad walked back to his horse and placed his foot in a stirrup.

'I asked him to save his people, lord bishop. To save them from raiders, foreign incursions and slavers.'

He hauled himself into the saddle as the others also walked to their mounts. He pointed at Andres.

'And after Harrien has been brought under the protection of the Sword Brothers, Jerwen will likewise be freed from tyranny. That I swear.'

On the way back to the village Conrad explained his plan to Andres and Hillar, afterwards both of them leaving the party to rejoin their men camped among the oaks approximately a mile to the west of the village. A few minutes after they had departed Hans and Anton began glancing behind apprehensively after seeing plumes of black smoke ahead, coming from the village.

'Everyone for miles around will be able to see that smoke,' warned Hans.

'That is the idea, my friend,' Conrad told him. 'So everyone in Varbola can see that Lumandu is occupied.'

'What if there are other enemy garrisons in the area, Conrad?' asked Anton.

'Then they will see what happens when the Army of the Wolf bares its fangs,' replied Conrad lightly.

Leatherface rolled his eyes. 'You won't be saying that if an army of heathens from hell pours out of that fort. No offence, bishop.'

Bernhard grinned like a mischievous child. 'No offence taken, dog of war.'

Conrad had the feeling that the venerable bishop was having the time of his life. He glanced right at the trees where Hillar and Andres hid their men. Ahead was the village in the middle of an expanse of flat land, part meadow, part arable land; all now covered in deep snow. The single track, in reality a small indentation in the snow, pointed like a spear at the buildings that stood dark and stark against the white background. Like most Estonian villages the hall of the chief stood in the centre of the settlement with huts, barns and animal pens around it. In front of the chief's hall was an open space where markets were held and where the villagers gathered when summoned by their lord.

Conrad and the others dismounted in front of the hall and led their horses into the building. In the open space Riki's warriors and Tonis and his wolf shields stood in their ranks. Once the horses had been secured in the hall Conrad and the others walked outside to take up their positions. He called Leatherface over, pointing to two barns at right angles to the hall on the right side of the open space.

'Get your men in those two barns, in the hay lofts.'

The veteran mercenary looked across to the huts opposite the barns, on the other side of the space.

'*Half* my men will be in the barns. The rest will be among those huts so we can shoot at the enemy from two directions.'

'Tell them they are not to shoot until we have rescued Riki,' Conrad ordered.

Leatherface raised an eyebrow. 'You are going to snatch Riki from under the noses of the enemy, Brother Conrad?'

'Something like that.'

'Then may God go with you, for sure as hell no one else will.'

He offered his hand to Conrad and called his men together to brief them before the enemy came. If the enemy came.

Two mounted sentries were posted just to the north of the village to watch the track for any movement. It was now approaching midday and Conrad was worried that the garrison had not taken the bait. The two fires that had produced the smoke were continually fed to ensure unbroken smoke pillars. But as the time passed and men walked up and down to stop their limbs from going numb, Conrad began to feel a knot tighten in his stomach. He imagined Riki's body hanging from the ramparts or, worse, him being tortured for the amusement of the fort's commander. Leatherface and his men loitered in the haylofts, checking their weapons and quivers. The fifty Harrien, now leaderless, stood to the right of Tonis' wolf shields – a hundred and fifty men in mail armour, helmets and felt boots ready to form a shield wall to keep the enemy amused until the Jerwen and Rotalians launched their surprise attack. It was deathly quiet and the tension was unbearable. Then there was a great cheer as one of the sentries rode into the space. He jumped from his pony and headed for Conrad. Immediately everyone broke ranks to gather round to hear what he had to say.

The bearded Harrien took off his helmet and tucked it under his arm.

'Enemy approaching, *Susi*.'

'How many?'

'Hundreds.'

A ripple of excitement coursed through the warriors, tinged with trepidation.

'To your positions,' shouted Conrad. He pointed at the sentry. 'Go and fetch your companion.'

He rushed back to the hall's doors where Hans and Anton stood with Bishop Bernhard. Tonis began shoving his men into position as the Harrien closed the space between them and the wolf shields.

'If I can ask you to remain here with Hans and Anton, lord bishop,' requested Conrad. 'I have work to do.'

Bernhard drew his sword. 'Not likely. I came here to fight.'

Hans looked at Conrad in alarm.

'I would advise against it, lord bishop.'

Bernhard looked around at the men in front of him closing ranks, the blue sky above and the snow underfoot. He closed his eyes and breathed deeply.

'If God wills that this day is to be my last on earth then so be it, but He would not want me to stand meekly by while good men are fighting and dying, and neither can you. So attend to your duties, lord marshal, and allow me to attend to mine.'

They found him a helmet and a shield bearing a leering wolf's head and placed him behind the rear rank of the wolf shields. One hundred and fifty men arrayed in three ranks was a thin shield wall, but their task was to hold the enemy until reinforcements came. Conrad held out his hand for Hans and Anton to perform their pre-battle ritual. Bernhard spotted it. Without asking he placed his hand on top of theirs.

'Oh, Lord,' he said loudly, 'watch over Thy servants and give them victory over the heathens this day.'

'As dust to the wind.'

'As dust to the wind,' they all replied.

Conrad left Hans and Anton with the churchman and he made his way over to the Harrien, walking around their right flank to the centre of the line. He pointed to the haylofts and the huts beside which crossbowmen were sheltering.

'I want ten men to accompany me to rescue your lord when the enemy appears. The crossbowmen will cover our withdrawal.'

Everyone volunteered so he selected the ten nearest and then waited for the enemy to arrive. He did not wait long.

The Ungannians left their ponies outside the village, aside from their commander, standard-bearer and half a dozen of the latter's guards, and Riki. He was riding next to the commander as his warriors flooded into the open space to form a shield wall around fifty paces in front of Conrad's men. The shields of the Ungannians bore a golden eagle symbol and presumably so did the banner held by the standard bearer, though it hung limply in the windless air. Chiefs began shouting at their men to form a shield wall and Conrad saw that although the front ranks all wore helmets, many among those behind had either no head protection or were wearing leather caps. That was the good news; the bad being that more and more were entering the village. He put on his helmet, took his shield off his back and slipped his left arm through the inner straps. He saw Riki looking over at him as the enemy commander began pointing at the white-uniformed figure standing in front of the Harrien warriors. Then he witnessed Riki making a lightning-fast swing with his right arm to ram his dagger into the Ungannian's neck, before spurring his horse forward towards one of the gaps in the enemy line. The horse shot forward as Conrad raised his sword and ran towards the enemy.

'To me.'

The ten selected men kept pace with him as Riki came towards them, followed closely by the Ungannian horsemen determined to spear him. Two fell from their saddles, the rest

515

pulling up sharply. Conrad gave thanks for the expertise of Leatherface and his men. He heard a great cheer, stopped to push up his helmet as Riki halted his horse and vaulted from the saddle.

'Good to see you my friend,' he shouted.

But Riki was staring past him at the sound of cheering that was getting closer. Conrad turned to see Tonis leading the wolf shields in a headlong charge. In his enthusiasm to rescue Riki he had forgotten to inform Tonis that he would lead a small group to snatch Riki from the enemy. When Tonis had seen him rush forward he had led the Saccalians into the charge. Not to be outdone, the rest of the Harrien were following. His plan to stand on the defensive was in tatters as the wolf shields and Harrien crashed into the enemy.

The Harrien warriors cheered and slapped Riki on the arm as they rushed past the pair to clatter into the enemy. The Ungannians, momentarily stunned by the loss of their leader and the sudden assault, gave ground. But their chiefs were screaming and shouting to rally their men. They put themselves in the front ranks and soon a furious mêlée began. And then numbers began to tell.

Riki, his face half hidden by his helmet's wide nasal guard, drew his sword and grinned.

'I brought the enemy so that you may slaughter them, *Susi.*'

He ran back to join his men, thrusting his sword into enemy bellies, disappearing among a forest of helmets. Conrad praying that Andres and Hillar were on their way, yanked down his helmet, pulled the axe from his belt and went to join the battle.

In a shield wall, as long as those in it are disciplined, well-armed and trained, once the two sides clash the press of bodies makes it hard to wield weapons to maximum effect. And if shields are kept tight to bodies then casualties can be remarkably light. But in a swirling, free-for-all mêlée weapon strikes come from every direction and loosed arrows and crossbow bolts add another element of danger. Confusion was everywhere and so were enemy weapons.

Conrad tripped over a dead body and stumbled forward, the back of his helmet taking a blow as he did so. He instinctively swung his axe backwards and turned to see a warrior similarly armed clutching a great two-handed axe with a wickedly curved blade. The warrior screamed and chopped down with his weapon to literally cleave Conrad in half. The Sword Brother made no attempt to parry the blow or stop it with his shield. To do so would split his shield, sever his arm and quarter his body. He leapt aside as the iron blade missed him by inches. He rammed his shield forward into the warrior and barged him to the ground. But all thoughts of finishing him off were abandoned as he heard a wild scream to his right and turned just in time to see a man, bare headed and unarmoured, running at him clutching a spear with both hands. Having no time to get out of the way he went down on one knee and tried to deflect the spear. But he was too late and the point went through the leather and wood to miss his arm by a whisker. He swung his axe and chopped it forward to embed it in the forehead of his assailant, who suddenly stopped screaming, grunted and collapsed to the ground.

Conrad wrenched free his weapon just in time to face a circle of enemy warriors. He appeared to be the only one of his army left alive as he threw his now useless shield to the ground transferred his axe to his left hand and drew his sword. The ground, formerly covered in snow and ice, was now slush mixed with blood and littered with dead and dying men. Four assailants faced him but his chief concern was his footing.

'Keep moving; in battle if you stop moving you will be cut down as sure as night follows day.'

The words of Brother Lukas, the man who had taught him how to fight, had been seared into his mind. The sounds of battle, of weapons clashing and men shouting and screaming filled his helmet as the warrior in front of him swung his hand axe, a wild swing that did not have the reach to harm Conrad. Conrad lunged forward to drive his sword point into the man's left thigh.

The warrior crumpled as an axe blade gashed Conrad's right arm, slicing through the chainmail and aketon underneath to cut flesh. He winced as a stinging sensation shot through his arm but he instinctively slashed right with his blade, gashing the axe man's neck, forcing him to stagger backwards. He spun and saw the spear-armed warrior behind him, whom he thought would have run him through while was he pre-occupied with his other assailants, standing as if frozen. The man then gently toppled forward on to the ground, a spear lodged in his back.

Other missiles hissed through the air, an arrow glancing off Conrad's helmet, another hitting the enemy on his left. It struck him in the left leg and he staggered slightly. But he was a large man with a thick beard and his battle rage kept him on his feet. He came at Conrad with a succession of axe blows, the brother knight using his own axe to either deflect or block the blows. But the strikes were powerful and Conrad was forced back. He heard horns being sounded and a crescendo of war cries but had no idea who they belonged to. He stepped back and tripped over a dead body, falling on his back. The bearded brute hollered in triumph, spread his arms to signal his impending victory and let out of mournful groan as two crossbow bolts slammed into his chest, piercing his mail corselet. With his last ounce of strength he forced himself forward, dropped his shield, clutched his axe with both hands, raised it above his head and straddled Conrad. The Sword Brother propped himself up with his left hand and thrust his sword upwards into the man's genitals. The warrior gave a high-pitched scream and fell silent as another crossbow bolt went into his neck just below the larynx. He toppled forward to land on Conrad's arm, pinning him to the ground.

Conrad's left arm felt as though it had been immersed in a fire and his right arm was also throbbing. He tried to move but any attempt to remove his arm from under the dead warrior resulted in a searing pain shooting through his shoulder. He shouted out in frustration and wished he had not as six helmeted figures suddenly loomed over him, all wearing leather armour breastplates and armed with blood-smeared axes and swords. He stared up at them through the vision slits of his helmet and prepared to die.

'Are you hurt, *Susi*?' shouted one above the din of battle.

Relief coursed through Conrad.

'Shields, shields,' the one who had spoken to him shouted.

More warriors grouped round as the man knelt beside him.

'Get that stinking bastard off my arm,' shouted Conrad.

The warrior gestured to his comrades who hauled the corpse away. Then one grabbed Conrad's left hand and tried to pull him to his feet. The brother knight emitted a blood-curdling shriek of pain. The warrior let go and he fell back on the cold, wet ground.

'Get this helmet off,' Conrad said through gritted teeth.

His helm was yanked off.

'My left arm is broken,' he told them.

As a wall and roof of shields formed around them the warriors assisted him to his feet, his left arm dangling uselessly by his side, the axe strap still wrapped around his wrist. His right forearm was also bleeding.

'The battle is won, *Susi*,' grinned the warrior with the sword, who Conrad guessed was a chief judging by his expensive mail armour, age and sword. He then noticed the insignia on his and his men's shields: a stag.

'You are Lord Hillar's men?'

He nodded. 'Yes, *Susi*. We reached the village from the north and attacked the Ungannians from behind while the Jerwen entered the settlement from the other direction. The fighting will not take long now.'

Conrad, exhausted and in great pain, gave him a thin smile and then his feet gave way under him.

'Get him some water,' shouted someone and moments later a water bottle was held to his lips. He drank the cold liquid and managed to stabilise his footing. Then he noticed that there were no sounds of battle, just moans and cries coming from those who had been wounded. He looked up and saw that grey clouds had replaced the blue and he spotted small snowflakes in the air. They took him to the chief's hall that was soon filled with other wounded men where a healer set his left arm between two splints and bandaged his right.

Darkness soon enveloped the village as parties counted the dead and loaded the bodies on carts for cremation outside the village. The Army of the Wolf brought its ponies into the village and packed them in the barns, those of the Ungannians too. Of the latter nearly three hundred had been killed, the majority falling when Hillar and Andres had led their men into Lumandu. Thankfully both Tonis and Riki still lived, though their men had suffered many dead and wounded following their reckless charge. He was also relieved to see Hans and Anton, both of whose surcoats and chainmail were ripped and had links missing. But they were both unhurt.

'Where's the bishop?' Conrad asked.

'Administering to the dying,' replied Anton, 'and saying mass over the dead before they are cremated.'

'He is most unhappy that they won't be buried,' added Hans, 'but he demurred when Hillar told him that if he felt so strongly about it then he could dig their graves himself.'

'Make sure he doesn't get a chill,' said Conrad with concern, 'at his age we can't be too careful.'

'He gets annoyed about the constant references to his age, Conrad,' said Hans. 'He has a fiery nature.'

Conrad was in great pain but he insisted on holding an impromptu council of war, at which he issued his orders after Riki informed him that there was but a handful of men left guarding Varbola. A fire had been started in the hall, around which the wounded were gathered, the horses having been taken to nearby barns. But there were gaps in the roof and walls and the wind had increased to make the interior cool. Conrad shivered in his cloak.

'Riki, I must ask you to return to Varbola to demand its surrender. At least you will have Tonis, Andres and Hillar for company.'

He looked at his friends and Leatherface. 'It is important that there are no Sword Brothers or mercenaries present. The fort's fall should be to fellow Estonians.'

'What if the commander rejects our demands?' said Hillar.

'Then we will have to storm the fort,' replied Conrad. He looked at Riki. 'But I would prefer a bloodless end to our campaign.'

'There are perhaps a score of men left in the fort, *Susi*,' said Riki. 'You wish to offer them safe passage to Ungannia?'

Conrad nodded. 'Yes.'

'So we can fight them again when they rejoin Kristjan?' complained Andres.

Conrad winced as pain shot through his broken arm. 'That can't be helped.'

He screwed up his nose as a sickly sweet aroma entered his nostrils.

'Why is it that roasting human flesh smells so different from animal meat?' asked Tonis.

'The pyres will be burning all night,' Andres told him. 'If the wind changes then perhaps the smell will blow towards the fort.'

'Those inside will know that their comrades will not be returning by now,' said Conrad. 'The hours of darkness will increase their fears and uncertainties. Ensure you arrive at the ramparts at dawn.'

They saluted and went back to their men. Conrad called Leatherface back. His face was grey and his shivering had increased.

'No fighting for you for a few weeks,' grinned the mercenary.

'I wanted to thank you for saving my life earlier.'

'We thought that big brute would get you even after putting a couple of bolts in him. Amazing what blind fury can do. You were lucky we had clear shots after you decided to charge the enemy and create mayhem.'

Conrad grimaced. 'That was not supposed to happen.'

'Still, all's well that ends well.'

'It will be if tomorrow has a favourable outcome.'

The garrison of Varbola surrendered the fort the next day on a guarantee of safe conduct out of Harrien. Twelve men mounted on ponies rode from the gates west towards Ungannia. That day the Army of the Wolf took possession of Varbola and Conrad, as Marshal of Estonia, appointed Riki as its governor.

Chapter 11

'Somewhere warmer, perhaps.'

It was winter outside and the land was blanketed in snow but the temperature in the palace was even chillier as Domash sat on his throne and brooded. Gleb paced up and down in front of him, trying to cheer his master.

'Perhaps we could go to Suzdal,' he suggested, 'or Kiev even.'

The mayor's handsome face was a mask of misery. For years he had enjoyed the patronage of Prince Mstislav, using and abusing his position as mayor of Pskov to enrich himself, bed the wives of the city's boyars and merchants and raid foreign lands with impunity, safe in the knowledge that the ruler of the Kingdom of Novgorod was his friend and master. He had been appointed *posadnik* of Pskov by Mstislav and believed that his rule in the city was permanent. But now the prince was gone, sent on his way by Novgorod's *veche* following the dismal failure of the campaign against Reval. When a delegation from the city had arrived at the siege lines before Reval with the news that they no longer required Mstislav's services a mighty rage had possessed the prince. He had threatened to kill the city officials with his own hands and gave orders that his army would immediately march east to exact revenge on the *veche*.

The next day Grand Prince George announced that he was sick and tired of the endless siege and was returning to

Suzdal. He offered Mstislav and his family sanctuary in his city, an offer that was accepted when Novgorod's *Druzhina* refused to obey Mstislav's orders and promptly left to return with the delegation from the city. In light of these developments Domash, suddenly unsure about his position, had decided to take Pskov's troops back to their homes. But Gleb and the other *Skomorokhs* ensured the continuing loyalty of what remained of the *Voi*, who were ecstatic that they were going home. And the *Druzhina* were similarly glad to be away from the infernal defence works of Reval. But once back at Pskov Domash knew that it was only a matter of time before orders came from Novgorod demanding his banishment or even his arrest. He had decided to flee before either happened.

'I think Suzdal is out of the question, Gleb. I have no wish to be the brunt of Mstislav's fury. And they wouldn't give you a warm welcome in Kiev. They burn *Skomorokhs* there, I have heard.'

'So I would get a warm welcome,' smiled Gleb.

'You're well liked here,' said Domash, 'you might as well stay. You don't have to come with me.'

Gleb puffed out his cheeks. 'Without your protection, lord, I think the priests and merchants would soon have me tied to a stake in the marketplace.'

Domash slumped on his throne. 'How did it come to this?'

He looked at the guards standing around the walls and wondered if any remained loyal to him. He dismissed the idea.

His gloom deepened as he considered his diminishing options. He had just turned forty and had no desire to become a wandering, penniless sword for hire. Perhaps Prince Boris at Polotsk might offer him a temporary home. He looked at Gleb and remembered the deep hostility of Polotsk's Orthodox priests towards the *Skomorokhs* and discounted the idea. The whole wretched situation was demoralising. A steward entering the chamber brought him back to the present. He stared at the thin, insipid individual and foreboding within him grew with every step he took.

The man halted and bowed to Domash. 'A delegation from Novgorod has arrived, highness. The commander is in the hall and requests an audience.'

Domash's mouth went dry and a knot tightened in his stomach. Gleb looked at him with alarm. The *veche* had moved fast, too fast. They were caught like rats in a trap. Gleb stared at him. The steward stared at him and he stared back.

'Are you available to see him, highness?'

'What? Yes, I suppose I am. Show him in.'

The steward bowed smartly, turned and walked briskly to the doors.

'Well,' reflected Domash, 'at least we won't have to worry about where we are going to flee to, Gleb.'

The *Skomorokh* scuttled over to stand beside his lord. Domash smiled grimly. He had to admit that for all his derogatory comments Gleb was loyal; the only one who was in the entire city. It was immeasurably sad. His sadness turned to mild annoyance when he saw the figure of Yaroslav Nevsky enter the chamber, his burnished helmet tucked under his right arm. His thin face wore a serious expression as he marched towards the dais. Domash thought that sending the man whom he had previously given sanctuary to after his banishment from Novgorod to arrest him was particularly cruel of the *veche*.

Yaroslav halted and bowed. 'Greetings, lord, I hope you are well.'

'Until now,' replied Domash.

'I am here as a representative of Novgorod's *veche*, lord,' continued Yaroslav. 'To clarify your position regarding the city's new rulers.'

Domash's ears pricked up. 'My position?'

'The *veche* desires your pledge of loyalty, lord, as Mayor of Pskov.'

Domash sat up. 'My first loyalty has always been to the Principality of Novgorod, Yaroslav. If the *veche* is happy with me to continue as *posadnik* of this city then I will endeavour to do so to the best of my abilities.'

Yaroslav grinned broadly. 'They are very happy for you to remain so, lord.'

The mood in the chamber changed instantly to relief and gratitude. Domash stood and offered his hand to Yaroslav.

'I trust you and your family have settled in well at Novgorod.'

'They have, lord.'

Domash placed an arm around his shoulders. 'Good. Tonight we will celebrate the dawn of Novgorod's new era. An era of peace and prosperity, I hope.'

'God willing, lord.'

Domash was all smiles as he watched Yaroslav leave the chamber. After the doors had been closed a feeling of utter relief swept over him and he flopped back down in his high-backed throne.

'You must be the luckiest bastard alive,' remarked Gleb.

*****

'Now that the spring has arrived, lord, perhaps you should take time to visit your sister?'

Kristjan sat back in his chair and examined Indrek, the man who had been his father's right-hand man for as long as he could remember. His beard was now heavily laced with grey and his hair was thinning but he still retained his powerful physique and commanding air. He knew he was a brave and fearless warrior but wondered if age was starting to whittle away at his courage.

'I have no time,' hissed Taara's chosen one.

'She would appreciate seeing a member of her family,' said Indrek, undeterred. 'I know she gets lonely.'

Kristjan sprang from his chair. 'Lonely? If I don't devote all my time to military affairs then she will soon have plenty of company. Except that they will all be wearing white tunics and mail armour. If she wants to have the Sword Brothers for

529

company then by all means I will go and sit with her while Ungannia burns.'

Indrek said nothing but feared his homeland would soon be burning anyway. The previous summer and autumn had been a peaceful and bountiful time. War had stayed away from Ungannia and the harvest had been good. But now the winter snows had melted he knew that the Sword Brothers would be venting their fury on the kingdom.

Kristjan began pacing, occasionally touching the silver torc around his neck.

'It is little wonder that the gods are angry with Estonia. I take Fellin with ease only for the imbeciles that I left to garrison it to give it up without I fight. I capture Varbola, the strongest fort in all Estonia, without raising a sword and the garrison manages to get itself slaughtered outside its walls by the Sword Brothers. I am surrounded by idiots.'

He looked at Vetseke standing beside Indrek. 'Excepting you, prince, you have remained a steadfast ally throughout my time of trial.'

The great hall of the fort atop Toome Hill had been cleared of petitioners, guards and servants, its thick oak doors shut to allow Kristjan some peace. He found the day-to-day business of dealing with merchants, traders, craftsmen, commoners and mystics tedious to say the least. Whereas Indrek made time for the inhabitants of Dorpat, lending a kindly ear to their grievances, Kristjan thought their lives miserable and their words unworthy of his semi-divine ears.

'It is a pity, prince,' continued Kristjan, 'that your Russian friends could not have supported me more at Reval. Another week and the port would have fallen.'

Vetseke stifled a laugh. 'It was unfortunate I agree, lord.'

'The answer is plain enough,' continued Kristjan, 'you will go to Novgorod and request more Russian troops for our fight against the Sword Brothers. Only this time they will be under my command.'

'There is a new government in Novgorod, lord,' cautioned Vetseke. 'One that might not be so predisposed to sending its soldiers into the west.'

Kristjan waved a dismissive hand at him. 'Tell Novgorod that if they send me aid then it will share in my victory over the Sword Brothers.'

Indrek's eyes widened in alarm. 'Might it be better to seek an accommodation with the Bishop of Riga, lord?'

Kristjan retook his seat. 'Better for whom, Indrek?'

'For your kingdom and its people, lord.'

'The gods are watching over Ungannia, Indrek,' replied Kristjan. 'It is not coincidence that of all the Estonian kingdoms only Ungannia is free from foreign occupation, either that or is a ravaged husk.'

He touched the torc to emphasise his link to the gods. 'This year I intend to defeat the Sword Brothers once and for all, to shatter the myth of their invincibility.'

'It is a dangerous strategy, lord,' warned Indrek.

'Dangerous for the Sword Brothers, I agree,' said Kristjan. 'Now I have a headache and you both may leave.'

Indrek and Vetseke bowed their heads and walked from the chamber, leaving Kristjan to brood alone. Indrek said nothing to the Liv prince as they strolled from the hall into the fort's compound. It had been raining but now the sky was filled with white clouds and the air smelt cool and fresh.

'Well, prince, at least you have a reason to leave now.'

Vetseke, his green cloak spotless and his hair well groomed, turned to face the older man.

'What do you mean?'

Indrek gave him a wry smile. 'You must know that in the summer the Sword Brothers will be marching straight here to settle affairs with Kristjan. It would be a foolish man who willingly runs back into a burning building that he has just escaped from.'

'For years I have been a landless prince condemned to a wanderer's life. There comes a time, Lord Indrek, when a man grows tired of such an existence and desires an end to it all.'

*****

Riga was a city transformed. The spectre of the pox had long been banished, the burial pits and endless processions to inter the dead having been replaced by bustling markets and a thriving populace. The end of the pestilence had resulted in the lifting of the quarantine so once again the city became a destination for those in Livonia who wished to sell and buy goods. In addition, the end of the Danish blockade had meant that once again the Dvina became a thoroughfare for trade. Many ships and boats filled the city's docks, bringing crusaders from Germany and fur, flax, timber, tar and hides from Novgorod, Polotsk and the Lithuanian kingdoms, though the latter were still embroiled in a civil war that showed no signs of ending and which adversely affected their trade. The jetties were crammed with single-masted riverboats bearing names written in Cyrillic, while moored at the longer quays were the great cogs that had brought Bishop Albert and his crusader army from Lübeck. Officials went among the rows of vessels methodically making note of their names and cargoes, the latter incurring port charges according to their value. The city treasury, emptied during the pestilence and blockade, was gradually being refilled as the lifeblood of trade began to flow again.

Away from the heaving docks and streets packed with Livs, Rigans, Russians and newly arrived German soldiers, the Bishop's Palace was a haven of peace and order. Gardeners tended to immaculate rose beds and guards in the red livery of the garrison stood sentry at the gates and around the stone palace itself. Inside white-robed priests and red-uniformed servants, mostly fresh-faced teenage boys on the specific orders of the archdeacon himself, moved silently along its corridors and among its well-appointed rooms. Each of which was provided with rich tapestries and furniture imported from Europe, the larger ones with sumptuous fireplaces, well lit with dozens of beeswax candles. The bedrooms, reserved for the bishop, archdeacon and high-ranking guests, were all equipped with great beds. They had a heavy wooden frame and springs made of interlaced strips of leather overlaid with a feather mattress, sheets, quilts and pillows. Each bed was curtained, with linen hangings that were pulled back in the daytime. They were closed at night to provide privacy. The palace was always tightly guarded, of course, but the archdeacon insisted that one of the young servants always slept in his chamber for additional security.

Stefan now sat with his two uncles in one of the palace's withdrawing chambers, attended by two male servants who poured fine wine into silver-gilt wine flagons with swan handles engraved with the cross keys symbol of Riga.

Bishop Albert had arrived at Riga two days before to a rapturous reception from the city's population, no doubt buoyed by the hundreds of knights and their retainers that also came ashore from their mighty cogs. It was generally accepted that this year would see the final subjugation of the pagan Estonians, though the archdeacon had more pressing matters to put to his uncle.

'I regret to inform you, uncle, that since you have been away the Sword Brothers have become a law unto themselves. They continually undermined my authority as de facto ruler of Livonia, culminating in the murder of several members of the garrison of Riga.'

Albert leaned back in his chair and sipped at his wine. He caught the eye of his brother Hermann who gave a slight shake of his head.

'I heard about the incident at Wenden. Most regrettable.'

Stefan leered. 'Then I have your permission to have Conrad Wolff arrested?'

'You do not,' replied Albert.

Stefan choked on his wine. 'But, dear uncle, he killed some of my, that is your, men, having first interfered in a legally sanctioned execution of a witch. Such knavery cannot go unpunished.'

Albert sighed. 'I know that the Sword Brothers can be blunt at times, but if I was to arrest the man whom I made Marshal of Estonia, the man I might add who also saved my life, killed Lembit and has raised an army that serves the interests of the Holy Church, it would cast me in a bad light.'

He pointed to the window. 'There are many among the crusaders that came with me from Germany who have expressed a desire to fight alongside Conrad Wolff, such is his reputation. I will not and cannot have him arrested on the eve of our great crusade.'

'And the garrison of Wenden, uncle,' said Stefan testily, 'are they to escape justice as well?'

'To send a detachment of the garrison of Riga to arrest one of Wenden's brother knights was foolhardy in the extreme, Stefan. How do you know Master Rudolf and his men were not provoked, or even attacked?' replied Albert.

535

He looked at his brother. 'Hermann, what is your opinion in this matter, seeing as you were present when this girl, this supposed witch, was rescued from the stake?'

Hermann considered for a moment. 'I found Conrad Wolff to be reasonable in the affair, which is more than can be said for the members of the Rigan garrison.'

'I object to that, uncle,' said Stefan through gritted teeth. 'The garrison of this city safeguards Riga.'

'And its governor,' added Hermann caustically.

Stefan's eyes narrowed. 'May I remind you, uncle, that I was appointed by your brother to preserve the interests of Livonia in his absence?'

'And may I remind you that I am a prince of the Holy Church,' replied Hermann, 'and that the role of an archdeacon is to be a bishop's assistant, not his adviser.'

'Enough,' ordered Albert. 'The matter is closed for the moment. I need the Sword Brothers for the coming campaign in Ungannia. Of more immediate concern is the whereabouts of Bishop Bernhard. Has he returned to Dünamünde?'

Hermann looked at Stefan and smiled. 'He is in the north with Conrad Wolff and his army. He found the atmosphere at Riga not to his liking, or perhaps it was the company. I received word from Wenden that he is safe and well and currently residing in Varbola, a stronghold captured by the Marshal of Estonia in the winter just passed.'

'You see, Stefan,' said Albert, 'how important Conrad Wolff is to our mission in this land.'

Stefan said nothing as he sat on his silk-covered chair and fumed in silence.

'So, brother,' said Hermann, 'we march to capture Dorpat.'

Albert nodded. 'It is most strange that Ungannia, formerly a loyal ally of Riga, suddenly became its chief foe. Why this should be I cannot fathom.'

Stefan shrugged. 'Who knows the workings of the pagan mind, uncle, save only the Devil? Only by banishing paganism can reason and justice be planted in this land.'

'Master Rudolf at Wenden has informed me that Russian soldiers have been fighting alongside the Ungannians,' said Hermann. 'If this is the case, then we may be fighting them in Ungannia itself.'

Albert waved over one of the servants and placed his empty flagon on the silver tray he carried. The boy bowed and retreated.

'It cannot be helped. Ungannia has betrayed our trust and must be punished. There can be no sanctuary for those who commit crimes against God.'

He looked at his nephew. 'And that is what we are here for, what the Sword Brothers exist for: to serve God. Not to advance our own personal interests or those of the Buxhoeveden family. But to establish the kingdom of God in Livonia and Estonia. Remember that, Stefan, when you are conducting your personal feud against the Sword Brothers.'

For the archdeacon it was a chastening meeting. In his uncle's absence he had ruled Livonia like a king, treating it as a personal fiefdom, the area around Riga at least. Now Bishop Albert had returned and his wings had been well and truly clipped. It was an experience he found most disagreeable. He said no more on the matter of the Sword Brothers but he was determined to redouble his efforts to clip *their* wings and that of Conrad Wolff, the low-born baker's son.

*****

For the first time in years Rotalia was free of foreign incursions. The outposts along the coast deterred Oeselian raids, which in truth had declined markedly of late anyway, and the rebuilt fort of Leal meant Hillar could dispatch men to every part of his kingdom. He was not actually a king but a governor, made so by Conrad and confirmed by Bishop Bernhard. When the spring came Hillar returned to Leal while Conrad and the rest of the Army of the Wolf stayed at Varbola. There the Marshal of Estonia's broken arm mended itself and he recovered his strength. Riki, delighted to be home at long last, gladly accepted baptism in the cold waters of a nearby river in return for him becoming governor of Harrien. His men, now numbering forty after the hard fight at Lumandu, also agreed to have their heads ducked under the water to wash away their sins and become members of the Catholic faith.

It was a good time. The rivers and streams were filled with pure, fast-flowing melt water, the forests teemed with elk, deer and wolves and the meadows with hares and buttercups. Among the trees the thick snow disappeared to reveal lush undergrowth and in the wetlands there was a profusion of bog moss, cotton grass and bog whortleberry. But more heartening than the changing landscape was the return of villagers to their homes. Not many at first, the news of a Harrien leader once again in Varbola being slow to travel throughout the land. Many of the villages, especially in the north of the kingdom that had been raided by the Danes, remained empty, their inhabitants having been either killed or taken as slaves long ago. But further south people came out of their hiding places in the forests and returned to their homes. Those village elders still alive gathered together to hold parish meetings and elect a parish elder, the elders in turn electing a county leader.

From Varbola Riki sent out riders to all the villages requesting reports of how many people lived in each settlement so as to paint an accurate picture of the state of Harrien. As the weeks passed a steady stream of reports were sent to Varbola, along with young men making their way to the fort to offer their services to the new 'elf warrior'.

'Who?'

Bishop Bernhard scratched his head as two young men were escorted from Varbola's great hall, having been accepted into Riki's service.

'That was the name given to Alva, lord bishop,' answered Riki, 'the last leader of the Harrien to sit in this hall.'

'They think you are a reincarnation of him?' asked Bernhard.

Riki nodded. 'Some do, though I dissuade them of the notion.'

'You should indulge it,' Conrad told him, 'Alva was a great leader of your people.'

'He fought against you, *Susi*,' said Riki.

Conrad laughed. 'So did you, my friend, at one time.'

The Harrien leader was sitting in one of the two chairs on the dais, the other having been given to Bishop Bernhard on account of his age. Conrad, Hans and Anton stood on one side; Riki's two most trusted lieutenants on the other. A pair of guards escorted another potential recruit into the hall, a boy no older than thirteen or fourteen. Like his race his hair was blonde and his eyes blue. He had a handsome face, though it wore a scowl. He paced between the two guards, one carrying a sword in a scabbard. They halted in front of the dais.

'Name?' said Riki.

'Jaan,' replied the boy. 'I have come to offer my sword to you, high one.'

One of the guards held out the sword. 'He came with this, lord. Probably stole it.'

Jaan's eyes flashed with anger. 'I did not steal it. It belonged to my father.'

'Where is he?' asked Riki.

The boy's eyes filled with pain. 'Dead. Murdered by the Danes.'

'Where are you from, boy?' asked Riki.

'Maardu.'

'Near Reval?' Riki was impressed. He looked at the tatty leather shoes on his feet. 'You walked here?'

Jaan nodded.

'And the rest of your family,' enquired Conrad, 'where are they?'

Jaan looked at the Sword Brother, unsure who he was and yet knowing that he must be an important person if he was standing next to Riki.

'Dead,' he answered flatly.

'I remember another youngster whose family had been killed, Conrad,' said Hans, 'who came to us an orphan with a desire to kill the enemy. She turned out all right.'

Jaan studied Conrad closely. 'You are the one they call *Susi*?'

'I am,' replied Conrad, 'but I have no authority here. Governor Riki rules in Harrien.'

'You are too young to join my war band, Jaan,' Riki told him. 'But you may stay here at Varbola and work in the kitchens or stables until you reach sixteen years.'

'I have a right to avenge my parents,' shouted Jaan.

'If you want to do so,' said Riki calmly, 'then the first thing you need to do is obey orders. You may keep your sword, Jaan, but you must learn how to use it before you stand beside me in battle.'

541

He indicated to the guards that the youngster's time was over. They grabbed his arms and manhandled him from the chamber.

'It is good for Harrien that it breed such firebrands,' said Bishop Hermann, 'though I doubt he will be happy mucking out stables. I have seen that sort of desire in men before. You should take him with you when you next march, Riki.'

Before he could answer one of the guards reappeared and walked to the dais, saluting Riki.

'There is a courier from Wenden, lord, with a package for you.'

'For me?' Riki was confused.

'Excellent,' said Conrad. 'I did not think it would get here so quickly. It is a gift for you, Riki.'

The courier was ordered to enter, a Liv in a green tunic and mail shirt carrying a large bundle wrapped in hides. He was a big man but found the package awkward and heavy to carry. Conrad asked him to place it on the reed-covered floor before Riki. He pulled his dagger, walked forward to cut the string around the hides and asked Hans and Anton to assist him. He discarded the hides and unwrapped the large white banner, Hans and Anton each held up a side as Conrad stepped back. Riki stood in amazement as he looked at the standard, which had a red lynx with great claws against a white background edged with gold.

'The good textile workers at Wenden laboured hard to create this, Riki,' said Conrad, 'A fitting standard for the new leader of Harrien, I think.'

'It is magnificent, *Susi*,' said Riki, extending a hand to touch the red lynx.

It was not the only banner that was presented to the commanders of the Army of the Wolf. Conrad also gifted standards to Andres, Tonis and Hillar, all of them depicting the symbols of their respective kingdoms and all made from the finest materials. The morale of the army rose and so did its numbers. Those crusaders that had been at Leal, plus the ones that had remained in Saccalia, were concentrated at Varbola under the command of Bishop Bernhard. Those that had made the winter journey to Leal had all recovered their strength and made the trip to Harrien without incident, as did those from Saccalia. The result was that four hundred crusader foot soldiers mustered outside the fort at the end of May to be inspected by Conrad and the bishop. A few days later they were paraded again, this time being joined by the other contingents of the army. Afterwards the man elected to be the commander of the crusaders, a dour-faced individual named Ulric, spoke to Conrad.

'The men aren't happy, lord.'

'Oh? They look healthy enough and now they all have some sort of armour after the victory at Lumandu.'

He shook his head. 'It's not that, lord.'

'Then what is it?'

'No standard, lord. The pagans have new standards and we don't have one.'

Conrad thought it was some sort of joke until he looked at Ulric and saw that his expression was glummer than normal. It was really extraordinary that his men's top priority was a piece of cloth rather than weapons and armour. But then he realised that soldiers attached great importance to banners. Would he not sacrifice his own life to preserve Wenden's standard? Of course he would. And Novgorod had gone to war over the loss of one of its banners at Dorpat. The cloth still resided at Wenden, in Master Rudolf's office.

'You are right, Ulric. Your men shall have a banner.'

Riki summoned the best seamstresses and weavers from the surrounding villages and put them to work creating a flag. There was no silk or gold edging available so the banner would be made of wool with the design on each side being sewn linen. Conrad thought it trivial at first, but as the days passed he became more interested in its design. Bishop Hermann, Ulric and the crusader commanders spent many hours in a hut in the fort's compound thrashing out the details. And as they did so and then conveyed their instructions to the women who had been charged with creating the banner, the chief topic of conversation in Varbola was when it would be completed. Leatherface tried to get the bishop drunk so he would reveal its design to him and thus win the sizeable sum that had been wagered on the standard's pattern. But the bishop had drunk the mercenary under the table, the latter having to be carried by Conrad and Hans back to his hut, unconscious.

It took a month to create the banner and when it was finished it was escorted under armed guard from the hut where it had been created to the fort's main hall. There it was placed on a table in the centre of the chamber where Bishop Hermann blessed it. Those monks who had journeyed to Varbola with the crusaders were also in attendance, holding a vigil through the night over the sacred standard. No one was allowed into the hall while this was going on. After being thus consecrated the banner was then fixed to a staff with a traverse bar at the top so it would never hang limply and would be visible even when there was no wind.

Warriors filled the fort's walls and towers when the bishop carried the banner from the hall to present it to his men. Riki's signallers blew their horns as Ulric's men, drawn up in a square, knelt and bowed their heads. Conrad, Hans and Anton stood with Leatherface in a tower overlooking the compound crammed with civilians. He smiled when he saw Jaan among the crowd, spade in hand, craning his neck trying to see what was going on.

Bishop Bernhard said a prayer, his words clear and loud in the warm morning air. Conrad and his friends bowed their heads as the bishop implored God to protect His banner and the men that carried it. He tapped Leatherface on the arm to indicate he should do likewise. After he had finished the bishop ordered his men to stand and he handed over the banner to

Ulric, to loud cheers from the crusaders and accompanying acclaim from the assembled warriors and civilians.

The design showed a yellow bishop's mitre on a white background, the mitre adorned with three blue crosses to symbolise the Holy Trinity. Beneath was a red rose, the symbol of the city of Lippe in honour of Bishop Bernhard. Beneath the mitre and rose was a scroll bearing the motto *episcopi spurii*.

'What does that mean?' asked the illiterate Hans.

Conrad had no idea, having no knowledge of Latin.

'The bishop's bastards,' said Anton, who could not only read Latin but write it as well.

Thus did the bishop's soldiers have their banner and, their morale high, prepared to march with the Army of the Wolf. Only one question remained: where would they march to?

Two weeks later Conrad called together the commanders of his army to inform them of his plans. They gathered in Varbola's great hall, around an old oak table that had reputedly been made by the gods. The mood was relaxed and confident. Riki had settled into his new position and was becoming accustomed to settling disputes and giving his judgement to his people. Hillar was kept fully abreast of affairs in Rotalia by Koit, which continued to be free from Oeselian raids. Only the stout and courageous Andres appeared slightly glum, no doubt thinking about his homeland that was under the control of the tyrant Kristjan.

Hans was munching on a small pie filled with meat and herbs as the rest were served with beer and honey mead. Bishop Bernhard sat at one end of the table, Riki at the other, as Hans finished his pie and tore off a chunk of bread a servant had place before him.

Conrad banged the end of his dagger on the table to get everyone's attention.

'We have received news from Wenden that Bishop Albert has landed at Riga with an army. Master Rudolf has informed me that Dorpat will be the objective of the coming campaign.'

The others banged their fists on the table to show their support.

'Ungannia will not be able to withstand the bishop's army combined with the Sword Brothers,' stated Conrad.

'Or indeed your army, Conrad,' said Bernhard, which resulted in more fists hitting the table top.

Conrad held up his hands to request quiet. 'But first I intend to occupy Jerwen.'

Andres looked at him in surprise.

'That's right, Andres. You and your men have been away from their homeland for too long. The Army of the Wolf will therefore free Jerwen before it marches south to assist in the capture of Dorpat.'

Conrad thought he detected tears in Andres' eyes but the big Jerwen raised his cup to Conrad and downed his beer in one gulp.

'Go and tell your men, Andres, that they are marching to free their families, villages and farms. We leave in two days.'

*****

Novgorod's *veche* was packed with the city's finest as a grim-faced Mikhail Vsevolodovich stood before the assembled delegates. He had accepted their offer to be the new prince of Novgorod. He was a member of the ancient and prestigious Rurik dynasty, a descendant of the Varangian Prince Rurik who had been invited by the people of Novgorod to be the ruler of their city some three hundred and fifty years before. He had been away from the city for some months, having taken part in a great campaign against a cruel enemy from Asia. A coalition of Russian princes and Cumans had gathered in the Ukraine to stop these infidel raiders who some called Mongols. Rumours had reached northern Russia of subsequent events but now the *veche* was informed of what had happened by one who had been there.

'Eighty thousand Russian soldiers were deployed in battle order near a river called the Kalka,' said Mikhail. 'We greatly outnumbered the eastern devils and were confident of victory. What followed I can only attribute to God deserting us for the enemy horsemen charged and unleashed deadly volleys of arrows. Hundreds were cut down before our own horsemen had a chance to reply.'

There was a collective groan as he continued his tale of woe.

'When our horsemen charged the enemy retreated. But it was only a ruse to lure them away from the rest of the army. The enemy suddenly turned and engulfed our mounted warriors. None returned. And then the slaughter began. The enemy, all horsemen and armed with spears and bows, rode around our men and peppered them with arrows. For hours they shot at our men, gradually whittling down our numbers until the sons of Russia could take no more. They ran. We tried to rally them but to no avail. Only darkness saved the army from total annihilation.'

He cast his head down and spread his long arms.

'How many men rallied after the battle, highness?' enquired Yuri Nevsky.

'Twenty thousand survived the battle,' reported Mikhail, 'though only because the Mongols did not follow up their victory.'

Sixty thousand men killed was almost an incomprehensible number. Men looked at each other in despair and alarm. What if these Mongols returned and headed north instead of west?

'We must look to our own defences,' said Mikhail. 'The strength of Novgorod must be directed towards the defence of this kingdom. There can be no more expeditions against the Danes or Sword Brothers.'

This declaration was met with warm applause. Mikhail held up an arm and the hall fell silent.

'The defences of this city are strong and the Mongols have no siege engines. They are raiders and plunderers so we should not be unduly alarmed.'

More applause greeted this declaration. Mikhail smiled, knowing that if the Asian horsemen returned they would probably overrun the Kingdom of Novgorod with ease. He had never seen such ferocious and, crucially, well-organised horsemen and he feared their return.

Afterwards Yuri Nevksy and his son accompanied the prince back to the kremlin. The members of the *veche*, glad to be rid of Mstislav and his expensive foreign wars, returned to their grand houses in a satisfied mood. They had been shocked by the news of the catastrophe at the Kalka but comforted themselves that the Ukraine was hundreds of miles away from Novgorod. Trade had been restored with Riga and Europe's desire for squirrel pelts was as insatiable as ever. The party had an escort but there was no need: the people were delighted that Prince Mikhail now ruled over them. They crowded round but kept a respectful distance, bowing their heads to him as he passed.

Inside the kremlin they found Prince Vetseke waiting for them. When the commander of the guard informed Mikhail that the prince desired an audience he had no idea who he was.

'A pagan, highness,' Yuri Nevsky explained, 'who was favoured by Prince Mstislav. He and his men were once employed by him in the northern regions to gather pelts. He has been fighting alongside the Ungannians against the Sword Brothers recently.'

Mikhail stopped and looked at the tall, clean-shaven individual who wore a green cloak and a sword in a red scabbard.

'Prince Mstislav gave him some soldiers to aid him in his fight, highness,' said Yaroslav Nevsky.

'Did he indeed?' uttered Mikhail thoughtfully. He waved Vetseke over.

'He speaks Russian?'

'He does, highness,' replied Yuri, 'after a fashion.'

Vetseke was escorted to the prince by a pair of guards, who used their spear shafts to prevent him getting within striking distance with his sword. The commander of the guard demanded the Liv's weapon. Vetseke pulled the sword from its scabbard and handed it over. He bowed to Mikhail.

'What brings you to Novgorod, Prince Vetseke?' asked Mikhail.

'I come with a request from Kristjan, the leader of the Ungannian people, lord,' answered Vetseke. 'He desires aid in his fight against the heretical Bishop of Riga and the Sword Brothers.'

'You mean soldiers?' said Mikhail.

Vetseke nodded. 'Yes, lord.'

Mikhail stroked his brown curly beard. 'And if Novgorod aids this Kristjan, will it help him defeat the servants of the Church of Rome?'

'No, lord.'

They all looked at Vetseke in surprise.

'Your answer does not aid your cause, prince,' said Mikhail. 'Why should I send Russians to aid a kingdom that according to you is already lost?'

'Because it is better for Russian soldiers to be fighting the Sword Brothers in Ungannia rather than in their own territory, lord.'

Mikhail looked at Yuri who gently shook his head.

'Come back to the palace tomorrow, Prince Vetseke,' said Mikhail, 'when I will give you my answer.'

Vetseke bowed his head and backed away. The commander of the guard gave him back his sword and his men escorted him towards the gates. Mikhail watched him go.

'What is the news concerning the Bishop of Riga and the Sword Brothers?' he asked Yuri Nevsky.

'Our merchants report that the bishop has landed at Riga with a large army of crusaders, highness. In addition, the Marshal of Estonia has conquered a substantial area of that land.'

'Who?'

'A Sword Brother, highness,' answered Yuri, 'who leads an army of pagan Estonians. He reportedly has the favour of the Bishop of Riga.'

Mikhail considered for a moment. 'I am apt to give our valiant Liv some assistance. He is right when he states that it is better for the bishop and his soldiers to be occupied in Ungannia rather than turning his gaze further east.'

He looked at Yaroslav. 'Send word to the mayor of Pskov that he is to furnish Prince Vetseke with military aid. Emphasise that no members of the city's *Druzhina* are to march west. I do not wish to alienate the city's boyars as my predecessor did here. I will inform our valiant Liv of his good fortune tomorrow.'

*****

Conrad had Andres collect all his Jerwen warriors at Varbola prior to marching back into their homeland. As mid-summer came and passed four hundred men were assembled outside the fort, which despite its great size had become cramped with the Army of the Wolf, the 'bishop's bastards' and many women and children. Riki issued orders that many of his own men were to relocate to nearby villages to alleviate the press of people. But that was but one of Riki's worries as he sat in his hall listening to his people airing their grievances. The bishop, who seemed to be getting younger by the day so invigorating did he find the surroundings of Varbola, offered to be an adviser to the young warlord and now ruler of his people An offer that was gladly accepted. Riki also asked Conrad to be a part of these proceedings, feeling that the presence of *Susi* would expedite matters more speedily.

'You mean make people less inclined to disagree with you if I am backing you up.'

553

Riki smiled. 'Yes, *Susi.*'

The bishop, ensconced in a high-backed chair beside the blonde-haired Harrien leader, nodded approvingly.

'You are learning how to be a courtier, Riki.'

'I preferred him when he was a warlord,' muttered Conrad.

The petitioners were allowed into the hall where their cases were put before Riki. Mostly they concerned disputes over land and livestock, but increasingly young women arrived with members of the 'bishop's bastards' asking permission to marry the foreign men. The latter, being recruited from the lower orders of German society, were only too glad to have attractive, voluptuous, blonde-haired girls requesting to be their wives. It was the same today as a striking girl in a blue linen skirt and white woollen tunic walked up to Riki arm-in-arm with a man in a gambeson who appeared to be twice her age.

'We wish to be married, lord,' she declared in Estonian.

Riki pointed at her husband-to-be. 'To him?'

'Yes, lord.'

Riki looked at the bishop who spoke to the soldier in German.

'Marriage is not to be entered into lightly, my son. I hope your intentions to this young woman are honourable.'

'Yes, lord bishop,' he smiled, revealing at least two missing front teeth.

'And what if you marry this girl,' said Conrad, 'and then decide to return to Germany after having taken her virtue?'

The man looked horrified. 'Return to Germany, lord? Not a chance in hell, begging your pardon, lord bishop. I was a labourer in Saxony, lord, and every winter I nearly starved. I slept in ditches, under bridges and sometimes had to beg for food in towns. But here there is plenty of land, the forests and rivers are full of game and fish, so I can grow and hunt my own food.'

He slapped the girl on the backside. 'And feed a family if we are so blessed.'

'Poor girl,' mumbled Conrad.

'Lord?' the soldier asked.

'Nothing,' replied Conrad.

Riki turned to Conrad. 'Years of warfare have emptied many villages of young men, *Susi*. If I am to rebuild this kingdom then the young women must have husbands.'

'You are still a soldier,' said Bernhard sternly, 'and there is a chance that you may not return from the forthcoming campaign against Dorpat.'

The man nodded solemnly. 'I know that, lord bishop, and so does she. But God willing I will live to see my old age and watch my children grow up.'

Riki looked at Conrad who shrugged his shoulders. Bishop Bernhard seemed pleased by his reply and so the Harrien leader gave his consent, to the delight of both mismatched parties. But Riki seemed pleased that Harrien women would be giving birth to future warriors and the bishop was delighted because he knew that any such marriages would be conducted according to the Christian practice.

For his part Conrad had more pressing matters to attend to and three days later rode beside his two friends and Andres at the head of four hundred Jerwen warriors mounted on ponies. Scouts rode ahead and on the flanks to guard against being surprised by the Danes or any of Kristjan's men. Andres discounted the idea.

'The Danes hide behind their walls at Reval, *Susi*, that is the rumour that reaches my ears.'

'And what of Jerwen?' asked Hans, 'is it still an ally of Kristjan?'

'Kristjan has been very generous with Jerwen lives,' Andres told him, 'he is no friend of my people.'

They were striking east, towards the ancient capital of the Jerwen people, the hill fort of Kassinurme. The site had reportedly been occupied for seven thousand years and was believed to have magical powers. Conrad was worried that it would be heavily defended.

'We cannot storm Kassinurme, *Susi*,' Andres told him. 'For a Jerwen to attack our most sacred site would be sacrilege.'

'Then how do we take it?' asked Hans.

'We do not,' answered Andres.

The three Sword Brothers were confused but five days out from Varbola, in a rolling plain flanked by thick spruce forests, the scouts returned with news that a sizeable force of warriors was approaching on foot. Estimated to be around two hundred, they carried many symbols on their shields and were led by an ugly fat man dressed in rags.

Hans laughed. 'This should be easy enough. We can match their shield wall and then use the wings to envelop them.'

'Another victory for you, Conrad.'

Andres turned in the saddle. 'There will be no battle. Will you accompany me, *Susi*, to speak to their leader?'

'Are you mad?' Anton said to him. 'They will cut you down, especially Conrad when they see the insignia on his surcoat and shield.'

'I ask *Susi* to trust me in this matter,' replied Andres as dark shapes appeared a quarter of a mile or so ahead.

The day was warm and the air sweet with the aroma of meadow grass and buttercups. The standard of Andres held by a warrior behind them hung limply in the still air, the tails of ponies swishing away the army of midges that always plagued the lush summer landscape.

'Very well,' said Conrad, 'let us go and try to win with words instead of swords.'

He dug his spurs into his horse's sides and the caparison-covered beast walked forward. Andres did the same and the pair headed towards the warriors who were now deploying from column into line as they formed a shield wall. Behind them they left four hundred confused and worried men.

'This leader,' said Conrad, 'you have fought beside him before?'

Andres shook his head. 'He is not a warlord, *Susi*, he is a holy man like Bishop Bernhard.'

'A spiritual leader, then?'

Andres nodded and then fell into silence. The horses walked on and the gap between them and the now formed shield wall got shorter. Conrad noticed that there were no birds in the sky as they approached the line of warriors drawn up three or four deep. Andres' men sported the bear symbol of Jerwen on their round shields but the warriors that faced the pair carried shields that bore more ancient insignia: the sun cross, pentagram, plaited lattice, elk antlers, eight-pointed star and sunflower. Standing a few paces in front, armed only with a staff, was a rotund man in rags who watched the riders with a disinterested air.

'His name is Rustic,' said Andres quietly, 'and he wields great power.'

Conrad raised an eyebrow in surprise. During his childhood he had seen beggars in Lübeck better dressed. But he knew that many holy men of the pagan religion lived as hermits in the forests and looked like vagabonds so he said nothing. Andres halted half a dozen paces from the mystic and dismounted. Conrad did the same. Rustic said nothing while behind him the warriors stood silent in their ranks. The Jerwen leader and Sword Brother faced the forest dweller.

'I received your message, Andres son on Paavu, saying that you wished to put an end to the suffering of your people,' said Rustic, ignoring Conrad. 'And yet you come with an army at your back.'

'An army of Jerwen, Rustic,' replied Andres, 'men who wish to return to their villages and homes to work the land once more.'

'There are many who have promised such things,' remarked Rustic derisively, 'only to drench the land in more blood. Why should you be any different to them?'

Andres held out a hand to Conrad. 'This is Brother Conrad of the Sword Brothers, the man called *Susi* among the Estonian people, who has brought peace to Rotalia and now restored a leader of the Harrien in Varbola. With his help I intend to restore peace and prosperity to Jerwen, my homeland.'

Rustic tilted his head at Conrad. 'Even though you wear the uniform of our enemies I salute you, *Susi*, for in our culture when a wolf is encountered he should always be greeted with kind words. The more so if he is the physical embodiment of the spirit wolf of the forest.'

'Thank you, sir,' replied Conrad, bowing his head in return, 'I sincerely hope we can agree on a settlement that is beneficial to us all and avoids unnecessary bloodshed.'

Rustic peered into his eyes. 'Others may call you *Susi* but I see a *toonehundid*, a wolf sent by the gods to protect their people. The gods work their magic in strange ways.'

He turned back to Andres. 'South of the Mother of Waters is Kristjan, who has taken the name Murk in honour of Taara. He believes that Jerwen is his domain.'

'He is deluded, Rustic,' said Andres. 'I have witnessed the cruelty he has inflicted on the people of Saccalia and Harrien, and he has wasted the lives of many Estonian warriors at Reval for no purpose save his own vanity.'

Behind Rustic the warriors banged their spear shafts against the inside of their shields to indicate their support of his words.

'Fine words,' admitted Rustic, 'though I learned long ago that talk is cheap and actions speak louder than words.'

'With your blessing,' said Andres, 'we would like to travel through Jerwen.'

'To make war on Ungannia?' asked Rustic.

Andres nodded.

'Kristjan has declared war upon my order,' said Conrad, 'and has killed many innocents. He cannot be allowed to continue his depredations.'

'Dorpat is very strong,' said Rustic.

'It will not survive our assault,' stated Conrad. 'A great army gathers to the west that will sweep Kristjan away.'

'And after that, wolf spirit?' asked Rustic.

'After that another kingdom of Estonia will be free from tyranny.'

'But not foreign occupation. The religion of the men of iron spreads like a dark shadow over this land. Once Ungannia has been conquered it will be subjected to the will of the new religion that seeks to crush the ancient ways of this land.'

'With all due respect, sir,' replied Conrad, 'I think you are misguided.'

Andres looked alarmed but Conrad continued.

'My order has not desecrated the ancient groves and sacred places of your people. And if I had done so then I would not have hundreds of Estonian warriors under my command, men who serve me of their own free will and not because they are forced to do so. You are free to go to Varbola and Leal, sir, to speak to the leaders of the people of Rotalia and Harrien if you do not believe me. I cannot answer for all the men of iron, but I was appointed by Bishop Albert to be Marshal of Estonia and I say to you that I have no intention of replacing one tyranny with another.'

Once again the warriors rapped their hafts against their shields. Rustic waited for the noise to die down before speaking to Andres.

'To you, Andres, son of Paavu, I say this. You may lead your men through Jerwen south to Ungannia. There the gods will decide your fate and that of Kristjan. Afterwards the one favoured by the gods shall take up residence in Kassinurme as the true ruler of the Jerwen people. This is my decision.'

He looked at Conrad. 'Even though you have won great victories and fame, your time of trial is yet to come, wolf brother.'

With that he turned, pointed his staff to the east and walked through the shield wall. His men promptly about-faced and followed him, leaving Conrad and Andres alone, their animals munching the grass.

'You will soon be sitting in the hall of that hill fort,' Conrad told him, 'for as night follows day Kristjan will not be able to withstand the army that he will be facing at Dorpat.'

Andres watched the warriors becoming smaller as they marched east.

'I wonder how many of my people are still with Kristjan?'

*****

'Deserted?'

Kristjan threw his dagger on the table and touched his silver torc. He shrugged at Indrek.

'No great loss. The Jerwen are women when it comes to fighting. We still have enough men to man the walls and the fort.'

Indrek did not bother to protest. For weeks he had been organising the defence of Dorpat, the great trading centre of Ungannia beside the Emajogi River, the ancient Mother of Waters that was a major trade route with Novgorod via Lake Peipus to the east. He had given orders that deer, elk and boar were to be hunted, their carcasses butchered and the meat smoked to provide the garrison with food during a siege. He had worked tirelessly to strengthen the earth and timber rampart that surrounded the town and Toome Hill, atop of which stood the hill fort. But as he was doing so Kristjan's disastrous campaign in the north had cost him hundreds of men. Worse, his volatile and cruel nature had mostly destroyed any loyalty the other Estonian tribes had towards Ungannia. The trickle of deserters from among the Jerwen and Wierlanders had turned into a flood, made worse by the news brought by merchants that Bishop Albert had landed at Riga with a large crusader army. The result was that Kristjan's foreign volunteers now consisted solely of the mad, religious fanatics, criminals and those without a home.

Kristjan drank from his cup of beer. 'In the coming fight I want only men who are beloved of the gods and who believe in our cause.'

'Beloved of the gods, of course, lord,' said Indrek listlessly, his eyes surrounded by black rings.

He spent his time among the people of Dorpat, many of whom feared for their lives as the inevitable clash with Bishop Albert got nearer. Indrek had wanted to evacuate the women and children before the siege commenced but Kristjan would have none of it. He told his deputy that men fight better when they are defending their families.

Kristjan poured some beer into a cup and handed it to Indrek.

'Here, you look terrible.'

'Lack of sleep will do that, lord.'

Kristjan picked up his dagger and began turning it in his hand.

'It is important to bring in all the people from the surrounding villages before the crusaders arrived.'

Indrek did not bother to tell him that the villagers had fled days ago, a few to Dorpat; most to secret hiding places deep in the forest.

'Send soldiers to burn the villages,' ordered Kristjan.

Indrek spat out his beer. 'Lord?'

'I do not wish to provide the bishop with lodgings for his soldiers. See to it.'

Indrek would disregard that order. Kristjan spent most of his time in the fort, hardly bothering to venture down the hill into the town.

'What about your sister, lord?'

'My sister?'

'She is vulnerable at Odenpah now that it no longer has a garrison.'

Maarja's face had been terribly scarred by the pestilence that had killed her sisters and parents and people believed that Odenpah was cursed. As a result she lived there with only a small number of loyal servants. The garrison had deserted long ago, along with most of the slaves and workers. Kristjan waved the dagger in the air.

'I have more pressing matters to think about than the welfare of my diseased sister. She can lock Odenpah's gates if she feels threatened.'

Indrek sighed. 'With your permission, lord, I must get back to the town.'

A guard entered the ill-lit hall, saluted to Indrek and reported to Kristjan.

'Prince Vetseke has returned, lord.'

Kristjan's face lit up. 'Show him in.'

The Liv entered the chamber moments later, immaculate in a pair of new leather boots, spotless green cloak, mail shirt, his sword in its red scabbard. He gave Indrek a friendly smile and bowed his head to Kristjan.

'Greetings, lord, I bring reinforcements from the Kingdom of Novgorod. Three hundred archers, a gift from Prince Mikhail and the Mayor of Pskov.'

Kristjan clapped his hands together. 'You are most welcome, prince. Tonight I will feast you and your Russians in this hall to celebrate your and their arrival. Indrek, see that the prince's men are allotted quarters. They must be tired after their journey.'

'If you would follow me, lord prince,' said Indrek.

Vetseke bowed again to Kristjan. 'Until later, lord.'

Kristjan wore a broad smile as Indrek walked with Vetseke from the hall.

'So, you came back.'

'As I said I would.'

Indrek gave him a wry smile. 'Just in time for the inferno that is about to engulf us.'

Chapter 12

The great crusade against Dorpat commenced in the middle of July, the army that had landed at Riga finally moving northeast after an interminable delay caused by Master Thaddeus insisting that the siege engines that were to be used against the pagan town were constructed before the march. He set his engineers to work at Wenden, Kremon and Segewold organising the collection of timber and construction of mangonels and trebuchets that would join the army on its way to Dorpat. Once built they then had to be disassembled and their component parts loaded on to four-wheeled wagons, though some of the mangonels, the smaller ones, were fitted with solid wooden wheels so they could be towed by teams of oxen.

There was a great service in Riga's cathedral on the day before the army's departure, the stone building packed with knights, squires and priests who knelt with heads bowed as Bishop Albert asked God to bless their forthcoming campaign.

Because the Lithuanian kingdoms were embroiled in a civil war Grand Master Volquin decided that it was safe for the order's castles along the Dvina to each contribute twelve brother knights, thirty sergeants, forty crossbowmen and the same number of spearmen to the undertaking. The same number was to be provided by the castles of Kremon, Segewold and Wenden so that the Sword Brother complement for the campaign totalled just over eight hundred and sixty men. The castles along the Dvina still retained garrisons to deter any Lithuanian incursions, which was considered highly unlikely.

Conrad received a request to march the Army of the Wolf towards Dorpat from Master Rudolf, who also made the same request of Sir Richard at Lehola. Conrad had moved back to Varbola with Andres and his men following the curious encounter with Rustic, which had cheered his Jerwen commander enormously.

'So let me get this right,' said Leatherface, one leg impertinently draped over the arm of his chair, 'if you beat Kristjan then you get the keys to your kingdom, so to speak.'

'That is correct,' answered Andres.

Leatherface grinned impishly. 'Looks like you will be sitting in your hill fort before autumn comes, then, for as sure as a bear shits in the woods Dorpat won't be able to withstand the army that is marching against it.'

Conrad winced at his inappropriate words and made an apologetic face at Bishop Bernhard, who waved away his silent atonement. He had convened a council of war to decide the army's course of action as it mustered at Varbola. The hall was hot and smelt of leather and sweat. Young servant girls ferried beer and water from the kitchens, in addition to bread, cheese and apples, though only Hans had an appetite. The warlords sat around the table on which food and drinks were piled, occasionally swatting away a fly that landed on sweating cheese. Technically Leatherface should not have been in attendance but his humour, vast experience and blunt tongue had endeared him to the Estonian leaders who had known him for years. For his part Bishop Bernhard found the mercenary's flippancy refreshing.

'Because of our commitments in Rotalia and Harrien,' said Conrad, 'I intend to take only two hundred Rotalians and the same number of Harrien to Dorpat.'

He looked at Riki. 'I assume you will stay here, at Varbola, to administer your new kingdom, my friend.'

Riki shook his head. 'I have had a gut-full of listening to complaints. It makes my head throb so I will be coming with you. But I shall leave Varbola well garrisoned.'

Conrad looked at Hillar. 'And you, my friend, will you go back to Rotalia?'

He smiled. 'Like Riki I feel the need to wield my sword before it becomes rusty through lack of use. Besides, Koit has affairs well under control at Leal.'

'That's the thing when you stand at the back of a shield wall, Hillar,' smiled Tonis, 'you never get a chance to use your weapons. You should stand with me in the front rank with the rest of my Saccalians.'

Hillar threw a chunk of bread at him.

Conrad looked at Bishop Bernhard. 'I assume your eminence will turn over command of your soldiers to Ulric for the forthcoming campaign?'

'Why?' asked the bishop. 'Do you think I am unfit to lead them?'

'No, lord bishop,' said Conrad, 'not at all, but the fight for Dorpat will be a hard one and in view of your eminence's great age I would…'

'If you mention my age again,' growled Bernhard, 'I will excommunicate you.'

'That's you told,' said Leatherface.

'I would not worry, Conrad,' said Hans, 'Master Thaddeus' siege engines will probably batter Dorpat into submission so we won't need to storm the place.'

Bernhard looked unhappy. 'I hope not. There is little point in gathering an army if it is not going to be used.'

'Very well,' said Conrad, 'we move out in two days.'

Just over fourteen hundred men left for Dorpat, four hundred of which were led by Bishop Bernhard and the grim-faced Ulric. Aside from a small number of mounted scouts and horses to carry the commanders they marched on foot, accompanied by ponies loaded with tents and others pulling carts containing spare weapons, ammunition and armour. For their part the commanders walked on foot leading their mounts most of the time, Conrad insisting that the bishop ride at all times. So he did, riding up and down the column shouting encouragement, threats and obscene jokes.

'I wonder why he became a priest,' said Conrad. 'He is the most unholy man I have ever encountered.'

'I heard he was appointed by the pope himself to preach the word of God in Livonia,' Anton told him. 'But eschewed the opportunity to become a bishop straight away, preferring instead to enter a monastery as a monk.'

'To start at the bottom,' said Hans.

Anton nodded. 'Can you imagine it? To be a humble monk at the age of sixty; incredible.'

'And now he is over eighty and I am responsible for him,' added Conrad glumly.

A warrior wearing a leather cuirass and carrying the bear symbol of Jerwen on his shield ran up to them.

'We have apprehended a boy, *Susi*, a Harrien, who was following us. He is demanding to see you, says you know him. Do you wish me to break one of his ankles so he cannot follow us?'

'No,' said Conrad, 'I will at least see him before you break one of his limbs. It would be impolite not to do so.'

'Especially as you know him,' grinned Hans.

Conrad handed his friend the reins of his horse and walked back with the warrior to where two of his comrades were holding the arms of a teenage boy.

'Well, Jaan,' Conrad said to him, 'you are lucky that I am in a good mood otherwise these men would have broken your leg. Let him go.'

He shook his arms free and pointed at one of the warriors.

'He has my sword.'

'He has my sword, *sir*,' Conrad rebuked him. 'What are you doing here?'

'I wish to avenge my father.'

The warrior thrust his father's sword into the boy's arms. Conrad nodded to their commander who walked back with his men to the Jerwen column.

'Follow me,' Conrad said to the boy as he turned and made his way back to Hans and Anton. The day was warm and he had pulled his mail coif off his head. Even so he was still sweating as he walked back up the column, warriors raising their spears in salute as he did so.

'This is not a game, Jaan,' he said, 'we go to war.'

'I want to fight,' came the voice behind him.

Conrad shook his head. 'We will see if you can.'

The army marched ten miles that day, where possible keeping to forest tracks in an effort to avoid the swarms of midges that inhabited the meadows, especially the ones that contained lakes or flanked rivers and streams.

That night, as hundreds of two-man tents were pitched beside a forest of spruce and the early night air was filled with the sounds of chopping as men collected wood for temporary stables and lean-tos, Conrad ordered Jaan to erect the tent of the three Sword Brothers and then make a fire.

'After that you can cook our meal and then we will see if you can use the sword you carry around with you.

'I got tired of mucking out stables and did not leave Varbola just to pitch tents and cook meals.'

Conrad pulled his axe from his belt, gripped the shaft near the blade and gave Jaan a hefty whack on his upper arm with the other end of the haft.

'Don't be impertinent,' Conrad told him. 'This is an army not a camping expedition. Everyone obeys orders here.'

Jaan rubbed his arm. 'You don't, *Susi.*'

Conrad laughed. 'You think I am taking this army to Dorpat because I feel like it? I obey orders like everyone else; like you will if you wish to stay with us.'

'Who gives you orders, *Susi?*'

'The Bishop of Riga.'

'And who gives him orders?'

'His Holiness the Pope. Now get that fire started. Brother Hans gets very angry if his meal is not prepared on time.'

He caught sight of Jaan staring admiringly at the red insignia on his surcoat.

'Perhaps you wish to become a brother knight of our order.'

Jaan's eyes lit up. 'Yes, *Susi.*'

'It will take you seven years. Seven years of hard work, dedication and obeying orders. There is no mystery to becoming a knight, Jaan, it just takes time and a desire to earn the insignia I wear. If you feel you are up to it then stay with us. If not, then return to Varbola in the morning. The decision is entirely yours. But while you are making your decision get that fire started and the meal cooked.'

The boy was very quiet that evening, and after he had cooked what Hans described as an excellent stew he fell asleep in the brother knights' tent as the three friends sat around the fire. The night was cool and cloudless, the sky filled with a myriad of twinkling stars.

'Do you realise it is fourteen years since we arrived in Livonia,' reflected Anton. He saw Hans eating an apple. 'And after all that time Hans still looks half starved.'

Hans threw the apple core at him.

Conrad peered into the flickering flames. 'Sometimes it seems like yesterday and at other times my life before Livonia is like a dream.'

'A good or bad one?' asked Hans.

'Good,' answered his friend, 'though not at the end.'

They heard the rustle of boots on the ground and saw three figures approaching: Bishop Bernhard, Ulric and Leatherface. The Sword Brothers stood as the trio stopped in front of the fire.

'Just doing the rounds,' grinned the mercenary.

'Your men are well trained, lord marshal,' said Ulric. 'Ponies stabled, carts placed in a wagon park, tents pitched and guards posted in no time at all.'

'They have had lots of practice,' Conrad informed him.

'My bastards are catching up, though,' grinned the bishop. 'This campaign should see them become more like fighting men than civilians dressed up as soldiers.'

'It is very late, lord bishop,' said Conrad, 'you should get your rest before tomorrow's march.'

Bernhard pointed a bony finger at him. 'One more word from you about my supposed infirmity, lord marshal, and I will write personally to the pope requesting that you are placed in charge of the Curia's latrines.'

'The bishop fancies a spot of scouting tomorrow,' said Leatherface. 'Ain't that right, your holiness?'

'Just to blow the cobwebs from my mind,' stated the bishop.

Conrad sighed. 'I would prefer you to stay with the army, lord bishop.'

'And I would prefer if you stopped trying to deprive an old man of a bit of fun.'

Knowing that he would not win the argument Conrad gave up.

'After Dorpat falls,' Bernhard said to him, 'you will take your army north?'

'I will,' replied Conrad. 'The only kingdom left to be freed will be Wierland, which is currently ravaged by the Danes and the Russians.'

'Those two powers might have something to say about your plans, Conrad,' said Bernhard.

The Sword Brother smiled grimly. 'It will be to their detriment if they do.'

But the immediate concern was Dorpat and over the following four days the army continued its march towards the town. The Jerwen enjoyed marching through their homeland and Andres directed the army on a route that took it close to many villages. Scouts, including the bishop, rode ahead to announce the forthcoming arrival of Andres and his men, so that when the army passed villagers stood by the side of tracks waving and cheering. Attractive young girls placed garlands of wild flowers around the necks of handsome warriors and ruddy faced children ran alongside the column cheering and screaming at the men carrying spears with whetted points and wearing burnished helmets.

There was no sign of Kristjan's soldiers as the Army of the Wolf moved towards the River Emajogi, the waterway that marked the border between Ungannia and Jerwen. The army reached the northern bank of the river on a humid day at the end of July, approximately five miles from Dorpat. Scouts were sent splashing across a ford of the slow-moving river to ascertain the whereabouts of Bishop Albert's army. A camp was established and parties on foot sent east along the river to gather information from the villages along the Emajogi concerning the availability of boats and barges that could transport men across the river. The mounted scouts returned with the news that a great army composed of Livs, Sword Brothers and crusaders surrounded Dorpat. On hearing this news Conrad, Hans, Anton and Bishop Bernhard immediately rode south to report to Bishop Albert.

It was late afternoon by the time they reached the crusader camp, a vast sprawl of tents, temporary stables, campfires, wagons and carts that circled Dorpat. Actually that was incorrect. The town had originally been a small settlement built on Toome Hill next to a great bend of the Emajogi. The hill fort was a thousand feet from the river and as decades passed buildings were erected between the hill extending east to the river, eventually the whole was surrounded by a ditch, behind which was an earth rampart topped by a timber wall. Gates were sited in the southern and northern walls and the docks fronted the river at the eastern end of the town.

The horsemen were stopped by a mounted patrol of Sword Brother sergeants who escorted them to the bishop's pavilion directly west of the hill fort on Toome Hill. Already teams of engineers were directing parties of workmen to assemble the siege engines that would batter the walls, two large trebuchets being sited to hurl rocks at the hill fort itself. More parties were ferrying wood from the great pine and spruce forest surrounding Dorpat, resembling lines of ants as they brought firewood, building material for mantlets and a siege tower into the camp. The warm summer air mingled with wood smoke, the smell of horses and animal and human dung to produce an aroma that was unique to a besieging army.

The sergeants left Conrad and his companions outside the bishop's pavilion where servants dressed in the red and gold livery of Riga took their horses and a steward went inside the large canvas structure to announce their arrival. As they waited for the man to return Conrad noticed that the merlon that was attached to the top of the sidewalls was decorated with dozens of cross keys insignia. The steward returned and invited the Sword Brothers and Bishop Bernhard inside where Bishop Albert and his brother waited in the reception area.

There was a warm reunion between Albert, Hermann and Bernhard, the first two dressed in mail armour and red surcoats emblazoned with gold cross keys and edged with gold. For his part Bernhard was dressed in a simple grey tunic, leather cuirass and brown leggings.

'It is good to see you, my friend,' said Albert, smiling when he saw the sword strapped to Bernhard's waist. 'I trust you have enjoyed the hospitality of the Marshal of Estonia?'

Bernhard jerked a thumb at Conrad. 'He's a great commander but fusses over me like a mother hen. Thinks I'm going to keel over at any time.'

'Quite right, too,' said Albert as Conrad, Hans and Anton bowed their heads to him.

'Your army is near, lord marshal?' asked Albert.

'Five miles to the north, lord bishop. Fourteen hundred men ready to assist your crusade against Dorpat.'

The bishop smiled. 'Excellent. Tonight I want you to attend a banquet so that all the army's commanders can be gathered together.'

Bernhard stayed with his two fellow prelates while Conrad and his friends rode to the Sword Brother camp north of Dorpat. The quarters of Grand Master Volquin and the chapel tent were in the centre, circled by the tents of the masters, brother knights, sergeants and mercenaries. After leaving their horses at the stables they immediately sought out Master Rudolf, who conveniently was in the grand master's tent partaking of some fine German wine.

'Well,' said Rudolf, 'the wanderers return.'

They saluted Volquin who ordered them to pour themselves some wine. It was among the best that Conrad had tasted.

'A gift from Duke Fredhelm,' said Volquin to Conrad. The latter stared blankly back at him.

'The commander of those who have taken the cross in Livonia, Conrad,' continued the grand master. 'He is a friend of Rudolf's father and Bishop Albert has made him general of all those who came from Germany.'

'Two thousand, seven hundred soldiers,' said Rudolf, 'including three hundred Flemish crossbowmen, which must have cost someone a lot of money if the gold required to keep our mercenaries happy is anything to go by. How is the commander of my crossbowmen, by the way, still alive?'

'And prospering, master,' Conrad told him. 'He and Bishop Bernhard have become firm friends.'

'A bishop and a godless dog of war,' remarked Rudolf, 'who would have thought it.'

'Refill your cups,' Volquin told Hans and Anton, 'you have all done well these past twelve months, ridding Estonia of that bastard Kristjan.'

'Estonia is not yet free of him, grand master,' cautioned Conrad, 'he is in Dorpat.'

'And will be squealing on the end of a lance within the week,' promised Volquin. 'What have you heard of the Russians, Conrad?'

'The Russians, grand master?'

'Only Novgorod can save Dorpat now,' said Volquin.

Conrad looked at his friends. 'We have heard no reports of Russian soldiers near Dorpat, grand master.'

Volquin smiled. 'Then Kristjan is finished. Bishop Hermann intends to live there after Dorpat has fallen. His brother has made him Bishop of Dorpat, subject to confirmation by His Holiness the Pope, which means there will be a Sword Brother garrison in that hill fort, which means I will need a new master to command it.'

He looked at Conrad. 'Would you be interested in such a position, Conrad?'

Conrad was momentarily speechless. 'You flatter me, grand master.'

He thought of commanding a garrison of the order but then remembered he had matters to attend to in Estonia.

'But I must humbly decline.'

'You aim higher, Conrad?' probed Rudolf.

'No, master, but there is unfinished business in Estonia.'

'What unfinished business?' asked Volquin.

'Wierland still remains under Danish tyranny, grand master,' replied Conrad. 'Bishop Albert made me Marshal of Estonia and I will not abandon my duties. No offence, grand master.'

'Well,' said Volquin, draining his cup, 'it looks as though I will have to find myself another candidate for master of Dorpat.'

He looked at Hans. 'What about you, Brother Hans?'

Hans, appalled at the idea of leaving his friends, came up with the perfect excuse. 'I cannot read or write, grand master.'

Volquin walked over to the table on which the jug sat. 'And you, Brother Anton?'

'Neither can I, grand master.'

Volquin refilled his cup. 'I did not know, Rudolf, that Wenden is full of illiterates.'

He raised his cup to Conrad. 'To you, Conrad, Marshal of Estonia and lion of the north. You have been invited to the banquet tonight?'

Conrad nodded, as did Hans and Anton.

'Well don't drink too much and kill Nordheim with your sword. I received a grave admonishment from Bishop Albert concerning your altercation with the garrison of Riga and the subsequent bloodbath at Wenden.'

Conrad made to protest but Volquin held up a hand to him.

'Just be thankful that you do not have to live in Riga and put up with the pomposity of Archdeacon Stefan and his nefarious schemes.'

The banquet was excellent and, notwithstanding the presence of Nordheim who sat next to Bishop Albert and ignored all the Sword Brothers present, the fine wine and generous amounts of food made for a most pleasant evening. Conrad and his friends had laughed with Sir Richard, Fricis and Rameke and expressed disappointment that the latter had not brought Kaja.

'She wanted to come,' he told them, 'but I could not bear the thought of her being placed in danger. So I left a very unhappy wife at Treiden.'

Conrad smiled to himself as he remembered a time when Kaja had saved his life by spearing an enemy soldier in battle. She must have been fuming at having been left with the other women.

Conrad and his friends slept among the Sword Brothers, attending Prime Mass before eating breakfast with the other brother knights. It had been good to see Lukas and Walter again, not so good clapping eyes on Henke, who was as provocative as ever. He was nearly forty now and if anything more brutish and opinionated than ever. He planted himself opposite Conrad and his friends.

'So,' he said to Conrad, 'I hear your army of heathens has taken most of Harrien and Jerwen.'

'That is correct, brother.'

'You'll be fancying a crack at Reval, no doubt,' Henke grinned.

'Reval is Danish,' replied Conrad guardedly.

But Henke would not let it go. 'I heard you turned down becoming Master of Dorpat after it has fallen. So that leaves me to believe that you have bigger fish to catch.'

'I am a simple brother knight of our order, Henke,' replied Conrad. 'One who obeys orders.'

'Simple, yes, but I know you have the favour of Bishop Albert and that old fool Bernhard. In any case you three will have to shift for yourselves soon. There are a dozen novices at Wenden who are soon to become brother knights and they will be filling your places.'

'That's ridiculous,' said Anton.

Henke grinned maliciously. 'Is it? You've all been away for so long that everyone thinks you are dead.'

He rose from his bench. 'Perhaps you soon will be when we attack the fort. I thought the Ungannians were your allies,' he said to Conrad.

'It is difficult to believe,' replied Conrad.

Henke looked confused. 'What is?'

'That you think,' sniffed Conrad.

Henke curled his lip at him and walked away.

'Oaf,' said Conrad.

'What if he's right?' asked a concerned Hans. 'About us losing our place at Wenden.'

'Perhaps you should have accepted the bishop's offer of Dorpat, Conrad,' mused Anton.

'Henke is just trying to cause trouble,' insisted Conrad. 'Just concentrate on the coming battle and worry about trivia afterwards.'

The next day a council of war was held in Bishop Albert's pavilion. The area where they held it still stank of sweat, wine and roasted meat as servants hurriedly arranged trestle tables side by side, over which they spread white linen cloths. On the way to the council of war Conrad ran into Master Thaddeus, as usual appearing deathly pale but at the same time resplendent in his red surcoat.

'Ah, Conrad, you have returned from your northern adventures. We have all been enthralled at Wenden by your progress against the enemy. You remind me of Saladin, though of course he was a Saracen.'

'Who?'

Thaddeus rolled his eyes. 'A great Saracen warlord who captured Jerusalem and whom I encountered at Acre, though not on the battlefield I am glad to say.'

'Your siege engines are nearly ready?' enquired Conrad.

'They *are* ready,' declared Thaddeus, 'though Lord knows my patience has been sorely tested getting them here and assembled in time. It is my destiny to be constantly surrounded by fools. And I have been put in charge of all the non-combatants, which is enough to test the tolerance of a saint.'

He went on to explain that Bishop Albert had marched to Dorpat with a total of nearly five thousand fighting men. But there was an additional eight hundred non-combatants that were essential to the functioning of an army. They included engineers, pioneers, miners, smiths, carpenters, novices, armourers, wagon drivers, veterinaries, surgeons, priests, monks, hawkers, cooks, pages, servants and whores.

'Whores?' queried Conrad.

'They are good for maintaining the morale of the baser sort of soldiery,' he answered.

Conrad noticed that he had a leather tube tucked under his arm, the contents of which were revealed when they reached the bishop's pavilion. Servants at the entrance offered the pair wine in silver chalices, Conrad bowing his head to the three bishops and Grand Master Volquin as he walked to the table. Thaddeus ignored everyone, tapped the end of the leather tube and unrolled the piece of parchment that fell out. He huffed and puffed as he attempted to flatten it out. There was a map of Dorpat sketched on it.

'I need paperweights,' said Thaddeus as he failed to prevent the ends of the parchment rolling up. He pointed to the pectoral crosses around the necks of bishops Albert and Hermann.

'They will do; if I may borrow them.'

Duke Fredhelm handed over his dagger and Sir Richard did the same, so all four corners of the vellum were pinned to the table top.

'Excellent,' said Bishop Albert. 'My lords, if you will step up to the table.'

Conrad stood beside Rameke and stared at the map.

'Later today,' said Albert, 'Master Thaddeus' engines will commence their work, the trebuchets shooting at the hill fort on Toome Hill. The mangonels and crossbowmen will shoot at members of the garrison on the walls around the town. Tomorrow the general assault will begin.'

Volquin was surprised. 'Should not the siege engines be allowed to work longer, lord bishop?'

Albert shook his head. 'I wish Dorpat to be stormed quickly as a demonstration of God's power against the pagans. I do not want to be here for weeks, especially if the Russians are tempted to assist the Ungannians.'

He pointed to the south of the town and smiled at the Liv leader. 'King Fricis' brave Livs will assault the southern wall and our valiant crusaders,' he smiled at Duke Fredhelm, 'will attack in the west and north. In the north the attack will also be supported by the Sword Brothers.'

Volquin pointed at the river that bordered the east of the town. 'And in the east?'

Bishop Albert smiled at Conrad. 'The Army of the Wolf, already camped to the north of the river, will cross the waterway and assault the town from the east.'

He looked at Sir Richard. 'I would esteem it a great favour, my lord, if your men could support this assault.'

Sir Richard gave Conrad a grin. 'It would be an honour.'

'What about the fort, lord bishop?' asked Rudolf, 'it is a very strong position.'

'And because it is so strong,' answered Albert, 'we will focus on the town first. Once it has fallen we can concentrate our resources against the fort.'

'It is most important that the town falls into our hands relatively unscathed,' Hermann told them. 'Please impress upon your men that they are not to embark on wanton destruction.'

'That might be difficult,' said Bernhard, 'once soldiers storm a town they tend to give full vent to their fury, especially if there are women to be had.'

'Then inform them that rape is preferable to arson,' said Hermann. 'I want Dorpat to be a stronghold of the Sword Brothers and the Holy Church, not charred ruins that we have to rebuild from scratch.'

'Are there any questions?' asked Bishop Albert.

'I request a delay to the assault, lord bishop,' said Conrad.

Albert frowned. 'Why?'

'I have fourteen hundred men to get across the river,' said Conrad. 'The Ungannians have impounded all the boats and barges on the Emajogi at Dorpat. They are not stupid. So my men will have to build rafts to cross the river, which will take at least two days.'

'And Sir Richard's men will also have to be taken into account,' added Thaddeus.

Volquin looked at Albert studying the map. 'An assault against all four sides of the town stands more of a chance of overpowering the garrison, lord bishop.'

'He's right Albert,' said Bernhard.

'Very well,' Albert agreed. 'Conrad, you will inform us when you have constructed your rafts.'

'Yes, lord bishop,' said Conrad.

After the meeting Conrad spoke to Rameke.

'Kaja complains that we hardly see you these days, Conrad.'

'Affairs keep me in the north, my brother.'

Rameke looked towards the town and hill fort. 'Many of the people inside the town will be dead in a few days. I thought the Ungannians were your friends.'

'So did I,' said Conrad.

He returned to the Army of the Wolf in the company of the Duke of Saccalia and his men and issued orders to create a hundred and fifty rafts to transport them and Sir Richard's men across the river – a distance of around three hundred feet. After a brief meeting with his commanders it was decided that it would be better if the rafts were constructed near the camp and then once in the water towed south to face Dorpat by ponies rather than build them in full sight of the garrison. So the warriors put down their shields and spears and picked up axes, saws, chisels and ropes, parties being detailed to fell trees, others being responsible for hauling the logs to the riverbank where men waited to lash them together. Scouts were still posted to warn of any enemy approach but everyone else became woodsmen.

Conrad and his two friends, stripped to the waist, chopped down trees and then trimmed them of their branches. A sweating Jaan assisted, taking delight in shouting 'have a care' as a tree that had been notched and sawn on the opposite side crashed to the ground. Afterwards he and the Sword Brothers descended on the tree to hack at it with axes to cut it into manageable pieces.

Jaan pointed at a maple tree. 'We should avoid that one, and any oaks too. They are harder to cut and move and don't float as well as pine, fir and spruce.'

Anton walked past a dead tree towards a living spruce but Jaan pointed at it.

'Standing dead trees should be used because they do not contain water and so are lighter.'

'You seem to know a lot about making rafts,' said Conrad.

'My father taught me, *Susi*,' the boy replied sadly.

'He was obviously a talented man,' said Conrad.

'After we have finished the rafts we will cross the river and capture the town?' said Jaan, his eyes afire with the thought of slaying enemies with his father's sword.

'*We* will,' Conrad told him. 'You will be staying on the northern riverbank to guard the carts and ponies.'

Jaan snatched at an axe and began furiously chopping at the branches on the felled tree, mumbling under his breath.

The logs were towed to the Emajogi where the rafts were constructed. The current was at its slowest and the river at its lowest level at the height of summer. The logs were lined up side by side and lashed to connector logs placed on top at right angles to those underneath. Oars were also constructed to steer the rafts across the river when the time came. That time was two days later when they had been completed and towed to their positions facing the town. When his preparations were complete Conrad sent a swimmer downstream to cross the river and deliver a message to Bishop Albert that the Army of the Wolf and Sir Richard's soldiers were ready to attack.

*****

The day of the assault dawned dry and warm. As the sun crept over the forest canopy in the east and turned the clouds in the sky from black to orange, Kristjan stared out at the crusader army that surrounded his town. For two days the accursed instruments of Bishop Albert had pelted the town's defences with stones that had shattered the ancient timbers and shingle roofs of the towers. Some of his warriors had been decapitated by the missiles, after which Indrek had ordered that only a few lookouts should remain on the walls. It had been the same on Toome Hill, the large stones shot by the trebuchets arching into the air before smashing into the fort, shattering wooden walls, piercing thatched roofs and spreading alarm. And then Kristjan heard that a new army was gathering across the river, an army of fellow Estonians carrying the banners of Saccalia, Jerwen, Rotalia and Harrien. And had he had looked long enough he would have seen another banner among them, a white boar's head with golden tusks on a blue background. It was the standard of Sir Richard Bruffingham, Duke of Saccalia and friend of Conrad Wolff.

Indrek looked a shadow of a man, crushed by the thought that Dorpat would soon be a blazing inferno, its people either dead or enslaved, its warriors slaughtered trying to

589

defend their loved ones. But he remained to do his duty, to his people and his lord, the unhinged Kristjan.

'At least the infernal machines have stopped their damnable work,' observed Vetseke standing beside the pair, immaculate as ever in his mail cuirass, burnished helmet and green cloak.

'That is because they are going to attack,' said Indrek. 'Not even the Christians are stupid enough to hit their own men.'

'They are just stupid,' sneered Kristjan. 'Today Taara will grant me a great victory over the Sword Brothers. They will be destroyed as an offering to the God of War. Get the men to their positions, Indrek.'

He turned away from the army that was gathering around his capital and descended the log steps that led down to the fort's compound.

'Where are you going, lord?' enquired Indrek.

'The army that gathers across the river is the Army of the Wolf,' replied Kristjan, 'which is commanded by the man who betrayed my parents. After I have killed him I will return to direct the battle.'

He jumped into the saddle of his horse held by a guard and galloped through the open gates of the fort. Warriors came from the huts beneath the walls to scramble up the steps as their lord attended to a personal matter. And beyond the ramparts hundreds of men fell to their knees to receive the blessing of white-robed Cistercian priests.

Indrek looked at Vetseke but said nothing. What was there to say? They both knew that Dorpat was doomed, and so were they. But Indrek stayed because he had a duty to his mad chief and Vetseke because he was tired. Tired of running and tired of fighting an unending supply of crusaders and Sword Brothers. Once he had ruled the Kingdom of Kokenhusen but now his home was a Sword Brother garrison and his kingdom polluted with the Christian faith. He had given his trusty Livs, men who had been with him for years, the opportunity to save themselves but not one had left his side. They were too brave, too loyal and also too tired. And so they stayed, prayed to the old gods that they would have worthy deaths and waited for the crusader attack.

'These Christians like to dress gaudily,' said Vetseke as he rested his hands on the splintered timbers and stared at the bishop's army. Around him warriors stood in preparation to repulse the attack against the fort.

Vetseke turned to stare to the south where the dull browns, green and greys of Fricis' Livs were mustering in their ranks. He then looked to the north where the distinctive white surcoats and shields of the Sword Brothers were massed, and beside them more crusaders from Germany. An absolute silence had descended on the area as the Christian priests went among their flock to fortify their courage and ensure them that should they fall then a place in heaven awaited. The trebuchets and mangonel crews stood redundant, their machines having done their work.

Had Vetseke had knowledge of such things he would have been able to identify the various contingents within the bishop's army by the standards that fluttered in the breeze that had begun to blow. The largest formation was from Rostock, the knights wearing surcoats emblazoned with a yellow phoenix on a blue background, the coat of arms of the city. There were also the soldiers gifted by the Bishop of Bremen, their banners showing a silver key at a forty-five degree angle on a red background. Standards from Hamburg showed a white castle on a red background and those of Prüm displaying a white horse on a red background standing on a field of green, beneath which was a red cross against a white and blue background. There were militiamen from Lübeck, their shields painted red and white – the colours of the city. The crossbowmen of Flanders wore gambesons dyed yellow, their banners showing a black lion rampant on a yellow background. And around the Bishop of Riga and his brother Hermann were his bodyguard commanded by Manfred Nordheim, every man wearing a red surcoat sporting two crossed gold keys, the red caparisons of their horses also sporting the same insignia.

Vetseke offered his hand to Indrek. He and his Russians and Livs had elected to battle Fricis' warriors who were massed beyond the southern ramparts. They clasped forearms.

'May the gods be with you,' said the prince.

'And you,' replied Indrek whose former hostility towards the Liv had given way to a grudging respect.

Vetseke gave him a slight nod before walking to the steps and descending to the compound to collect his horse. There was a sudden cacophony of trumpet blasts beyond the walls followed by a great cheer and then the assault began.

*****

Conrad knelt and held his sword before him as Bishop Bernhard asked God to give the army victory over the heathens this day. The Sword Brother smiled, his army still contained many men who had not converted to the Catholic faith, preferring to worship the old gods rather than the new religion. Others, their friends and comrades, had converted and also knelt as monks who had followed the 'bishop's bastards' from Germany went among them to bless their weapons.

After Bernhard had finished Conrad and his friends rose as the old man turned and looked across the smooth waters of the Emajogi towards the docks of Dorpat. It was crowded with barges and riverboats: vessels that had been gathered in before the army had arrived. Hillar, Riki, Andres and Tonis came to Conrad and his friends by the riverside, which was crowded with freshly made rafts. The water level was low and the riverbank sandy and dry, the air already warm. Rivulets of sweat ran off Sir Richard's bald crown as he arrived in his armour, helm tucked under his arm.

'God's teeth it's hot,' he complained.

The wind carried the sound of a multitude of trumpet blasts and they all craned their heads towards the west.

Bernhard rubbed his hands with glee. 'It's started. God be with you all. I will see you on the other side.'

Sir Richard looked at Conrad in confusion but the Sword Brother merely shook his head. The bishop walked away to be with his men. The Duke of Saccalia watched him go.

'He is very old to be taking part in an assault, even if we are expecting minimal resistance.'

'Don't tell him that,' warned Hans, 'otherwise he will have you excommunicated, like he did with Conrad.'

Sir Richard was surprised to say the least. 'You have been excommunicated?'

'Nearly,' said Conrad. 'The bishop seems determined to be in the thick of battle one last time.'

He turned to his commanders. 'To your rafts, my friends.'

They nodded and departed, all around those who would cross the river taking their positions on the rafts. Short spruce oars had been furnished to propel the vessels across the water, distributed among men kneeling by the sides. Another man at the rear pushed off with a long pole.

As was customary before a battle Conrad and his two friends gathered in a circle and extended their arms to place their palms one on top of the other. It was Anton who spoke.

'We remember our friends, Bruno and Johann, and seek to fight as bravely as they did. Let us be as true and keen as our sword blades that we may scatter our enemies. As dust to the wind.'

They embraced and walked to the nearest raft, Leatherface shaking his head.

'Hurry up, you will miss all the fun.'

Each raft was loaded with ten men, six of whom were designated rowers. The plan was for the rafts to cross in two waves because otherwise the frontage would be too wide for all of them to land within the docks area. In the first wave each raft carried a crossbowman to provide missile support once the docks were reached and the men stormed ashore.

There was a slight breeze and current but neither were strong enough to alter the course of the seventy-five rafts that edged towards Dorpat, the grunts of the rowers as they dipped their oars in the blue water mingling with the muted sounds of battle coming from across the river.

Leatherface licked his lips. 'This should be easy enough.'

Conrad peered ahead and thought he saw movement. Not people but one of the boats moored to one of the jetties. Then he saw individuals on the jetties, dozens of them. And then he heard the shout.

'Enemy boats, enemy boats.'

Conrad did not know who called the warning but soon men were pointing towards the docks where three, four, a dozen and more riverboats were suddenly being rowed towards the rafts. Wide in the middle and with their single sails furled, they formed into a line and headed straight for the centre of the first-wave rafts. The latter were around mid-point in the river and had stopped dead, the second wave drifting into them as they did so.

'Keep rowing, keep rowing,' screamed Conrad left and right, gesticulating with his arms that the rafts should move.

Oars dipped in the water as arrows were shot from the riverboats, their pointed prows cutting through the water as men pulled on their oars. The dozen boats were closing fast on the rafts and arrows began arching into the sky as archers on board shot at the rafts. Leatherface placed his foot in the metal stirrup on the fore-end of his weapon and pushed it down to draw the bowstring, hooked on a metal claw attached to the front of his belt, along the crossbow's stock until it slipped over the catch of the lock. He pulled a bolt from his quiver as an arrow hit the arm of a rower beside him. The man cried out in pain and dropped his oar in the water, collapsing on the logs.

'Don't miss,' Conrad called to Leatherface, putting on his helmet and pulling the shield off his back. Hans and Anton did the same as those warriors on the raft that weren't rowing, all of them wolf shields, held up their shields as a defence against the arrows.

The mercenary placed the stock of his weapon to his shoulder as one riverboat closed in on the raft, standing at the prow a young, powerfully built warrior with shoulder-length fair hair and wearing a mail corselet. Through the vision slits of his helmet Conrad could see that he also wore a silver torc around his neck. He held a sword in his hand and on his left side a large round shield bearing a golden eagle insignia. He recognised the warrior – Kristjan. The rowers suddenly plunged their oars in the water and held them in place to slow the riverboat, which came to a juddering halt and then bumped into the raft. As it did so Kristjan leapt on the logs and came at Conrad as Leatherface released his trigger and killed a warrior immediately behind him.

Chaos enveloped the line of rafts as the Ungannians smashed into them and boarded the log vessels. Designed to carry ten men they were suddenly platforms for desperate mêlées. The result was a series of splashes as men were wounded and fell overboard or lost their footing and slipped off the rafts.

Kristjan attacked Conrad with a series of side strikes with his sword, the other warriors that had been on the riverboat crowding behind him. He blocked the blows with his shield, the blade cutting the leather covering and chipping the wood underneath. Conrad brought his sword up to shoulder height and thrust it at Kristjan's face; a tempting target as he wore no helmet. But the young Ungannian had very quick reflexes and ducked the point, ramming up his shield to force Conrad's sword up while he jabbed his own blade forward to skewer the Sword Brother. But Conrad could also move fast and he feinted right, Kristjan's sword slicing through his surcoat.

In the tight confines of the fighting area it was impossible to keep out of the way of weapons being wielded and an axe struck the side of Conrad's helmet, temporarily disorientating him. Kristjan laughed in triumph and whipped his blade forward to deliver a diagonal cut that sliced through the chainmail on Conrad's upper arm. He felt a sharp spasm of pain shoot through his arm and shoulder but instinctively leapt forward to smash his shield into Kristjan's chest. Another spasm of pain went through his left side but Kristjan staggered back, tripping over a dead man on the raft. Conrad aimed a vertical cut to his adversary's head, the blade missing the top of his skull but the point slicing deep into Kristjan's cheek as it came down.

The Ungannian cried out in pain and frustration as Conrad again smashed his shield into him, forcing him back towards the riverboat. His ears still ringing, Conrad again raised his sword to thrust it into Kristjan's face, which was now bleeding heavily. The Sword Brother sensed victory but the pair were suddenly forced apart when two grappling warriors barged into them, knocking Conrad backwards. He saw Kristjan scramble into the boat and then disappear as he collapsed on its deck. The two tussling warriors fell into the water, leaving the path clear for Conrad to board the boat. But he heard a muffled voice shouting 'Hans, Hans' and turned to see Anton face down on the raft trying to haul Hans out of the water.

He rammed his sword back in its scabbard and knelt down to grab Hans' other arm. In full mail armour and helmet his friend was in danger of drowning despite the efforts of Anton. Conrad's left side was on fire as he pulled with all his strength. Slowly, with supreme effort, he and Anton managed to haul Hans from the water and on to the raft. Conrad pulled off his helmet, gasping for air and rolled on to his back, exhausted. To see a leering, bearded monster with a two-handed axe standing over him. He was helpless, transfixed, as the wild-eyed warrior lifted his weapon above his head to cleave Conrad in two.

The brute grunted 'huh' as a crossbow bolt slammed into his right armpit, wavered on his feet, the axe still hoisted above his head, but did not fall. Conrad desperately tried to scramble to his feet but he lost his footing on the wet logs and fell to his knees. He heard a low groan and saw another crossbow bolt hit the warrior, this time in his chest. This time he dropped the axe, fell to his knees and then had his face reduced to a red pulp as Anton bludgeoned him with his mace. He kicked the now dead warrior away and grabbed Conrad's arm to haul him to his feet.

There were three wolf shields left alive on the raft, plus Leatherface and the three Sword Brothers. The rest either lay dead on the logs, were floating in the river or had disappeared under the water. The Ungannians who had boarded the raft had suffered the same fate, though the boat they had rowed from Dorpat was nowhere to be seen. And neither was Kristjan.

Conrad raised a hand to the mercenary. 'My thanks.'

Hans staggered to his feet and grinned at his friends. 'I thought I was fish meal.'

There was still some fighting going on where riverboats had collided with rafts but the majority of the latter were still rowing towards Dorpat. Indeed, it appeared that some had already reached the docks. Conrad picked up an oar.

'Come on, let's try to reach the other side.'

The others likewise grabbed oars and began paddling, though their progress was slow.

'That was Kristjan, wasn't it?' said Hans.

Conrad nodded.

'Well, at least he's dead and one less thing to worry about,' shouted Anton.

Conrad looked around at the bodies floating in the water and the riverboats, now empty or filled with dead men, drifting away on the current. He certainly hoped he was.

When they reached the docks they found Sir Richard and Bishop Hermann organising their men. The tar-making shops, workshops, barge and rope-making yards and blacksmiths' forges were all deserted. Hillar, Tonis, Riki and Andres had mustered the Army of the Wolf around two large warehouses that were both empty. Conrad's left arm was throbbing with pain as he sought out the bishop and Sir Richard. Tonis gave him a shield with a wolf's face as he had lost his own and also a new helmet with a nasal guard as his helm had been badly dented. Bernhard and Sir Richard were both unhurt.

'That was a surprise,' remarked the bishop regarding the assault of the riverboats, 'but futile and now there appears to be no enemy to stop us marching into the town.'

'We will leave some men here to guard our line of retreat should we need one,' said Conrad. He looked at Bernhard and was going to suggest that the bishop should remain with those men, but changed his mind as a frosty gaze dared him to speak so.

'Very well,' said Sir Richard, 'let us be away.'

Two hundred men were left to guard the docks, drawn from the four Estonian contingents in Conrad's army. The rest formed up in four compact formations led by Riki, Tonis, Hillar and Andres respectively, shuffling forward between seemingly empty huts and buildings, the 'bishop's bastards' on their left and Sir Richard's men on their right. Ahead the sound of battle became louder as they inched forward into the town of Dorpat.

*****

Indrek was dead. From the ramparts of Toome Hill he had seen the crusaders attacking the northern and southern walls, their soldiers scrambling up the high earth bank clutching scaling ladders that they placed against the timber walls. Rocks and javelins were hurled down on the climbers, and at the foot of the wall on the town side the two hundred Ungannian archers loosed volley after volley at the attackers. But the Sword Brother crossbowmen and those from Flanders picked off the warriors on the walls to allow the crusaders to get a foothold on the ramparts. Such were their numbers that soon the Sword Brothers and crusaders were in possession of the entire northern wall.

No attackers scaled Toome Hill and Indrek realised with horror that the crusaders had no intention of attacking the hill fort. So he gathered together the majority of the garrison and led them down the hill to strike the crusaders and Sword Brothers flooding over the northern wall. His attack was unexpected and well delivered and after only a few minutes his warriors had cut the Hamburg and Bremen militias to pieces. And for a moment it appeared that the enemy might be defeated, that Dorpat might be saved and the Bishop of Riga's army defeated. But more and more crusaders came over the walls – soldiers from Prüm and Lübeck – to reinforce the hard-pressed knights and squires of Duke Fredhelm and the brother knights and sergeants of the Sword Brothers. And from the walls the order's crossbowmen joined with their mercenary counterparts from Flanders to shoot a deadly rain of iron-tipped death upon the Estonians. The fighting around the walls was furious but gradually the crossbowmen whittled down the Ungannians with deadly efficiency, and in this combat Indrek was shot through the left eye and killed instantly. News of his death spread and Estonian morale began to crumble.

At the southern wall Vetseke's Russian archers reaped a rich harvest of Liv dead shooting from the walls. Fricis' men had few archers and no crossbowmen but they did have a siege tower covered in thick hides that they pushed towards the walls. A thousand Liv warriors assaulted the southern wall and two hundred of them were killed or wounded by arrows before they reached the defences. But once they did they flooded over the wall. The siege tower was pushed forward until it was flush to the wall, the earth rampart having been dug away by miners during the preceding days. The siege tower's drawbridge was lowered and Rameke led the assault against the defences. After a brief but fierce mêlée on the walls Ungannian resistance crumbled and Rameke led the advance into the town.

'Indrek has fallen, lord.'

Vetseke stared past the Liv warrior who had delivered the message to see the distinctive white surcoats of the Sword Brothers moving up Toome Hill towards the fort. He turned to look at the miserable remains of his command: a score of Livs, perhaps thirty Russian soldiers armed with shields and swords and fifty or so Pskovian archers, the survivors of the three hundred that had started the battle.

'We head for the river,' he told them, 'that is our only escape route out of this town. Move.'

The archers covered the retreat to the river, shooting at any of Fricis' men who appeared behind them. Inside huts women and children trembled and cried as the sounds of battle reached their homes. Soon crusaders and Livs were pulling women from the huts and ripping their clothes off prior to raping them. Any who interfered were butchered. This suited Vetseke and his men who were able to slip away to the river unnoticed. To run straight into the Army of the Wolf and its allies.

*****

Conrad was alerted to the fact that resistance had been encountered by the terrible screams, bellowing and snorts of cattle held in pens by the side of the market square. He also heard the cries of men and knew that a battle was developing on the left.

'To the bishop's men,' he called, breaking into a quick run, the Estonians behind him doing the same.

He saw the animal pens, cattle inside them and the 'bishop's bastards' advancing to attack a small group of archers and foot soldiers who were running into the market square. The archers were shooting at the bishop's men with alacrity, their missiles well aimed and finding their targets.

The archers, seeing a mass of warriors bearing down on them, directed their aim away from the bishop's men and managed to unleash a volley. But then the Estonians engulfed them. Conrad, his left shoulder afire from pain, was in the forefront of the attack, sword in his right hand and axe in his left, though it would be difficult to wield the latter if pressed. His men screamed their feral war cries and raced at the archers and few soldiers defending them. There was a brief clatter of weapons and Conrad saw a man wearing a green cloak surrounded and fighting for his life, a red scabbard at his hip. He remembered a cheerful little girl called Hele sitting on his horse and seeing her dead body after a battle at a river and the pain in his shoulder disappeared.

He ran at Vetseke and raised his axe to strike at the Liv's neck. The latter instinctively raised his shield to deflect the blow as Conrad spun the axe in his hand to bring down the spike on the opposite side of the axe head on Vetseke's shield. The metal embedded itself in the wood. Conrad yanked down his axe to wrench the shield away from its owner, who stumbled forward at the exact moment when the Sword Brother screamed in rage and plunged his sword into the mouth of Prince Vetseke. The point went through his mouth and exited the rear of his neck. Conrad collapsed on the ground as the dead Liv fell backwards and all around Vetseke's men disappeared under a blur of axe and sword strikes.

'That's for you, Hele,' whispered Conrad.

Conrad was sitting on a rung of an animal pen, the surviving cows still bellowing and snorting in alarm behind him, having his shoulder bandaged when a distraught Ulric found him.

'*Susi*, that is lord marshal, you must come quickly.'

Hans and Anton, the former still dripping wet, the latter not a scratch on him, helped their friend to his feet. They walked to where the 'bishop's bastards' were standing in groups, concern etched on their faces.

'Get these men into a defensive posture,' shouted Ulric at his commanders, angrily pushing his way through those standing around.

His commanders began issuing gruff orders to establish some sort of order. Conrad stepped over dead bodies, their faces and bodies pierced by arrows, until he came to a group of monks kneeling beside a body. He saw a priest clutching at the wooden crucifix around his neck, his eyes closed as he chanted prayers. He was rocking to and fro as he said the words.

'Shut that blasted noise,' he heard a weak voice order. 'You've already given me the last rites so let a man die in peace.'

The pale-faced priest stopped rocking, opened his eyes and fell silent, his mouth opening and closing in helplessness. Conrad saw Bishop Bernhard on the ground, his head supported by one of the monks, an arrow lodged in his right shoulder, another in his left leg. By the large red patches surrounding the shafts it appeared the heads had penetrated deep into the bishop's flesh. Conrad knelt beside the wan prelate. He took the old man's hand. It was cold and bony.

'Well, Conrad,' his voice was getting fainter by the minute, 'the battle is won?'

'The battle is won, lord bishop.'

Bernhard gave him a thin smile. 'I have a request of you.'

'Name it,' replied Conrad.

'Look after my men after I have gone. They are mostly rascals and the like but they have stuck by me and I would not have them treated basely. With the right leadership they could become much better than they are. I would like them to be a part of your army.'

'It shall be so, lord bishop,' promised Conrad, 'I will inform Bishop Albert of their bravery and steadfastness and they…'

'He's gone, lord,' said the monk cradling the bishop's head.

Conrad closed his eyes as Hans and Anton knelt beside the body and the priest began reciting a prayer for the deceased.

Thus died Bernhard, Lord of Lippe and Bishop of Semgallia. They wrapped his body in Anton's unblemished white cloak and his men carried him aloft outside the town to Bishop Albert's pavilion where he was received with great ceremony and much mourning.

Dorpat had fallen. The cost in lives had been high, both among the attackers and defenders, almost the whole of the garrison being wiped out in the battle. The fort atop Toome Hill, emptied of its garrison by Indrek so he could launch his counterattack, fell without a fight, the Sword Brothers taking possession of it and flying the flag of their order from its ramparts to show the whole world that once more the Holy Church had triumphed over paganism. As a reward for their heroism Bishop Albert decreed that the town should be sacked for two days, which meant that the Ungannian women and children were raped and abused for a further forty-eight hours.

Conrad was glad he did not have to witness the depravity and abuse of a people he had once counted as allies. Instead, and after he had requisitioned a number of cattle and a pair of oxen and had the animals placed under guard, he and a small party of horsemen were sent south to reconnoitre the fort of Odenpah, which was rumoured to be well defended. If it was, then Bishop Albert would once again need his army and Thaddeus' siege engines because the fort was a mighty stronghold.

He rode south in the company of Hans, Anton, Sir Richard and his knights – over a hundred men in mail armour riding horses protected by caparisons. The mood among the mounted party was sombre. Everyone had liked the plain-speaking Bernhard, especially Conrad. He would be sorely missed.

'He had a long and interesting life,' said Squire Paul behind his lord, 'not many men in this world can say that.'

'He should have been with bishops Albert and Hermann,' said Conrad, 'not taking part in the siege.'

'It was what he wanted,' Sir Richard stated, 'you gave an old man his last wish. He had a good death.'

Conrad thought of the bishop lying on the ground with two arrows stuck in him, his lifeblood leaking into the dirt. He thought it a sordid, unworthy death. But then, all death suffered on the battlefield is brutal and bloody.

When they arrived at Odenpah they found a most strange scene. There were no travellers on the road that led to the fort's outer gates, which were wide open. There were no herds of sheep grazing on the lush meadow grass either side of the road, no guards in the towers or at the gates. In fact no signs of life at all.

'Odd,' grunted Paul.

'It might be a trap,' warned Jaan behind Conrad. As he could ride Conrad had brought him along because he thought he should see the great stronghold of Odenpah, once home to Kalju and his wife Eha, former friends of Conrad.

'Strange sort of trap,' replied Paul. 'I admit there could be dozens of archers hiding behind the walls and in the towers but why would they leave the gates open?'

'Why indeed?' said Conrad who spurred his horse forward. 'Stay here,' he ordered Jaan as Hans and Anton also rode towards the gates, as did Sir Richard.

'If you all get killed,' Paul shouted after them, 'who will command all these fine knights?'

'You will,' Sir Richard called back. The knights laughed at this, earning them a rebuking stare from Sir Richard's squire.

Odenpah had two walls, one surrounding the lower level, the second encompassing the upper plateau of the hill on which it sat. Beyond the outer northern wall was Lake Alevijärv, its waters blue and smooth. Normally small fishing vessels would be on the lake but today there were no boats.

The party rode to the outer gates and halted a few paces from the wooden bridge that spanned the water-filled moat, which had been constructed on the orders of Master Thaddeus when the Sword Brothers had helped to defend the fort. In a different time.

Sir Richard peered up at the towers either side of the gates.

'It must be deserted,' he said.

'What do you want?

The voice above them gave them a start and all four drew their swords and placed their shields in front of them as a defence against arrows. Conrad winced as he did so; his shoulder still hurt.

'Why do soldiers come to Odenpah?' the faceless voice demanded.

'We are here on the orders of Bishop Albert,' Conrad shouted back, 'to demand the surrender of this fort to him and the Holy Church.'

They sat motionless on their horses awaiting a reply. None came but then an individual, a stout elderly man wearing brown leggings and a green tunic appeared between the open gates. He carried no weapons and wore nothing on his balding head, his thinning hair hanging around his shoulders. He began chuckling.

'The bishop might not wish to take possession of this place if he knew the truth.'

'And what is the truth?' asked Conrad.

'That this place is cursed,' answered the man. 'It is home to no one except a small band of loyal followers who stayed when everyone else fled. No one comes to Odenpah anymore. People avoid it and with good reason. It is a place of pestilence and death.'

'And yet we came,' said Conrad, spurring his horse forward across the bridge. The others followed. He halted his mount a few paces from the man.

'Dorpat has fallen and Kristjan is dead,' Conrad announced. 'The Bishop of Riga and his army are currently resting at Dorpat before marching to this place.'

The man peered at the insignia on Conrad's surcoat. 'So the Sword Brothers have killed Kristjan as well. Only one member of Lord Kalju's family still lives. Have you come to kill her too, Sword Brother?'

'I am here to kill no one,' replied Conrad.

The man looked at the sword in his hand. 'Your demeanour suggests otherwise.'

Conrad sheathed his sword. 'I would like to speak to her.'

The man looked surprised. 'The lady Maarja sees no visitors.'

'Then please convey a message to her. Tell her that I was a guest of her parents once and she may remember me. My name is Brother Conrad, Marshal of Estonia, who some call *Susi.*'

The man's eyes widened in recognition of the last name. 'I will tell her.'

He turned about and marched off.

'What's happening, Conrad?' called Sir Richard.

Conrad wheeled his horse around. 'I am waiting to see if the mistress of the fort will see me.'

Sir Richard and his friends frowned in confusion but he turned his horse back to face the entrance and waited. The quiet began to unnerve him as he stared at the empty compound beyond the gates. But after what seemed like an eternity the man returned.

'The lady will see you, Conrad Wolff, but you must leave your horse and weapons here.'

'And my friends?' asked Conrad.

'They too must remain here.'

Hans and Anton were unhappy but Conrad did not sense any threat and so readily agreed. His guide said nothing as they walked through the outer compound to the steps cut in the hill leading to the higher, inner stronghold. When they had reached the small gate to the inner compound Conrad asked if he and Maarja were the only inhabitants of the fort.

'There are a few others who elected to stay with our mistress, though she wanted us all to depart and leave her alone with her affliction.'

Conrad remembered the attractive young girls who were Kalju's daughters.

'Her affliction?'

But the man would say no more as they walked past the empty huts, stables, armoury and animal pens in the inner compound to the doors of the great hall. Inside the hall, once the home to Kalju and his family and bodyguard, the entrance hall was deserted and the feasting chamber dimly lit. Only a few torches flickered on the great oak pillars that supported the high roof and there was no fire in the great hearth at the far end of the hall near to where the dais was positioned. It took a few moments for Conrad's eyes to adjust to the gloom as he followed his guide to the dais where a figure clothed in black was sitting, a black veil covering her face. The old man bowed his head and stepped aside. Conrad also noticed two guards armed with spears flanking the dais, each of which eyed Conrad cautiously.

'It has been many years since you sat in this hall with my parents, Conrad Wolff.'

The voice was that of a teenage girl, slightly high pitched but soft and calming.

'Many things have happened since then, lady,' said Conrad. 'It is my regret that you and your family have suffered so during that time.'

Maarja leaned forward slightly, the veil hiding her face. 'I have been told that Dorpat has fallen and Kristjan is dead.'

'It is so, lady,' replied Conrad.

'Alas for my brother, he was always filled with rage and hatred. Even before the Sword Brothers killed my parents and sisters he held a grudge against you, Conrad Wolff.'

'Forgive me, lady, but I do not understand.'

'Do you not remember the time at the feast when your actions angered Kristjan?' asked Maarja.

'Not that, lady,' said Conrad. 'Forgive me, but I know that the Sword Brothers did not kill your family.'

Maarja sighed gently. 'When a gift arrived for my parents, a chest filled with expensive clothes for my mother and sisters and bearing the insignia of the Sword Brothers, they believed that it had been sent by you, Conrad Wolff. They remembered you with kindness, and even when their bodies were eaten away by a terrible affliction they did not believe that you were capable of such devilry.'

Conrad fell to his knees and clutched his hands together.

'I swear, lady that I have no knowledge of this chest that was sent to your parents. This I swear on the souls of my dead wife and son. May I be struck dead in front of you now if my words are false.'

Maarja used a hand to indicate that he should rise. He noticed that it was covered with scars. A chill went down his spine – they were the marks of the pox.

'I believe you, Conrad Wolff, because my mother believed you above all to be an honest person, devoid of malice and treachery.'

Overcome by pity, Conrad walked forward so he could take the unsightly hand and kiss it. But the guards levelled their spears to deter him. But as he withdrew he caught a brief glimpse of the girl's face behind the veil. He wanted to sob as he realised that it too was covered in the unsightly scars of the pox.

'You must go now, Conrad Wolff. I am tired. You may tell the Bishop of Riga that he may storm this fort and kill me. I will offer no resistance. Indeed I would welcome death to be free of the curse that afflicts me.'

'No harm will come to you or your servants, lady that I promise.'

With the fall of Dorpat the whole of Ungannia was now under the control of the Bishop of Riga. Hermann was made Bishop of Dorpat and plans were implemented to build a stone castle on Toome Hill. And, almost unnoticed, Andres and his

Jerwen warriors marched north where they were met by a foul-looking man in rags who escorted them to the ancient and sacred Kassinurme hill fort. Riki and his men returned to Varbola, taking with him the 'bishop's bastards', and Hillar marched back to Rotalia. Conrad stayed at Dorpat to enjoy the company of Rameke and Sir Richard and to make plans for the final stage of the conquest of Estonia.

But before he did he embarked on an errand to fulfil a vow he had made.

*****

'If you are Marshal of Estonia and we are your deputies,' said Hans, 'positions of some importance, I might add, why are we herding cattle like common drovers?'

Anton said nothing but Conrad could tell that he too was unhappy. He was sitting in his saddle with a long face, staring ahead and refusing to speak. In front of them were half a dozen cows; behind them the pair of oxen being led by an equally dejected Leatherface.

'May I remind you we all took a vow of obedience, poverty and chastity,' replied Conrad.

'I didn't,' muttered Leatherface.

Conrad ignored him. 'So high or low ranks are irrelevant when it comes to being a brother knight of the Sword Brothers. I made a vow to someone and now I am fulfilling it, which is more important to me than being the Marshal of Estonia.'

A cow broke wind loudly in front of them and another defecated, causing Hans to shake his head and sigh loudly. The cattle were moving slowly through a green and peaceful land, the blood, death and stench of Dorpat having been replaced by the pleasing aroma of pine and the sights of majestic eagles in the sky, hares in the long grass and roe deer at the forest edge. It was hard to believe that a few days earlier they had been fighting for their lives in battle. Now all they had to worry about were six cows and two oxen. The latter were being controlled by ropes fastened to their nose rings. The three mounted Sword Brothers were directing the cows from behind. During the day it was easy enough to move the beasts, the lessons they had learned earlier when they had been collecting Kaja's dowry being put into practice. At night the animals had to be corralled together and guarded from wolves and even the odd bear that came sniffing out the camp, Leatherface killing one on the first night with a bolt through its brain. But the expedition was largely uneventful aside from Hans' incessant complaining and Anton's sullen silences.

On the fourth day they neared an Ungannian village that looked very similar to the dozens of others within the kingdom.

'Do you recognise this place?' Conrad asked his companions.

'No,' muttered Hans.

Anton shrugged and Leatherface was too busy yanking the ropes pulling the oxen to notice.

'It is called Restu,' announced Conrad proudly.

Blank faces stared back at him. He frowned at them.

'Let me give you another clue. Do you remember two old men and two boys from that village who offered battle when we were stealing their cattle?'

'Ah, yes,' said Leatherface, 'when you rode forward on your own without waiting for me to accompany you. Very foolish. It only takes a lucky throw of a spear to bring down even a mighty Sword Brother.'

'Well this is the place,' replied Conrad. 'I told the old man that I would bring back his cattle and so I have.'

'These aren't his cattle,' said Anton, 'they are from Dorpat.'

'I'm sure the villagers or indeed the cattle won't mind,' his friend replied.

'We are about to find out,' said Leatherface, pointing ahead to where a group of people was walking from the village.

Dressed mostly in linen shirts, trousers and skirts, some wearing hats in the summer heat, a quick glance revealed there to be more women than men and of the latter most had white or thinning hair. Conrad wondered where all the men of fighting age were. He realised with a shock that they had probably all been killed following Kristjan. He hoped that some were still making their way home but doubted it.

'Say nothing about the fall of Dorpat,' he told the others before the villagers arrived. 'I don't want to plant the idea in their minds that their men aren't coming home.'

'Why not?' grunted Hans. 'It's true.'

The villagers were led by a man with a white beard and hair that fell to his shoulders – the same individual who had tried to prevent Conrad from stealing the settlement's cattle when he and the others had last visited Restu.

'Stay here,' said Conrad.

He dismounted and pulled down the mail coif that covered his head as the old man led the villagers towards him. This time he carried only a spear. A boy, whom Conrad assumed was his grandson, also carried a spear and a couple of the other elderly men held bows. Their leader held up an arm to halt the villagers as he continued to walk forward purposely. Conrad stepped towards him until they were only a few paces apart.

'Greetings, friend,' he said. 'I have come to return your cattle, as I promised I would.'

The old man rested the end of his spear on the ground and peered past Conrad to stare at the cattle that were munching on grass. He also saw the oxen.

'Did you steal the oxen from another village, Sword Brother?'

Conrad was slightly taken aback that the old man had not been more grateful.

'They are the property of my order and are for your village, too. A gift from the Sword Brothers.'

Now it was the elderly man's turn to be discomfited.

'Well, I thank you for that. They will be invaluable to assist in the ploughing this year. Many of our menfolk have

618

failed to return from the war, though their wives are hopeful that they may still see them before the leaves turn brown.'

Conrad knew otherwise. 'I hope so, sir.'

The man turned and raised his arms to get the attention of the villagers.

'Our cattle have been returned and the Sword Brothers have given us a pair of oxen as well.'

His words were met with joyous acclaim from the villagers who rushed forward to take possession of the beasts, the cattle scattering in alarm as they did so. Leatherface threw the ropes attached to the oxen to a gangly teenage boy.

'You're welcome to them,' said the mercenary.

Another youth ran up to his grandfather. Conrad smiled. The last time he had seen the boy moving fast he had been trying to run him through with a spear. This time he wore a beaming smile instead of a hateful scowl.

'Have you been practising your skills with a spear?'

'Yes, sir. My grandfather has been teaching me.'

Conrad looked at the sinewy old man with skin like leather. He had the appearance of a man who had seen his fair share of fighting in his long life.

'A good teacher, I'm sure. What is your name?

'Arri,' replied the boy.

'I have something for you.'

Hans and Anton sat in their saddles smiling as the young women and old men of the village gathered in the cattle and began patting the oxen. To them they were just two beasts of burden but to the villagers they were the means that would allow them to plough the fields to plant their crops. As such they were a gift more precious than gold. Conrad walked to one of the packhorses that carried tents and supplies and extracted something wrapped in a red cloth. He walked back to Arri and handed it to the boy. The youth's eyes lit up when he removed the cloth to reveal a sword in an iron scabbard bound with leather.

'It is called a *myech*,' Conrad said as the boy pulled the blade from its scabbard and marvelled at the straight, two-edged blade. 'It is Russian but now belongs to you.'

'What do you say, Arri?' said his grandfather sternly.

'Thank you, sir,' whispered a stunned Arri.

'I'm sure your grandfather will teach you how to keep it clean and use it well,' smiled Conrad.

'Help the others to get the cattle into the village, Arri,' commanded his grandfather.

Arri grinned broadly at Conrad, carefully replaced the sword in its scabbard and ran off to help gather in the cows, scabbard clutched to his chest.

'You are very clever, Sword Brother,' said the old man.

'How so?'

'You give a fine sword to a boy knowing that by doing so he will remember you with affection and perhaps yearn to be like you.'

Conrad feigned surprise. 'I found it lying on the ground and thought it could be put to good use, that is all.'

'Its owner was very remiss in mislaying it.'

Conrad's lips curled into a thin smile as he remembered the dead Russian bodies around the warrior with the green cloak he had killed at Dorpat.

'He has no use for it any more. If your grandson has a mind in the future to become a soldier rather than a farmer, send him to me. He will be warmly received. And now, sir, I must leave you.'

Conrad nodded at the man and turned to walk back to his horse.

'What hear you of the war?' the grandfather called after him.

'There is no war,' said Conrad, 'Ungannia is at peace.'

'What is your name Sword Brother? In case my grandson decides to take you up on your offer.'

'Conrad Wolff, Marshal of Estonia.'

The three Sword Brothers and Leatherface left the inhabitants of Restu happy and one boy deliriously so. Now free from their bovine guests they could make good progress back to Dorpat as the afternoon sun abated in its fury.

'That was a generous gift for a total stranger,' said Anton.

'It was not a gift, it was an investment,' Conrad told him.

Anton gave him a bemused look.

'Now that the war against Ungannia is over,' announced Conrad, 'we have to ensure that its people are loyal to the Sword Brothers. Today we have ensured that those who live in the village of Restu are our friends, not our enemies.'

'Loyal to the Sword Brothers or loyal to you, Marshal of Estonia?' queried Leatherface.

'They are one and the same,' Conrad told him.

Chapter 13

The crowd shouted 'Lamekins, Lamekins' as the prince escorted the body of Duke Butantas to the tent of Duke Arturus. Soldiers were deliriously happy; a mixture of disbelief and relief that they not only still lived but had won another victory. A victory snatched from the jaws of defeat in the valley of the Venta River. The river, some eighty miles south of the Dvina, flowed from the heartland of Samogitia and Arturus believed that a small, mobile army marching alongside the Venta could deliver a fatal blow to the Kingdom of Samogitia. So he had collected three thousand horsemen and the same number of foot and had led them into the heart of Duke Butantas' domain, only to run into an army three times the size of his own.

Abandoning his wagons and wounded, Arturus had retraced his steps through the Venta Valley, every day enemy horsemen harassed his retreating army. The Kurs had been disheartened to discover that they faced not only the Samogitians but also the Aukstaitjans, for unknown to Arturus Butantas had convinced Duke Kitenis to send him reinforcements. Butantas had reasoned, convincingly, that if Samogitia fell to the Kurs then Aukstaitija would suffer the same fate. No one trusted Vsevolod, 'the Russian', whose duplicity was well known. And so Kitenis had despatched horsemen and foot soldiers to Butantas. These and his son conducted a skilful campaign against the Kurs. Whilst their foot created a cordon around Arturus' army Ykintas had darted in with groups of horsemen to torment the Kurs, inflicting a steady stream of casualties. The morale of the Kurs plummeted and that of their enemies soared and after five days of incessant harassment Butantas believed that one final assault would finish the Kurs and rid the world of the heinous Duke Arturus. But he had reckoned without the genius of Prince Lamekins.

The Kur army had been boxed in on an expanse of flat plain against the river, the soldiers of Butantas surrounding them on three sides with the horsemen under Prince Ykintas mustered in the centre with their backs against a great forest of birch. The duke and his son had expected the Kurs to recommence their march west, towards Kurland, but instead Arturus' men attacked. The assault was furious and unexpected and was led by Lamekins at the head of the Kur horsemen. They charged through the bleary eyed Samogitian foot soldiers and smashed into Ykintas' horsemen. Ykintas himself fought bravely but was soon separated from his men who were pushed back towards the forest under relentless pressure. When they were forced back into the trees their discipline collapsed and they fled, whereupon Lamekins rallied his tired horsemen and led them back onto the plain to attack the enemy foot.

Butantas, leading the foot soldiers of Samogitia and Aukstaitija, was now being assaulted from two sides and his men began to give way. For four days they had been chasing the enemy west and had believed that the Kurs were on their last legs. But instead of a glorious victory on the morning of the fifth day they were being cut to pieces. Many ran, more were killed in the fighting but at the end of the morning there were no Samogitians or Aukstaitijans in sight, only a carpet of their dead. Among them was Duke Butantas.

'Behold Duke Butantas, lord,' smiled Lamekins, his chainmail ripped and his helmet dented, 'the late ruler of Samogitia.'

Arturus, himself bleeding and looking half dead, walked from the entrance of his tent and embraced his deputy, to more cheers.

He raised his arms. 'Kurland.'

His men chanted 'Kurland, Kurland,' as the duke ordered the body to be taken away and beckoned Lamekins inside. They both flopped down into chairs, exhausted.

'What are our losses?' asked Arturus.

'Around five hundred of our horsemen fell today, lord,' replied Lamekins, 'though more of the enemy did so.'

Arturus pointed at him. 'I will not forget this day, Lamekins. Only your brilliance stood between our victory and what should have been our deaths. I was stupid to believe that I could conquer Samogitia with so few men. I will not make the same mistake again.'

Lamekins smiled. 'As the gods are smiling on us we should take advantage of their generosity and pursue the enemy.'

Arturus rubbed his tired eyes. 'If the gods exist, which I doubt, I am sure they have better things to do than smile on us.

Besides, our men are on their last legs. We return to Kurland and prepare for next year's campaign.'

'What about Vsevolod, lord?'

Arturus leaned back in his chair. His whole body ached from having little sleep in over a week.

'Our scheming Russian friend has no allies, which means he has no one to do his fighting for him, which means that he will make no offensive moves against us.'

'Then we will complete the conquest of Samogitia next year, lord?'

Arturus rubbed his eyes and looked at his deputy. 'We are in the happy position of being able to choose what enemy shall fall to us first, Lamekins. Samogitia or Selonia.'

*****

Once again Selonia and Nalsen had been spared a Kur invasion. The harvest had been a good one, the people were well fed and healthy and the autumn signalled that the campaigning season was over for another year. Yet a sense of doom permeated every facet of life in those two kingdoms. Men's hearts had been cheered when they heard the news that Duke Arturus was leading an army into Samogitia for it meant that the Kurs would not be making war on them. But the mood of the people had darkened with the news that the elderly and frail *Kriviu Krivaitis*, the high priest of their religion, had finally died. His body had been cremated in the sacred grove near to Panemunis where the eternal flame burnt. The *kriviai*, the white-robed priests who expounded the will of the gods to the people, declared a month of mourning and gathered to choose a successor, the one who would have been chief priest having been killed by Arturus. But the absence of a *Kriviu Krivaitis* was seen as an ill omen and the people were cast into the pit of despair by the news of the defeat and death of Duke Butantas.

Mindaugas was all for mustering an army and marching to the aid of Prince Ykintas, who had taken refuge with his wife and an entourage in the east of Samogitia. Rasa, egged on by Morta, had also recommended such an action but Vsevolod had vetoed it. He had no desire to suffer the same fate as Butantas, though he did not tell his wife and son-in-law this, and in any case he doubted if any army he put in the field would fare any better against the Kurs than the soldiers of Butantas.

Vsevolod stopped and looked out from the battlements of Panemunis. Beyond the wooden palisade extended a land of unbroken greenery. It was a vision of lush forests, rolling plains, hillocks covered with white birch groves and glittering blue lakes. He rested his hands on the top of the wooden battlements.

'I want you to deliver a letter for me.'

Aras stopped and looked surprised. 'Letter, lord?'

Vsevolod looked left and right to ensure no guards were within earshot.

'The letter I am about to write to the Bishop of Riga. I want you to take it to Riga and deliver it personally.'

Aras, dressed in black boots, leggings and a thick leather tunic, stroked his neatly trimmed beard.

'May I enquire the nature of this correspondence, lord?'

Vsevolod again made sure that they were far enough away from the nearest tower so as not to be heard.

'Before I answer tell me this, Aras. Do you think that we can prevail if we march against Arturus, as Mindaugas desires?'

'No,' stated Aras flatly.

'And do you believe that Panemunis will be targeted next year when Arturus once again casts his gaze to the east.'

'Yes.'

'Then I am faced with a dilemma,' said Vsevolod. 'To do nothing will result in Arturus arriving at the gates of this fortress. To take action will result in the destruction of my army, after which Arturus will arrive at the gates of this fortress anyway. Feel free to interrupt me if you disagree with anything I say.'

Aras remained silent.

'Our allies,' continued Vsevolod, 'such as they are, lie dead, demoralised or reluctant to leave their kingdoms. We are alone, Aras, and to compound our misfortune that old idiot chief priest decided that he would die at a most inappropriate time.'

Aras looked at the prince. He was immaculately dressed in a white tunic in the Byzantine style with narrow wrist-length sleeves and a high-cut neckline, over which he wore a red dalmatica with wide, straight sleeves shorter than the tunic's and belted at the waist. His green leggings matched the colour of his boots and the white, fur-lined cloak he wore was clasped at the right shoulder by means of a silver griffin brooch. Many of his chiefs and elders derided Vsevolod for what they saw as his effeminate dress but the former ruler of Gerzika never abandoned his Russian roots.

'So you are asking the Bishop of Riga for aid, lord?'

Vsevolod smirked. 'Not aid, Aras. I will invite him to cross the Dvina to take possession of Semgallia, thus creating a bulwark between us and Duke Arturus.'

Aras' black eyes narrowed.

'You disagree?' asked Vsevolod. 'If you have a better proposition then by all means tell me.'

'The Christians crossed the Dvina before, lord. It did not end well for the Bishop of Riga. But if he accepts your offer then you invite an angry bear into Lithuania, one that will be reluctant to leave.'

Vsevolod brought his hands together.

'Let me put another image into your mind. If the Bishop of Riga and Kurs lock horns and bleed each other white, who benefits? We do. It gives us time, Aras. Time to rebuild our strength, to forge a new alliance while the Catholics and Kurs kill each other.'

Aras said nothing as he stared at the landscape of Selonia.

'I would have your opinion,' snapped Vsevolod. 'Speak freely.'

'I have heard that the Bishop of Riga has recently won a great victory in Estonia.'

Vsevolod nodded.

'Now that Riga is no longer blockaded,' continued Aras, 'it grows rich from trade with Novgorod and Polotsk. Both it and the Sword Brothers are stronger than they were when they first crossed the Dvina. My worry is that this time they will prove too strong to eject from Semgallia, lord.'

'That is a price I am prepared to pay,' said Vsevolod grimly, 'for the alternative is too dreadful to even consider.'

'And Viesthard?' asked Aras.

'Viesthard?' scoffed the Russian. 'He clings on to Tervete like a chick in the nest of a high tree buffeted by the wind. Why should I consider a man who cannot even hold on to his own kingdom, what's left of it?'

He turned to his trusted general.

'The mission calls for tact and diplomacy, Aras, that is why I am sending you personally. And speaking of tact, I see no reason to mention this scheme to Princess Rasa and definitely say nothing to Mindaugas.'

Aras smiled weakly. 'He would find little merit in what you are proposing, lord.'

'He would see none,' said Vsevolod firmly. 'But what my son-in-law must realise is that politics is above all a pragmatic business. It's all very well charging off to war with other impressionable young men, but when the dust has settled, calmer, more rational minds have to clear up the mess.'

'It might be an idea to send a token force to aid Prince Ykintas,' suggested Aras, 'at the very least to provide an escort for him and Princess Elze should they be forced to flee Samogitia.'

Vsevolod rapped his fingers on the wooden wall. 'Very well, I will despatch some horsemen to appease my wife and eldest daughter. But Mindaugas will remain here. If he goes to Samogitia he will only hatch a mad scheme with Ykintas to strike at Arturus that will result in nothing except their deaths.'

Aras wondered which scheme was the most insane: to fight Arturus or to invite the Bishop and the Sword Brothers into Lithuania?

*****

While the Bishop of Riga had assailed Dorpat and Ungannia in southern Estonia, further north Reval remained unmolested. Fleets of cogs transported supplies and soldiers to the port, sailing together to deter attacks by Oeselian longships. Occasionally a vessel fell out of line, was surrounded and boarded, its crew either killed or taken as slaves and its hold plundered. But in general the line of communications between Denmark and Reval remained relatively secure. But no goods transited through the port, the Novgorodians preferring to trade with Riga via the Dvina, especially after the loss of Russian lives during the siege of the port. So Reval became a military base, an isolated Danish outpost on the Gulf of the Finns.

The latest flotilla to land at the port had brought food, weapons and armour and a message for Count Rolf, the governor. After reading it he led a party of horsemen from the town ten miles south to a small hill fort, an outpost, one of several that the Danes had taken possession of. Set on top of a sandstone outcrop on the edge of a pine forest, it had once been the refuge of local villagers. But the villages were now empty and their inhabitants had either fled, been killed or taken as servants to work on Reval's defences. If the latter then most of them were also dead, a consequence of the ill-usage they had been subjected to. This part of Harrien was largely devoid of native inhabitants, a fact that Rolf was glad of as he and his men rode by impenetrable thickets and skirted festering bogs. It was one less thing to worry about.

The hill fort, in truth nothing more than four timber walls constructed on top of a bank of earth with one watchtower in a corner and a single gate for an entrance, was home to a small garrison of ten men – a sergeant and nine spearmen and a few ponies that were used for communications with Reval. The men lived in a single wooden hut inside the fort with another hut for their stores. From the top of the watchtower a sentry could see for miles around, and could warn of the approach of another army intent on besieging Reval. But no army had come; indeed, no activity of any kind had been detected in the green wilderness for some time.

Today, though, the fort was the scene of high activity. First the brave and arrogant Count Albert had arrived with his dozen knights, all mounted on destriers covered by red caparisons sporting white nettle leaf motifs. The count, bored by garrison duty, often rode out on these expeditions, like a knight of old in search of a dragon to slay. On every occasion he rode back to Reval disheartened that he had found no dragon or natives to battle. He also liked to think that these excursions to the small outposts that ringed Reval boosted the morale of their tiny garrisons, though truth be told the opposite was the case. The common soldiery found him boorish and loud. They were glad to see the back of him and his warhorses that invariably dumped large amounts of dung inside their forts.

The commanding sergeant groaned when the sentry shouted down from the watchtower that the governor himself was approaching at the head of a column of horsemen. More dung to shovel! The fort had a large enough compound to accommodate the two parties of horsemen, the beasts being tethered to wooden rails while the governor and Count Albert walked together back out of the fort. Overhead a pair of black storks cut through the air as Rolf handed the younger man the letter.

'It is from the Archbishop of Lund. He is raising an army to rescue the king, your uncle, and his son from their imprisonment.'

Albert took the letter and began reading it.

'The archbishop is requesting your return to Denmark, together with your men and the crossbowmen that the king despatched to Reval when he was still at liberty.'

Albert finished reading and nodded thoughtfully. 'The archbishop leaves the decision in your hands, Rolf.'

'I know that you are bored to distraction here, Albert, and yearn to return to Denmark. I will not stop you.'

He took the letter from Albert. 'In truth I would join you if my responsibilities here did not prevent me.'

'Every effort should be made to secure the freedom of the king,' said Albert.

Rolf nodded. 'I agree.'

Albert looked at the fort. 'What about Reval, though? Will you be able to hold it if the Russians come back?'

'As long as the port remains open I can hold Reval,' stated Rolf. 'In any case I doubt the Russians will return any time soon, not after the losses they suffered last time. But the king's liberty is more important than Reval and its garrison. I could always request reinforcements from the garrison of Narva if things become pressing. Notwithstanding that its commander has become a law unto himself of late.'

'Once we have defeated Count Henry and his rebels we will return to Reval and complete the conquest of this land,' asserted Albert.

Rolf pondered for a moment, remembering the reverses they had suffered at the hands of the Oeselians, the humiliation of being rescued by the Sword Brothers and the subsequent capture of King Valdemar.

'Let us hope so, Albert. You and your men will be able to leave on tomorrow's tide if you ride back with me.'

Rolf watched the cogs leave the Bay of Reval, on board all of Count Albert's soldiers plus the three hundred crossbowmen originally sent by Valdemar. They had proved invaluable during the siege but Rolf comforted himself that he still had five hundred soldiers to defend the port, the defences of which remained formidable. He was certain that any assault against the walls of Reval would result in bloody failure. In any case it was now autumn and no enemy would commence a siege with the prospect of seeing its army freeze to death in the snow and ice of an Estonian winter.

*****

Conrad clapped his hands together in a futile effort to restore the feeling to his fingers. Despite his mittens he had been crouching by the side of the fir tree for too long and now the cold was beginning to permeate his limbs. Like his friends he was well wrapped in woollen underwear, woollen leg wraps under his thick leggings and snug felt boots on his feet. His cape was also made of felt and was a lot thicker than the standard Sword Brother issue. Like Hans and Anton he still wore his aketon, gambeson and hauberk but had dispensed with mail chausses on his legs. It was difficult keeping chainmail free of rust when fighting in winter and so they did away with unnecessary items. He heard a chewing noise behind him and turned to see Hans eating a piece of cured meat.

'We should get back to camp, Conrad,' he said, 'we will freeze to death if we stay here any longer.'

635

'He's right,' added Anton, looking at the long shadows cast by the sun. 'It's starting to get dark.'

The summer at Dorpat seemed like another age. In the aftermath of the great victory Brother Walter of Wenden, whose piety, bravery and steadfastness was known throughout the Sword Brothers, was made Master Walter and given command of the order's new castle at Dorpat, which would be built on the site of the hill fort on Toome Hill. Rudolf made Brother Lukas Wenden's deputy commander. With Ungannia conquered Bishop Albert, greatly satisfied, returned with the army to Riga to celebrate God's victory in the cathedral. The Army of the Wolf was dispersed to its strongholds in Harrien, Jerwen and Rotalia, though Tonis had returned to Saccalia to undertake his new duties as Count of Fellin. Conrad was sad to see him leave but it made perfect sense. He was a Saccalian and a veteran of many battles and campaigns and greatly respected throughout his native land. So he travelled back with Sir Richard. To compensate for the loss of his Saccalians, Conrad's command of the 'bishop's bastards' was confirmed, which pleased him enormously. They returned to Varbola and their wives with Riki and his Harrien.

Conrad and his two friends had been ordered to remain at Dorpat by the Bishop of Riga, who had summoned him to his pavilion in the days after the battle. The prelate had declined an opportunity to be accommodated in the hill fort on account of the smell of death still permeating the town as hundreds of bodies were consigned to funeral pyres beyond the walls.

Christian dead were buried, pagans were cremated and the nauseous aroma of roasting human flesh hung in the summer air like an invisible low-lying cloud. The smell permeated clothing and stuck in the back of the throat and no matter how many battles he fought in Conrad was convinced that he would never get used to it.

At the pavilion he found Bishop Albert, his brother Bishop Hermann, Grand Master Volquin and Master Rudolf seated at a trestle table over which had been draped a white cloth. To one side was a smaller table also covered in white, on which stood a large silver cross. Two of Nordheim's guards showed him into the reception area where the bishops and two commanders of the Sword Brothers sat facing him. Albert and Hermann both wore white mitres, though their attire was martial: mail hauberks and red surcoats emblazoned with the gold cross keys motifs. Conrad bowed his head.

'Welcome Brother Conrad,' said Albert, 'Marshal of Estonia and now lord of nearly all that land. Your service to the Holy Church and the Order of the Knights of Christ has been exemplary these past two years.'

Volquin and Rudolf rapped their knuckles on the table to indicate their support for the bishop's words. Hermann smiled and Conrad blushed.

'I was merely performing my duty, lord bishop.'

'God uses people like you, Conrad,' said Albert. 'Many men do their duty to a greater or lesser degree, but what you have achieved in Estonia has been nothing short of remarkable.'

Once again the seated Sword Brothers rapped their knuckles on the table.

'After the Lord's great victory at Dorpat His word is now heard from the Dvina to the Gulf of the Finns. My brother will be made Bishop of Dorpat and the town will be strengthened as a bulwark against the heretic Orthodox Russians in the east.'

Conrad thought this eminently sensible.

'I also intend to make Odenpah a stronghold of the Sword Brothers,' continued Albert, 'so that the flame of rebellion will never again burn in Ungannia. I have conferred with Grand Master Volquin and Master Rudolf and they agree with my decision to make you the Master of Odenpah.'

Conrad was stunned. 'Me, lord bishop?'

'Grand master?' said Albert.

'You have led armies, defeated enemies and brokered agreements to the benefit of Livonia, Conrad,' stated Volquin. 'It is time your accomplishments were rewarded.'

'And Dorpat would feel more secure knowing that the Master of Odenpah was the Marshal of Estonia,' added Hermann.

'You are most generous, lord bishop,' began Conrad, 'but...'

Albert held up a hand to him. 'The matter is not open to debate, Conrad. Consider the offer of becoming master a direct

638

command from the Bishop of Riga on behalf of His Holiness the Pope.'

So that was it. He was to be made Master of Odenpah whether he liked it or not. He should have felt proud but in truth he felt hard done by.

'You do me great honour, lord bishop. Thank you.'

'Excellent,' beamed Albert, 'all's well that ends well.'

'I have a request, lord bishop,' said Conrad.

'Regarding?' queried Albert.

'The lady Maarja, lord bishop.'

Albert looked quizzically at his brother, who shrugged his shoulders. Volquin and Rudolf were equally mystified.

'The lady Maarja is the current resident of Odenpah, lord bishop,' explained Conrad, 'she is the sister of Kristjan, instigator of the late rebellion against Livonia.'

'She intends to resist us?' asked a concerned Rudolf.

Conrad looked forlorn. 'Alas, master, she lives at Odenpah with a few servants, a victim of the pox that has scarred her face and hands.'

The two bishops crossed themselves and held their pectoral crosses that dangled on silver chains around their necks.

'May Christ have mercy on her,' said Albert.

'You have been told this?' asked Volquin.

'I have been there to see her suffering myself, grand master.'

'That was brave,' said Hermann.

'Or foolhardy,' Rudolf rebuked him.

'There is no pestilence at Odenpah, master,' said Rudolf, 'just an empty shell where once there used to be a mighty stronghold held by a great warlord. The lady Maarja is the only surviving member of Kalju's family and I will not see her evicted from her home to become a beggar in her own land. If I am to be Master of Odenpah then that is my first order.'

Rudolf frowned at his insolence but Albert merely retained a calm disposition.

'We are not heathens, Master Conrad. We do not make war on women, children and the weak, much less those who have been afflicted by a terrible illness.'

'We shall build a leper house,' announced Hermann, 'a place of sanctuary and healing near to her home where she can live in peace until she departs this life.'

'I will ask her if that is acceptable, lord bishop,' said Conrad.

'Perhaps we should build her a palace instead,' remarked Rudolf caustically.

'It would be politic to show her civility and mercy,' replied Conrad calmly. 'Though she has been shunned by her own people because of her affliction to slight her in any way would make the Sword Brothers look petty and vindictive.'

'You have your answer, Master Rudolf,' said Albert. 'It shall be as you wish, *Master* Conrad.'

The meeting over, Conrad walked back outside the pavilion to where Hans and Anton were waiting.

'Well?' said Hans.

'I have been made Master of Odenpah,' replied Conrad flatly.

'You don't seem very pleased with your promotion,' observed Anton.

Conrad gave him a sly look.

'Well, one benefit is that I can appoint my own deputies, I believe. So you two are coming with me.'

Rudolf came from the pavilion and walked over to the trio.

'I would have a word alone with Master Conrad,' he said to Hans and Anton.

They saluted him and went to collect their horses, leaving Conrad and Rudolf alone. Around them hundreds of men in uniform were cleaning their armour, riding their horses from camp to mount patrols or practising drills to keep them occupied. Squires and pages brushed horses and mended their masters' clothes and engineers oversaw the dismantling of siege engines. It was the scene of an army preparing to return home.

'So Wenden says goodbye to one of its more illustrious sons,' smiled Rudolf. 'It makes sense that the Marshal of Estonia should be based in that land.'

'I suppose so, master' muttered Conrad.

Rudolf sighed. 'All right, what is troubling you? When the bishop informed you of your elevation to master you had the appearance of a man who had just been sentenced to death.'

'Wenden was my home for many years, master,' said Conrad glumly. 'I will miss it and those who live there.'

Rudolf was momentarily lost for words. 'You will?'

Conrad nodded.

'I will keep that to myself. If word gets out that the Marshal of Estonia is not a remorseless killer then our enemies may no longer be cowed into submission.'

'If I am killed I request that I am buried with my wife and son in Wenden's cemetery.'

'If we manage to retrieve your body I think that can be arranged,' said Rudolf in a matter-of-fact fashion.

'I would like Hans and Anton to be my deputies, master,' asked Conrad.

'As they too are never at Wenden and are your deputies anyway that is most sensible.'

Conrad was cheered by Rudolf's answers. Wenden's castellan tugged his elbow.

'Let us walk.'

He watched a party of mounted sergeants riding past, kettle helmets glinting in the sun.

'The bishop takes the army back to Riga to celebrate our victory but the grand master has ordered that some of the order's soldiers should remain in Estonia. He wants them to join with your men to test the Danish defences around Reval.'

Conrad was surprised. 'We are at war with the Danes, master?'

'No, but while the Danes are preoccupied in northern Germany the grand master is of the opinion that the Sword Brothers should let them know that Estonia does not belong to them.'

Conrad was tempted to ask about Rudolf's father, Count Henry, but then remembered that the count had been responsible for Johann's death and thought better off it.

'Word is,' continued Rudolf, 'that the Danes are raising an army to crush the German lords who have sided with my father.'

'Your father risks much by his actions,' said Conrad. 'Valdemar does not seem the forgiving type.'

Rudolf laughed. 'If my father is defeated on the battlefield then he will die with a sword in his hand, of that I am certain.'

'And if he wins, master?'

'Then power in the Baltic will change forever and Reval's position will become most precarious. Let us pray that happens.'

Conrad would pray for a German victory against the Danes but also for the death of Count Henry at the moment of victory.

'One more thing,' said Rudolf, 'this is Sword Brother business. Bishop Albert has enough to occupy him and does not need to know. And that goes for his brother, too.'

'Yes, master.'

'You don't have to call me "master" any more, Conrad. We are of equal rank now.'

'Yes, master.'

Rudolf shook his head and walked away. In the distance black smoke began to rise into the sky as another funeral pyre was lit.

In the days following Conrad returned to Odenpah with a message from Bishop Albert assuring Maarja that though the Sword Brothers would have to take possession of Odenpah, he would personally make provision for her future wellbeing and comfort. To this end he vowed to sponsor a leper hospital a short distance from Odenpah, complete with a generous allocation of land for farming and livestock. He and his brother Hermann ordered the release of funds from Riga's treasury to build the stone hospital, with a small manor house to accommodate Maarja and her servants. Wicked tongues said that this generosity was not only to display the wealth and piety of the two bishops, but also to act as penance for the outrages they had allowed at Dorpat.

Whatever the reason in the years following the leper house at Odenpah was seen not as a centre of sinful penitents but as a refuge for the godly, those who endured Christ-like suffering and purgatory on earth but who were guaranteed a place in heaven. This was in no small measure due to Maarja herself, who's gentle and forgiving nature elicited sympathy and pious concern throughout the whole of Ungannia. It was said that Bishop Hermann visited her regularly to seek her forgiveness and advice.

*****

Maarja had always thought that September was the loveliest month. Summer in Ungannia was beautiful, the air warm but also scented heavily with the aroma of pine, birch and fir after the frequent rains fell. In the early mornings the bog fields were often covered with light grey mists, which when she was a young girl she had believed were filled with tiny fairies that danced over the surface of the water. But now the deciduous trees were beginning to lose their leaves and as they did so the forests were splashed with autumn reds and golds. The short, refreshing summer showers were giving way to constant drizzle and the temperature was falling, the sky often overcast and forbidding. But Maarja loved this time of year because the days were often still and cool and filled with mist and she imagined that the unseen fairies living within it came to the very walls of Odenpah, and perhaps even inside.

She smiled and continued her digging. She enjoyed spending her days kneeling on a cushion and turning over the soft soil of her flowerbeds in the inner compound. She was seeding a new bed of cornflowers with her trowel, her mittens covering the ugly scars on her hands. The cornflower grew in abundance in the wild, of course, but she liked to cultivate it within the fort's walls, along with snapdragons, miniature roses

645

and lilies. She was becoming quite an accomplished gardener, or so her servants told her. They were very kind.

Maarja stood and stretched her back. She looked into the grey sky and saw through her veil a pair of grouse flying overhead. How she envied the birds that could go where they wanted, free to travel to far-off lands. She became aware of a presence behind her and turned to see her brother standing a few paces away, a hard expression on his once handsome face, now disfigured by a red-raw wound, his blue eyes full of hatred.

'Hello, Kristjan.'

'Sister.'

His voice was harsh, unfeeling. He was still tall and powerful but he looked tired, his hair bedraggled and his clothes dirty.

'I have come for father's gold,' he said.

Maarja sighed. 'No kind words for your sister, Kristjan? Has your heart hardened so much that you have no thoughts for your family.'

'If my heart has become stone as you say,' he replied, 'it is because our enemies have made it so.'

She walked forward with outstretched arms to embrace him but he recoiled from her show of affection.

'I am here for the gold, Maarja, nothing else. Ungannia is full of enemies and I cannot delay.'

She let her arms drop to her side. Kristjan had always been headstrong and aggressive but now he appeared wholly consumed by bitterness, indifferent to her fate and that of his people.

'Your people need you, Kristjan.'

'My people?' he shouted, causing her to jump. 'My so-called people have deserted and betrayed me. They have proved themselves unworthy of my leadership and that is why the gods have abandoned them. They failed at Reval, Varbola and Dorpat. Do not speak to me of the Ungannians.'

He started walking up and down, waving his arms in the air, one hand on the hilt of the sword at his hip and the other continually touching the torc around his neck.

'You think I passed the test of Taara to waste my time on those who are unworthy? You are wrong.'

She waited for his anger to subside before she spoke to him.

'Will you at least take refreshment with me, brother?'

He nodded, his cheeks still flushed, his mouth twisted into a sneer. They walked to the great hall, its wooden doors carved with images of the golden eagle, for hundreds of years the proud symbol of Ungannia, now a reminder of a lost age. The old steward, a man who had been at Odenpah when Kristjan had been a babe in his mother's arms, ordered servants to fetch food and honey mead. Kristjan did not sit in his father's chair as he snatched the cup from the nervous servant girl and once again began pacing.

'I will go east, to Novgorod. They have their own men of iron, thousands of them, with which to crush the Sword

Brothers. With the gold I can raise my own soldiers, an army of mailed horsemen to retake this land from the barbarians.'

Maarja lifted her veil to drink her mead. A look of disgust spread across Kristjan's face.

'Does my appearance revolt you, brother? That is all I have known since I was struck down by the pestilence: fear and loathing. How ironic, then, that those whom you call enemies should show me tenderness, kindness and respect.'

Kristjan threw his cup to the floor. 'Who? Tell me.'

Maarja sipped at her cup and placed it on the table, replacing the veil over her disfigured face.

'I have been visited by the Sword Brother who once came to defend this place, Kristjan. Surely you remember Conrad Wolff? He is a great man now but such is his humility that he tried to take my hands in his and kiss them as a sign of respect.'

'I have sworn to kill Conrad Wolff. He is the one who killed our parents.'

'How blind are you, Kristjan?' said Maarja. 'Do you not see that it is your foolishness, your arrogance that has led you to the dire situation you find yourself in? You made war on the Sword Brothers because of your vanity, and lost. And you also lost the lives of many of our people. And for what?'

But he would hear no more and stormed from the hall. He immediately went to a storeroom to acquire a spade before walking to the area immediately behind the hall. Maarja collected two guards and followed him, the sky darkening overhead, small spits of rain blowing in the wind. The area behind the hall was the site of chicken coops, pigsties and goat pens, a patch of mud and dung usually visited only by those who tended the animals. There was no treasury at Odenpah but Kristjan knew that his father had secreted a horde of gold behind his hall and he now frantically dug at the earth in one of the sties, the pigs squealing and grunting in alarm as he did so. Maarja and the guards looked on as the sky darkened, the spit turning into large raindrops, Kristjan slowly becoming splattered with mud and filth. He hit something solid and called to the guards to help him. They looked at Maarja who gave her assent.

With their help he pulled the small chest from the glutinous mud, the rain now sheeting down to drench everyone. Kristjan hauled the chest out of the sty and smashed the lock with his spade. There was a clap of thunder and a flash of lightning followed by a howl of triumph as Kristjan lifted the lid and extracted a large leather pouch, inside of which was a collection of small gold ingots. He fell to his knees and stared at the pieces of precious metal, pushed them back into the pouch and rose to his feet.

'Tell Conrad Wolff that I will return to kill him,' he ordered Maarja, his wet hair matted to his skull, rain coursing down his face.

'Hate will eat away at you, Kristjan,' his sister told him, 'until you are an empty husk. It is not what our parents would have wanted for you.'

He smiled and then laughed maniacally, throwing back his head as he did so, while overhead the sky shook with the sound of thunder.

'And their deaths is not what I wanted but it happened. Stay here, Maarja, and become a pet of the Sword Brothers if you wish. I will leave and fight to make Ungannia free once more.'

He left her standing in the mud and rain, took a pony from the stables and rode from the fort. She never saw her brother again.

*****

When General Aras arrived at Riga his first thoughts were how the port and city had grown. The harbour, now greatly expanded, was filled with vessels of all shapes and sizes. There were the great cogs that brought crusaders and their horses from Germany and shipped goods back to the markets of Lübeck and Denmark. Along the wooden jetties were moored dozens of riverboats, their Russian crews unloading the grey squirrel pelts that made Novgorod rich. Fishing vessels unloaded baskets of freshly caught Baltic herring and sprat for sale in the markets, the sea filled with a seemingly inexhaustible supply of these fish. As he and his guards shoved their way through the noisy press of sailors, merchants, dock workers and officials he could see that Riga was thriving.

He had arrived with a dozen of Prince Vsevolod's personal bodyguard, which in itself was an indication of the importance the prince attached to his mission. The men's expensive lamellar armour, blue tunics and leather boots made a good impression, as did the silver griffins on their shields. He knew how the Christians loved their heraldry and also how they despised the native inhabitants of the lands both north and south of the Dvina. As soon as his vessel had docked a port official, a thin man with a twitch, had stood on the jetty demanding to know the crew's business, if they were selling any goods and how long they intended to stay. He then presented the captain with a bill for docking fees. When Aras, who fortunately spoke German, informed him that he was an envoy from Prince Vsevolod on urgent business and had to see Archdeacon Stefan, he looked concerned and hurried away. He returned an hour later with Manfred Nordheim, the commander of Riga's garrison, who said that he would personally escort Aras to the bishop's palace, though his men would have to remain on the boat. The captain of the Russian guards was unhappy but Nordheim assured Aras that he was perfectly safe.

'This is a Christian city, general, not a pagan settlement. We do not kill envoys.'

Aras ignored the slight and agreed to accompany the commander to the Bishop's Palace. Nordheim was in a talkative mood, informing him that Bishop Albert had won a great victory in Estonia.

'The last pagan stronghold has fallen and now the Catholic Church rules all the lands from the Dvina to the Gulf of the Finns.'

Aras thought this was excellent news. If the Bishop of Riga had no distractions in Estonia then he would look more favourably on crossing the Dvina. Whether this would serve his lord's long-term interests was another matter.

'And the Russians,' enquired Aras, 'do they still make war upon Riga?'

'Look around you, general,' said Nordheim, gesturing with his right arm towards the heaving docks. 'There are many Russian merchants and vessels here. Novgorod desires peace so it can sell its goods to the good people of Germany.'

Aras had also seen boats with their hulls painted with the symbol of Polotsk – large ships sailing the waters of the Dvina – an indication that Prince Boris also had amicable relations with Riga.

'You are here to see Archdeacon Stefan?' probed Nordheim.

'Yes, commander.'

'Not Bishop Albert?'

'My lord felt that because he has had previous dealings with the archdeacon,' replied Aras, 'it would be better if he did so this time. He esteems the archdeacon a friend and ally.'

Nordheim remained expressionless. He doubted that the archdeacon had any friends and certainly not any pagan ones. But the fact that Vsevolod, whose duplicity was well known in

Riga, had sent his general to the city meant that whatever message was in the leather bag that Aras carried must be of the utmost importance.

'We are very pleased to see you, general,' smiled Stefan obsequiously.

The archdeacon was dressed in a magnificent red dalmatica that had gold decorative trim around the hem, sleeves and neckline. A solid gold cross hung from a golden chain around the portly churchman's neck and there were gold rings on his fingers. Those fingers were holding Vsevolod's letter, which the archdeacon proceeded to read, occasionally nodding his head as he did so.

They were in the ordered calm of one of the palace's withdrawing chambers, its walls covered with oak panelling, a fire burning in the great stone fireplace. Attractive young boys in red livery served the archdeacon, Aras and Nordheim with fine wine, fruit, cheese and freshly baked bread. Candles on silver stands illuminated the room as the autumn light faded outside the windows.

Stefan finished reading the letter. 'I hope you and your men will stay in the palace tonight, general.'

'You are most kind,' smiled Aras. 'When will you inform Bishop Albert of my lord's suggestion?'

'He is out of the city at the moment,' said Stefan, 'but I assure you that he will be informed the moment he returns.'

Nordheim was most courteous to Aras during his brief stay at Riga, showing him around the city and the castle where he had the garrison drawn up on parade for the Lithuanian's inspection. The commander of the garrison was not present at the meeting where Bishops Albert and Hermann were informed of Prince Vsevolod's invitation to cross the Dvina and seize Semgallia and Kurland.

'The last time we crossed the Dvina,' said Albert looking at his nephew, 'we were basely betrayed. Why should I take heed of this Russian prince who wants us to fight his battles for him?'

'We should not, uncle,' answered Stefan, 'but in his letter Vsevolod makes a pertinent point.'

'Which is?' asked Hermann.

Stefan handed Bishop Albert the letter and replied to Bishop Hermann.

'That if this Duke Arturus conquers all of Lithuania he will cross the Dvina to invade Livonia, just as the other pagan Daugerutis did eleven years ago.'

'Is that likely?' said Hermann. 'The Lithuanians were defeated then and Livonia is much stronger now.'

'These pagans are not rational beings, uncle,' replied Stefan. 'They are not far removed from animals and have retained the base instincts of four-legged creatures. They exist only to fight and procreate.'

Albert waved a hand at him.

'You are both wrong. Now that Livonia and Estonia are watered by the holy word I would be failing in my duty to God not to bring the teachings of the Holy Church to the pagans

654

south of the Dvina. It was always a matter of when, not if, we would again crusade in Lithuania.'

He held up the letter. 'This may aid us in our holy mission. That said, I will give the matter more consideration in the coming weeks. Winter will soon be upon us, so let us look forward to celebrating the birth of Christ. And let us also give thanks that Estonia is finally at peace.'

*****

Conrad saw the figure appear in the distance, a black shape plodding through the snow.

'He's here,' he said to Hans and Anton.

They stayed crouching among the trees to ensure that the approaching individual was alone and was not being followed or indeed the vanguard of an enemy patrol. But after a few minutes he could see that it was the Jerwen warrior that had volunteered to reconnoitre the ground ahead and so he stood and walked towards him. The man raised his hand to him as he continued to walk through the snow that lay thick on the ground. When Conrad reached him the warrior was sweating and panting.

'The position is very strong, *Susi*. The river runs by the eastern side of the settlement. The garrison is housed in a timber enclosure atop a bluff on the western bank of the river.'

'Is there a wall around the settlement itself?' asked Conrad.

'Yes, *Susi*.'

Conrad patted him on the arm. 'Get yourself some hot porridge and rest. You have done well.'

He walked back to the trees with the tired warrior where Hans and Anton waited. Two Jerwen warriors escorted the man back to the camp in the forest, leaving the three friends behind.

'Well?' said Anton.

'It's a strong position, as we suspected.'

'You will stick to your plan, Conrad?' enquired Hans.

Conrad nodded. 'I will. We have marched this far through the snow to get here and I do not intend to abandon the prize just because it is well defended.'

The prize he was speaking of was the settlement of Narva, a collection of huts and barns on the west bank of the river of the same name. Originally a Wierland fishing village, it lay six miles from the coast and around thirty miles northeast of the northern shore of Lake Peipus. The Narva River flowed from the lake to the Baltic and marked the frontier with Novgorod. When Wierland was a pagan kingdom Novgorod hardly bothered with the village of Narva, which hugged the high bluff on the western side of the river. This river was a formidable barrier, being between two and three hundred yards wide along its course, in parts almost double that width. As well as being a natural barrier the river was rich in aquatic life, including loach, grayling, salmon, lamprey, sturgeon and bream. This in turn spawned dozens of villages along its length and around the settlement of Narva itself.

Occasionally Novgorod would send raiding parties across the Narva to collect captives – women and children – to ship south for sale in the slave markets of Constantinople. Or sometimes just to kill and plunder. But mostly the pagan Wierlanders were left alone to live out their lives. Then everything changed with the arrival of the Danes who created the stronghold of Reval, but who also sent their soldiers east to seize the strategically important settlement of Narva, which was the gateway to Danish Estonia.

During his disastrous campaign against Reval Prince Mstislav had ignored Narva believing, quite rightly, that if the former fell then it would be easy to seize the much smaller and weaker Narva. But now the Sword Brothers were waging a campaign against Reval's outposts, capturing them one by one to isolate the Danish port. And Conrad was determined that the Army of the Wolf would seize Narva. For one thing it was the strongest outpost of the Danes in Wierland. If he took it then the Wierlanders would be free from Danish oppression and would most likely flock to his banner. And Wierland was the last Estonian kingdom that was not controlled by his warlords.

Those warlords now stood warming themselves around a campfire as Conrad explained to them and Sir Richard his intent to capture Narva. The air reeked of horseflesh, or more specifically ponies, a thousand of the beasts having carried the five hundred and fifty men to Wierland and another five hundred having transported their tents, spare clothing and weapons, fodder and food.

'We know that Narva has not only a Danish garrison,' said Conrad, 'but also that the commander, a rogue by the name of Dietrich von Kivel, has a large number of German mercenaries in and around Narva.'

'How many?' asked Sir Richard, a fur cap covering his bald scalp.

'At least as many as we have brought to this place, perhaps more, your grace.'

Leatherface spat into the fire. 'If they get wind of us and retreat inside the palisade then with their numbers we'll never be able storm the place.'

'He is right, *Susi*,' said Andres. 'We have no siege engines and we will lose many men if we have to assault Narva.'

Conrad looked at their faces illuminated by the flames of the fire. He suddenly realised that if he ordered it they would fling themselves against Narva's defences leading their men, such was their loyalty to him. In that moment he felt like a king who could save or waste men's lives on a whim. Then he remembered that he was merely a simple brother knight, albeit one recently promoted to castellan.

'My friends, I have no intention of attacking Narva,' he assured them. 'I intend to fight the enemy in the open.'

'Why should they leave their fort, *Susi*?' asked Riki.

'I was wondering that,' added Anton. 'Only an idiot would leave a strong position to fight a battle in the snow.'

'An idiot or a tyrant,' replied Conrad. 'I have taken a keen interest in our friend Commander Kivel. I asked Andres and

658

Riki to send scouts into Wierland to not only reconnoitre the kingdom but also discover more about the Duke of Narva.'

'Is that his title?' said Hans, holding his hands to the flames.

'He is, by all accounts,' continued Conrad, 'a favourite of King Valdemar who bestowed the title on him before his departure for Denmark and subsequent imprisonment. He has taken advantage of the king's absence to aggrandise himself at the expense of the Wierlanders. But more importantly, he believes himself to be a great general, which we will use to our advantage.'

'You are confident that if we manage to lure this Kivel out of Narva we can defeat him, Conrad?' asked Sir Richard.

'With your help, your grace, I am certain of it,' smiled Conrad. He looked at the others. 'It might fortify your confidence to know that we will not be alone in our fight, if everything works out the way I hope it does.'

He was met by a circle of confused and quizzical expressions.

'Have you been at the ale?' teased Leatherface.

'Conrad has a secret that has been impossible to tease out of him,' said Anton, 'but his general air of smugness suggests that he is confident of victory.'

'All I will say is this,' said Conrad. 'It is my intention to free Wierland from the Danes and I will offer battle to this Kivel in the full confidence that we can defeat him on our own.

If not then we will withdraw and wait until the spring when we will return with a larger army.'

After the impromptu gathering the leaders returned to their men and Hans and Anton went in search of food. The camp had been established in a large pine forest just north of Lake Peipus and southwest of Narva. The trees afforded shelter from the harsh winds that often whipped up the lake and also provided firewood and materials for stables and lean-tos. Guards patrolled the perimeter and scouts were sent out every day to ensure the garrison of Narva did not venture from its warm stronghold until provoked. All the men who had marched to Wierland were volunteers, veterans of previous campaigns; men who were well armed and equipped and who could be relied upon in battle. Even Ulric's one hundred soldiers were now warmly clad and appropriately armed, a far cry from the miserable wretches that had journeyed from Germany in the company of Bishop Bernhard.

Conrad walked among them after the meeting, sharing jokes and listening to them reminiscing about Varbola and Dorpat. Their mood was relaxed and confident, sentiments shared by the other contingents in camp. Even Ulric seemed less morose than usual. Conrad shared some soup with 'the bastards' and then continued on his tour of the camp, stopping when he sensed he was being followed. He spun round and saw Leatherface holding up his hands.

'Don't run me through, Master Conrad, I was only seeking a bit of company.'

'You should take care,' Conrad admonished him, 'creeping around camp might get you shot by one of your own men.

The mercenary drew his cape around himself and quickened his pace to walk alongside Conrad.

'My boys are too well trained to shoot their commander. So, you reckon you can beat this Danish lord.'

'He's German, but yes, we can beat him.'

Leatherface chuckled.

'What's so funny?' asked Conrad.

'I was just thinking about the first time you were given a command, when Sir Richard was besieged by the Cumans.'

'I remember.'

'So do I,' smiled the mercenary. 'You could not come up with a plan and did not think much of the Saccalian rabble that you were leading. But you managed to forge them into a force that defeated the Cumans and relieved Sir Richard.'

Now Conrad smiled. 'I was lucky.'

'No, you had the ability; it just had to be teased out of you. You've come a long way since then, Master Conrad, Marshal of Estonia.'

Conrad stopped and looked around at the tents, groups clustered around campfires and the rows of ponies under temporary shelters.

'In the spring it will be fifteen years since I first stepped foot in this land. I sometimes wonder where those years went.'

'Easy,' said Leatherface. 'Fighting wars and killing enemies.'

Conrad walked on. 'And now we are close to bringing the war to an end. Estonia is almost ours and next year the bishop will look to the conquest of Oesel.'

Leatherface smiled ruefully. 'This war might be coming to an end but there will be others to fight, mark my words. That's the thing about crusades, Master Conrad, there is an endless supply of heathens to either convert or send to hell.'

'All the more work for you, then.'

'Me? I reckon that I've got a couple of years left in me at most. These winters wreak havoc on my tired old body.'

'So your plan is still to buy that alehouse in Riga, then?' said Conrad.

Leatherface gave him a wink. 'That and acquire a young wife with child-bearing hips.'

Conrad shuddered. The thought of him mauling a young woman was truly appalling. Later, when Hans and Anton were asleep on the floor of their crowded conical tent, Jaan also deep in slumber, Conrad strapped on his sword and went to the tents in the centre of the camp where the supplies and spare weapons were stored. It was a numbingly cold night, still and silent, his breath misting in front of him. A sentry, a Jerwen, snapped to attention as he approached.

'All is quiet?'

'All is quiet, *Susi*.'

He walked to one of the tents, its flap tied shut, looked around and then untied the straps to give him access. Inside were spare cloaks, shields and surcoats bearing the emblem of the Sword Brothers, all stacked on a table constructed from pine branches to stop the damp seeping into the wood, leather and cloth. The capes and surcoats were wrapped in hides tied with leather cords. As a pale light entered the open flap his eyes got accustomed to the dim interior and focused on one bundle on top of the pile. He laid a hand on it, closed his eyes and said a silent prayer that they would come. But he could wait no longer. Eventually the whereabouts of the camp would be reported to Narva's garrison and he wished to retain the element of surprise. He opened his eyes. The die was cast for good or ill.

The next morning the warriors mustered well before dawn in their contingents with 'the bastards' in their companies, the cold, damp air making men cough and wipe their runny noses. In January northern Estonia only had six hours of light each day so it was imperative that Sir Richard and his horsemen were goading the enemy garrison when dawn broke. Squires and knights shivered and then sweated as they checked the shoes of their horses. Winter horseshoes were wonderful things, being equipped with spikes that gave the animal traction on snow and ice, preventing a horse from slipping. But they also had to be checked several times a day to ensure that compressed snow had not built up under the hoof, which could lead to bruising. But he had to admit that even in the pre-dawn gloom, once covered with their blue caparisons sporting a white boar's head with gold tusks they looked very impressive.

Sir Richard and his knights wore the same colours on their surcoats and shields, and even the lesser knights, those men who had originally come with him from England who had no squires, rode horses protected by padded caparisons. In truth Sir Richard's two classes of knights were no different from each other and his squires were all over the age of eighteen and veterans of the wars in Livonia.

Sir Richard, his helm resting on his saddle, spoke to Conrad as his men filed out of camp. Squire Paul, ever the faithful if insubordinate servant, stayed beside him. They had gone over the plan and reconnoitred the ground and now all that remained was to put the scheme into action.

'What if they refuse to accept my challenge?' said Sir Richard.

Conrad shrugged his shoulders. 'Then we will withdraw, your grace, and warm ourselves by our fires until the spring. But I am confident that they will be unable to resist the temptation. If all else fails let Paul insult them. That should be enough to draw them out.'

'I will not lower myself to reply,' sniffed Paul.

'God be with you, Conrad,' said Sir Richard.

'And you, your grace.'

He wheeled his warhorse around and joined the rear of his column of men, Paul accompanying him. Conrad walked back to his tent where Anton and Hans waited, like him dressed in their mail armour and white surcoats, shields slung on their backs. They also wore thick woollen leggings on their legs instead of mail chausses and thick felt boots on their feet. Jaan stood beside them dressed in a gambeson that was too large for him, holding a short spear in his hand.

'You will stay here with the camp guards,' Conrad told him. 'And don't sneak away and try to catch up with us.'

'I want to fight,' he complained.

'And I want wings so I can fly into Narva,' replied Conrad. 'But wanting and having are two different things so you will stay here and prepare our evening meal.'

Jaan looked around in frustration at crossbowmen checking their bowstrings and the full quivers hanging from shoulder straps, warriors tucking hand axes in their belts and 'the bastards' adjusting their helmets. The air tingled with the prospect of battle, he could almost taste it, and he wanted to be a part of the great adventure.

'Your time will come, Jaan,' Hans told him. 'We were like you once.'

'And we had to obey orders, just like you do,' Conrad told him.

The three Sword Brothers walked to the head of the column of foot soldiers to lead the advance out of the forest. Their destination was Lake Kadastiku, only half a mile northeast of the forest. Like most inland lakes in Livonia and Estonia it froze in November and the ice did not melt until the following May. Now, in the depths of winter, it was an expanse of thick, iron-hard, snow-covered ice.

The pace was slow to conserve stamina, no one speaking as the dawn at last began to break to herald a cloudless, bitterly cold day. The sky turned pink, blue and orange as a pale sun peeked above the treeline. There was no conversation, just a crumping sound as boots trod in the snow and mail armour rustled as men tramped through the whiteness. The majority carried round shields covered with leather and rimmed with iron to withstand blows on their edges. In comparison 'the bishop's bastards' were equipped with almond-shaped shields painted with red crosses and they now wore mail armour over their gambesons. Every man wore a helmet and was armed with either a spear or an axe. It was a testimony to their success in battle that every man was also armed with a sword, a collection of blades captured from the Oeselians, Russians, Danes and Ungannians.

Kadastiku Lake was surrounded by evergreen forest, a bell-shaped expanse of water that in spring and summer was surrounded by low, sandy shores but now was buried beneath snow and ice. There were a few islands in the lake: thin strips of land where trees and shrubs grew. Conrad's men tramped across the ice towards the largest of these islands in the middle of the lake, now a row of pines some two hundred paces in length rising up from the white.

'This will be our position,' Conrad told his commanders. 'We will form a line in front of the trees and wait for Sir Richard to return.'

'Followed by the enemy,' said Hans.

'God willing,' replied Conrad.

Anton looked around at the snowy wilderness. 'If God bothers with this forlorn place.'

The tribal contingents of the Army of the Wolf were intimately acquainted with their drills and formations by now. They had marched and fought together for over four years and represented a veteran formation second only to the Sword Brothers themselves. Master Rudolf had lent Conrad fifty of the order's crossbowmen, Sir Richard having brought the same number. Leatherface, appointed commander of all of them, now went among them to slap a few arms and shake more hands. He had no need to bellow orders or make threats. He knew his missile men knew their craft and so his task was to reassure them that they were the best at what they did.

It was the same with the Estonians. Tonis, having jumped at the opportunity to rejoin the Army of the Wolf, Hillar, Riki and Andres stood among their men sharing jokes, indulging in idle chatter and enquiring after their wellbeing. Conrad placed the Jerwen on the right of the line, with the Harrien, Rotalians and Saccalians standing beside them from right to left. Everyone knew that the place of honour in the battle line was on the right, though they knew not why, and so Andres and his men thought it very prestigious that they should be placed there. Conrad placed Ulric and his men on the extreme left of the line, next to Tonis' men. Because they were on the flank they would be exposed to frontal and flank attacks but Conrad believed that they had earned the right to be given an important position in the battle line. The crossbowmen, who also had shields on their backs, were positioned all the along the line, just behind the front rank, ready to shoot volleys of bolts into an attacking enemy. The Army of the Wolf presented a compact mass of brown and green, bristling with spear points glinting in the sunlight and topped by a sea of gleaming helmets. Behind the row of pines thick snow covered the shrubs around them.

Leatherface came up to Conrad who was standing a few paces ahead of the front rank, peering at the line of trees that marked the edge of the frozen lake.

'Three hours of daylight left,' he said to the mercenary.

'It only takes a few minutes to win a battle,' came the reply.

'If there is a battle,' complained Conrad, scanning the area in front for any signs of movement. He turned and walked back towards the warriors drawn up five deep and standing in close formation, though not too close that they would not be able to use their weapons.

'You should be careful what you wish for,' said Leatherface, who suddenly sprinted back to the shield wall.

'Load your weapons,' he shouted before disappearing behind the line of shields.

Conrad stopped, turned and saw horsemen at the northern end of the lake, men in blue surcoats riding horses covered in caparisons of the same colour. Sir Richard's men. The commanders of the Estonians and 'bastards' shouted orders and signallers blew horns to sound the alarm as Conrad walked back to his position beside Hans and Anton in the middle of the line, among Hillar's Rotalians. Hillar himself stood in the front rank, alongside his biggest and most powerful warriors, his thick leather cuirass protecting his large chest and an axe in his hand. Conrad took his shield off his back and slipped his left forearm through the straps on its inner side as Sir Richard cantered towards the white-clade figures. The warriors began banging the hafts of their spears and axes on their shields in salute as he approached. He raised his lance in acknowledgement and brought his warhorse to a halt in front of Conrad. He removed his helm, his face framed by the mail coif underneath.

'They took the bait, Conrad.'

He turned and pointed his lance at a break in the trees at the far end of the lake.

'There appears to be more of them than we envisioned.'

Conrad peered across the dazzling white surface of the lake to see black shapes clustering in the gap. He could see no horsemen.

'They have no riders, your grace?'

Sir Richard looked back at the increasing numbers of men on foot swarming on to the lake.

'They did have when they were pursuing us.'

'Perhaps they got lost in the snow,' opined Conrad.

Sir Richard raised his land to him, replaced his helm and rode to rejoin his men who were taking up position behind the pines, to the rear of the shield wall. The plan was for them to be a mounted reserve that would deliver the coup de grâce to win the battle.

The enemy foot were still massing on the far side of the lake, drums banging and banners held aloft. They were around five hundred paces away, thus making it impossible to identify the standards. As the minutes passed the extent of their line increased as more and more foot soldiers came from the trees to form up on the lake. The Army of the Wolf stood silently in its ranks, waiting for the enemy to attack.

All eyes were gazing towards the northeast where the enemy foot soldiers were massing, shouting and banging their spears on their shields to add to the din of banging drums and horn blasts. And create a perfect distraction for the enemy horsemen that suddenly charged out of the trees to the Army of the Wolf's front, no more than four hundred paces away.

They charged not in an ordered formation, knee-to-knee, but as a disorganised mass, dozens of them. They were led by Danish knights covered in mail armour from head to foot, wearing full-face helms, yellow surcoats and carrying long, almond-shaped shields painted yellow and sporting a red cross. Black and yellow caparisons, the bottoms of which flapped around wildly as they bore down on the packed ranks of Conrad's men, covered their mounts.

'Aim at the horses,' shouted Leatherface to his crossbowmen as the charging horsemen suddenly parted to divide left and right to sweep around the flanks of the Army of the Wolf.

There was a succession of cracks as crossbowmen released their triggers to send bolts shooting through the air. To miss their targets.

'Stop shooting!' screamed Leatherface as the horsemen thundered past.

Behind the knights were German mercenary horsemen, men wearing knee-length mail hauberks split at the waist, and round helmets with nasal guards. Caparisons did not protect the horses and their riders carried javelins instead of lances, which they now hurled at the warriors as they passed. Iron points pierced wooden shields to fracture arms and cut flesh. The crossbowmen among 'the bishop's bastards' and Jerwen managed to shoot a number of horses as they passed, the beasts screaming in pain and crashing on the ice. But then the horsemen were behind the island, attacking Sir Richard's men in a furious mêlée. Conrad's reserve had disappeared.

'Arrows,' someone shouted.

Conrad looked through his helmet's vision slits to see thin black shafts in the sky and instinctively crouched down to make himself a small target and brought up his shield. There were a series of thuds as the arrows hit shields, snow and flesh, followed seconds later by groans and screams as men were hit. They ignored the wounded and stayed under their shields as another volley of iron-tipped missiles landed among them, then a third and a fourth. Each volley inflicted casualties – wounded with a few dead – and then the arrows ceased and the air was filled with hundreds of war cries as the enemy foot attacked.

Under cover of the arrow volleys they had marched closer to the Army of the Wolf, the members of which barely had time to get to their feet before being hit by the full fury of the enemy charge. Conrad had no time to rise as a warrior holding a large-bladed war axe came at him, shield strapped to his back, his weapon gripped with both hands above his head, ready to split open Conrad's helm. He heard a loud crack, saw the bolt go through the man's leather cuirass and braced himself as the fatally wounded man clattered into him. He thrust his sword beneath the man's armour and pushed upwards to ensure he would die and shoved the corpse back into the warrior behind him. Leatherface behind Conrad shot this man in the eye and reloaded his weapon, staying close to the Sword Brother as axe blows and spear thrusts rained down on the Army of the Wolf as it was assailed on three sides.

Hillar was swinging his axe expertly, splintering shields and splitting spear shafts, while Hans and Anton were wielding their maces against the sea of enemy soldiers to the front. They were a mixture of Wierlanders armed with axes and spears and German mercenaries equipped in knee-length mail hauberks

672

and almond-shaped shields and armed with seven-foot-long spears, swords and daggers.

A crossbowman behind Conrad and Hillar emitted a high-pitched scream as a spearmen thrust his weapon between them and pushed the point into his left thigh. In a deft movement Hillar hacked down with his axe to splinter the shaft and then flicked his wrist to whip the blade up to shatter the spearman's jawbone.

The Army of the Wolf was slowly forced back as the press of enemy soldiers surged forward and chopped and hacked at the Estonian shield wall. Every man in Conrad's army knew that to become separated from the men next to him meant certain death, and so they tried to retain their formation. But as one man fell under a deluge of axe blows or was pierced by spear points, those next to him pulled him from the fray and took a step back to stop the enemy surging through the gap. Slowly but surely the Estonians were being pushed back towards the line of trees behind them.

Hans lunged forward and crouched to swing his mace to smash the kneecap of the soldier he was fighting before springing back to bludgeon the helmet of the spearman that was about to skewer Conrad. The latter killed a Wierlander who had wounded Hillar, plunging his sword into the man's thigh and then lifting his shield to parry an axe that came at him out of nowhere. He hauled Hillar back and another Rotalian took his place, but they were both forced back by a sudden surge of the enemy, men screaming with fury as they threw themselves

673

forward, raining down blows on the shields of Conrad's men, searching for an opening.

The press was now so tight that the front ranks were shoved against each other, making it difficult to move. A stinking bearded man mountain directly in front of Conrad, their faces only inches apart, head-butted the Sword Brother's helm. But his efforts only resulted in his own helmet's nasal guard being pushed inwards. He roared in frustration, his foul breath seeping into Conrad's helmet. Conrad was hit twice in quick succession by enemy blades that did not pierce his helmet. Then there was a hiss and a slight blow on the helm's right side and he saw a great hole in his adversary's throat. It must have been a crossbow bolt shot between him and Hans. It was either a superb shot or a bolt that had been loosed wildly. Whatever it was it killed the man in front of him and also wounded the one behind, having gone straight through the brute's throat. Conrad gave a mighty heave and pushed the corpse back. It collapsed backwards, forcing the man behind to give way. Conrad rammed his sword forward into the mail hauberk of the wounded spearman, the bolt lodged in his right shoulder. He in turn staggered back, allowing Conrad to step on the corpse at his feet and strike with his sword over the shoulders of the wounded spearmen into the face of another German mercenary behind. Hans and Anton were with him, their maces grey blurs as they aimed them at enemy faces in front of them. Another crossbow bolt flashed through the air to strike an enemy soldier. Then another and another and

674

gradually the impetus of the enemy assault slackened and then dissolved.

The fury of the close-quarter combat in the shield wall had lasted for perhaps ten minutes but it had seemed like ten hours. The Army of the Wolf, battered, bloody and having suffered casualties among each of its contingents, stood in ragged ranks behind a tideline of dead and dying.

'Shoot at them, shoot at them.'

Conrad heard the voice of Leatherface as the mercenary urged those of his crossbowmen who still lived to keep shooting at the enemy. Seconds later there was a thwack as he released his trigger, then more as his men took aim and shot at the retreating enemy. But they stopped and reformed their ranks less than fifty paces away.

Conrad saw a crossbow lying at his feet, its dead owner beside it. He placed his blood-covered sword back in its scabbard and picked up the weapon. Like Hans and Anton he always wore a double-pronged claw on the front of his belt for just such an occasion. He loaded the weapon using a bolt taken from the dead man's quiver and shot it at the enemy. As he reloaded and shot the crossbow again the warrior behind held his shield above his head, for everyone knew that the enemy's archers would soon be shooting their missiles from their rear ranks in preparation for another attack.

Leatherface and his surviving men were working like fury to expend their remaining ammunition. They and everyone else knew that they would probably not endure another charge because the enemy now formed a thick semi-circle around their position.

Conrad shot the last bolt from the dead man's quiver and tossed the crossbow aside. He shoved up his helmet. Hans and Anton did the same. They looked at each other and knew that they were about to die on this frozen lake in northern Estonia. As Conrad held out his right arm the shooting gradually faded and then stopped as all the crossbowmen ran out of ammunition. Hans smiled and placed his hand on top of his friend's, Anton's on top of his.

'As dust to the wind.'

They repeated the words and then embraced. There was no need for further words. They were friends and brothers, united by an eternal bond that could not be broken. The only thing that remained was to die well.

Opposite enemy commanders finished reorganising their men and stood in the front ranks, among the Wierlanders resembling the Army of the Wolf in appearance, save for their leather armour instead of mail. Conrad wondered why the Estonians were fighting for the enemy but had no time to ponder the riddle. The German mercenaries turned their long shields towards Conrad's men and lowered their spears, ready to charge forward. And men on both sides waited, waited for the archers to fill the sky with arrows that would fall on the Army of the Wolf like raindrops in a thunderstorm. Conrad put on his helmet and picked up a round Rotalian shield, his own having been hacked and splintered to render it useless. And waited.

There was a loud blast of trumpets that shook the air and the Army of the Wolf locked shields, huddled together preparing for the deluge. But then the ground began to shake as the trumpets sounded again but no storm of arrows came. Instead a great groan came from the enemy's ranks, which quickly became a crescendo of shouts as their ranks fragmented and then fell apart. Conrad brought down his shield and looked to the right, from where the rumble was coming from. He saw banners and iron-tipped lances and gave a shout. And soon the Army of the Wolf was shouting and cheering and holding weapons and shields aloft as dozens of horsemen in lamellar armour charged across the lake and plunged into the now fleeing enemy.

Conrad fell to his knees and clasped his hands together in prayer as the horsemen rode among the fleeing foot soldiers, spearing them with their lances and then going to bloody work with their swords and axes. For surely his deliverance was an act of God. The Christians among the Army of the Wolf did the same, thanking God for sending these armoured avengers who were slaughtering the enemy with gusto.

'You lucky bastard.'

Conrad got off his knees, removed his helmet and turned to see a smirking Leatherface, crossbow in hand, not a scratch on him.

'The power of prayer,' replied Conrad, 'you should try it some time.'

The mercenary was unconvinced. 'Mmm. If it was the power of prayer then the good Lord wouldn't have sent Russian horsemen to save you, seeing as the Sword Brothers and them don't see eye to eye on religious matters.'

Hans grabbed Conrad's arm and embraced him. 'It is a miracle, Conrad, a miracle.'

Anton joined the celebrations as hardened warriors wept with joy and embraced each other, watching as a detachment of horse archers followed their heavily armed comrades to add to the slaughter. The horsemen continued the butchery to the far side of the lake and beyond, hunting down the tired, frightened garrison of Narva through the pine trees. When they left, the surface of the lake was covered with dead bodies, ravenous crows and birds of prey descending in droves to pick at the still warm flesh.

'So much for the field of glory,' remarked Leatherface sarcastically.

Horns suddenly sounded from within the Army of the Wolf, prompting exhausted, bruised and bleeding men to pick up their shields and face front as a party of horsemen, two score or more, approached them. They presented a magnificent spectacle: every rider wearing lamellar armour over a *kol'chuga* and on his head a *shishak* with a brass nasal guard and a red plume. Mail aventails covered necks, shoulders and faces. Their almond-shaped shields protecting their left sides from chin to knees were red and edged with blue. Each man carried a lance with a red pennant and was also armed with a sword, dagger and a *topor*.

The Army of the Wolf stood in silence once more as a rider at the head of the detachment removed his helmet and pulled down his aventail so he could speak.

'I seek Master Conrad of the Sword Brothers if he still lives.'

The man spoke impeccable German, albeit with a thick accent.

Conrad stepped forward. 'I am Master Conrad.'

The horseman spurred his horse to where Conrad stood on the ice, the Sword Brother ordering his men to stand down. An audible collective sigh of relief rippled through the ranks behind him.

The Russian looked at Conrad's' damaged chainmail, his ripped, blood-covered surcoat and tired eyes.

'I am Yaroslav Nevsky, official envoy of his highness, Prince Mikhail, ruler of Novgorod. I am here to collect an item of some value to the prince and the people of Novgorod, which I believe is in your possession.'

'Your appearance is most timely, lord,' replied Conrad, 'though I would have wished you had arrived a few hours earlier.'

'My scouts kept me fully abreast of the events at this place, as well as the movements of the garrison of Narva.'

'I fear Narva is still held by the Danes, lord,' said Conrad.

Yaroslav gave him a knowing smile. 'My soldiers have possession of Narva, Master Conrad. As surety for the return of that which is in your possession, you understand.'

'Of course,' Conrad smiled back.

The rumble of horses' hooves on the ice prompted Yaroslav's men to close around their lord but Conrad held up his hands when he spotted blue caparisons.

'It is merely our horsemen,' he said. 'Have no fear.'

Sir Richard pulled up his horse in front of Conrad and stared at the Russians. The Army of the Wolf banged the ends of their spears on the ice to welcome the Duke of Saccalia.

'I am heartily glad to see you, your grace,' said Conrad.

'We fought a running battle with the Danish horsemen,' replied Sir Richard, 'but we could not get the better of them.'

He nodded at the Russians. 'Not until they arrived.'

'And Kivel?' asked Conrad.

'Got away with most of his knights,' lamented Sir Richard.

'I am forgetting my manners. Lord Nevsky,' said Conrad, 'this is Sir Richard Bruffingham, Duke of Saccalia.'

Yaroslav tilted his head politely at Sir Richard and looked at Conrad.

'It is time to exchange goods, Master Conrad. Novgorod's property for Narva.'

As the sun began to drop quickly on the horizon Conrad gave the order to march back to camp. There was an awkward moment when the Russians galloped ahead, leaving Conrad

680

standing on the ice. But Sir Richard ordered three of his knights to surrender their horses to allow the Sword Brothers to ride the half-mile back to camp. Once in camp Yaroslav dismounted when Conrad disappeared and reappeared a few minutes later with the banner than had been wrapped in hides. He bowed his head as he handed it to the Russian noble, who ordered two of his men to dismount and take hold of each end of the cloth.

Hans, Anton and Sir Richard watched as Yaroslav examined the banner. He smiled in satisfaction and then closed his eyes as he ran his hands over the red flag embroidered with two black bears each side of a throne. He ordered the flag to be wrapped in a cloak.

'You have fulfilled your part of the agreement, Master Conrad,' said Yaroslav formally. 'I will ride back to Narva. Tomorrow I will transfer it to your stewardship in completion of the agreement between the Kingdom of Novgorod and the Sword Brothers.'

'It will be my honour, lord,' replied Conrad.

Yaroslav barked an order, mounted his horse, raised his hand to Conrad and Sir Richard and departed for Narva as the foot soldiers of the Army of the Wolf began to arrive back in camp.

It had been a most extraordinary day.

The battle on the ice had been a close-run thing. One in five of the Army of the Wolf was either wounded or dead. But the arrival of the Russians had broken the Danish army and the corpses of its members were still littering the surface of the frozen lake when Conrad, his two friends, Sir Richard and his knights rode the two miles to Narva to meet with Yaroslav Nevsky the next day. The new Master of Odenpah was tired, with black rings round his eyes, mostly because of the exertions of the previous day but also because he had been kept awake into the early hours explaining to those who now rode with him how he had managed to enlist the support of the Russians.

It had been relatively straightforward but did involve persuading Master Rudolf into giving up the banner of Novgorod. It had been captured at Dorpat when the oafish Henke had provoked an incident in which Villem, Kalju's son, had been killed. After Bishop Albert had captured Dorpat Conrad had written to Master Rudolf and despatched letters to Novgorod, using the Russian traders who used the River Emajogi to transport their goods as mediators. It had taken many weeks but eventually Prince Mikhail agreed to support the capture of Narva in return for the banner and an assurance from the Marshal of Estonia that he would not wage war against Novgorod. But it was the banner, the holy icon that had been lost at Dorpat that had enticed the Novgorodians to send their soldiers west once again. Its return to the city of Saint Sophia would mend relations with the Sword Brothers and give a huge boost to Prince Mikhail's authority.

'So you see, Hans,' Conrad chided his friend as they rode through the crisp snow on the way to Narva, 'being able to read and write has its uses.'

'Not for me,' replied his friend, 'I am a lowly brother knight not a general.'

'You have done well, Conrad,' said Sir Richard, 'Narva is an important outpost. Can I take it that the Sword Brothers are intent on eventually capturing Reval itself?'

'You can, your grace,' said Conrad grimly. 'The Danes and their allies are no friends of the Sword Brothers. Their king tried to destroy Livonia and my order and now it is time to return the favour.'

When they arrived at the gates of Narva, the wooden stronghold on the bluff above the river framed against a brilliant blue sky, Russian foot soldiers were marching from the settlement. To one side observing the lines of spearmen, archers and carts containing their supplies was Yaroslav Nevsky, once again resplendent in his lamellar armour and burnished helmet. Today he and his men had fur-lined red cloaks around their shoulders, the material falling down to the hindquarters of their horses. It was once again a bitterly cold day and mist could be seen at the nostrils of the beasts.

At least today Conrad and his friends were attired in pristine white surcoats, replacement helmets that had been polished until they shone by Jaan, their horses draped in white caparisons bearing the colours of the order. Sir Richard's knights looked equally impressive in their liveries, though perhaps not as magnificent as the rich boyars of Novgorod. After the death and gore of the previous day today was all about splendour, manners and the exchange of compliments.

Conrad noticed that the banner that had sat in a drawer at Wenden for years was not on show when he pulled up his horse before Lord Nevsky and his horsemen. No doubt it was being carried back to Novgorod in a special chest, guarded by a host of soldiers.

Lord Nevsky held up a hand. 'Greetings, Master Conrad. I am pleased to see that the new day sees you well and refreshed after your exertions yesterday.'

Conrad laughed. 'You are too kind, lord.'

'And greetings to you, Sir Richard, Duke of Saccalia,' smiled Yaroslav. 'It is my fervent hope that you will accept my invitation for you and your friends to visit me in Novgorod where we may all hunt together.'

Sir Richard bowed his head. 'That would be most agreeable, my lord.'

The Russian nudged his horse forward until he was next to Conrad.

'Narva is yours, Master Conrad.'

He extended his hand. Conrad took it.

'I was at Wenden once,' Yaroslav told him, 'in the company of many Cumans to demand the return of the banner that you so nobly surrendered.'

Hans and Anton exchanged glances, knowing that they had been defending Wenden's walls during the Cuman attack, as had Conrad. But the latter now smiled.

'Let us hope that our two kingdoms can now enjoy the peace they so richly deserve, lord. That is what my bishop is most desirous of.'

'As is my prince,' said Yaroslav. 'God be with you, lord marshal.'

Yaroslav tilted his head at Hans, Anton and Sir Richard, turned his horse and trotted away from Narva's gates, followed by his horsemen.

'And with you, lord,' said Conrad as he watched the boyar depart.

They remained on their horses until the last of the Russians had departed, a long line of foot soldiers and horsemen marching south towards the frozen Lake Peipus and thence east to Novgorod. When Narva was empty they spurred their horses through the gates and into the settlement of wooden buildings, riding through the dwellings and into the timber stronghold. Like most ancient fortresses it contained a feasting hall surrounded by outbuildings that functioned as stables, barracks, armouries, storerooms and forges, the whole surrounded by a timber wall and towers.

Conrad dismounted and walked to the steps that led to ramparts, Sir Richard directing his men to conduct a search of the fort. Hans and Anton followed their friend to the battlements and stood beside him as he gazed at the River Narva below, now frozen solid until April. To the north was the Baltic and south lay Lake Peipus. Conrad turned his eyes towards the west where a long line of men on ponies was making its way towards the settlement – the Army of the Wolf. Like a boy that has discovered a great prize he grinned at his friends. He was now Castellan of Narva and Lord of all Wierland.

Epilogue

To His Holiness Pope Honorius III from Albert, Bishop of Riga and Commander of the Livonian Brothers of the Sword, the Holy Guardians of the Bishopric of Riga, Bishopric of Dorpat and the Catholic region of Livonia.

Holy Father,

You will be well acquainted with the great perils and trials that Livonia was subjected to during the unfortunate dispute with King Valdemar and the subsequent blockade that was imposed upon your bishopric. To add to the great discomfort that this land was subjected to the Lord seemed fit to test us further with an outbreak of the pestilence that claimed many innocent souls that He saw fit to transport to heaven.

But after the whole kingdom did penance and prayed for deliverance the Lord saw fit to reveal to the Sword Brothers a way to save the kingdom, whereby they went with joyous hearts into the black depths of paganism to deliver King Valdemar to safety.

In recognition of this, King Valdemar and the Sword Brothers, united in their love of the Holy Church, were reconciled and now share a mutual respect for each other that can only benefit our holy crusade in the Baltic.

I am compelled to draw to Your Holiness' attention the selfless efforts of a member of the Sword Brothers whom I have alluded to in previous missives to the Curia. Brother Conrad, formerly of the garrison of Wenden, was appointed Marshal of Estonia and has worked tirelessly to ensure that the Holy Church has triumphed in that kingdom. He recently crushed a dangerous pagan insurrection and assisted in our great and victorious crusade against Dorpat. As a reward for his bravery and piety I have promoted him to Master of Odenpah, a former pagan stronghold close to Dorpat.

The joyous news that the Catholic Church now rules from the River Dvina to Reval means that I can now plan a fresh crusade south of the Dvina to reclaim the Bishopric of Semgallia from the pagan Lithuanians. I do this not only to plant the seeds of the true faith in the soil of Lithuania but also in honour of Bishop Bernhard of Semgallia who was martyred at Dorpat.

'Given this twentieth day of February in the year of our Lord one thousand, two hundred and twenty-five and the ninth year of your pontificate.'

Printed in Great Britain
by Amazon